Romances w

They are se
Mediter

Latin LOVERS

Anne Mather, Kay Thorpe
Michelle Reid

Three complete novels from these three international bestselling authors of more than 260 books, which have sold in excess of **71 million** copies worldwide.

THE SPANIARD'S SEDUCTION
by
Anne Mather

THE ITALIAN MATCH
by
Kay Thorpe

THE UNFORGETTABLE HUSBAND
by
Michelle Reid

First published in Great Britain 2006
by Harlequin Mills & Boon Limited, Eton House,
18-24 Paradise Road, Richmond, Surrey TW9 1SR

The Spaniard's Seduction, The Italian Match and *The Unforgettable Husband* were first published in Great Britain in separate, single volumes.

ISBN 0 263 84983 X

108-0206

Printed and bound in Spain
by Litografia Rosés S.A., Barcelona

THE SPANIARD'S SEDUCTION

by

Anne Mather

Anne Mather has been writing since she was seven, but it was only when her first child was born that she fulfilled her dream of becoming a published author. Her first book, CAROLINE, met with immediate success, and since then Anne has written more than 150 novels, reaching a readership which spans the world.

Born and raised in the north of England, Anne still makes her home there with her husband, two children and, now, grandchildren. Asked if she finds writing a lonely occupation, she replies that her characters keep her company. In fact, she is so busy sorting out their lives that she often doesn't have time for her own! An avid reader herself, she devours everything from sagas and romances to suspense.

CHAPTER ONE

IT HAD rained in the night, and when Enrique stepped out onto his balcony at six o'clock the morning air brought a feathering of goosebumps over his flesh.

Of course it was very early, too early for the pale thread of the rising sun to give any warmth to the day. He should still be in his bed—or rather in Sanchia's bed, as she had expected—instead of standing here, brooding over something that alone could bring an unwelcome thinning of his blood.

His long fingers curled impatiently over the iron railing. It was still much warmer here, even at this ungodly hour of the morning, than it had been in England, he recalled, not altogether wisely. Despite the fact that early June in Andalusia meant blue skies and long days of hot sunshine, London had been cool and overcast while he was there, making him glad to be boarding the plane to come back home.

Only to find *that* letter waiting for him…

He scowled. He didn't want to think about that now. He'd spent far too many hours thinking about it already and it was all too easy to allow his anger to overtake his common sense. The realisation that, if his father hadn't been so ill, the letter would have been delivered to him filled him with outrage. It was only because Julio de Montoya was in the hospital in Seville that the letter had lain unopened on his desk until Enrique's return the day before.

His hands tightened on the railing, his fingertips brushing the petals of the morning glory that climbed the pillars beneath his balcony. Raindrops sparkled, creating a rainbow of colour on the pearly-white blossoms, drawing his eyes lower to where a veritable waterfall of jasmine and bougainvillaea spilled their beauty in the courtyard below.

Enrique had always believed his home was the most beautiful place on earth, but this morning it was difficult to empty his mind of intrusive thoughts, destructive thoughts. Even the sunlight glinting on the spire of the church in the valley below the *palacio* brought him no pleasure today, and he turned back into his apartments with a barely controlled feeling of frustration.

The letter was lying on the floor beside his bed, thrown there after he had read it for the umpteenth time at three o'clock that morning, but he ignored it. Even though the temptation was to pick it up and read it once again, he put the impulse aside and, stripping off the silk boxers which were all he wore to sleep in, he strode into the adjoining bathroom.

He ran the shower hot at first, using its pummelling spray to warm his chilled flesh. Then, after thoroughly cleansing his hair and body, he turned the thermostat to cold. The shock of the ice-cold water sharpened his senses, and, feeling more ready to face the day, he turned off the taps and stepped out.

A pile of towels were stacked on a rack beside the shower cubicle and Enrique wrapped one about his hips before taking another to dry his straight black hair. His jaw was rough, evidence of the night's growth of beard, and, slotting a towel about his neck, he studied his reflection in the mirror above the handbasin with a critical eye.

He looked as rough as his jawline, he thought grimly, scraping a hand over his chin. His olive skin had a sallow cast and his deep-set dark eyes were hollowed by the dark circles that surrounded them. Narrow cheekbones flared above thin lips that were presently set in a forbidding line, and although women seemed to find his appearance appealing he could see no attraction in his hostile face.

But then, that was what came of burning the candle at both ends, he conceded. He'd flown back from London only the previous morning, and had spent the afternoon in meetings that would have been exhausting at the best of times. Then Sanchia had expected him to spend the evening with her; more than the evening, as it had turned out. Though much to her disappointment he had declined. Nevertheless, it had been after two o'clock when he'd crawled into bed—but not to sleep. The letter had made sure of that, and he scowled again as he thought of it lying there, waiting for him to pick it up, waiting for him to deal with it.

And he would have to deal with it. Soon. Before his father came home from the hospital, which might be in the next few days. When he'd spoken to his mother yesterday evening, she'd been overjoyed to report that the surgery her husband had undergone had proved so successful. Now, with care and a certain amount of luck, Julio de Montoya should have several more years of active life ahead of him. That was so long as nothing untoward happened to hinder his recovery.

Like that letter.

Enrique's jaw compressed and, after smothering the lower half of his face with foam, he reached for his razor. Dammit, what did that—*bruja*—hope to achieve? And who was the child—if there really was a child—who had reputedly written the letter? No kin of his, he was sure. Or of Antonio's. Cassandra had probably invented the whole thing. So what game was she playing?

Cassandra...

His hand slipped and the razor sliced into his cheek. Swearing as blood dripped onto the towel around his neck, Enrique groped for the tap. Then, after sluicing his face with cold water, he waited for the blood to congeal. What the hell was wrong with him, he wondered, letting that letter cause him such grief? He had to get a hold of himself, and damn quick. He'd done it ten years ago and he could do it now. He had no intention of letting that woman ruin his life. Again. She might be Antonio's widow, but she had no connection with this family. None at all.

The cut had stopped bleeding by the time he'd dressed in loose cotton trousers and a black tee shirt. Deck shoes slipped easily onto his narrow feet and he used a comb on his still-damp hair. Then, despite his unwillingness to do so, he bent and picked up the letter and opened it once more.

It was only a short letter, written in a distinctly childish hand. Had Cassandra used her left hand to write it? It might explain the immature scrawl, the evident effort taken to form the letters. A child of nine could have written it, he supposed, but as he refused to accept its content he couldn't accept its validity.

The temptation to tear the letter into shreds was appealing. He doubted if even Cassandra would have the nerve to write again, and once it was destroyed he could forget all about it.

But he couldn't do it. Despite his suspicions, despite the fact that Antonio's untimely death meant he had no nieces or nephews, a sick kind of curiosity demanded to know what was at the bottom of it.

Even the paper offended his sensibilities. A single sheet of lined notepaper, the kind a stenographer might use to take notes at a meeting, or, more likely, a sheet torn from a child's notepad, just to reinforce the illusion of innocence.

Innocence!

His lips curled as he spread the page between his fingers and read again the message that had so angered him.

Dear Grandpa,

You don't know me and Mum says you don't want to but I don't believe that. I'd like us to be friends and that's why I've got Mum to bring me to Spain on holiday this year. We're coming on June 12 and we're staying in Punta del Lobo at the Pensión del Mar. I know it's by the sea, but I don't know if it's a long way from Tuarega, but anyway you could come to see us. I'm sure Mum would like to see you whatever she says.

With love from your grandson, David de Montoya.

Enrique's teeth clenched. How dared she call her child de Montoya? he thought savagely. If indeed there was a child, he reminded himself again. But, if so, he had to be some bastard born after Antonio was dead and buried. And Enrique knew—

But that was a path he had no intention of being drawn down. Whatever he knew or didn't know about Cassandra was not in question here. His only concern was in ensuring that his father never saw the letter, never suffered the pain of knowing that once again Cassandra Scott—de Montoya, dammit—was trying to insinuate herself into his family.

His fingers curled about the cheap sheet of paper, screwing it into a tight ball in his palm. He didn't want to look at it. He never wanted to see it again. But he had the feeling that, whatever he did, nothing would erase the memory of the words.

He aimed the ball of paper at his wastebin, and then dropped his arm again. If he left the letter there, someone might be curious enough to wonder what it was and unravel it. Unless he was prepared to tear it into pieces and put it into the lavatory, or set fire to it, he would have to dispose of it elsewhere.

Which was what he would do, he decided, neither of the other alternatives having much appeal to him. He refused to consider he might have any unacknowledged motive for hanging onto the missive. It was, after all, the only evidence he had that Cassandra had tried to reach his father.

Smoothing the letter out again, he opened a drawer in his bedside cabinet and slipped it between the pages of his missal. An ironic smile touched his lips at the incongruity of its resting place, but at least he was fairly sure that no one else was likely to find it there.

That still didn't solve the problem of what he was going to do about it, he reflected later, after the maid had served him strong black coffee and warm brioche at a table set beneath the arching canopy of the colonnade. At this hour it was extremely pleasant eating breakfast outdoors, and normally this was the time of day when Enrique reviewed the work that had been done the previous day and consulted his managers' reports of work in progress. As his father's deputy—and in recent weeks the nominal head of the de Montoya corporation—Enrique took his responsibilities seriously. It was infuriating to think that this morning his thoughts were constantly bombarded by the knowledge that it was already June the fifteenth and Cassandra—and possibly her son—were only thirty miles away at Punta del Lobo.

Had the boy—if there was a boy—already found out how

far it was from Punta del Lobo to Tuarega? Was it conceivable that Cassandra might go so far as to come to the estate?

Unable to sit still with such a prospect for company, Enrique picked up his coffee and walked restlessly across the courtyard to where a stone nymph cooled her heels in the waters of the fountain. He paused beside the stone basin and tried to calm his thoughts with the sight of the cream waterlilies that floated in the pool. The *palacio* circled three sides of this central courtyard, the fourth edged with purple azalea and scarlet oleander, whose mingled perfumes found little favour with him this morning. A warm breeze blew up from the valley, tumbling the drying strands of his thick hair over his forehead, and he thrust them back with impatient fingers.

Dammit, why now? he wondered, taking an absent mouthful of his coffee. After almost ten years, why choose this time to break her silence? Was it possible she'd read about his father's illness? Did she think the old man might be more—approachable now, having been faced with his own mortality?

It was possible. Indeed, it was the only explanation that made any sense. Putting aside the unlikely premise that this boy, David de Montoya—he baulked at using that name—had written the letter, what else did he have? So what did he intend to do about it?

Cassandra stood on the sand, shading her eyes as she watched her son playing in the water. He'd made friends with a German boy who was also staying at the *pensión* and they'd spent the past couple of hours competing with each other on the plastic floats they'd hired from the beach attendant. This cove was the ideal place for children, and, although she'd had misgivings when she'd booked the holiday, there was no doubt that they were both benefiting from the break.

But it was already nearly five o'clock and Cassandra could feel her shoulders prickling in spite of the layering of sunscreen she'd applied and reapplied during the afternoon. Three days was not long enough to become completely acclimatised, and, although her skin wasn't as sensitive now as it had been when they'd arrived, she knew better than to risk getting burned.

David didn't have that problem. His skin already possessed a stronger pigment, and, even though she'd insisted on his wearing some protection, he didn't seem to be affected by the sun. Which wasn't unexpected considering his ancestry, Cassandra thought wryly. Not even nine years spent in a cool northern climate could significantly alter the pattern of heredity, and his skin was already acquiring a deeper tan.

Which she couldn't hope to emulate, she reflected, brushing the sand from her arms with slim fingers. She rarely tanned, her pale skin turning pink or red, depending on the circumstances, and then reverting to a creamy white again as soon as the heat subsided. But at least she didn't suffer the ignominy of freckles, even if her unruly mass of hair was more red than copper.

She glanced about her and noticed that the beach was emptying fast. Most people were making their way back to the hotels and *pensiónes* that dotted the hillside below the small town of Punta del Lobo, and Cassandra mimed to her son that it was time they were leaving, too. The beach was used almost exclusively by tourists and, like her, Cassandra guessed they were all looking forward to a cool shower and a change of clothes before venturing out for the evening meal.

Because of David, Cassandra ate earlier than many of their fellow guests. Europeans often had dinner at nine or even ten o'clock in the evening, but as David was invariably up at dawn, by ten o'clock Cassandra was wilting, too.

Still, it was nice to eat at one of the outdoor cafés or *tapas* bars that thronged the small square, and Cassandra looked forward to the glass of wine she usually allowed herself with the meal. Well, she was on holiday, after all, she defended herself, bending to pick up her beach bag and the towels lying on top of it. It had taken long enough, goodness knew, for her to feel sufficiently confident to make the trip.

She straightened and looked about her once again. Despite the fact that this bay was at least an hour's drive from Tuarega, she couldn't completely dispel the apprehension that gripped her when she was alone like this. This was the de Montoyas' territory, after all, and it wouldn't do to forget it.

Not that she truly expected to see anyone she knew. None of them knew they were here and she was a fool to anticipate anything unexpected happening. It would be too much of a coincidence if any member of the de Montoya family turned up in Punta del Lobo. She was worrying unnecessarily.

All the same, when David had once again broached the idea of them coming to Spain on holiday, she had demurred. She supposed he'd been six or seven years old when he'd first asked if they could go to Spain, and it had been comparatively easy at that time to find excuses not to go. This year she hadn't been able to put him off, and, telling herself that Spain was a big country, she'd given in.

She'd had second thoughts, of course, when David had chosen Andalusia, but she'd had to admit that it was one of the most attractive areas in the brochure. And, not wanting to provoke more questions, she'd swallowed her inhibitions and booked it. Despite her fears, no one at the *pensión* had questioned their identity. After all, Punta del Lobo was not Cadiz. She was sure they would be safe enough there.

Her father thought she was mad, of course. But then, Mr Scott had always maintained that she should never have told David his father had been a Spaniard. Though how could she not? she argued. His name was so distinctive. It was only now, as David got older, that she could see her father might have had a point.

But not now, please God, she mused, as her son ran up to her, spraying her with seawater. Horst was with him and Cassandra smiled at the German boy with genuine warmth. Horst's parents had gone to Seville for the day, but the boy had wanted to stay with David and Cassandra had agreed to look after him. He was a nice boy and far more biddable than her son.

No surprise there, then…

Cassandra cut herself off. She had no intention of getting into the reasons for that; no desire to remind herself of the generations of proud arrogant genes that ran in his blood. God knew, it was hard not to think about it every time she looked at him, but somehow, over the years, she had managed to subjugate all her bitterness where her son was concerned.

And she couldn't imagine life without him; that was part of the problem. The fear that one day the de Montoyas might find out she had had a son was an ever-present anxiety, but after nine years she was becoming a little less apprehensive. One day, maybe, when David was fully grown and able to make his own decisions, she might tell him who his father had been. But that was far in the future and not something she even wanted to contemplate at this moment.

'Do we have to go?'

David had picked up his towel and was rubbing it vigorously over his hair. Cassandra smiled and handed Horst his towel before replying, 'I'm afraid so. It's getting late. Haven't you noticed? We're practically the last people on the beach.'

David grimaced. 'So?' he said, arching an imperious brow, and just for a minute Cassandra was reminded of his father's ruthless face.

'So, it's time we were getting back to the *pensión*,' she declared tersely, angry with herself for putting that connotation on him. It was because they were here, because of what she had been thinking, she realised, hiding her irritation. It wasn't David's fault that she was on edge.

'It has been a good day, Mrs de Montoya,' said Horst, his precise English almost better than David's. 'It was most kind of you to let me stay.'

'No problem,' said Cassandra, jockeying her son into putting on his shorts. 'We were happy to have you, weren't we, David?'

'What? Oh, yeah.' David grinned, and he and Horst exchanged a high-handed slap. 'I like showing him what a ditz he is when it comes to board racing.'

'Ditz? What is that, a ditz?' queried Horst, and then grinned himself when he realised the joke was at his expense. 'Jerk,' he said succinctly. 'I will not tell you what I could call you if your mother was not here.'

'Feel free,' taunted David, and, giving the other boy a push, he darted off along the beach.

Horst followed him, and pretty soon they were rolling and tumbling together, with a complete disregard for the clothes they had just donned.

Cassandra sighed, and after returning the two boards the boys had left to the attendant she started after them, easily overtaking them with her long-legged stride. Her ankle-length voile skirt was showing the effects of sand and seawater, too, and she draped David's towel about her shoulders to protect her smarting shoulders as she reached the cliff path.

The boys went up ahead of her, David the taller and therefore the quicker of the two. He was already a good-looking boy and she could imagine what a heartthrob he was going to be when he was older. So long as he didn't do what his father had done, she mused sombrely. That was one problem she did not want to have to deal with again.

The Pensión del Mar was situated near the top of the cliff path, a narrow-fronted building with a striped awning protecting its pristine white façade. Cassandra had been favourably impressed with its appearance and with the service offered which, considering what they were paying, was considerably cheaper than similar accommodation back home. The proprietor, Señor Movida, was a charming man, too, and he was doing everything he could to make their stay a happy one.

To Cassandra's relief, the small Fiat that the Kaufmans had hired was parked on the gravelled forecourt of the *pensión*, which meant that Horst's parents were back. In fact, Herr Kaufman was standing in the doorway to the *pensión*, watching for his son, and Horst bounded ahead to greet his father.

'Lucky dog,' muttered David enviously, and Cassandra cast a startled look his way.

'What did you say?'

'I said Horst is lucky having a father,' declared David gruffly. Then, before his mother could make any response, 'I wonder if there's been any post for us.'

'Post?' Cassandra blinked. 'Do you mean a letter? Who

would be writing to us? We just spoke to your grandfather last night on the phone.'

David shrugged. 'I don't know,' he said, not altogether convincingly, and Cassandra knew a sudden chill. But then Herr Kaufman was coming towards them and she was forced to put her own doubts aside.

'Thank you for looking after Horst, Mrs de Montoya,' he said warmly, his eyes moving appreciatively over her slender figure so that she became intensely conscious of her damp skirt. 'Has Horst been good?'

'He's been very good,' Cassandra answered swiftly, wondering if she was only imagining the avidity of his gaze. 'Did you enjoy your trip?'

'It was most enlightening,' replied the man, nodding. 'We visited many of the palaces and museums. Not something my son would be particularly interested in, I think.'

Cassandra forced a smile. 'I think not,' she agreed. 'I can't imagine David being interested in old buildings either.'

'I might be,' protested her son, but Herr Kaufman wasn't listening to the boy.

'Did you know that your name, de Montoya, is quite a famous one in Andalusia?' he asked conversationally. 'We have been reading some literature about this area, and it seems the de Montoya family is well-known both for the quality of the fortified wines they produce and for the magnificent bulls they breed on their estate just north of here. I do not suppose you are related to them, Mrs de Montoya?'

'No,' said Cassandra quickly, aware that David was now listening to Herr Kaufman with unusual interest. She gestured towards the *pensión*. 'Is that likely?' she asked, trying to make a joke of it, and then felt the fizzy soda she had consumed in the middle of the afternoon rise into her throat.

A man had just emerged from the building behind Horst's father and she felt the colour drain out of her face. Almost convulsively, she clamped a desperate hand on David's shoulder. The boy objected, but for once she was unaware of him. Her eyes were riveted on the newcomer. It couldn't be, she thought sickly. But it was. Enrique de Montoya had paused in the doorway of the *pensión* and was presently surveying the scene that greeted his cold dark eyes with a mixture of satisfaction and contempt.

Dear God, how could this be? she fretted weakly. She'd told no one but her father that she was coming here, to this particular address. People knew she was holidaying in Spain, of course. Her boss at the bookshop where she worked knew, for example. She'd had to tell him what she was doing when she'd arranged for the time off. But he wouldn't have told anyone. No one here, anyway. Certainly not the de Montoyas.

Her mouth dried. He looked just the same, she thought painfully: just as proud, just as arrogant, just as condescending as before. And just as attractive, though her attraction to him had been as crazy as that of the rabbit to the snake. He'd used that attraction, too, ruthlessly, and then expected her to do exactly as he'd wanted.

'Is something wrong?'

Herr Kaufman had noticed her pale face and Cassandra hoped with a desperate longing that it was only a terrible coincidence that Enrique was here. He'd seen them, but perhaps he hadn't recognised them. Well, her actually. He'd never seen David, didn't even know of his existence.

She had to get away. The urge to run was irresistible, and, without considering what David might think of her sudden change of plan, she tightened her hold on his shoulder.

'I've got a headache,' she told Herr Kaufman swiftly. 'It must be the sun. David, come with me. I need some aspirin. We'll just pop along to the *farmacia*—'

'Oh, Mum!' David was predictably awkward. 'Do we have to? We've just got back from the beach. I want a shower.'

'David!'

'Perhaps I can be of some assistance,' broke in Herr Kaufman, possibly seeing a chance to compensate her for looking after his son. 'I'd be happy to go to the *farmacia* for you.'

'Oh, no. I—'

But it was too late. Before she could formulate a convincing excuse, one which would allow her to escape before Enrique recognised them, a tall shadow fell across their little group. And a voice, one which she would have sworn she'd forgotten, cut into their exchange.

'Cassandra?' Even the way he said her name was horribly familiar. 'It is Cassandra, is it not? I am not mistaken?'

As if Enrique de Montoya would ever admit to being mistaken about anything, thought Cassandra wildly, forced to tip her head back to look up at him. He knew exactly who she was, and before she could do anything to protect her son Enrique's dark eyes had moved almost dismissively to the boy at her side.

'And this must be—David,' he continued, only to suck in a strangled breath when he saw the boy.

David! Cassandra blinked. How had he known her son's name? But before she found an answer to this, she saw the devastation his identity had wrought in Enrique's stunned expression. Yes, look at him, she wanted to scream accusingly. See what you did; see what you've lost!

But of course she didn't do anything of the kind. The de Montoyas were too polite for that. Besides, Herr Kaufman was still there, looking at Enrique with considering eyes, glancing from him to Cassandra and back again with obvious enquiry. He was probably wondering what someone who looked like Enrique de Montoya—who dressed like Enrique de Montoya—could have in common with a rather dishevelled English housewife. Enrique's three-piece suit and grey silk shirt were obviously designer-made, whereas Cassandra's clothes had never been particularly stylish, even when they were new.

'You are a friend of Mrs de Montoya?' It was the German who spoke, although David was close on his heels.

'Do you know my grandfather?' he demanded, and even as Cassandra was absorbing the shock of learning that her son knew something about this Enrique found his tongue.

'I—yes,' he said through clenched teeth, the look he cast at Cassandra full of emotions she couldn't hope to identify. 'I—I am your—' His harsh voice was strained. 'Your uncle,' he got out tightly. 'Enrique.' He took a laboured breath. 'I am—happy to meet you at last.'

'You are Enrique de Montoya? *The* Enrique de Montoya?'

Herr Kaufman was persistent, and although Cassandra could hardly blame him for being curious, she wished he would show some discretion.

Enrique was gradually recovering his composure, however. She could see it in the way he straightened his shoulders and looked at the other man with bleak assessing eyes. He'd weathered the blow she'd dealt him and now he was exercising damage control. He had no intention of allowing anyone else to see his real feelings, and his thin lips lifted in a cold smile.

'I have that privilege,' he said now, in answer to the other man's question. 'And you are?'

'Kaufman,' said the German eagerly. 'Franz Kaufman, *señor*.' He held out his hand. 'It is a great pleasure to meet you.'

Enrique hesitated long enough to make the other man uneasy before accepting the gesture. 'How do you do?' he responded, and then turned back to Cassandra.

'Are you really my uncle?'

David had been silent long enough, and at last Franz Kaufman seemed to realise he was intruding. 'If you will excuse me, Horst and I must go and see if my wife is ready to go into town,' he declared, and Cassandra saw Enrique's brow arch in acknowledgement.

He'd probably thought the other man was with her, she brooded bitterly. God, she wished he was, she thought, forgetting her own discomfort with Kaufman's familiarity earlier. But she wished she had some weapon to use against Enrique, something to hurt this man who had attempted to destroy her life.

CHAPTER TWO

THE silence after Franz Kaufman's departure was deafening. Enrique guessed it was up to him to answer the boy's question, but for all his appearance of calm he was as taut as a violin string inside.

God! He'd been so sure he knew what he was doing when he'd decided to come to the Pensión del Mar and confront Cassandra with her sordid little deception. So sure it was the only thing he could do to keep her away from his father. Instead, he was left with the distinct suspicion that he should have left well enough alone.

'I—yes,' he said, after deciding there was no point in denying their kinship. 'Antonio de Montoya was my brother,' he conceded obliquely, aware that Cassandra was looking almost as sick as he felt. 'You are David, I presume?'

Before the boy could answer, however, Cassandra grasped her son's arm and pulled him round to face her. 'What have you done?' she demanded harshly, her voice thick with emotion. 'What have you done?'

The boy had the grace to blush at his mother's obvious distress. 'I told you there might be some post for us,' he mumbled, trying to drag himself away from her. 'I didn't know—*he*—was going to turn up, did I?'

No, he hadn't known that, admitted Enrique to himself. But perhaps he should have suspected that such a bombshell would secure more than a casual response.

Unless... Unless the boy had assumed that his paternal grandfather knew of his existence?

'Did you really expect we might ignore your letter?' he asked now, supremely conscious of Cassandra standing stiffly beside her son, her whole being emitting the kind of hostility he'd never thought to have to face again. It was hard to remember that she had brought this on herself. It wasn't his fault that she'd chosen to keep her son's existence from them.

'No.' David swung round, evidently relieved to be distracted from his mother's fury. 'I knew you'd want to see me. I told Mum ages ago that I wanted to meet my Spanish grandfather, but she said you weren't interested in us.'

'Did she?' Enrique couldn't keep the bitterness out of his voice. 'But she told you how to get in touch with us, no?'

'No!' Cassandra was incensed. 'I wouldn't do such a—'

But David's excited voice overrode her protest. 'No, Mum didn't tell me anything. I got your address from my dad's passport,' he explained proudly. 'Mum keeps it in a box upstairs.' He gave his mother a defiant look as she tried to interrupt him. 'You do,' he insisted, clearly deciding he might never have another chance to defend himself. 'You know you do. Along with all that other stuff: Dad's wallet and letters and things.' He sighed ruefully. 'I'm sorry.' Although he didn't look it. 'I found the box when I was looking for—for something else.'

'What?' Cassandra's demand promised retribution, and David hunched his thin shoulders.

'My catapult,' he muttered, and she stared at him.

'You were looking for your catapult in my wardrobe?' she exclaimed scornfully. 'You expect me to believe that?'

'It's true.' David was defensive now. 'I'd already looked in your knicker drawer and—'

Cassandra uttered something unrepeatable, and despite the seriousness of the situation Enrique felt his lips twitch with uncontrollable mirth. There was something so ludicrous in talking about catapults and knicker drawers when moments before his whole life had shifted on its axis.

But his humour must have shown in his face because Cassandra turned on him, her anger dispersing any pretence of courtesy he might have made. 'You find it funny?' she demanded caustically. 'Well, of course, why would I expect anything different from you? No doubt you find the whole thing hilarious. You and your father can have a good laugh about it when you get home. Which I suggest should be sooner rather than later. Whatever you may think, there's nothing for you here.'

Enrique sobered. 'You think not?' he asked succinctly, and knew a momentary satisfaction when anxiety replaced the fury in her eyes. 'I beg to differ.'

Cassandra held up her head, and he had to admire the way she overcame her obvious dismay. 'I think we've said all there is to say,' she insisted tensely, but Enrique shook his head.

'Not nearly,' he responded coolly. 'And I have to tell you that the only reason I am here is because my father is in the hospital in Seville. He had what they call a triple bypass—yes?—ten days ago. Had he not had this operation, he would have received David's letter himself.'

Cassandra was obviously taken aback at this explanation, but although her lips parted she didn't say anything. It was left to David to express his concern and to ask if his grandfather would be home soon. 'We have to go home in less than two weeks,' he explained earnestly. 'Do you think he'll be back before then?'

'It doesn't matter whether he will or not,' declared Cassandra, proving that whatever Enrique had thought she had had nothing to do with the letter. 'I have no intention of allowing you to associate with—with the de Montoyas, David. We've managed without their involvement in our lives for the past nine years. I have no desire to change the status quo.'

'But I have,' cried David indignantly, a sulky curve pulling down the corners of his lips. Lips which were distinctly like his own, noticed Enrique unwillingly. 'They're my family, just as much as you and Grandad are.'

Enrique had never thought he would ever feel sorry for Cassandra, but he did then. Her face, which had been flushed with anger, became almost dangerously pale, and the hand she lifted to push back the heavy weight of her hair was trembling.

'But they don't want you, David,' she said, her voice breaking under the strain. 'Do you?' She looked at Enrique with eyes he was uneasily aware were filled with tears. 'Do you? Dammit, tell him the truth, can't you?'

* * *

It was after eight o'clock before Enrique got back to Tuarega. It hadn't been that late when he'd left Punta del Lobo, but he'd spent at least an hour driving aimlessly along the coastal road, trying to come to terms with what he'd learned.

God! His hands tightened on the wheel of the Mercedes. He couldn't quite believe what had happened. At no time had either he or his father imagined that the woman who had married his brother and who had been widowed less than twenty-four hours later could have conceived a child. And yet she had. There was no doubt that David was a de Montoya.

But she hadn't known a thing about the letter. Her reaction had proved that. As the boy had said, he'd taken it upon himself to write to Julio de Montoya. The letter had been posted before he and his mother had left England.

He groaned.

Of course, it was tempting to shift all the blame onto Cassandra. She should have known what her son had done. He was only nine years old, *por el amor de Dios*. How difficult could it be to keep track of his movements?

But he also knew that he was not speaking from personal experience. And just because the sons and daughters of his close friends were fairly biddable that was no reason to suppose all children were the same. Indeed, he thought wryly, it could be argued that David was already exhibiting facets of his de Montoya heritage.

At the same time he felt a searing sense of injustice that Cassandra had kept the boy's existence from them. And that, without David's intervention, they might never have learned that Antonio had had a son.

Yet could he wholly condemn her for it? After what had happened—after what *he* had tried to do—she probably thought she'd had every right, after Antonio was killed, to cut the de Montoyas out of her life.

But, God, his father was going to get such a shock. If he'd known of the boy's existence, Enrique knew he would have moved heaven and earth to gain custody of the boy. Whatever he'd thought of Cassandra, whatever he'd done to try and stop their marriage, David was his grandson. His only grandson to date. And, where Julio de Montoya was concerned, blood was everything.

Which was probably one of the main reasons why Cassandra had kept the information from them, Enrique acknowledged shrewdly. She knew better than anyone how ruthless his father could be—how ruthless *he* had been in pursuit of his father's wishes.

But he didn't want to think about that now. This was not the time to be feeling the twinges of conscience. He had to remember how Cassandra had seduced Antonio away from his family, his duty, and the girl he had been engaged to marry. She hadn't shown any conscience, any remorse, not even when—

He took a deep breath. No. He would not get into his own role in the affair. The fact that it had ended in tragedy was enough to warrant any sense of outrage he might feel. Cassandra had destroyed so much: Antonio's honour, his loyalty, his future. Was it possible that his brother had found out what a faithless bitch his new wife was and that was why he'd crashed the car as they drove to the south of England on honeymoon?

No! Once again, he couldn't accept that. If he did, it would mean that Antonio had found out what Enrique and his father had tried to do. Surely, in those circumstances, Cassandra would have wanted him to know, would have wanted him to suffer as she was surely suffering now.

His jaw compressed. Thankfully he had succeeded in hiding the extent of the devastation David's appearance had had on him. As far as Cassandra was concerned his shock had been short-lived, swiftly superseded by the anger he'd felt at her deception. No doubt she believed him to be entirely without feeling, and perhaps it was better if it stayed that way. But how the hell was he going to tell his father?

He shook his head. It would have been so much easier ten years ago. Then, Julio de Montoya had been a strong and dominant man, perfectly capable of handling any situation, with a merciless disregard for anyone who got in his way. He had ruled Tuarega with a rod of iron, and that was why he had found it so hard to accept when Antonio had defied him and insisted he wanted to marry the English girl he'd met while he was at college in London. Julio would have done almost anything to stop that marriage, even to the extent of sending his elder son to England with orders to use any means at his disposal to prevent it.

Enrique's nostrils flared with sudden self-derision. That he hadn't succeeded had always been a source of bitterness between himself and his father. He doubted Julio had ever forgiven him entirely for his failure, but his father had never known what had really happened, why Enrique had returned home without achieving his objective.

He could have stopped the wedding. If he'd told Antonio the truth, he was fairly sure his brother would have called it off. But he hadn't said a thing. Because he'd been too ashamed of what he'd done; because he'd had only disgust for his part in it. He'd flown back to Spain knowing that Cassandra had won.

But had she? Now he was not so sure, and he despised himself for his weakness where she was concerned.

It was dark as he drove up through the valley where his family had lived for hundreds of years. Lights glinted from narrow windows in the village and the floodlit spire of San Tomás's church was a reassuring sight. It was easy to believe that nothing changed here, that the ghosts of his ancestors would see and recognise the sights and sounds of other centuries in the immediacy of the twenty-first, but he knew better. There had been many changes, most particularly during General Franco's years as president. But fortunately the political climate in this rural area had never mirrored that found in the cities, and as he accelerated past the fields and paddocks where his *toros bravos*, or fighting bulls, were grazing, he felt a sense of pride in his family's achievements.

But that was short-lived. Thinking of his family reminded him that he had promised to ring his mother this evening. She was staying at the *apartamento* in Seville while her husband was in the hospital there and Enrique had said he would ring no later than seven o'clock. It was long past that time now, and he was ashamed to admit that for the past few hours he had given little thought to his responsibilities.

His mother would be sure to think that he'd forgotten, or that he simply didn't care. Since Julio's illness Elena de Montoya had become over-sensitive, looking for slights where none were intended, as if she was afraid that her husband's incapacity somehow affected her authority. Perhaps she feared that if Julio died Enrique would no longer have respect for her, which was ridiculous.

Still, it was true that since Antonio's death she had come to depend on him more and more. Julio's heart attack some months ago had only increased her demands on his time, and, although Enrique knew it was only to be expected in the circumstances, it wasn't always easy to balance his own needs with those of his parents.

Enrique brought the powerful car to a halt beside the arched colonnade that had once fronted a coach house and which now provided garaging for the estate's many motor vehicles. Years ago, Enrique's grandfather had kept a shining Hispano-Suiza here, and he remembered being allowed to ride in the front of the car on special occasions. He also remembered the punishment he'd received when the old man had found out he had taken the car out alone. He'd been afraid he'd never be allowed to have a car of his own.

But now was not the time to be having memories about the past. He knew it was seeing Cassandra again, meeting the boy, remembering what had happened ten years ago, that was responsible for his reminiscing about happier times. But the past wasn't going to help him now. Somehow he had to decide what he was going to do about the present, and, although he intended to ring his mother, there was no way on earth he could tell her where he had been.

Or what had happened, he conceded, nodding to the man who had emerged from the building to take charge of the car. As he strode across the forecourt to the magnificent entrance of the *palacio* his mind was already busy finding excuses for his tardy behaviour.

Hardly noticing the intricately carved doorway, with its

wrought-iron façade, he strode through a high-ceilinged entry that was distinctly Moorish in design. With a carved ceiling and tiled walls, this was the oldest part of the *palacio* and displayed its heritage in a dozen different ways. Enrique had always believed that Tuarega owed its name to the wild tribe of the Sahara, whose influence had spread beyond the shores of North Africa. But, whatever its history, there was little doubt that it owed its origins to the Saracen invaders who had occupied this part of Spain at the time of the crusades.

Generations of Spanish conquerors had followed them, of course, and much of the present building had been erected in more recent centuries. But the *palacio* had retained its atmosphere of light and coolness and space, successive craftsmen sustaining the delicacy of design that had characterised its Muslim architecture.

The courtyard, where he had eaten breakfast that morning, was immediately ahead of him, but Enrique turned left before reaching the outer doors, mounting a flight of marble stairs to an upper landing. One of the *palacio's* many retainers stopped him to ask if he had eaten, but Enrique wasn't interested in food. First he had to ring his mother, then he had to try and take stock of what his options were. And what he was going to do about them.

Cassandra had given him no latitude. As far as she was concerned he was sure she would prefer to consign him and all his family to hell. She hadn't even let him talk to David, with or without her presence. She'd dragged the boy away into the *pensión*, probably hoping that she never had to see him again.

Which was decidedly naïve, he conceded grimly, thrusting open the door into his apartments and consigning his tie to the nearest surface. Whatever his own feelings in the matter might be, there was no way he could ignore the fact that David was his nephew. His parting words to the boy—that they would meet again, and soon—had been met with a cold 'Over my dead body!' from his mother, but Enrique was not deterred. Whether Cassandra chose to make this easy or not was of no interest to him. David was a de Montoya. Sooner or later he would have to learn what that meant.

CHAPTER THREE

CASSANDRA propped her chin on her hands and stared wearily across the table at her son's sulky face. She ought to be really angry with him, and she was, but she couldn't help feeling the tiniest bit of sympathy, too.

After all, it wasn't his fault that she'd never told him the truth about his de Montoya relations. She'd always avoided any discussion of her late husband's family, hoping, pointlessly as it had turned out, that David would accept the fact that they and his mother just didn't get on. It wasn't as if he was short of an extended family. Cassandra's two sisters were both married with children of their own. David had aunts and uncles and cousins, as well as his maternal grandfather to call on. Foolishly, she had thought that would be enough.

Clearly, it hadn't been. Like his father before him, David was far too intelligent to accept her prevarication. But to go through her things, to seek out Antonio's passport and write secretly to Julio de Montoya without even telling her what he'd done... Well, she didn't know how she was going to forgive him for that.

She sighed, wondering what the chances were of them getting an earlier flight home. Not very good, she surmised, remembering how full the plane had been on the journey out. Besides, she'd paid for a two-week holiday package and if she wanted to change the return date she would obviously have to pay extra for their seats.

Not an option she wanted to consider. She had already spent over her budget in coming here and she was loath to ask her father to bail them out. That, too, would entail more explanations than she was prepared to face at present.

'Are you going to maintain this ridiculous silence for much longer?' she enquired at last, forcing her son to look up from the scrambled eggs and bacon he had ordered in spite of her protests. A fried breakfast was far too heavy in this climate, in her opinion, but David had not been in the mood to compromise. 'Because if you are,' she added, 'I'll leave you to it.'

David emptied his mouth of food, took a gulp of orange juice, and then regarded her with accusing eyes. 'Do I get a choice?' he enquired insolently, and Cassandra knew a totally uncharacteristic desire to smack him.

'I won't be spoken to like this, David,' she said, folding her napkin and placing it beside her plate. She, herself, had eaten nothing, and the sight of the greasy food was enough to turn her stomach. 'I realise you think you have some justification for acting this way, but you've got no idea what a nest of vipers you're uncovering.'

'A nest of vipers,' scoffed her son, around another mouthful of egg. 'You don't know what you're talking about. If you ask me, you're just jealous because Uncle Enrique liked me.'

Jealous!

Cassandra's nails dug into her palms. 'You think so?' she said, the urge to wipe the smug look off his face becoming almost overwhelming. 'And what would you know about it?'

'I know Uncle Enrique is nice, really nice,' declared her son staunchly. 'Gosh, you were so rude to him, Mum! It's a wonder he even wants to see me again.'

Cassandra pressed her lips together, feeling the unwelcome prick of tears behind her eyes. Oh, yes, she wanted to say, Enrique de Montoya wants to see you again. Now that he knows I have a son, he'll do everything he can to take you away from me.

But, of course, she couldn't tell her son that. She couldn't be so cruel. Apart from anything else, it was unlikely he would believe her. In David's world, people were exactly what they appeared to be; they said what they thought. They didn't lie or cheat, or use any means in their power to destroy someone else. Why frighten him unnecessarily? He would learn soon enough that the de Montoyas would do anything to gain their own ends.

'Anyway, I think you should tell him you're sorry when you see him again,' went on David, scraping up the last of his eggs with his fork. He looked up, his dark eyes a haunting reminder of the past. 'We are going to see him again, aren't we, Mum?'

Cassandra hesitated. 'I don't think so. I've decided to cut the holiday short,' she said, even though she hadn't decided any such thing until that moment. 'I'm going to find out whether we can get a flight home later today—'

'No!' David sprang up from his seat in dismay, and the family of holidaymakers at the nearby table turned curious eyes to see what was going on. 'I won't go,' he said, not caring what anyone else thought of his behaviour. 'You can't make me.'

'Sit down, David.'

Cassandra was embarrassed, but her son was beyond being reasoned with. 'I won't sit down,' he declared. 'I want to see Uncle Enrique again. I want to see my grandfather. Why shouldn't I?'

'Sit down!'

This time Cassandra got half out of her seat and, as if realising he wasn't doing himself any favours by making it impossible for his mother to face her fellow guests, he subsided unwillingly into his seat.

'Now, listen to me,' said Cassandra, her voice thick with emotion, 'you'll do exactly as I tell you. You're nine years old, David. I have every right to demand that you do as I say.'

David's expression was sulky, but Cassandra was relieved to see that there were tears in his eyes now. 'But why are you being so awful?' he exclaimed huskily. 'You always said you loved my father. Was that just a lie?'

'No!' Cassandra gave an inward groan. 'I did love him. More than you can ever know.'

'Then—'

'But your father wasn't like the rest of his family,' she continued urgently. 'He was—sweet; gentle. He—he was prepared to risk the wrath of his own family just so we could be together.'

David frowned. 'Are you saying they tried to stop you getting married?'

Cassandra's stomach lurched. 'Something like that.'

'So when you said you didn't get on with Dad's family, what you really meant was that they didn't get on with you?'

God, Cassandra really didn't want to talk about this.

'I—suppose so,' she agreed tensely.

'But that doesn't mean they don't want to know you now,' protested David, his eagerness showing in his face. 'Dad died, what? Ten years ago?'

'Nearly.'

'So...' He shrugged. 'They've obviously changed their minds. Why else would Uncle Enrique come here to meet us?'

'Because of *you*,' cried his mother fiercely, realising too late that she had spoken a little too vehemently. 'I mean,' she said, modifying her tone, 'naturally they want to meet you. You're your father's son.'

'And yours,' put in David at once. 'And once they get to know you—'

'They're not going to get to know me,' said Cassandra desperately. 'Haven't you been listening to a word I've said? I never want to see any of the de Montoyas again.'

David's face crumpled. 'You don't mean that.'

'I do mean it.' Cassandra felt dreadful but she had to go on. 'I know you're disappointed, but if we can't get a flight home, I'm going to see if it's possible for us to move to another *pensión* along the coast—'

'No!'

'Yes.' Cassandra was determined. 'I'm prepared to compromise. I know you've been looking forward to this holiday, and I don't want to deprive you of it, so perhaps we can move to another resort.'

'I don't want to move to another resort,' protested David unhappily. 'I like it here. I've made friends here.'

'You'll make friends wherever we go.'

'No, I won't.'

'Of course you will.'

'But—'

'But what?'

David shook his head, apparently deciding he'd argued long enough. 'Nothing,' he muttered, and then looked considerably relieved when Horst Kaufman and his parents stopped at their table.

The German family had been having breakfast on the terrace and now they all smiled down at David and his mother.

'Good morning, Mrs de Montoya,' said Franz Kaufman cheerfully. 'It is another lovely day, yes?'

'Oh—yes.' Cassandra managed a polite smile in return. Then, noticing their more formal clothes, 'Are you going off for the day?'

'Yes. We are going to Ortegar, where we believe there is a leisure facility for the children.' It was Frau Kaufman who answered, and Cassandra couldn't help but admire their grasp of her language. 'A water park and such. We wondered if you would permit David to come with us?'

'Oh.'

Cassandra was nonplussed. She hardly knew the Kaufmans and the idea of allowing David to go off with them for the day was not something she would normally countenance. But, she reminded herself, she was going to spend the day trying to change their hotel arrangements, and going off with Horst and his family might be just what her son needed to put all thoughts of the de Montoyas out of his head.

'Can I, Mum? Can I?'

David was clearly enthusiastic, and, putting her own doubts aside, Cassandra lifted her shoulders in a helpless gesture. 'I—I don't know what to say.'

'We would take great care of him, of course,' put in Franz Kaufman heartily, patting David on the shoulder. 'And as he and Horst get along together so well...'

'We do. We do.'

David gazed at her with wide appealing eyes, and deciding that anything was better than having him dragging after her all day, making his feelings felt, Cassandra sighed.

'Well, all right,' she agreed, earning a whoop from both children. 'Um—where did you say you were going?'

'Ortegar,' said Frau Kaufman at once, and Cassandra frowned.

'Ortegar?' she said. 'Where is that exactly?'

'It is along the coast. Near Cadiz,' answered Franz a little impatiently. 'Maybe twenty miles from here, that is all.'

And probably twenty miles nearer Tuarega, thought Cassandra, moistening her lips. She knew that because she had scanned the map very thoroughly before agreeing to David's choice of destination.

Her heartbeat quickened. David's choice of destination, she realised unsteadily. Goodness, how long had her son been planning to write to his grandfather?

'I'll go and get ready,' said David eagerly, and she wondered if he suspected what she was thinking. 'I won't be long.'

'I'll come with you,' murmured Cassandra, getting up from her chair and giving the Kaufmans another polite smile. 'If you'll excuse me.'

'We will be waiting out front.' Franz Kaufman nodded his approval, and Cassandra was left with the uneasy feeling that she had been out-manoeuvred by her son again.

David had already bundled a towel and his swimming trunks into his backpack by the time she reached their room. He had evidently raced up the stairs and she tried not to wonder if he was desperate to get away.

'Do you need any money?' she asked, picking up a discarded tee shirt from the floor, but David only shook his head and edged towards the door.

'I've got four hundred pesetas. That's enough,' he said quickly, and his mother stared at him.

'That's less than two pounds,' she exclaimed. 'You don't know how much it will cost to get into the leisure park.'

'You can pay Herr Kaufman when we get back,' said David impatiently. 'Come on, Mum. They're waiting for me.'

Not that urgently, thought Cassandra unhappily, but she had given her word. 'All right,' she said, accepting his dutiful peck on her cheek. 'Be good.'

'I will.' David headed out of the door with a triumphant grin on his face. 'See you later.'

* * *

Sanchia's red sports car was just pulling up outside the *palacio* when Enrique came out of the building. Sanchia herself, tall and dark and exotically beautiful, emerged from the vehicle, smoothing down the narrow skirt of the green linen suit that barely skimmed her knees.

Once his brother's fiancé, Sanchia had swiftly recovered from that fiasco. Within a year, she had married a distant relative of the Spanish royal family, and when her elderly husband died leaving her a wealthy widow, she had immediately transferred her affections to her late fiancé's brother, making Enrique wonder if that hadn't been her objective all along.

But perhaps he was being conceited, he thought now. Sanchia had been heartbroken when Antonio had married an Englishwoman and had then been killed almost before the ink on the marriage licence was dry. She had turned to him then, but he hadn't imagined that her plea for his affection had been anything more than a natural response to the circumstances she'd found herself in. After all, Sanchia's family had never had a lot of money and it must have been quite a blow when her wealthy fiancé abandoned her less than three months before their wedding.

In any event, Enrique had made it quite plain then that he was not interested in taking up where his brother had left off. He liked Sanchia well enough, he always had, but the idea of taking her to bed because his brother had let her down was anathema to him. He had been grieving, too, and not just because his brother was dead. He had let Antonio down, and he'd found it hard to live with himself at that time.

Now, things were different. Sanchia had been married and widowed, and he himself was that much older and more willing to accept that life could all too easily deal you a rotten hand. The relationship he had with Sanchia these days suited both of them. He doubted he would ever get married, despite what his father had had to say about it, and, although Sanchia might hope that he'd change his mind, she was not, and never could be, the only woman in his life.

Which was probably why he felt such an unexpected surge

of impatience at her appearance this morning. His thoughts were focused on what he planned to do today and Sanchia could play no part in that.

She, of course, knew nothing of the events of yesterday. Even though there'd been a message from her waiting on his answering machine when he'd got back last night, he hadn't returned her call, which probably explained her arrival now.

'Querido!' she exclaimed, her use of the Spanish word for 'darling' sounding warm and intimate on her tongue. She reached up to kiss him, pouting when her lips only brushed his cheek, before surveying his casual appearance with some disappointment. 'You are going out? I was hoping we might spend the day together.'

'I am sorry.' Enrique was aware that his navy tee shirt and cargo trousers were not his usual attire, but they were less likely to attract attention in a holiday resort than the three-piece suit he'd worn the day before. 'I have got—some business to attend to.'

'Dressed like this?' Sanchia twined her fingers into the leather cord that he'd tied at his waist. 'I cannot see you visiting one of your clients in a tee shirt.'

'Did I say I was going to visit one of my clients?' asked Enrique rather more curtly than he had intended. He disentangled her fingers from the cord and stepped back from her. 'It is a personal matter,' he appended, feeling obliged to give her some sort of explanation. 'Really. I have got to go.'

'Is it another woman?' she demanded, and just for a moment he felt a surge of resentment that she should feel she had the right to question his actions.

But then common sense reasserted itself. Why shouldn't she feel she had some rights where he was concerned? They had been seeing one another for months, after all.

'Not in the way you mean,' he assured her, his thin smile hardly a reassurance. Then, belatedly, 'Perhaps I can ring you later?'

Sanchia's lips tightened. 'You are not going to tell me where you are going?'

'No.' There was no ambivalence on that score.

Her mouth trembled now. 'Enrique…'

His irritation was totally unwarranted, and he despised himself for it. But, dammit, he wanted to get to Punta del Lobo before Cassandra had time to disappear again. 'Look,' he said reasonably, 'this does not concern you—us. It is—something to do with my father. A confidential matter I have to attend to.'

Sanchia's jaw dropped. 'Your father has been having an affair?'

'No!' Enrique was horrified that she should even think such a thing.

'But you said it did involve another woman,' she reminded him, and Enrique wished he'd kept his mouth shut.

'I also said, not in the way you mean,' he declared shortly. 'It is just—' *Dios*, what could he say? '—an unexpected complication.'

'That involves a woman?'

'Only indirectly.'

That, at least, was true, although Enrique could feel his stomach tighten as he thought of confronting Cassandra again. *Dios*, he hated that woman, he thought savagely. If only he could tell Sanchia how he really felt, she would have no further cause for concern.

'Muy bien.' She pivoted on her high heels and, waiting for him to fall into step beside her, she started towards her car. 'But you will ring me later this morning, *sí*?'

'Make it this afternoon,' said Enrique, suppressing a sigh. 'If I cannot reach you at home, I will call your mobile.'

'Which will not be switched off as yours was last night,' remarked Sanchia waspishly, inspiring another twinge of irritation. Dammit, when had they got to the point where every move he made had to be justified?

'I will ring,' he assured her, making no promises of when that would be. He swung open the door of the scarlet convertible. *'Adiós!'*

CHAPTER FOUR

CASSANDRA trudged back to the lodging house with a heavy heart. She had wasted the whole morning waiting to see her holiday representative to try and get David and herself transferred to an alternative *pensión*, but she was no further forward.

The trouble was, the kind of accommodation she and her son could afford was in short supply and, without paying a huge supplement and moving to a hotel, they were stuck. The young rep who was based at the nearby Hotel Miramar had been very polite, but after spending the morning dealing with other holidaymakers' complaints, she was naturally puzzled by Cassandra's request. Particularly as the only excuse she could offer for wanting to leave the Pensión del Mar was because Punta del Lobo was too quiet. The girl had probably thought she was used to frequenting bars and nightclubs, thought Cassandra unhappily. And what kind of a mother did that make her appear to be?

It was all Enrique de Montoya's fault, she thought resentfully. If he hadn't turned up and ruined what had promised to be the first really good holiday they had had in ages, she wouldn't have had to tell lies to anyone, or now have to face the prospect of David's disappointment when he discovered their options had narrowed. As far as she could see, she only had one alternative: to bring the date for their homeward journey forward. Whatever it cost.

And, as she approached the *pensión*, she was forced to admit that it wasn't just the de Montoyas' fault that she was in this position. David had to take his share of the blame. All right, perhaps she should have been more honest with him right from the beginning, but surely he had known that what he was doing was wrong? Wasn't that why he had kept the letter a secret from her?

She turned in at the gate of the *pensión*, tipping her head back to ease the tension in her neck, and then felt a quivering start in the pit of her stomach. As she looked ahead again, she saw a man rising from the low wall that bordered the terrace, where chairs and tables offered an alternative to eating indoors. The striped canopy, which gave the Pensión del Mar its individuality, formed a protective shade from the rays of the midday sun, but it also cast a shadow that Cassandra at first thought had deceived her eyes. But, no, she was not mistaken. It was Enrique who had been sitting there, waiting for her, like the predator she knew him to be.

But, as always, he looked cool and composed, his lean muscled frame emphasised by a tight-fitting navy tee shirt and loose cotton trousers. Despite herself, she felt her senses stir at his dark, powerful masculinity, and it was that much harder to steel herself against him.

'What are you doing here?' she asked, taking the offensive before he could disconcert her, and he gave her a retiring look.

'Where is he?' he demanded, looking beyond her, and she was inordinately grateful that the Kaufmans had taken David out for the day.

'He's not here,' she said, deciding to let him make what he liked of that. 'You've wasted your time in coming here.'

Enrique's eyes grew colder, if that were at all possible. He was already regarding her with icy contempt, and she was unhappily aware that again he had found her looking hot and dishevelled. But after a morning sitting in the open foyer of the Miramar, which was not air-conditioned and where she had not been offered any refreshment, she was damp and sweaty. Her hair, which she should really have had cut before she came away, was clinging to the nape of her neck, and her cropped sleeveless top and cotton shorts fairly shrieked of their chainstore origins.

But what did it matter what he thought of her? she asked herself impatiently. However she looked, he was not going to alter his opinion of her or of David, and, even if she'd been voted the world's greatest mum, the de Montoyas would still be looking for a way to take David away from her.

'Where is he?' Enrique asked again, and this time she decided not to prevaricate.

'He's gone out with friends,' she replied, making an abortive little foray to go past him, but he stepped into her path.

'What friends?' His dark eyes bored into her. 'The Kaufmans?'

'Got it in one,' said Cassandra, acknowledging that Enrique never forgot a name. 'Now, if you'll excuse me…'

Enrique said something that sounded suspiciously like an oath before his hard fingers fastened about her forearm. 'Do not be silly, Cassandra,' he intoned wearily. 'You are not going anywhere and you know it.'

She didn't attempt to shake him off. It wouldn't have done any good and she knew it. But perhaps she could get rid of him in other ways and she widened her eyes challengingly at him as she opened her mouth.

But the scream she'd been about to utter stuck in her throat when he hustled her across the gravelled forecourt of the *pensión*, his words harsh against her ear. 'Make a scene and I may just have to report Señor Movida to the licensing authorities.'

Cassandra stared at him. 'You can't do that. Señor Movida hasn't done anything wrong.'

'I am sure my lawyers could come up with something, if I paid them enough,' retorted Enrique unfeelingly, propelling her around the corner from the *pensión* to where his Mercedes was parked. 'And you, I am equally sure, would not risk that.'

Cassandra trembled. 'You're a bastard, Enrique!'

'Better a bastard than a liar, Cassandra,' he informed her coldly, flicking the switch that unlocked the car. 'Please get in.'

'And if I don't?'

Enrique regarded her with unblinking eyes. 'Do not go there, Cassandra. You are only wasting your time and mine. We need to talk, and you will have to forgive my sensibilities when I say I prefer not to—how is it you say it?—wash my linen in public?'

'Dirty linen,' muttered Cassandra, before she could stop herself, and Enrique's mouth curved into a thin smile.

'Your words, not mine,' he commented, swinging open the nearside door and waiting patiently for her to get into the car. And, when she'd done so with ill grace, unhappily conscious of her bare knees and sun-reddened thighs, he walked round the back of the vehicle and coiled his long length behind the steering wheel. Then, with a derisive glance in her direction, 'Do not look so apprehensive, Cassandra. I do not bite.'

'Don't you?'

Now she held his gaze with hot accusing eyes and then experienced a pang of anguish when he looked away. Was he remembering what she was remembering? she wondered, despising herself for the unwelcome emotions he could still arouse inside her. God, the only memories she should have were bitter ones.

His starting the engine caught her unawares. 'What do you think you're doing?' she cried, diverted from her thoughts, and he lifted his shoulders in a resigned gesture.

'What does it look like I am doing?' he enquired, glancing in the rearview mirror, checking for traffic. 'You didn't think we were going to sit here and talk?'

'Why not?'

'Humour me,' he said tersely, and although Cassandra was fairly sure that nothing she said or did would change his mind, she bit down on her protests. Why should she object when he was leaving the *pensión*? She might even be able to persuade him not to come back.

Or not.

'I'm not going to Tuarega with you,' she blurted suddenly, and Enrique gave a short mirthless laugh as he pulled out of the parking bay.

'I have not invited you to do so,' he observed drily, and she felt the flush of embarrassment deepen the colour in her cheeks. 'I suggest we find a bar where it is unlikely that either of us will meet anyone we know.'

'Don't you mean anyone *you* know?' she snorted, and he gave her a considering look.

'Does it matter?'

'Not to me,' she assured him coldly. 'I just want to get this over with.'

Enrique shook his head. 'We both know that is not going to happen,' he replied flatly. 'You should not have written to my father if you wished to keep your selfish little secret.'

'I didn't write to your father,' Cassandra reminded him fiercely. 'I wouldn't do such a thing.'

'No.' He conceded the point. 'I believe that now.'

'Now?' Cassandra was appalled. 'Do you mean you had any doubts?'

Enrique shrugged. 'I had my reasons.'

'What reasons?' Cassandra stared at him, and then comprehension dawned. 'My God, you did think I'd written the letter, didn't you? You honestly thought I'd want anything from *you*! Or your father!'

Enrique didn't answer her and she was left with the shattering discovery that his opinion of her hadn't changed one bit. He still thought she was a greedy little gold-digger, who had only latched onto his brother because she'd known what his background was.

Pain, like a knife, sliced through her, and she reached unthinkingly for the handle of the door. In that moment she didn't consider that they had left the small town of Punta del Lobo behind, that the car was in traffic and that they were moving at approximately sixty kilometres an hour. Her only need was to get as far away from him as possible as quickly as possible, and even the sudden draught of air that her action elicited only made her feel even more giddy and confused.

She didn't know what might have happened if Enrique hadn't reacted as he had. At that moment she didn't care. But, with a muffled oath, he did two things almost simultaneously: his hand shot out and grasped her arm, anchoring her to her seat, and he swung the big car off the winding coast road, bringing it to a shuddering stop on a sand-strewn verge above towering cliffs.

'*Estas loco?* Are you mad?' he demanded, and she realised it was a measure of the shock he'd had that he'd used his own language and not hers. Then, when she turned a white tear-stained face in his direction, his eyes grew dark and tortured. 'Crazy woman,' he muttered, his voice thick and unfamiliar, and, switching off the engine, he flung himself out of the car.

He went to stand at the edge of the cliffs, the warm wind that blew up from the ocean flattening the loose-fitting trousers against his strong legs. He didn't look back at her, he simply stood there, gazing out at the water, raking long fingers through his hair before bringing them to rest at the back of his neck.

Perhaps he was giving her time to regain her composure, Cassandra pondered uneasily, as sanity reasserted itself. But she didn't think so. Just for a moment there she had glimpsed the real Enrique de Montoya, the passionate man whose feelings couldn't be so coldly contained beneath a mask of studied politeness, and she suspected he had been as shocked as she was.

Nevertheless, however she felt about him, there was little doubt that he had saved her from serious injury or worse. He'd risked his own life by swerving so recklessly off the highway, taking the car within inches of certain disaster, just to prevent her from doing something which, as he'd said, would have been crazy.

What had she been thinking? She trembled as the full extent of her own stupidity swept over her. What good would it have done to throw herself from the car? What would it have achieved? If she'd been killed—God, the very thought of it set her shaking again—who would have looked after David then? Whose claim on her son would have carried the most weight? She didn't need to be a psychic to know that in those circumstances her own family would have been fighting a losing battle.

So why hadn't Enrique let her do it? Or was that what he was doing now? Reproving himself for allowing a God-given opportunity to slip through his fingers? No. However naïve it might make her, she didn't think that either.

She took a breath and then, pushing open her door, she got out of the car. She steadied herself for a moment, with her hand on the top of her door. Then, closing it again, she walked somewhat unsteadily across to where he was standing. The wind buffeted her, too, sending the tumbled mass of her hair about her face, but she only held it back, her eyes on Enrique's taut profile.

'I'm—sorry,' she said after a moment, but although she knew he'd heard her, he didn't look her way.

'Go back to the car.' The words were flat and expressionless. 'I will join you in a moment.'

Cassandra caught her lower lip between her teeth. 'You're right,' she said, forced to go on. 'What I did was crazy! I could have killed us both.'

Now Enrique did look at her, but she gained no reassurance from his blank expression. 'Forget it,' he told her. 'I have.'

Cassandra quivered. 'As you forget everything that doesn't agree with you?' she asked tremulously. 'And everyone?'

Enrique's features contorted. 'I have forgotten nothing,' he assured her harshly, and she shrank from his sudden antagonism.

'Then how do you live with yourself?' she was stung to reply, and with a muffled epithet he brushed past her.

'God knows,' he muttered in his own language, but she understood him. He headed for the car. 'Are you coming?'

The bar he took her to was in the next village. A whitewashed building on the road, it was open at the back, spilling its customers out onto a wood-framed deck above a pebbled beach. Further along, a black jetty jutted out into the blue water, and several small fishing smacks and rowing boats were drawn up onto a strip of sand. Old men sat mending their nets, and, judging by the clientele in the bar, this was not a venue for tourists.

Contrary to what Enrique had said earlier, the bartender knew exactly who he was, and it was obvious from the man's manner that he welcomed his customer. Cassandra guessed, nonetheless, that he was curious about who she was and why Enrique should choose to bring her here, but he knew better than to ask questions. Instead, he escorted them personally to a table on the deck that was shaded by a canvas canopy, and enquired politely what he could get them to drink.

'Wine?' suggested Enrique, looking at Cassandra, and at her indifferent nod he ordered two glasses of Rioja. 'It is served from a barrel here,' he explained as the man walked away, and Cassandra guessed he was only behaving courteously for the other man's benefit.

'What is this place?' she asked, taking her cue from him, and Enrique glanced towards the jetty before looking at her.

'San Augustin,' he said in the same civil tone. 'I used to come here a lot when I was younger. While I was a student, I worked behind the bar for a while until my father found out.'

'And stopped you?' suggested Cassandra unthinkingly, and he nodded.

'My father said a de Montoya should not—well, it is not important what he said,' he appended shortly. 'It is many years now.'

'Yet the bartender remembers you.'

'I did not mean it is so many years since I was here,' he explained. 'José and I, we know one another quite well.'

Cassandra began to smile and then pulled her lips into a straight line again. She was starting to relax with him and that was not good. She had no doubt it would suit him very well, but she had to remember why he had brought her here and it wasn't to exchange anecdotes about the past. Well, not that past anyway, she amended, with a sudden spurt of hysteria.

The bartender returned with their wine and a large plate of what she realised were *tapas*. But not the mass-produced *tapas* that were available in the bars in Punta del Lobo. Something told her that this was the real thing, the fat juicy olives, spiced with herbs, the batter-dipped prawns, the bite-sized pieces of crisply fried fish bearing little resemblance to what she'd seen so far. They smelled wholesome, too, and in other circumstances the cheese that was oozing out of the paper-thin rolls of ham would have made her mouth water.

'Is good, *señor*?' the man enquired, obviously having heard them speaking in English, and Enrique inclined his head.

'Muy bien, José,' he responded in his own language. Very good. *'Gracias.'*

The bartender smiled and went away, and Enrique indicated the food. 'Are you hungry?'

'Hardly,' said Cassandra, reluctantly taking a sip of her wine. She hoped it wasn't too intoxicating. She'd had nothing to eat that day and her stomach was already bubbling with apprehension. 'Why did you want to speak to me?'

Enrique hesitated. She noticed he wasn't interested in the food either and, like her, he seemed quite content to concentrate on his wine. His hands, brown and long-fingered, played with the stem of his glass, and she was mesmerised by their sensitive caress. It reminded her far too acutely of how those fingers had felt gripping her wrist, grasping her arm, stroking her naked flesh…

She took a laboured breath as somewhere nearby a guitar began to play. Its music, poignant at times, at others vibrantly sensual, tugged at her emotions, fanning the flames of memories she desperately wanted to forget. She should not have come here, she thought unsteadily. She was still far too vulnerable where he was concerned.

'I think you know why we have to talk,' Enrique said at last, his eyes intent. 'David is a de Montoya. You had no right to keep that from us.'

Cassandra pursed her lips. 'You're sure of that, are you?'

'What? That he is Antonio's son? Of course.'

'What makes you so certain?'

Enrique lay back in his chair, giving her a sardonic look. 'Cassandra, do not play games with me. We both know that he is the image of his father at that age.'

'Is he?'

'Do you wish me to produce a photograph as proof? No, I did not think so. The boy shows his Spanish blood in every way. His eyes, his colouring, his mannerisms. His honesty.'

Cassandra stiffened. 'His honesty?' she demanded caustically. 'Oh, right. You'd know a lot about that.'

A muscle in Enrique's jaw jerked angrily. 'Do not bait me,

Cassandra. What is it they say about glass houses? It is not wise to throw stones, no?'

Cassandra rested her elbows on the table, hunching her shoulders and curling her fingers behind her ears. It would be so easy to burst his bubble, she mused, so easy to explode the myth that David was Antonio's son, but it was seldom wise to give in to temptation, as she knew only too well. Much better to wait to allow the situation to develop, to keep that particular revelation up her sleeve. She had reason to believe that she might need it.

'All right,' she said, allowing him to make what he liked of that, 'perhaps I should have informed your father when David was born. But I had every reason to believe that he—that all of you—wanted nothing more to do with me.'

Enrique's nostrils flared. 'So you decided to take your revenge by keeping the boy's existence a secret from us?'

'It wasn't revenge,' exclaimed Cassandra fiercely, her voice rising. And then, aware that she was attracting the attention of other patrons in the bar, she lowered her tone. 'I mean it. I—I wanted nothing more to do with the de Montoyas.'

'Even though my father was Antonio's father, too? That he is David's grandfather? That David is his only grandson?'

'I didn't know that, did I?' muttered Cassandra, taking a reckless gulp of her wine and almost choking herself. She coughed painfully and her eyes watered and it was several minutes before she could continue. 'I assumed that you'd have married and had children of your own,' she got out at last.

'Did you really?' He was sceptical.

'If I ever thought about it,' she declared defensively. 'I—have to admit, it's not something that's given me sleepless nights.'

Which wasn't entirely true, but Enrique didn't need to know that.

'No,' he said now, his lips twisting. 'Why should you waste your time on something that meant so little to you?'

Cassandra arched brows that were several shades darker than her hair. 'Do you blame me?'

Enrique shrugged, and with sudden urgency she added, 'I've always wondered, what did you tell Antonio?'

Enrique shook his head. 'Why should I tell you? He obviously did not believe me.'

'No.' She looked doubtful. 'He never said anything about it to me.'

'Why would he?' Enrique was harsh. 'My brother, too, was an honourable man.'

'Too?' she mocked him. 'I hope you're not including yourself in that statement.'

'I meant my father,' he retorted coldly. 'And my nephew David, at least understands that family means something.'

'David has a family.' Cassandra quivered in remembrance of why they were here. 'An English family. Who love him.'

'He also has a Spanish family who would love him just as much,' replied Enrique inflexibly. 'Oh, this is getting us nowhere.' He raised his hand and summoned the bartender, but although Cassandra knew a moment's panic that he had decided not to continue their conversation, he merely ordered two more glasses of wine.

The bartender, who brought his order, looked a little dismayed to see that they hadn't touched the *tapas*, but he held his tongue. Cassandra guessed he had taken one look at Enrique's dark face and decided now was not the time to make comments. Instead, he sauntered away with a decidedly defiant swagger.

'Now,' said Enrique, when they were alone again, 'I suggest we try to find some common ground here.' He took a breath. 'We are agreed, are we not, that David is Antonio's son, yes?' And, getting no argument from Cassandra, he continued, 'Very well. It is therefore a question of deciding how and when I am going to break this news to my father.'

Cassandra's throat closed up. 'And then what?' She had the sensation of things moving too fast for her here, of them getting out of control. And she wasn't altogether sure what she could do to stop them. 'We have to go back to England in a couple of days.'

'No.' Enrique was very definite about that. 'You will not

be going back to England until this affair is settled. And, just to put the matter straight, I have to tell you that before you and the boy appeared yesterday I spoke with Señor Movida at the *pensión*. He was kind enough to tell me that your booking is for two weeks. Do we understand one another?'

Cassandra's mouth quivered. 'You think you've got it all worked out, don't you?' She rubbed the end of her nose with a trembling finger. 'You can't tell me what to do.'

'Oh, Cassandra.' Now he sounded weary. 'You must have known how it would be. David wants to know his family—*all* his family. Do you honestly think you have the right to deny him that?'

Cassandra didn't know what to think any more. Her attempt to get away from Punta del Lobo, to return to England without Enrique's knowledge, seemed pointless now. The de Montoyas knew of David's existence. A few hundred miles would not prove any obstacle if they wanted to see him. Besides, it was David's life, David's decision. His letter had proved that. So did she have the right to prevent him from meeting his grandfather if that was what he wanted?

'Will you take me back to the *pensión*?' she asked tightly, her doubts weighing heavily on her conscience. 'David will be back soon.'

'And what will you tell him?'

Cassandra gave him a bitter look. 'Anything but the truth,' she said coldly. 'Can we go?'

CHAPTER FIVE

PUNTA DEL LOBO was quiet in the early-afternoon heat. Most of the shops and boutiques observed the hours of *siesta*, opening again around five o'clock and staying open until late in the evening.

It looked so normal, but Cassandra knew the kind of dislocation that came from feeling one thing and experiencing another. The narrow streets of whitewashed buildings might look familiar, but inside she sensed that nothing was ever going to be normal again.

She was relieved to see that the Kaufmans' hired Fiat was back in its parking space, although she was not looking forward to explaining to David why she had been consorting with a man she had hitherto treated as the enemy. He was bound to wonder why she hadn't told him that Enrique was coming, and even though she could deny having any knowledge of the Spaniard's movements, she suspected David might not believe her.

And, to a degree, he'd have a point. Hadn't she secretly suspected that Enrique might turn up today? Wasn't that why she'd been eager to get away from the *pensión* herself that morning? Only it hadn't worked, she thought dully. She'd forgotten how persistent—how patient—Enrique could be.

The Kaufmans were gathered on the forecourt before the *pensión* and Cassandra expelled a heavy sigh. Although she was glad that they were back, she would have preferred not to have advertised that fact to Enrique. He wouldn't have known the Fiat was their car, and without their physical presence to alert him he might have been inclined to leave.

Yeah, right.

She blew out a breath. She was being naïve. Enrique had

come here to see David and he was hardly likely to go away again without achieving his objective.

This time, Enrique parked the Mercedes at the gate and Cassandra pushed open her door with a heavy heart. There was no sign of her son, but she guessed he'd gone into the *pensión* to find her. Summoning a smile for the Kaufmans' benefit, she walked slowly up the path, aware that Enrique was right behind her.

The Kaufmans didn't smile, however, and Cassandra felt the first twinges of anxiety prick at her senses. What was wrong? What had happened? Why were they looking so worried? Oh, God, was David all right?

'You're back early,' she said, stifling her fears beneath a mask of politeness. 'I'm sorry I wasn't here when—'

'Mrs de Montoya! *Señora!*' Franz Kaufman stepped forward then, his plump face flushed with unbecoming colour. 'I am afraid I have some very—disturbing—news.'

'David?' began Cassandra, panic-stricken. 'Something's happened to David—?'

'Calma, pequeña!' Once again, Enrique lapsed into his own language to reassure her. Then, looking at Herr Kaufman, he arched an imperious brow. *'Donde esta el chico?'*

Franz Kaufman looked nonplussed. *'Er—no hablo español, señor,'* he said apologetically, and Cassandra could almost taste Enrique's frustration.

'The boy,' he said, his accent suddenly very pronounced. 'David: where is he?'

Franz Kaufman looked from one to the other of them in some alarm. 'I do not know,' he said unhappily, and Cassandra was hardly aware that she had clutched Enrique's arm in her panic. 'He—he has disappeared.'

'Disappeared?' cried Cassandra, her face draining of all colour. 'What do you mean, disappeared? Where did he disappear? Have you lost him?'

'Cassandra…' Enrique's voice was more reassuring than she would have thought possible. 'Let Herr Kaufman explain what has happened. We will not achieve anything by making as yet unfounded accusations, no?'

'I am so sorry, *señora.*' Franz Kaufman addressed his remarks to Cassandra now, and she saw how both Frau Kaufman and Horst moved closer to him as he spoke, as if seeking his protection. 'We went, as you know, to the water park at Ortegar, and both the boys wanted to go swimming in the wave pool.'

'And?'

Now Enrique was getting impatient, and the German hurried on with his explanation. 'There were lots of children in the pool, and the last we saw of David—'

'The last?' whispered Cassandra faintly, her nails digging unconsciously into Enrique's arm, and he turned to give her a sympathetic look.

'He seemed so content,' continued Franz Kaufman helplessly, putting an unknowing possessive hand on his son's shoulder. 'Frau Kaufman and I, we felt quite able to leave the boys to play while we went to the cafeteria to have a coffee.'

'You left them?' exclaimed Cassandra, but once again Enrique gave her a warning stare.

'It was not our fault,' put in Frau Kaufman suddenly, apparently deciding her husband was being too conciliatory. 'Horst said that David told him he was going down the—what is it they call it, Franz? The chute, *ja*? Horst did not want to go with him.' She shrugged. 'David did not come back.'

'Oh, God!'

Cassandra felt sick. She had thought that things couldn't get worse, but they had. David could be anywhere, with anyone. Dear God, she had heard such stories about boys of his age being lured away by unscrupulous men. Right this minute, he could be fighting for his life—

She caught her breath. He might even now be lying at the bottom of the chute in the water park. She hadn't thought of that. Oh, God! What was she going to do?

A sob escaped her, and Enrique, who had been asking more questions of the other family, turned to her with sudden concern.

'Querida,' he said softly, using an endearment she had never thought to hear from him again. 'Cassandra, try and be

positive. It may be that David lost his way back to the wave pool. Ortegar is a big complex. He could be with the director right now, waiting for someone to come and collect him.'

'Do you think so?' Cassandra realised belatedly that she was still gripping Enrique's arm and immediately dropped her hands to her sides. She shook her head. 'I've got to go there.' She hesitated, and then added in a low voice, 'Will you take me?'

'I would be happy to take you, *señora*,' declared Herr Kaufman before Enrique could respond. He ignored his wife's disapproving glare and touched Cassandra's arm. 'It is the least I can do.'

'Oh, well—'

Cassandra was turning to him when Enrique spoke. 'That will not be necessary, *señor*,' he said firmly. 'David is my nephew. Naturally, I am the one to escort Señora de Montoya to Ortegar.'

'If you say so.' Herr Kaufman's manner was stiff now, as if Enrique's command of the situation had devalued his offer and he was offended by it. 'But I must say, we searched the complex very thoroughly, and there was no sign of your son, *señora*.'

Cassandra shook her head, unable to answer him. Didn't he realise that that was the last thing she wanted to hear? If David had disappeared, couldn't he allow her to hope for just a little while longer?

'That was why we came back here,' added his wife shortly. 'We cut our day short because we hoped that if David had got lost, he might have got a lift back.'

'A lift?' Cassandra's throat was dry. 'Who with?'

'There were plenty of English people there,' said Frau Kaufman defensively. 'He could have gone with any one of them.'

'But David's not like that,' protested Cassandra, and then, catching Enrique's eyes on her, she shut up. He was right. There was no point in attributing blame. She should know, better than anyone, that David wasn't always predictable.

The sound of a mobile phone ringing cut into their

exchange. It was close, but not that close, and she was hardly surprised when Enrique excused himself and headed for the Mercedes.

She watched him anxiously. There was no reason for her to feel apprehensive about that phone call, but she did. Yet that was stupid. No one knew that Enrique was with her. Certainly no one at the Ortegar water park.

Enrique picked up the small phone and flicked open the mouthpiece. *'Sí?'* she heard him say, with obvious impatience, and then whatever was being relayed to him from the other end of the connection caused his expression to darken in obvious disbelief.

Cassandra took an involuntary step towards him. Somehow, she didn't know how, she sensed that the call had to do with David, and she was suddenly reminded of her doubts earlier in the day. Doubts about David going to Ortegar, about Ortegar's closer proximity to the de Montoya estate…

Pressing a hand to her throat, she continued down the path, and Enrique watched her approach with dark, enigmatic eyes. *Please,* she prayed silently, *let David be all right.*

Enrique finished the call almost simultaneously with her reaching the car, and tossed the phone back onto the console. 'He is at Tuarega,' he said shortly, and she didn't know whether he was relieved or angry. He went past her to tell the Kaufmans, and Cassandra crumpled against the wing. A momentary dizziness assailed her. He was safe! David was safe! Thank God!

It was only when Enrique came striding back to the Mercedes that she felt the beginnings of her own anger towards her son. No wonder he had been so eager to go out with the Kaufmans, she thought bitterly. He must have known exactly what he was going to do. Only Enrique had thwarted him by coming here.

'Get in,' said Enrique, swinging open the door, and Cassandra looked up at him with wary eyes.

'Aren't you going to tell me how he got to Tuarega?' she asked, aware that it was difficult to keep the tremor out of her voice. But she felt so helpless, so angry with her son. She couldn't believe he had been so reckless.

'I will tell you on the way,' Enrique said tersely. 'Come: we are wasting time.'

Cassandra hesitated, but then, glancing back at the other family, who were still clustered together outside the *pensión*, she decided to do as he said. She didn't want to get into explanations with the Kaufmans, explanations she couldn't begin to justify. Time enough for that later, when she'd had the opportunity to gather her thoughts.

'I ought to get changed,' she murmured, reluctant to appear before any members of his family in her cropped tee shirt and shorts, but Enrique merely gave her a considering look.

'I thought you were worried about your son,' he remarked, and the gentleness that had been in his voice earlier had all disappeared now.

Cassandra frowned. 'I am.'

'Get in, then,' he directed, walking round the bonnet to get behind the wheel. 'It is an hour's drive to Tuarega. Better not to give him time to have second thoughts, no?'

Cassandra scrambled into her seat without further ado. 'Do you think that's likely?' she asked, unable to prevent the question, and Enrique grimaced.

'No,' he said, starting the engine. 'I think he is exactly where he intended to be all along. Unfortunately, there was no one but my steward around to welcome him.'

'Your steward?' Cassandra glanced sideways at him as the car pulled away from the *pensión*. 'Was that who rang?'

Enrique nodded. 'It was.'

'Your mother's away?'

'My mother is staying at the *apartamento* in Seville,' he replied. 'So that she can be near my father.' His lips twisted with sudden irony. *'Gracias a Dios!'*

Cassandra stiffened. 'You've changed your mind about telling your parents about David?' she asked swiftly, but his reaction mocked her fleeting optimism.

'You wish,' he retorted with a short unfeeling laugh, and her eyes dropped to her hands, twisted together in her lap.

What had she expected? she chided herself. Enrique's only concern was the shock it would give the older de Montoyas to learn that they had a grandson after all these years. He didn't care about her feelings. He never had. She had only to remember the way he'd ignored her at his brother's funeral to know that Enrique believed she deserved nothing but his contempt.

Her eyes filled with tears, blocking her nose and making it difficult for her to breathe. She turned her head away so that he wouldn't notice and stared out at the beauty of the scenery surrounding them.

They had left Punta del Lobo behind and the busy coastal area was giving way to bare plains and fertile valleys. *Cortijos*, or farms, where white-painted cottages hid amongst avenues of citrus fruits and olive trees, followed the contours of hills that were tinged with purple in the lengthening shadows of late afternoon.

This had been her husband's homeland, she reminded herself, rubbing an impatient finger along the ridge of her nose. He had been familiar with these hills, these valleys, and, because the blood of the de Montoyas ran in David's veins, wasn't it natural that he should feel some affinity with it, too?

She looked down at her hands again, only this time her eyes were drawn to Enrique's feet in their expensive leather loafers. He wasn't wearing any socks, she noticed, his narrow ankles disappearing beneath the uncuffed hems of his cotton trousers. They were loose-fitting around his calves, only defining the body beneath when they reached his knees and the powerful thighs above them. His tee shirt was tucked into the drawstring waistband, and the leather cords hung down between his legs, drawing her attention to the unmistakable bulge of his sex…

God!

She dragged her eyes away from his crotch, feeling a film of sweat breaking out on her upper lip. This was crazy! *Crazy!* How could she be thinking such thoughts about a man who had done his best to ruin her life? She must be out of her mind.

'I suppose you think it is all my fault?'

His words broke into the turmoil of her thoughts, and for a moment she could only gaze at him, uncomprehending. 'I beg your—?'

'For David's running away from the Kaufmans,' prompted Enrique, his brows drawing together when he saw her flushed cheeks and glittering eyes. 'What is it? What is wrong? Are you ill?'

Only stressed out, she wanted to say bitterly, but she could hardly blame him for the shameful direction of her thoughts. That was all her doing, and she despised herself for allowing sex to colour her reactions to him.

'Just—hot,' she said instead, raising her hands to lift the weight of her hair away from her neck. Despite the car's air-conditioning system, her body seemed to be on some other planet. And it was only when she realised how the action caused her breasts to press provocatively against the thin fabric of her top that she quickly lowered her arms again. She wiped a knuckle surreptitiously over her upper lip. 'Um—is it much further?'

'Perhaps—twenty minutes,' answered Enrique tightly, and she guessed he'd noticed her embarrassment. Or perhaps she'd embarrassed him, she considered wryly. Though it wasn't likely. Enrique de Montoya was always in control of himself and his actions.

She was easing her thighs off the seat, allowing some air to pass between her skin and the leather, when he glanced her way again. 'You are not comfortable?'

'I'm fine,' she lied hurriedly. Then, forcing herself to look about her, 'Herr Kaufman said that your father's estate is famous for the bulls it breeds.' She took a steadying breath. 'I didn't know he was a farmer.'

'A farmer?' Enrique spoke drily. 'Is that what Kaufman told you?'

'Isn't it true?'

Enrique shrugged. '*En rigor*—strictly speaking, that is—I suppose he is right. Anyone who is involved with the land can be called a farmer. But there is much more to it than that. Much more to breeding bulls than getting a cow with calf.

And, as it happens, my father is first and foremost a businessman. He knows about growing grapes. He knows nothing about breeding bulls.'

Cassandra understood. 'But you do, right?' Her lips tightened. 'I should have known.'

Enrique gave a harsh laugh. 'Why do I get the feeling that that is not a compliment?' he asked. 'What would you know about it?'

'I know that it takes a certain kind of person to breed bulls to be slaughtered in the bullring,' retorted Cassandra, uncaring if she was overstepping the bounds of politeness. When had Enrique ever cared what he said to her? 'It's cruel, barbaric!'

Enrique sucked in a breath. 'And therefore I am cruel and barbaric also?' he suggested with dangerous civility, and Cassandra knew a twinge of fear.

'I—don't know,' she muttered, not prepared to make any accusations. Then, because she despised her cowardice, 'Are you?'

'I dare say we will find out,' he responded bleakly, his long fingers flexing on the wheel. 'Right now I am more concerned with what your son may have said to Mendoza.'

Cassandra gripped the edge of her seat. For a few shameful moments she had forgotten where she was, what she was doing here. But now the knowledge that she was soon to see her son again brought a quiver of apprehension to ferment the turmoil in her stomach.

She had never expected to come here, to see the place where Antonio had been born, where he had grown up. She had never wanted to come here, she told herself fiercely. Had never wanted to meet the family who had rejected her while her husband was alive and were rejecting her still. It was David who was welcome here. Not her.

They were driving through another valley now, a green fertile valley with a pretty village clinging to the hillside above a rocky gorge. The spire of a church rose above a stand of pine and cypress trees and the road narrowed to pass between white-walled cottages where carts and loaded mules held their own against more conventional traffic.

'What—what is this place?' Cassandra ventured, after Enrique had already acknowledged the greetings of perhaps a score of men and women, some of whom dragged wide-eyed children out of the path of the car. Older inhabitants, mostly men, she noticed, sat smoking their pipes in the shade of flower-hung balconies, and they, too, raised gnarled hands to him as he passed. 'Is—is it Tuarega?'

'It is Huerta de Tuarega,' he conceded after a moment, as if reluctant to answer her. Then, leaning towards the windscreen, he directed her gaze upward. 'There is the *palacio*.'

Palacio? Palace? Cassandra's mouth dried. The building he had indicated was situated further up the valley, surrounded by a plateau of lush fields and orchards of fruit trees. A road, its tarmac black against the terraces of olive trees that grew lower down the valley, curved away ahead of them, but it was the *palacio* itself that caused such a rush of apprehension. It looked like a sprawling medieval fortress from this angle, she thought fancifully, having never imagined anything like this. How had David ever had the nerve to come here, uninvited and unannounced?

'Does it live up to your expectations?' enquired Enrique mockingly beside her, and she turned to give him a startled look.

'I didn't have any expectations.' She swallowed. 'I—I had no idea you lived in a—in a palace.'

'No?' He was sardonic. 'But Antonio must have told you where he lived, no?'

'Yes.' Cassandra automatically adopted a defensive attitude. 'He told me his family had an estate called Tuarega. In England, estates can be large or small. They're rarely controlled from a—a palace!'

Enrique gave her a considering stare. Then, apparently deciding to give her the benefit of the doubt, he shrugged. '*Muy bien.* I believe you. But do not be alarmed. *Palacios* in Spain are not so rare. And Tuarega is really only a country house.'

Cassandra reserved judgement. Whatever Tuarega was, it was vastly different from anything she was used to. As they drew closer, she could make out towers and crenellations, and the unmistakable tracery of Moorish architecture.

'It—must be very old,' she said stiffly, trying to distract herself from the moment when she would have to get out of the car and go into the *palacio*, and Enrique inclined his head.

'Some of it is, certainly,' he agreed. 'But over the years there have been modifications and additions, so that now it is—how would you say it?—a mish-mash of styles.'

Cassandra wouldn't have said that. She wouldn't have described something that was essentially so beautiful in quite those terms. Whatever its period, Tuarega was a home to be proud of, and for all his deprecating words she sensed that deep down Enrique felt that way, too.

The sight of a herd of cattle grazing in the pasture that adjoined the formal gardens of the *palacio* briefly diverted her. The beasts raised their heads to watch the car go by, and she guessed that these were some of the fighting bulls they had been talking about. Strong, sturdy, with dangerously sharp horns, they didn't look like the domestic cattle she had seen at home and she had no desire to get any closer to them.

If Enrique noticed her unwilling interest, he made no comment. For which she was grateful. Right now, she had other things to face, to contend with, and she was glad she hadn't known exactly what she was getting into when they'd left Punta del Lobo or she might never have had the nerve to come.

But she would, she chided herself impatiently. David was here. Her son was here. And, for all its size and magnificence, Tuarega was a place where Antonio had lived.

CHAPTER SIX

THE boy came running to meet them as they entered the arched foyer of the *palacio*. Sunlight was slanting down through the grilled windows set high on the walls, throwing a barred pattern across the marble-tiled floor. David's rubber-soled shoes squeaked as he came to an abrupt halt some distance from them. Clearly, he hadn't expected to see his mother, and Enrique wondered, not without some irritation, whether the child had any thought for her feelings at all.

'Mum!' he said, his mouth tilting down at the corners. Then, twisting his gaze to her companion, his expression changed. 'Tio Enrique!' He was evidently proud of his pronunciation and he gave his uncle a delighted smile. 'I've been waiting to see you.'

Cassandra said nothing, and the awkward silence that followed his outburst was broken only by the appearance of an older man behind him. Enrique guessed Mendoza had been indulging in a little *siesta* and he evidently hadn't expected his charge to come rushing to greet them. Maybe he'd not heard the car, but David's ears were younger, and sharper, and in this place the sound of an engine could be heard for miles.

'Señor,' he exclaimed, with some humility. *'Lo siento mucho. El niño—'*

'No importa, Carlos.' Enrique broke into the man's apologies with a reassuring smile. 'Naturally, David is eager to speak to his mother; to apologise for his behaviour, *sin duda*. Is that not so, David?'

He arched a warning brow and the boy, clearly disconcerted by this turn of events, pulled a sulky face. 'You don't understand,' he protested, glancing defiantly towards his mother. '*She* was going to take me away.'

'We do not say "she" when we are speaking of our mothers,' Enrique reproved him sharply, even though the boy's words had only confirmed his suspicions about Cassandra's intentions. If he hadn't turned up at the *pensión* as he had, he might well have found himself compelled to employ a private investigator to find her. He breathed deeply and then added, 'How did you get here?'

David's chin jutted. 'Didn't *she* tell you?' he asked insolently, in deliberate contravention of his uncle's words. Then, when this didn't provoke the reaction he'd expected, he muttered sullenly, 'I got a lift.'

'A lift!' Cassandra spoke for the first time, her consternation evident. 'From Ortegar?'

'Where else?' This wasn't going at all the way David had expected and Enrique wondered what he would have done if he'd been here when the boy arrived. Taken him back to his mother, probably, he conceded drily. He had no desire to be accused of kidnapping. 'The Kaufmans weren't interested in what I did,' David continued. 'They dumped Horst on me and then cleared off to the bar.'

'That's not true.' Cassandra cast a shocked look at Enrique before chastising her son. 'Besides, you like being with Horst. You've played together all holiday.'

'All holiday!' David mimicked her. 'We've only been here for four days, Mum! And who said I liked him? He's a wimp.'

'Well, you were keen enough to go out with him and his parents this morning,' she cried, and David pulled a face.

'Haven't you figured out why?'

'That will do.' Enrique decided he had heard enough. 'Your mother asked you a question earlier. How did you get from Ortegar to Tuarega?'

'I answered her,' exclaimed David defensively, but Enrique was beginning to understand that Cassandra might well have her hands full with this young tyrant.

'To say you got a lift is not an answer,' he retorted coldly. 'From whom did you get this lift? I assume it was not with someone you knew?'

David shrugged. 'I know him now,' he said. Then, meeting Enrique's dark accusing eyes, he hunched his shoulders. 'Oh, all right. He was a wagon driver, yeah? Big deal! He even spoke English almost as well as you do. We talked about England's chances of qualifying for the World Cup.'

'Oh, David!'

Cassandra was clearly horrified and Enrique knew a quite inappropriate urge to comfort her. The boy was here, after all, safe and sound. Whatever risks he had taken, and however he deserved to be punished, she should not blame herself for his behaviour.

'I suppose the Kaufmans came moaning to you because I'd gone missing.' David was apparently unrepentant. Then, on a different tack, 'I thought you swore you'd never come here.'

'You wish,' said Cassandra tightly, recovering a little of her spirit. 'Have you any idea how worried I've been about you?'

'Oh, Mum!' David pushed his hands into the pockets of his shorts and scuffed his feet against the veined tiles. 'You must have guessed where I'd gone. Why else did you get in touch with—with him?'

He jerked his thumb towards his uncle and Enrique was amazed to discover that he badly wanted to take this young man in hand.

'Your mother did not have to get in touch with me,' he stated crisply. 'As a matter of fact, we had lunch together, and it was not until we got back to the *pensión* that we discovered you had disappeared. Or so the Kaufmans assumed. Without prior knowledge, they had no way of knowing where you had gone.'

David had listened to this statement with steadily increasing indignation, however. 'You had lunch together?' he cried accusingly. 'Why wasn't I told you were going to see one another again?'

Enrique gave him a half-amused, half-disbelieving look. 'I beg your pardon?'

'David—'

Cassandra tried to intervene, but her son was far too full of resentment to listen to her. 'I would have liked to have had lunch with you,' he exclaimed petulantly. 'Yesterday, you said you wanted to see me again. You were angry because Mum wouldn't listen to you. I bet that was why she sent me off with the Kaufmans. Just to get me out of the way.'

'David!' said Cassandra again, and Enrique couldn't let her defend herself alone.

'*Eres una—*' he began, and then cut himself off before he said something he would regret. 'The world does not revolve around you, *niño*,' he said instead. 'What your mother and I do is nothing to do with you. Do you understand me? You will never again question her actions or mine.'

David looked as if he would have liked to challenge him, but he evidently thought better of it. Dragging his feet, he moved closer to his mother, before saying sullenly, 'I want to go back to the hotel.'

Cassandra was clearly at a loss for words, and once again Enrique intervened. 'Not yet,' he said flatly. 'Your mother is tired. She needs some refreshment. I suggest we all adjourn to the patio. I will ask Consuela to bring us some iced tea.'

'I don't like iced tea,' muttered David, nudging his mother's arm. 'Can't we go? I don't like it here.'

Enrique realised that Cassandra was in a cleft stick. On the one hand she was probably relieved that he had exploded the boy's myth of a fairy godfather, but on the other she must know that giving David his own way wasn't going to do her any favours either.

'Shall I ask Consuela to attend to the matter of the refreshments?' suggested Mendoza, in his own language, and Enrique gave him an affirmative nod.

'*Gracias, Carlos,*' he agreed, then gestured towards the gallery that led to the courtyard at the back of the house. 'Will you come this way, Cassandra?'

He wasn't absolutely sure of what her reaction would be, but David grabbed her arm. 'I don't want to stay here,' he protested. 'Can't we get a taxi or something?'

'I, myself, will take you back to the *pensión*later,' essayed Enrique firmly. 'Cassandra?'

She was obviously torn two ways, but Enrique was not used to being thwarted by a nine-year-old child. 'Do not be so selfish, David,' he said, more pleasantly than he would have liked.

'You wanted to come here. Not your mother. It is only fair that you allow her to see a little of the place where your father was born and raised.'

David wouldn't look at him. 'Please, Mum,' he appealed. 'This place is old and creepy. Let's go home.'

Cassandra hesitated. Then, meeting Enrique's eyes, she said, 'Your—uncle is right. You were the one who wanted to come here, David. You can't expect to have it all your own way.'

'You would say that!' David was furious now. 'You don't care about me at all.'

'Por el amor de Dios!' Enrique's patience was at an end. 'I am beginning to doubt that you are a de Montoya, after all. Can you not show your mother some respect?'

David's eyes filled with tears, proving that for all his sulky belligerence he was still just a child at heart. 'Are—are you going to let—him—speak to me like that?' he asked tremulously, and Enrique waited with resignation for Cassandra's reply. Surely this was the opportunity she had been waiting for. And he had given it to her.

'Where did you say we could have tea?' she enquired instead, meeting Enrique's cynical gaze with searching eyes. 'I—should like a drink, if it's not too much trouble.'

He knew a fleeting sense of the initiative being taken from him, a disturbing pang of something that might have been pain in the pit of his stomach. *Caray*, but she never failed to disconcert him. And what was he doing, inviting her to have tea with him, when only the day before he had wanted to hurt her, to inflict a little of the pain on her that she had caused his family—*caused him*?

His momentary lapse meant his tone was cooler than it might have been when he said, 'Follow me,' and led the way along the vaulted gallery to the central courtyard at the back of the *palacio*.

Immediately, the beauty of his surroundings soothed him. At this hour of the afternoon, with long shadows providing welcome oases of shade beyond the shadows cast by the colonnade, the courtyard was a peaceful place. It was where his father used to sit in the late afternoon also, and Enrique had only recently come to appreciate its tranquillity after an exhausting day at the winery.

'What a—beautiful place!'

It was Cassandra who had spoken, surprising him by walking past him to admire the pool where the sound of running water was a constant delight. She rested her hands on the rim of the fountain, leaning forward to inhale the perfume from the lilies, and Enrique was instantly aware of the way the action caused her khaki shorts to ride up the backs of her legs.

Such long legs, he noticed unwillingly, as he had noticed once before, slim and shapely through the calves and thighs, deliciously rounded at the curve of her bottom—

Dios!

He turned abruptly away, half afraid that the boy who was still hanging behind him might have noticed his distraction. This was the woman who only yesterday he'd assured himself he hated. How could he look at her now with such passion when he knew what she had done to him, to his family? He must be mad!

Thankfully David had noticed nothing amiss. He was intent on kicking the fallen petals of a blossom he had found lying at his feet and Enrique felt a rekindling of the sympathy he'd felt towards his nephew the previous day. He must not lose sight of the real victim here. And it was certainly not Cassandra.

The appearance of a plump woman carrying a tray aided his recovery. *'Gracias, Consuela,'* he thanked her, after she had set her burden down on the table. Then, in her own language, 'I will let you know if we need anything else.'

'Sí, señor.'

Consuela, whom he'd known would be curious about the visitors, cast a startled glance at David as she withdrew, and Enrique resigned himself to the fact that any decision he might have made concerning the boy had essentially been taken out of his hands. It was one thing to trust Mendoza to keep his mouth shut and quite another to expect the woman who had been here since he and Antonio were children to remain silent about what she'd seen.

But he'd known that, he acknowledged, his eyes drifting once again towards the fountain. He'd known exactly what would happen when he'd suggested that Cassandra should stay. He would have to think seriously about what he was going to tell his mother before any rumour of the boy's identity reached her ears.

Cassandra turned then and came back to where the table was situated in the shade of the balcony, and Enrique made an effort not to stare at her. But, *Dios*, it was hard not to. Her hair was a tawny halo of red-gold curls that tumbled carelessly about her shoulders. It was longer than it had been ten years before, but just as fiery in the sunlight. He recalled how soft it had felt between his fingers—how surprised he'd been to discover in her nakedness that the colour was natural…

He hid the emotion that twisted his face by staring down at the tray Consuela had brought. Such thoughts were anathema to him, an affront to himself and his memories of his brother, and he despised himself for them. *De acuerdo*, she had not yet been married to Antonio when he'd known her, but that had been only a formality. It was no excuse for what he'd done.

Yet, she had still been a virgin…

'The village looks so small from here,' she murmured, clearly as discomfited by the situation as he was, but at least her words dispelled his painful introspection.

'Are you thirsty?' he asked, adopting a polite expression for David's sake, if nothing else. He indicated the tall glasses of iced tea with their delicate lacing of lemon slices. *'Por favor!'*

Cassandra glanced at him warily. 'I am a little thirsty,' she conceded, but he noticed that when she took the glass he offered she made sure she didn't touch his fingers with hers.

Well, that was as it should be, he told himself grimly, a pulse jerking in his temple nevertheless. Bringing her here had not been the wisest thing he'd ever done, on several counts, and he had to believe that it was the ever-present reminders of his brother that were making him so aware of his faults and hers. All the same—

'May I have a cola?' asked David at his elbow, and he

realised that the boy had come to join them. Thanks to Carlos, no doubt, there were several cans of the popular soda on the tray, the metal running with condensation in the heat.

'Por supuesto,' he said absently, his mind still involved with what he had been thinking. And then, realising the boy didn't understand him, he changed it to, 'Of course.' He lifted a can and flipped the tab before handing it to him. 'There you are.'

'Thanks.' David took the can, but instead of drinking from it he bit his lip. 'I'm—sorry, Uncle Enrique,' he said. 'Sorry I was thoughtless, I mean.' He cast his mother a rueful glance. 'I didn't mean to worry you, Mum.'

Cassandra looked taken aback and Enrique guessed David wasn't always as willing to back down. 'We'll talk about it later,' she said quickly, taking refuge in her glass. Then, with an obvious effort to be civil, she licked a pearl of moisture from her lip and added, 'This is delicious. Iced tea never tastes like this back home.'

Which was as good as saying she would talk to David when they were alone, Enrique conceded drily. This whole situation was rapidly losing any credibility at all. *Dios*, what did she think she was doing here? How was she going to justify what had happened to herself? Sooner or later she would have to accept that there was no alternative. One way or another, Enrique and his father were going to have a role in David's life.

David had moved away now, carrying his soda across to the fountain that his mother had been admiring earlier, and Enrique moved closer to Cassandra. 'I spoke to my mother last evening,' he said, forcing her to look up at him. She shouldn't imagine that because David was here he wouldn't say what he thought. He'd tried talking to her earlier in the day and that had not been a success. She had to be made to see that avoiding the issue was going to achieve nothing.

'Really?' she said now, and he knew a moment's regret when he saw the guarded look in her eyes. It was obvious she was still not prepared to compromise with him, despite what had happened. Her spine was very stiff as she continued, 'Is that supposed to mean something to me?'

Enrique took a deep breath. 'She told me that my father is making good progress,' he said evenly. He didn't add that she'd been put out by his failure to ring her at the time he'd promised or that he'd mentioned nothing about what he'd been doing all day. 'She hopes he will be able to return home in a matter of days.'

Cassandra lifted her slim shoulders. 'I'm happy for you.'

'Are you?' Enrique felt a quite compulsive desire to shock her. 'Why? Because it means David will get to know his grandparents that much sooner?'

A hand fluttered to her throat and, for all her efforts to appear composed, he could see the fear she was trying so hard to hide. 'You are joking?'

'I do not make jokes, Cassandra.' Enrique despised the wave of sympathy she aroused in him, and his words were unnecessarily harsh as he added, 'You are fighting a losing battle. Admit it. The boy has shown how he feels about it. All right, perhaps his method of achieving his ends left a lot to be desired. I accept that. But you are not going to get anywhere if you insist on denying him his right to know his Spanish family.'

Cassandra swallowed. He saw the way the muscles in her throat worked to hide the emotion she was fighting. Then, setting her glass down on the tray, she said tightly, 'Will you allow me to ring for a taxi to take us back to Punta del Lobo?'

Enrique sighed. 'I have told you: I will take you back to the *pensión* myself. There is no need for you to call a taxi.'

She shook her head. 'I would prefer to.'

'And can you afford it?'

His words were unforgivable, and he regretted them as soon as they were said. But it was too late. She had heard him, and his careless tongue aroused her as a polite denial would never have done.

'Of course, I would expect you to say something like that,' she told him in a low scornful voice. 'That is all you care about, isn't it? You and your father both. That was why you were so against me marrying Antonio, wasn't it? Because I didn't have any money. Because in your world having no money equals gold-digger, right? Well, you know what? I'd rather possess a poverty of the wallet than one of the spirit!'

She was staring at him now, her eyes wide and filled with righteous outrage. Dark lashes, unmistakably damp with tears, shaded pupils that were an incredible shade of blue, and he felt their condemnation in every pore of his being. For the first time in his life he was aware of his own arrogance, of the cynicism that had coloured all his dealings with this woman. And for the first time, also, he felt himself to be at not only an emotional but a psychological disadvantage, too.

'Lo siento,' he found himself saying softly. 'I am sorry. I should not have said what I did.' He paused. 'Will you forgive me?'

Cassandra rubbed the end of her nose with her knuckle. 'Do you care?' she demanded with a sniff, and before he could prevent it his hands had reached out to grip her arms just above her elbows.

It was a mistake. Her skin was like satin, soft and warm and deliciously sensitive to the touch. He knew that any pressure he brought to bear would leave dark bruises on her flesh and, for an insane moment, he wanted to do just that. To put his mark on her; to have the rest of the world see exactly what he'd done.

It was insane. He knew that. But that didn't stop him from feeling as he did. His eyes searched her face, wanting to see some matching emotion in hers, and settled on the parted fullness of her mouth. It was wide and sweet, her tongue hovering nervously over her lower lip, and for one mindless moment he wanted to touch it, to taste it, to allow his tongue to probe deeply into that hot moist cavern…

But it didn't happen. Although he was sure Cassandra was aware of the unexpected intimacy between them, she didn't respond as he had. With a muffled cry, she wrenched herself away from him, and David, who had been casting nervously surreptitious glances at them from the safety of the pool, now came awkwardly back to his mother's side.

'What's wrong?' he asked, his dark eyes, so like Enrique's own, moving from his mother to his uncle and back again.

'You're not still mad, are you, Mum? I was afraid you weren't going to let me see Uncle Enrique again, that's all.'

But that wasn't all, thought Enrique grimly, struggling to regain a sense of balance. Touching Cassandra had briefly torn aside the veneer of indifference that had sustained him. He'd forgotten how soft her skin was, how seductively feminine was her scent. For a few crazy seconds he'd wanted her to remember how it had once been between them without considering how dangerously attractive such a memory might be to himself.

Now, however, he had to reassure the boy, and, putting the destructive knowledge of his own weakness aside, he said harshly, 'Your mother knows there is no way she can prevent you from meeting the rest of your family.' He looked at Cassandra now with challenging eyes. 'Is that not so?' And when she didn't reply, he added, 'We will discuss this again tomorrow, no? When you have had time to recover from the shock of David's disappearance.'

CHAPTER SEVEN

ENRIQUE arrived as Cassandra was having breakfast the next morning.

Well, calling several cups of strong black coffee breakfast was pushing it a little, she conceded, but after the events of the past few days her appetite was practically non-existent.

She had certainly been in no mood for dinner the night before and although she'd taken David, at his suggestion, to a local pizzeria, she had had a struggle swallowing more than a few mouthfuls of her pasta.

David had been on his best behaviour, of course. He'd spent the first hour apologising for worrying her and the Kaufmans, and when he'd seen the German family later in the evening, he'd made a point of speaking to them personally. She didn't know what exactly he'd said to them. She told herself she didn't want to know. His attitude was far too reminiscent of his father and how charming he had been when he'd wanted his own way.

Nevertheless, David had got his own way and they both knew it. Whatever Cassandra said now, whatever she did, she had the weight of the de Montoyas' involvement hanging over her, and she wouldn't have been human if she hadn't felt betrayed in some way.

Yet, despite her misgivings, she couldn't prevent the thrill of recognition she felt when Enrique appeared in the doorway to the terrace, his eyes swiftly scanning its occupants in search of herself. Or in search of David, she amended bitterly. She had to remember this man was David's friend, not hers.

All the same, she was intensely aware of him. His tall dark figure, dressed more formally this morning in a pale grey button-down shirt and black trousers, was undeniably striking. And when he located her table beside the rail of the terrace and started towards her, his progress was monitored by more than one pair of curious eyes.

Cassandra felt the colour rise up her throat as he stopped beside her table. *'Puedo?'* he asked, which she thought meant, May I? But he didn't wait for her permission before pulling out the chair opposite, swinging it round and straddling it with his long legs.

She was immediately conscious of the fact that she hadn't bothered to put on any make-up that morning. Not that she wore a lot. But she usually used an eyeliner and a lipstick because of her fair colouring. However, with David still asleep, she'd merely sluiced her face in the tiny bathroom that adjoined their room and pulled on the tee shirt and knee-length trousers she'd worn the evening before.

'You're very early,' she said, unconsciously defensive. 'David isn't up yet.'

'It is not David I wish to speak to,' replied Enrique, before glancing round for a waiter. With enviable ease, he summoned the man and ordered coffee for himself, even though Cassandra was sure the little *pensión* didn't normally cater to visitors. Then, meeting her unwilling gaze with his own, 'Did you sleep well?'

Cassandra pushed nervous fingers through her hair. 'I suppose that's a polite way of saying I look a mess,' she declared, stiffening her spine. 'What do you want, Enrique?'

'I want to speak with you.' The waiter returned with his coffee and he pulled a note out of his pocket and pressed it into the startled man's hand with a quick, *'Gracias!'* Then, facing her again he added, 'Do not be so anxious, Cassandra. This need not be as unpleasant as you fear.'

'Want to bet?'

Cassandra's response was muffled as she looked down at her cup but he heard her. 'I mean it,' he said. 'It can be hard or easy. It is up to you.'

'Oh, right.' She looked up then. 'As long as I let you do exactly as you like, I'll find it easy. If I object, you'll fight me.' Her lips twisted. 'What a choice!'

Enrique shook his head. 'I do not want to fight you, Cassandra.'

'But you will if you have to.'

'If you attempt to deny my father the right to meet his grandson, I must.'

Cassandra made a scornful sound. 'And that's supposed to reassure me?'

Enrique drew a deep breath. 'I am not your enemy, Cassandra.' His long fingers tightened on the back of the chair. 'Why can you not understand my feelings? The boy is a de Montoya. You do not deny that?' And, when she didn't protest, '*Aquí tiene*, is it not reasonable that he should have the chance to learn about his heritage?' He paused. 'At this moment, he is my father's only hope for the future. Though, of course, he does not know it yet.'

Cassandra stiffened. 'What are you saying?'

Enrique sighed. 'I should have thought it was perfectly obvious.'

Panic gripped her. 'Are—are you implying that—that David—'

'Will one day be heir to Tuarega?' Enrique finished for her. 'It is very possible, yes.'

'No!' Cassandra was appalled.

'No?' Enrique arched a dark brow. 'Why not?'

'Because you—you are your father's eldest son. It is—it is your son who will inherit Tuarega.'

'And if I do not have a son?' Enrique stared at her, his eyes enigmatic in his dark face. 'It is entirely possible. I do not intend to marry, therefore—'

'But you must.' Cassandra shook her head. 'David's my son. *Mine*. He doesn't need what—what you're offering.'

'Does he not? Can you make that decision for him?'

'No, but—' Cassandra caught her breath. 'Enrique, he's just a child!'

'I know that.' Enrique lifted his shoulders in a dismissing gesture. 'And I am not suggesting that he should be faced with such a choice until he is older. Much older. But that does not mean that he should not be given the chance to learn about his Spanish family, to avail himself of the advantages we can give him.'

Cassandra shook her head. 'You can't do this.'

But they could, and she knew it. Had always known it, if she was honest. She'd told herself that Antonio's family didn't deserve to know about David, but what she'd really been doing was saving herself from further heartbreak.

'I want him to come and stay at Tuarega,' continued Enrique levelly. 'I think he should spend the rest of his holiday there.'

'You're not serious!' Cassandra stared at him disbelievingly. 'You have to give me some time—'

'For what?' Enrique's eyes were wary. 'To poison his mind against me?'

'No.' She would never do that. 'But it's too soon.'

'I disagree.' Enrique was implacable. 'It is the most sensible solution. He will enjoy it.' He paused. 'You both will.'

'Both?' Cassandra's jaw dropped. 'You expect me to come with him?'

'I am not entirely inhuman, no matter what you think of me,' replied Enrique flatly. 'I am not suggesting taking the boy away from you. That was never my intention. But perhaps it is time to put the past behind us.'

Cassandra couldn't think. 'We can't do that.'

'Perhaps not.' He had the grace to look slightly discomfited now. '*No haga este!* Do not do this, Cassandra.' He pushed his untouched coffee cup aside. 'Be reasonable, I beg you.'

'As you are?' Cassandra made a helpless gesture. Then, 'All right,' she said heavily. 'Ask David if he wants to spend the rest of his holiday at Tuarega. I can't stop you. But don't expect me to go with you.'

'Cassandra!' His use of her name was anguished, and she glanced anxiously about her, half afraid their conversation was being monitored, too. 'When are you going to realise that what is done cannot be undone? I did not write that letter. David did. Can you not try and understand how he feels?'

Cassandra couldn't look at him. 'David's a child,' she persisted. 'What makes you think he'll want to go to Tuarega? What is there for him? He gets bored very easily.'

'Does he?' Enrique considered her words. 'Well, you may be right. There is no beach at Tuarega, it is true. No shops or fast-food restaurants within walking distance.'

'David isn't interested in shopping,' Cassandra admitted unwillingly. 'But he does like the beach. He likes to swim.'

'Bien.' Enrique was philosophic. 'We do have a swimming pool, *por lo menos*. That may be some compensation.'

And, of course, it would be. Cassandra had to be honest with herself. Not to mention the fact that there was space at Tuarega; acres and acres of space, grazed by Enrique's bulls and probably horses, too. David could swim; he might even learn to ride. He would begin to appreciate how much she had deprived him of.

Cassandra's stomach hollowed. What Enrique and his father had to offer was overwhelming, *terrifying*. How could she hope to compete with the wealth and influence of the de Montoyas? Her son was too young to understand what she had had to pay for that wealth and influence.

'It is time you met your in-laws, too,' continued Enrique persuasively. 'My father has mellowed somewhat in his old age. When he learns about David, he will not turn you away.'

'Won't he?'

Cassandra wished she could believe him. Considering the lengths to which Julio de Montoya had gone to ensure that the wedding between her and his younger son did not take place, Enrique's words did not fill her with any degree of optimism. Besides, she wasn't at all sure she wanted to meet the man who had attempted—with his son's help—to ruin her life.

Even so, she couldn't deny that Enrique had a point. Perhaps she was being selfish in attempting to deprive David of the chance to choose between them. Just because she had suffered at the hands of the de Montoyas there was no reason to believe that her son would.

'I promise I will see that you—and David—enjoy your stay in my family home,' declared Enrique, watching her with his intent dark eyes, and she shivered. 'Please: say you will come.'

* * *

Enrique was in his father's study when Sanchia de Silvestre de Romero was announced.

Squashing the immediate sense of irritation he felt at her appearance at this time, he abandoned the schedule he'd been working on and got to his feet as Consuela showed the young woman into the room.

As always, Sanchia looked sleek and sophisticated, her dark hair coiled into a chignon at the nape of her neck, her sleeveless sheath fairly screaming its designer label. But today, for some reason, he found her appearance far too formal for a casual visit, and he wished she had rung before turning up like this.

'You will not believe it, *querido*!' she exclaimed, apparently unaware of the tension in his expression. She waited until Consuela had withdrawn, closing the door behind her, and then circled the desk to where he stood, reaching up to bestow a lingering kiss against his taut cheek. 'Do you know, your man, Mendoza, stopped me in the *salón* and asked me if I was expected? Such insolence! I told him I did not need an appointment to see *mi amante*, no?'

Enrique gave a small smile. But it was an effort, nonetheless. 'Carlos is aware that I am extremely busy, Sanchia,' he said, irrationally annoyed by her familiarity. He was not her lover. They had slept together a handful of times as much at her behest as his. 'Unless it is something urgent, I regret I will have to ask you to excuse me.'

Sanchia's lower lip jutted. 'You are sending me away? Again?'

Enrique stifled a sigh. 'I am sorry. As I say, I am very busy, Sanchia. I have to go to Sevilla this evening, to see my father, and there are things that must be done before I leave.'

Sanchia gazed at him. 'But Consuela says you have guests at the *palacio*. Surely you are not going to Sevilla and leaving your guests alone?'

Enrique bent his head so that Sanchia wouldn't see his exasperated closing of his eyes. He would have to speak to Consuela, he thought impatiently. To warn her not to gossip to the Señora de Silvestre de Romero as if she were already a member of his household. Which she would never be, however much she might presume upon it.

'Who are these guests?' Sanchia went on in the same proprietary tone. 'Are they exporters, dealers, what? Have they come to see the bulls?'

'They are—family,' said Enrique reluctantly, aware that Cassandra would not approve of his description. But there seemed little point in lying about it. Sooner or later, Sanchia was going to find out who they were.

'Family?' Sanchia's eyes brightened. 'Who? Your Tia Alicia? Your cousin Sebastian and his wife? Oh, I do like your Tia Alicia. She knows so much about your family—'

'It is not Tia Alicia,' said Enrique flatly, steeling himself to tell her exactly who his visitors were, when there was a knock at the door. Guessing it was Consuela again, come to ask if they would like some refreshments, Enrique called, 'Come!' with some relief at the diversion.

His deliverance was short-lived, however. It was not Consuela who pushed open the heavy door and stepped into the room. It was David, and he gazed curiously at his uncle's visitor before saying cheerfully, 'This is some place, Uncle Enrique. It's taken me ages to find you.'

Sanchia's face was a picture of consternation, and if Enrique hadn't felt so exasperated at the boy's intrusion he might well have found the situation ludicrous. After all, he had probably looked much like her when he saw David for the first time, but he shouldn't forget that, apart from her shock at seeing the boy, Sanchia was also looking at the son of the man she herself had expected to marry.

No one spoke, and it was David who broke the uneasy silence that had fallen at his entrance. 'Did I do something wrong, Uncle Enrique?' he asked with boyish candour, and Enrique guessed he was remembering what had happened the day before. 'Um—Mum said I could come down and find you, if I wanted to.'

Did she?

Enrique didn't voice the words, but they presented themselves, nonetheless. Had Cassandra sent her son down here to embarrass him? Because if she had, she had certainly succeeded.

'Nothing is wrong, David,' he assured him now, speaking in English and realising he was being overly suspicious. It was unlikely that Cassandra—or David, for that matter—could have known of Sanchia's arrival. He had had his father's housekeeper accommodate their guests in rooms at the opposite end of the *palacio* from those occupied by the family and unless someone else had been gossiping this was just an unfortunate coincidence.

'That's all right, then.' David gave Sanchia another speculative glance but it was obvious he could hardly contain his excitement. 'I've seen the swimming pool, Uncle Enrique. It's huge!'

'Quien—?' It was obvious that Sanchia was having difficulty in getting her words out. '*Quien este, Enrique?* Who is this?'

'My name's David de Montoya.' Once again, the boy forestalled his uncle. 'Mum and me are going to stay here for the rest of our holidays. Isn't that great?'

Sanchia didn't answer him, but she turned uncomprehending eyes on Enrique, and he came round the desk to put a hand on his nephew's shoulder.

'He is right,' he said, speaking in English again, deciding that perhaps this was the easiest way, after all. 'David is Antonio's son.'

'Antonio's son!' Sanchia looked horrified. Then, in their own language, 'Antonio did not have a son.'

'Oh, but he did,' said Enrique swiftly, aware that David was listening to this exchange and must have sensed her antipathy. 'David is nine years old—*sí*, David?'

Sanchia shook her head, as if to clear it, and then returned to the offensive. 'But—how do you know that he is Antonio's son? Who told you that he is?'

'Este seria!' Enrique's impatience was obvious. 'Be serious, Sanchia,' he exclaimed, his eyes flashing an unmistakable

message of warning. 'Have you looked at him? He is a de Montoya. He is the image of my brother at that age.'

'Or of you,' retorted Sanchia shortly. 'He bears a resemblance to both of you, but that does not mean—' She broke off, aware that she was doing herself no favours by voicing her doubts. Then, with hardly less censure, 'Do you tell me that you have invited—that woman to stay at Tuarega?' Her dismay contorted her expression. 'Enrique, have you taken leave of your senses? Do you want your father to have another heart attack? He will if he discovers you have had that—that *puta* here behind his back!'

'Es suficiente!' Enrique silenced her with the harsh words, aware that the anger he felt at her outburst was out of all proportion to the offence. *Dios mio*, only days ago he would have agreed with her. 'Nothing is being done behind my father's back,' he continued tightly. 'As it happens, I am going to Sevilla this evening for that very purpose. To speak to my mother. To discuss with her the best method to proceed.'

David was looking worried now. 'Something is wrong, Uncle Enrique!' he exclaimed, turning to look up at him, and for the first time Enrique saw a trace of his mother's fragility in his face. 'What are you talking about? Why is—she—so cross?'

Sanchia's nostrils flared. 'I need to speak to you alone, Enrique,' she said coldly, ignoring the boy's appeal and continuing to speak in Spanish. 'Why do you not ask—David—' Her lips thinned as if in distaste. 'Why do you not get the boy to ask Mendoza to accompany him on a tour of the *palacio*. You and I have matters to discuss.'

Enrique squeezed David's shoulder and then let him go to move back behind his desk. 'I regret I do not have the time to discuss anything at present,' he said, speaking English for the child's benefit. 'Perhaps we can continue this at another date, Sanchia.'

Sanchia's teeth ground together. 'You present me with a *fait accompli* and expect me to accept it, just like that?' she demanded. 'No apologies; no explanations. Simply the bald fact that the woman who ruined my life is staying here, with you, as a *guest*! *Dios*, Enrique, what do you think I am?'

Enrique expelled a wary breath. 'I know it must have been a shock, Sanchia—'

'A shock!' She uttered a mirthless laugh. 'If you had wanted to destroy me, you could not have chosen a better way.'

'Oh, please, Sanchia!' Enrique wished David wasn't hearing this but there was no way he could send him away without it appearing that he had indeed trespassed on his uncle's hospitality. 'Are you not being a little over-dramatic? I doubt that meeting Antonio's son is in any way destructive to your peace of mind today. It is almost ten years since my brother died.'

Sanchia gasped. 'And you think I should have forgotten how he deserted me for—for that—?'

'In the name of God, Sanchia!' Enrique lapsed into his own language to put an end to this. 'How can you expect me to believe that Antonio ruined your life when less than six months later you married Alfonso de Romero?'

Sanchia's mouth opened and closed, but no sound came out and, deciding he could not let David listen to any more of this, Enrique came round his desk again and smiled down at his nephew.

'Perhaps Señora de Romero is right, David,' he said gently. 'Do as she suggests and go and find Carlos. He will be happy to show you the rest of the *palacio*.'

David gave Sanchia a doubtful look. Then, returning his attention to his uncle, he asked, 'Will I see you again after—after Señora de Romero has gone?'

'Later,' declared Enrique firmly, propelling the boy towards the door. 'Now, go. You will find Carlos in the orangery. Do you know where that is?'

'I'll find it.' David looked a little mutinous now. 'What shall I tell Mum? Is Señora de Romero a friend of hers, too?'

Enrique was pretty sure that David knew she wasn't but he refused to get into that. Nevertheless, as he turned back to

Sanchia, he couldn't help the treacherous thought that he understood perfectly why Antonio had preferred Cassandra to Sanchia.

He always had...

CHAPTER EIGHT

CASSANDRA didn't see Enrique again that day.

According to David his uncle had gone to Seville, and Cassandra could only assume he had gone to see his father. To bring him up to date on current events? she wondered uneasily. It seemed the most likely explanation, yet Enrique had said that his father was recovering from major surgery. Did he really intend to risk his recovery by giving the old man another shock?

Or was she inventing reasons why Enrique shouldn't tell Julio de Montoya about David? After all, it was Enrique's father who called the shots at Tuarega, and, so long as the old man wasn't involved, she could still kid herself that she and her son could leave here at the end of their holiday with no harm done.

Yeah, right.

Deep inside, Cassandra knew there was no hope of that. From the moment David had devised his plan of writing to his grandfather, she had been on a collision course with Julio de Montoya. It was just a pity that it had taken weeks for her to find out about it.

David, himself, had come back from his exploration of the *palacio* full of excitement about where he'd been and what he'd seen. And, to a degree, Cassandra could understand his feelings. There was no doubt that Tuarega was the most beautiful place she had ever seen, and the rooms she and David had been given were nothing short of magnificent.

The *palacio* itself was divided into several apartments, each with its own courtyard and patio, all of which were interconnected by covered walkways or colonnades. Flowers spilled from dozens of tubs and planters, curled about the narrow white columns that supported the roof, and tumbled from balconies in exotic profusion.

Cassandra knew, because Señora de Riviera, the de Montoyas' housekeeper, had told her in heavily accented English, that Enrique and his parents occupied the main apartments that overlooked the courtyard, where they had had tea the afternoon before. But she and David had been accommodated some distance from there in a sunny pavilion with its own long reflecting pool outside, where tiny tropical fish swam amongst saucer-sized water lilies.

Cassandra wondered if their rooms had formed part of the *seraglio*, or harem, when Tuarega had been a Moorish stronghold. They were certainly set apart from the rest of the building, though the paintings and murals that adorned the walls and ceilings in her bedroom and bathroom seemed to give the lie to that supposition. Surely there was too much eroticism implicit in the images of semi-naked women bathing and anointing their bodies with what appeared to be perfumed oils to warrant that belief, but she still suspected the choice of accommodation had been a deliberate one on Enrique's part.

Nevertheless, the spacious *salón*, with its rich carpets and heavily carved furniture, was in no way inferior to the rest of the *palacio*. Some of the artwork was undoubtedly priceless, and the jewel-bright cushions that were strewn about the floors and sofas gave each room a glowing brilliance.

Adjoining the *salón* was an equally impressive dining room. Carved chairs were set about a granite-topped wrought-iron table, and a gold candelabrum supported several heavily scented black candles, giving the room a distinctly foreign ambience.

David had his own bedroom, of course, and, to his delight, his own bathroom, too. Like her own bedroom and bathroom, they were equipped with every possible convenience, which didn't make it any easier for Cassandra to face the prospect of him returning home.

The Kaufmans had been sorry when she'd told them that she and David were leaving the *pensión*. She'd felt obliged to give them an explanation after the fiasco of the day before and, although she felt sure that Franz Kaufman, at least, had put a different interpretation on her decision from the real one, she was not prepared to justify her actions to him. Let him think that she'd been as eager as her son to make contact with her Spanish in-laws, she thought. It was easier than to try and explain something which, even to her own ears, sounded very unlikely.

Señor Movida had expressed his regret at their departure. Although he would be able to re-let their rooms without too much difficulty at this time of year, he had assured her that he was going to miss her friendly face about the place. Which had touched Cassandra a little. It was good to know that someone cared.

Awakening at Tuarega the next morning did cause her some misgivings, however. Despite the fact that she and David had enjoyed a delicious supper in their own apartments last evening, and her fears that Enrique intended to monopolise her son's time had not been realised, she was not foolish enough to believe that she was going to have much say in his activities from now on. Enrique had brought them here so that David could get to know his Spanish family, his Spanish heritage. Allowing him to spend all his time with his mother was unlikely to accomplish this and she might as well accept it.

Even so, as she left her bed and trod barefoot across the cool marble tiles to the balcony that adjoined her room, Cassandra found her thoughts straying into another area. Over supper, David had admitted that his uncle had had a visitor when he'd gone to his study the previous afternoon. Ignoring her question as to whether he had been trespassing, David had gone on to explain that the visitor had been a young woman, who had been cross with his uncle for reasons he didn't understand.

They'd been speaking mostly in Spanish, he'd said, and Cassandra had been diverted from her own doubts about David's behaviour to speculate on who the young woman might be. It seemed obvious to her, if not to her son, that this woman resented their arrival, but why? Was this Enrique's girlfriend? His fiancée? Her lips twisted with unconscious irony. How she wished she could discredit him. Although she had no quarrel with the other woman, Enrique deserved a taste of his own medicine.

But it was no use wasting her time on such futile schemes. If he was engaged to this woman, it was nothing to do with her. Still, it seemed there was at least one more person to whom David's presence at Tuarega was not proving very appealing. Who was she? Cassandra wondered again, gripping the balcony rail with nervous fingers. And why did she care?

It was another beautiful morning. It was still fairly early but the sun was up, and the tiles of the balcony were already warm beneath her feet. Unlike her bedroom. She'd discovered that, although their apartments were not air-conditioned, the thickness of the walls prevented them from getting too hot. But out here, with the sun shining down out of a cloudless sky, she did not have any protection.

There seemed to be few people about that she could see. In the distance, beyond the jasmine-covered grille that edged the patio, a man was working in the gardens that surrounded the *palacio*, and somewhere the steady drone of a lawnmower broke the stillness. Even so, she was suddenly conscious of the scarcity of her attire—the oversized tee shirt she used to sleep in exposing far too much thigh for her liking—and, deciding to go and find her son, she abandoned the balcony in favour of her bedroom.

When she ventured into David's room, however, she found her son was gone. His bed had been slept in: the tumbled sheets were evidence of that. But his sleeping shorts lay discarded on the floor and, when she checked, she found the clothes he'd worn the day before had disappeared.

Cassandra sighed. She wasn't worried exactly. It was unlikely he'd ventured far from the *palacio*, and there were any number of staff around to see that he came to no harm. All the same, she couldn't help feeling a bit disappointed that he hadn't told her where he was going. This was their first day here, after all, and he should know she was as anxious as he was to get her bearings.

There was no point in stressing over it, however, and, going back to her own room, Cassandra took a quick shower before getting dressed. But, as she surveyed the clothes she'd brought with her, she couldn't help wishing she'd packed more summer dresses. Not that she had an extensive wardrobe, of course, but she had left several cotton dresses at home in favour of shorts and cut-offs, and cropped shirts of one sort or another.

She eventually decided to wear knee-length trousers in a soft cream micro-fibre with one of her less skimpy tops tucked firmly into the waistband. Then, securing her hair in a ponytail, she thrust her feet into heelless pumps and left her room.

Finding her way back to the main part of the *palacio* was not so easy, however. Accompanying Señora de Riviera along these corridors the previous day, Cassandra had been too overwhelmed by the beauty of her surroundings to pay a lot of attention to their actual direction. It was not until she emerged into another sunlit courtyard that she had to acknowledge that she was lost.

Crossing the paved path that circled another pool, this one with its own ornate fountain spilling water into a marble basin, she walked to the edge of the courtyard and looked out over a fertile landscape. Below her, the ground fell away gradually to the valley floor, wide terraces providing room for the acres of what she surmised were orange trees, judging by the overpowering scent of citrus that filled her nose. She wondered how many trees there were. Hundreds, certainly; possibly even thousands. But they were just a small part of the estate that was Tuarega, and she was reminded of how unreal her presence here seemed.

'What are you doing?'

Enrique's voice startled her, and she glanced round almost guiltily to find him standing beside the fountain. She hadn't heard his approach. She'd been too intent on her thoughts. And it was disconcerting to find him there, lean and dark and somehow menacing, watching her.

'I—got lost,' she admitted, deciding there was no point in lying about it. 'I was looking for David and—well, I seem to have missed my way.'

'Ah.' Enrique inclined his head and strolled towards her, not stopping until he, too, could see down into the valley. 'Are you admiring my father's fruit trees?'

'I was trying to estimate how many there were,' Cassandra conceded, pushing her hands into the back pockets of her trousers and lifting her shoulders in an awkward gesture. 'Are oranges easy to grow?'

'Comparatively so,' agreed Enrique, his dark eyes cool and assessing. 'They have their problems, as do we all. The fruit fly has not been totally eradicated, and a good grower is always alert for any pest which might damage his crop.' His lips tightened. 'Are you really interested, Cassandra? Or is this simply a way of avoiding the obvious?'

'The obvious?' Cassandra wasn't entirely sure she knew what he meant. 'You mean David? Do you know where he is?'

'He is with Juan Martinez, my chief stockman,' said Enrique at once. 'He came out to the paddocks this morning as we were examining the new calves.' He paused, and then went on slowly, 'It was not an entirely sensible thing to do. These cattle are not like your English domestic breeds. They have moods, temperament. An abundance of spirit. Without proper supervision, it is easy to see how accidents can happen.'

Cassandra's throat dried. 'Are you telling me that David was in danger? That these animals are killers?'

'No.'

'But you are. Or at least that's what you implied.'

'I said, entering the paddocks without giving any thought to what he might be getting into was reckless,' amended Enrique patiently. 'Contrary to popular belief, bulls do not attack without provocation.'

'So you say.' But Cassandra was dismayed. 'I think it's appalling!'

A muscle in Enrique's jaw jerked. 'Exactly what do you find appalling?' he asked harshly, and Cassandra knew a sudden sense of alarm. 'Me?'

'Of course not.' Though she wasn't being totally truthful.

'I meant breeding—breeding animals to be slaughtered in the bullring.' She took a breath. 'You know how I feel about it. I told you the other day.'

'And what exactly do you think your English farmers do with the bulls they breed?' he demanded, stepping closer to her, and Cassandra felt the heat rise up her face. It was hot outdoors, but it was an inner heat that was lifting her temperature, beading her upper lip with moisture, causing a rivulet of perspiration to funnel down between her breasts.

'That's—different,' she declared staunchly, lifting a protective hand to her throat.

His eyes darkened. 'How is it different?'

'Because—because they're slaughtered for food.'

'Really?' Enrique regarded her intently, so close now she could feel the heat of his body, too. 'And you think that killing beasts before they're half grown is acceptable, *sí*?'

'People eat beef. They're bred for a purpose.'

'And so are my bulls,' Enrique informed her flatly. 'Plus the fact that a bull is already four years old before he enters the bullring. A more reasonable lifespan than—what? Eighteen months or so?'

Cassandra shifted her weight from one foot to the other. 'You have your opinion. I have mine.'

'Ah, yes.' Enrique regarded her from beneath lowered lids. 'But you do not think my opinion matters, do you, Cassandra? And we are not just talking about my bulls, here.'

'What do you want me to say?' Cassandra spoke quickly, wishing she could put some distance between them. But he had trapped her between his body and the trellis of flowering vines behind her that edged the courtyard and she was intensely aware of how vulnerable she was. 'We're here, aren't we? You can hardly claim that that was my decision.'

'No.'

He conceded the point, but he continued to regard her in such a way that a spark of real fear ignited inside her. He was so powerful, so disturbing; so male. And what she was most afraid of was her own unwanted awareness of him as a man. She could remember too well how abandoned he had once made her feel. How helpless; how eager; and ultimately how ashamed...

'This is not an easy situation for any of us,' he continued at last, his mouth acquiring a dangerously indulgent softness. 'We share too many memories, you and I.' He lifted his hand and, to her dismay, he stroked a long mocking finger down her cheek and along her jawline. 'Couldn't you at least try and understand my feelings?'

Cassandra jerked her head away from his questing touch, rushing into speech to destroy the sudden intimacy between them. 'I—I don't know what—what you expect me to—to do,' she stammered wildly, desperate to get away from him. 'I—I'm sorry if our being here is putting a strain on your love-life, but I—that's not my fault—'

'What did you say?' His harsh response banished any pretence of understanding. With anger darkening his expression he reached for her, one hand circling her upper arm, the other curling about her nape and jerking her towards him. He thrust his face close to hers. 'What are you talking about?'

Cassandra was shocked out of her inertia. 'Oh, please,' she cried, trying futilely to prise his fingers from her arm. 'You know what I'm talking about. David saw you with her yesterday afternoon. He said she wasn't very impressed to see him.'

Enrique ignored her efforts to try and free herself. 'Saw me with whom?' he demanded grimly, apparently uncaring that he was embracing her in full view of anyone who cared to walk along the upper landing of the building that surrounded them on three sides. From a distance, no one would know his true feelings. 'Talk to me, Cassandra. Tell me who you think she was.'

Cassandra felt impotent. 'I don't know who she was, do I?' she exclaimed. 'You don't share your secrets with me.'

'No,' he agreed harshly. 'But you are prepared to speculate, are you not?'

'Enrique—'

'I will tell you, she is not my—what would you say? My girlfriend, *sí*? Her name is Sanchia, Cassandra. Sanchia de

Romero. She is the woman my brother was going to marry before he became—before he met you!'

Cassandra swallowed. 'I—I don't believe you.'

'Why would I lie?'

Why indeed?

Cassandra gazed up into his dark face with troubled eyes, the idea that Antonio's ex-fiancée was still a regular visitor in this house filling her with dismay. 'I—didn't know,' she excused herself lamely, wishing she hadn't spoken so impulsively, and Enrique's mouth compressed into a thin line.

'There is a lot you do not know, Cassandra,' he told her grimly, but he was looking at her differently now, his expression taut with suppressed emotion. 'Do you think you are the only one of us who has any feelings at all?'

Cassandra couldn't speak, couldn't move, couldn't drag her eyes away from his. A moment before she had been afraid of his anger; now she was afraid of herself. His hand about her arm wasn't hurting her any more. It abraded her flesh with an entirely sensual movement, his fingers at her nape flexing against her skin.

His thumb found the tender hollow below her ear and a pulse leapt nervously beneath his touch. Her shallow breathing couldn't prevent her breasts from brushing constantly against his chest, her nipples hardening to pebbles beneath the cloth of her sleeveless shirt. His thigh had parted her legs in an effort to keep his balance, and every nerve in her body felt as if it was on red alert. She could feel herself succumbing to his sexuality, her body weakening instinctively in response to his.

'This is not wise,' he said roughly, his eyes moving almost compulsively to her mouth, and she realised he was as aware of what was happening as she was.

'Then let me go,' she pleaded unsteadily, though she made no attempt to move away. And Enrique sensed that she was susceptible to this sudden intimacy between them. It was evident in the dark fire that blazed suddenly in his eyes.

'I will,' he said savagely, but his actions belied his words. His head dipped until his lips were only a few inches away from hers, his breath warm and sensual. 'I must,' he added barely audibly before he bent even lower and touched her mouth with his.

The fire that erupted between them was as uncontrollable as it was instantaneous. As it had been once before, Cassandra recalled in her last lucid moments before the hungry ardour of his kiss drove all other thoughts out of her head. Hardly aware of what she was doing, she gave in to the needs she'd been fighting ever since she'd encountered Enrique again on the forecourt of the *pensión*. Needs that involved clutching his warm neck with her fingers, burrowing closer to him, easing her aching nipples against the muscled hardness of his chest.

'Dios mio,' he muttered against her lips. *'Te deseo.'* And although Cassandra's grasp of his language was limited at best, she was fairly sure he was saying he wanted her.

Which was madness. Yet, when his tongue probed her lips before plunging deeply into her mouth, she met it with her own, allowing them to mate in a sensuous dance of desire. She was drunk with passion, seduced with longing, lost in the dizzying whirl of the senses.

Enrique's hand cupped the back of her head, angling her mouth to make it easier for him to kiss her. Easier for him to go on delivering those long, drugging kisses that had ignited the flame inside her. He was oblivious of his surroundings, holding her against him with an urgency that suffered no rejection, pressing his hips against hers so that she quickly learned how aroused he was.

She knew her shirt had come free of her trousers when Enrique's hand gripped the bare skin of her midriff. Sliding up beneath the hem of the shirt, his thumb massaged the soft skin beneath her breast. She wound her arms about his neck in mindless surrender. She wished he would touch her breasts; she wanted him to hold them; and for the first time in her life she understood the advantages of not wearing a bra.

She didn't know which of them heard the sound of footsteps first. She thought perhaps that she did. Certainly, she was instantly aware of the sudden chill in the air that had previously been swelteringly hot. But it was Enrique who lifted his head; Enrique whose whole body stiffened in sudden recognition,

Enrique who drew a hoarse breath and somehow managed to regain the initiative by putting her behind him.

'Mamá!'

Cassandra understood that word without any difficulty at all. His mother! Her knees felt as if they were about to buckle beneath her. That his mother should find them in such a compromising situation was bad enough. What she would think of her for allowing it to happen didn't bear thinking about.

'Enrique.' The voice that answered him was at best shocked, at worst blatantly hostile. *'Que pasa? Estas loco?'*

Cassandra stiffened. So, his mother thought he was mad, did she? Well, that was scarcely surprising in the circumstances. She must have been mad, too, to let him touch her.

'Speak English, Mamá.' Enrique's response was amazingly cool considering that only moments before he had been making violent love to her. All the same, Cassandra wondered how he was going to explain his actions. In fact, he didn't. 'I did not expect you to arrive so early.'

'Obviously not.' Señora de Montoya's rejoinder was like chipped ice. 'You had far more—pressing matters to attend to, I see.'

'Do not be sarcastic, Mamá. It does not suit you.' Enrique glanced behind him. 'Allow me to introduce you to your daughter-in-law.'

'I think not.'

The contempt in the woman's voice was galling, but Cassandra could hardly blame her. It had been what she was thinking herself, after all. She pulled down her tee shirt and ran smoothing hands over the strands of silky hair escaping from her ponytail. Her swollen mouth would be impossible to disguise, she thought, so perhaps it was just as well.

'You will have to meet her sooner or later,' Enrique was saying calmly, but his mother seemed indifferent to the fact that there was a third person present.

'You expect me to speak to her after this—this fiasco?' she exclaimed incredulously. '*Dios*, Enrique, I cannot believe you are acting this way. After all these years, I am expected to forget what happened to Antonio?' She gave a gasp. 'Never!'

'You are overreacting, Mamá.' Enrique was polite, but inflexible. 'As you say, it is ten years since Antonio's death. Life goes on.'

'And what is that supposed to mean?' His mother was obviously taken aback at this apparent defence of his brother's widow. 'Am I to understand that you are attracted to her? That you are infatuated with her as Antonio was before you? *Dios*, Enrique, I thought you had more sense.'

Now Cassandra had heard enough. She refused to hide behind Enrique as if she was afraid of meeting Antonio's mother. She surely deserved the chance to defend herself. Stepping round her unwanted protector, she confronted the irate little woman across the courtyard.

'Believe me, Señora de Montoya,' she said, annoyed to hear the tremor in her voice, 'I did not choose to be here.' She cast Enrique an accusing look before continuing, 'And nor did I instigate what happened just now. Your son—accosted me as I was looking for David. If you want to blame anyone, blame him.'

Elena de Montoya absorbed this outburst in silence, studying the other woman with critical eyes so that Cassandra was instantly aware of her own shortcomings. In a short-sleeved silk dress in a becoming shade of blue, Elena made up for in presence what she lacked in stature. She was no more than five feet one or two inches tall, but her coronet of sleek black hair and high heels gave her added height. In addition, a double string of what Cassandra guessed were real pearls encircled her throat, and her watch and rings sparkled with jewels. Her appearance would not have disgraced a royal investiture, thought Cassandra wryly, guessing the older woman had dressed this way deliberately. Girded for battle, she reflected, feeling inadequate in her cut-off trousers and cotton top. If only she'd known that Enrique's mother was coming today.

But Elena apparently had no intention of indulging in any verbal sparring with her. 'David?' she said instead, turning back to her son. 'That is the boy's name, is it not? Antonio's son? Where is he?'

'He is watching Juan examine the calves,' replied Enrique

at once, without looking at Cassandra, and she realised with a sense of outrage that his mother was not going to demand any further explanation from him. Whatever she said, whatever she did, Cassandra was the one Elena blamed; Cassandra, who would feel the chill of her displeasure. Cassandra could only hope that David would forgive her if ever the truth of this encounter was exposed.

CHAPTER NINE

'IS THAT agreeable to you, Enrique?'

Miguel de Guzman pointedly cleared his throat after asking the question and Enrique, who had been staring unseeingly through the long windows of the boardroom, turned uncomprehending eyes on the three other men who were gathered at one end of the long polished table.

'I—beg your pardon?'

'I asked if you were willing to allow Viejo to experiment with the vines he brought back from Italy,' explained Miguel patiently. 'Naturally, his experiments would not interfere with current production but, as we all know, without experimentation many of our finer blends would not have been discovered.'

'That is true,' echoed one of his fellow directors, and Enrique inclined his head in acknowledgement.

The famous story of how a wine-maker in the mid-nineteenth century accidentally shipped a barrel of the crystal-clear wine his uncle favoured to England, instead of the dark sweet wine that had been ordered, was the stuff of legend. The wine, subsequently called Tio Pepe, in honour of Manuel Gonzales's uncle, was now one of the top-selling wines in the world, and vintners were constantly experimenting with unique combinations of soil and grape and climate, as well as ageing methods, in the hope of discovering some new favourite.

'I am sure you are right,' Enrique said now, but he had little interest in their concerns today. He had a headache; had had a headache for the past three days, actually. And although he knew he owed it to his father to give his full attention to the business, it was difficult to concentrate when he hadn't had a decent night's sleep since David's letter had arrived.

It had been a stressful week, and ever since his mother's arrival at Tuarega things had gone from bad to worse. The whole household had been left in no doubt as to her feelings and although she had returned to Seville now, Enrique knew it was a temporary reprieve at best.

'Are you all right?'

Miguel de Guzman was looking at him with some concern and Enrique guessed a little of the strain he was feeling must be showing in his face. But, dammit, he had reason to be stressed. His mother had found him kissing the woman he'd sworn he despised more than anyone else on earth.

Yet, when he'd been kissing her, he hadn't despised her. When he'd held her in his arms, when he'd pressed her slim lissom body against his, he'd wanted nothing so much as to—admit it!—bury himself in her soft flesh. He'd wanted, he couldn't deny it, to make love with her, and if his mother hadn't come upon them as she had…

He raked his scalp with agitated fingers. That was what had made his contact with his mother so awkward. Elena de Montoya had been angry at first. He'd known that. But she'd soon recovered and she'd done her best since then to make it easy for him to put the blame elsewhere. She'd wanted him to blame Cassandra. She'd wanted him to say that the woman he had to remember was Antonio's widow had invited his attentions, had encouraged him to take advantage of her so that she could use it against them later.

But he hadn't been able to do it. Which was why he and his mother had failed to have any meaningful conversation while she was here. Cassandra had been foremost in both their minds; Cassandra had stood between them.

Not so with David, however. Although the boy had been somewhat in awe of his Spanish grandmother, he had shown a touching desire to get to know her. Enrique knew that the boy's behaviour left a lot to be desired as far as his mother was concerned: he was far too outspoken for one thing and he didn't behave towards his elders with the respect that Enrique and his brother had had drilled into them from an early age. But although Señora de Montoya had had mixed feelings about the whole situation, she had had to accept that David was her grandson and that her son had had no choice but to tell her about it.

In the end, Enrique had taken the letter to Seville and shown it to his mother. It had seemed the simplest, and possibly the kindest, way to break the news to her. And, although she'd initially expressed doubts about David's parentage, those doubts had ceased, as Enrique's had, as soon as she'd laid eyes on the boy. It was up to her now when, and how, she would tell Enrique's father. Until then, Enrique could only wait and hope that learning he had a grandson would prove a stimulant to Julio's recovery.

Which didn't make his situation any easier, he acknowledged, pulling the file under discussion towards him. It was hard enough to concentrate on everyday things like sleeping and eating at regular times without having to take on the responsibility of making decisions that might affect the future of the estate. All he could think about was that Cassandra was back in his life; Cassandra was at the *palacio*. And that, however eagerly she'd appeared to respond to his lovemaking, her feelings towards him were as hostile as ever.

'I—would prefer we put off taking a vote on this until my father is capable of participating in the discussions,' he said now, aware that he was disappointing them but unable to do anything about it. How could he pass judgement on something so important when he wasn't willing to look beyond the next few days?

The men took his decision resignedly. They weren't prepared to argue with Julio de Montoya's chosen successor, and, with a few polite expressions of goodwill for his father's recovery, they left the boardroom.

Enrique rose at their departure and went to stand at the window. Gazing out at the sweep of the Bay of Cadiz, visible from the elevated heights of the de Montoya building, he massaged the back of his neck with a weary hand. He had handled that well, he thought ironically. Julio would be furious if he knew how ineffectual his contribution had been. His father was depending on him to keep De Montoya y Hijo on course in his absence, but Enrique wondered if he wouldn't have been wiser to appoint Miguel de Guzman as his deputy instead of himself.

He scowled, balling a fist and pressing it against the carved wooden shutters that were folded back against the wall beside the windows. What was wrong with him, for God's sake? Why couldn't he stop thinking about Cassandra and concentrate on the fact that in less than a week his father would be home from the hospital? His mother had said that Julio's doctor was delighted with his progress and that, although he was sixty, Julio apparently had the constitution of a much younger man. It was his father's health that was important, he told himself now, not his own maudlin desire for a woman who had been out of reach as long as he'd known her…

Enrique had been introduced to the woman his brother intended to marry just two weeks before the wedding was due to take place.

He had flown to England on his father's orders to do whatever was necessary to stop the marriage. But, although Julio had told him to warn Antonio that he'd cut him off without a peseta if he went ahead with his plans, Enrique had known that that was a sure-fire way of achieving the exact opposite of what he wanted. Like himself, Antonio had been stubborn, and just quixotic enough to announce that his father could do his worst. And mean it.

In consequence, Enrique had devised a different strategy. He'd had no choice but to admit that his father had sent him, but he'd pretended he was on their side, that he was in favour of the marriage.

It had been pathetically easy to delude Antonio, he remembered, with a pang. His brother had been so open-hearted, so innocent. So sure that what he was doing was right that he hadn't suspected that Enrique might have a different agenda from his own.

In the beginning, Cassandra had been suspicious of him. Perhaps she'd realised even then that he was not to be trusted, though she'd managed to hide her feelings from Antonio.

And, after a few days, even she'd seemed inclined to accept him at face value. After all, he'd been the only member of her future husband's family apparently willing to come to the wedding, and she must have been able to see how delighted Antonio was that he was there.

Antonio had spent much of his time at the university, Enrique remembered. He had been working for his finals. With a degree in art history, he would have had no difficulty in getting a job with or without his father's approval, but it had meant that Enrique and Cassandra had spent a lot of time alone together. Her job at the local library had been much more flexible, and Antonio had insisted that she should get to know his brother.

Looking back now, Enrique knew a reluctance to reexamine his feelings at that time. When had he determined that the only way to stop the marriage had been to seduce her himself? When had he finally decided that his brother was making a mistake and it was up to him to prove it?

God, how arrogant he had been! Of course, he'd been convinced that she was only marrying Antonio because of what she expected to get out of it. Antonio's declaration that it had been love at first sight had sounded far too convenient, and he'd been sure that if Cassandra thought *he* was attracted to her, too, she'd instantly see the advantages of marrying the elder son. He was his father's heir, after all. Not Antonio.

He blew out a breath. Had he really thought it would be that simple? All right, he had only been twenty-four, and life had still been painted in colours of black and white, but he found it hard now to credit his belief in his own infallibility.

Nevertheless, he had sensed that Cassandra was aware of him. No matter how she'd tried to hide it, he'd seen the way she'd looked at him, the way she'd listened intently to everything he'd said. She'd thought she was just being friendly, but Enrique had recognised the signs. Unfortunately, she hadn't until it was much too late to save herself.

And he hadn't been totally indifferent to her, he remembered grimly. She had been—she was—a beautiful woman, and, with short skirts and bare legs, she had been much different from the constrained Catholic girls he'd known back home. In Spain, even today, young women of good families did not go about so freely. They were guarded and protected until they had a ring on their finger.

Perhaps that was what had attracted Antonio to her, too, although his brother had always been drawn to tall slim women with long legs and high breasts. Even without the curly mass of red-gold hair that tumbled about her shoulders, she'd been stunning, and Enrique had to concede that he wouldn't have been human if he hadn't found her stunning as well.

But it wasn't just her looks that had appealed to him, he acknowledged. In the days they had spent together, it had been her warmth and her personality that had made the task he had set himself so enjoyable. But also so difficult. She had shown him parts of London he hadn't known existed, sharing her knowledge generously, making him laugh with the many anecdotes she could recite about the famous people who had once lived in the city.

Perhaps that was when she'd started to lower her guard with him, Enrique reflected. She'd still been wary of him, of course, still unconvinced, perhaps, that both brothers would be prepared to defy their father in such a way. She'd known that Julio de Montoya was not in favour of their marriage, and that had made her cautious of trusting his deputy. But, gradually, Enrique had gained her confidence, and, despite himself, he'd been drawn to her unaffected charm.

So much so that he'd begun to resent the evenings when his brother had joined them, remembered Enrique bitterly. He wasn't proud of it, but he'd resented his brother touching her in ways he himself had wanted to touch her. And when Antonio had put his arms around her, and kissed her, Enrique had felt emotions he didn't even want to identify today…

Cassandra was sitting in the shade of the balcony outside their apartments when David came to find her.

She hadn't seen her son since early that morning. Now that his grandmother had gone back to Seville, he'd taken the first opportunity to go and find Juan Martinez. And, although

Cassandra was always anxious when he was out with the stockman, she'd accepted Carlos Mendoza's word that no harm would come to him at the *palacio*.

'He is *el patrón's* heir,' he'd said simply, and Cassandra had wondered if he knew how true that was.

But of course he didn't. None of them did. David was Antonio's son; Julio de Montoya's grandson. That was enough.

She and Carlos had struck up an unlikely friendship. Enrique's major-domo had done his best to make her feel at home at the *palacio*, and it was he who had taken her to the small chapel in the grounds and shown her where her husband was buried. Antonio had joined his ancestors in the stone *sepulcro* that bore his family's name, and Cassandra had stood for several minutes, feeling the peace that enveloped the place stealing about her.

Elena de Montoya was a different matter, however. Yet, despite her outrage at finding her son kissing his brother's widow, she, too, had recognised at once that David was a de Montoya. And although, to Cassandra's knowledge, she hadn't shown any affection towards him, she had spent several hours talking with him, learning about him, about his life in England, resenting her daughter-in-law's presence at these interviews, resenting her for keeping his existence a secret for so long.

Not that Cassandra cared what Enrique's mother thought of her. Elena de Montoya hadn't wanted to know her ten years ago and there was no doubt she'd prefer not to have to acknowledge her now. But, in that respect, David's attitude had been pivotal, and the older woman had been forced to behave at least politely towards her daughter-in-law when her grandson was present. They'd maintained a stiff formality that was as cold as it was artificial, but thankfully David had been too overawed at meeting his grandmother at last to notice.

Yet, she appended uneasily. Sooner or later, he was going to recognise the hostility for what it was, and then what excuse would she make? Cassandra didn't want to think about that now. She had too many other problems to contend with. Not least, Enrique...

Not that she'd spent any time alone with him since the morning of his mother's arrival. The memory of the scene Elena de Montoya had interrupted was too painful to consider objectively, and since then she'd done everything she could to keep out of his way. Fortunately, David wasn't expected to join the family for dinner because of his age, and, consciously or unconsciously on their part, it had given her the perfect excuse to stay with her son.

Of course, that hadn't prevented her from thinking about Enrique, and about what might have happened if his mother hadn't interrupted them. My God, she thought incredulously, she'd thought she was immune from any sexual attraction to him. Despite her awareness of Enrique, she'd really believed that nothing he did could make her lose control.

How wrong she'd been. As soon as he'd touched her, as soon as he'd fastened his lips to hers, she'd been like putty in his hands. And when he'd thrust his tongue into her mouth she'd been helpless. She'd had no defence against the raw emotion that had torn her defences aside.

Now, as she looked at her son, she had to acknowledge that, even in the few days that they'd been here, David had changed. She didn't know how exactly. She wouldn't have thought anything his grandmother had said to him could have caused the breach. He was more tanned than he'd been when they left Punta del Lobo, and he'd stopped putting the gel on his hair that had proved such a bone of contention before they'd left England. Now, his hair gleamed glossy and black in the sunlight, as thick and lustrous, though perhaps not as long, as Enrique's. But the change wasn't just physical. David seemed more confident; more respectful; older, even. He was beginning to behave as if he belonged here, she realised with sudden apprehension. As if Tuarega, and not the small semi in Hemmingway Close, was his home.

The realisation made her irritable, and her voice was that much sharper than it should have been when she said, 'Where have you been? It's almost two o'clock! Have you had lunch? Did you wear a hat as I told you?'

David's mouth compressed. 'I don't need a hat, Mum,' he

exclaimed, answering her last question first. 'Uncle Enrique doesn't wear a hat. Why should I?'

Cassandra's lips tightened. How tired she was of hearing Enrique quoted at every turn. David had shown no particular desire to spend more time with his grandmother, but Enrique was different. He obviously had great respect for his uncle, however much he might initially have resented him for disciplining him when he'd run away.

But then, that was hardly surprising, Cassandra conceded. Enrique was exactly the kind of dominant male her son would admire. Her own father had inspired affection, but David had always been able to run rings around him. Enrique was different. Dear Lord, did she need any more proof than she had already?

'Your—uncle doesn't need a hat because he was born here,' she told her son now, her voice clipped and impatient. 'He's used to this climate, David. You're not.'

'I'll get used to it,' said David carelessly, lifting his thin shoulders in a dismissive shrug. 'Where is Uncle Enrique anyway? I thought he'd be back from Cadiz by now.'

'He may well be,' said Cassandra, closing the book which had been lying open and unread on her lap. 'You're not his keeper, David. Enrique comes and goes as he pleases. You should know that.'

David sighed. 'What's wrong, Mum?' he exclaimed, not without justification. 'Why are you so crabby? I only asked where Uncle Enrique was. I wanted to tell him what I'd been doing today.'

Cassandra stiffened. 'What have you been doing?'

'Are you really interested?' David left her side to saunter across to the pool, dipping his hands into the cool water and splashing it over his wrists. 'All you ever do is spoil things. I know you didn't want to come here, but I don't see why you can't enjoy it anyway.'

Cassandra caught her breath. 'I—I don't spoil things,' she protested, aware of a slight tremor in her voice. 'David, that's an awful thing to say. And totally unfair. I was worried about you, that's all. You're just a child. You may enjoy watching the animals, but you shouldn't forget that they're dangerous.'

'Horses aren't dangerous,' retorted David, swinging round to face her. 'That was what I wanted to tell Uncle Enrique. Juan has found me a horse of my own. I've been riding round the paddock all morning.'

'A horse?' Cassandra didn't know whether to be relieved or dismayed. 'Do you mean a pony? Boys of your age don't ride horses, do they?'

'Uncle Enrique did,' said David, and Cassandra wanted to scream that *Uncle Enrique* was no role model for him to imitate.

'Anyway, Duquesa is a mare,' he went on, evidently proud of his achievement. 'She's not as big as Santa Cruz, that's Uncle Enrique's horse, but Juan says she's not a *caballito* either.'

'What is a *caballito*?' asked Cassandra, frowning, and then saw her son's face brighten with delight. But he was looking over her shoulder, not at her, and she was hardly surprised when Enrique answered her.

'It means a hobbyhorse,' he said, crossing into her line of vision. 'I told Juan to find a mount for David. If he has chosen Duquesa, he has chosen well.'

Cassandra looked up at him with hostile eyes. He was standing with his back to the sunlight, which meant his dark face was unreadable from this angle. But in a light grey suit that complemented his powerful frame, the jacket hooked lazily over one shoulder, he was still impressive. Impressive and disturbing, she thought uneasily, aware that even the air had quickened since he had stepped into the courtyard.

'I don't remember anyone asking me if David should be allowed to ride,' she said a little jealously, getting up from the low cushioned lounger where she had been sitting, and shading her eyes with a slightly unsteady hand.

'Oh, Mum!' Once again, David showed his impatience at her negativity. 'Why shouldn't I learn to ride? Everyone rides around here.'

'I don't,' retorted Cassandra at once, and saw Enrique's eyes take on a sardonic glint.

'That can be arranged,' he said smoothly, completely outwitting her defence. 'I myself will teach you. You will enjoy it. It will enable you to go freely about the estate. Is tomorrow too soon for your first lesson?'

Cassandra drew a breath. 'I don't wish to learn to ride, thank you,' she said, earning another exasperated sigh from her son. 'I just meant I would have liked to have been consulted about David's activities. He is still my son, however much you might wish it wasn't so.'

'What are you talking about, Mum?' Too late, Cassandra realised she had spoken rather rashly. 'Why should Uncle Enrique wish you weren't my mother? You were his brother's wife.'

'Your mother is a little annoyed with me, that is all, David,' inserted Enrique swiftly. 'I think perhaps it would be a good idea if you went to your room for a rest. You must be tired. Riding can be very exhausting. Besides, I wish to speak to your mother alone.'

'Oh, but—'

David was about to object when he thought better of it. And Cassandra, who resented the idea that Enrique could control her son far more easily than she could, quickly endorsed his words. 'Yes, do that, David,' she said, as if her contribution was the deciding factor. 'We'll continue our discussion later.'

David looked less happy at this interjection, but Cassandra couldn't help that. She had no real desire to be left alone with Enrique, but David had to learn that she was not abrogating her responsibility for him just because he considered his uncle's orders carried more weight. She was his mother. Her opinion mattered.

Nevertheless, she was incredibly tense. And, when David disappeared into the building behind them, she was uneasily aware of Enrique watching her with dark brooding eyes. But what was most disturbing was the realisation that he'd had no compunction about invading her part of the *palacio*. She had thought she was safe here. How wrong she had been!

'Stop looking at me as if you do not trust me,' he said abruptly, flinging his jacket onto the chair beside her. 'I know you have been avoiding me, but it is not necessary.'

'Isn't it?' Cassandra couldn't stand still under his abrasive scrutiny. 'Has your mother warned you not to overstep the mark again?' she asked sarcastically, stepping out into the sunlight. 'It's good to know that someone has some control over you.'

Enrique's eyes flashed with sudden anger. 'My mother knows better than to try and tell me what to do,' he retorted harshly. And then, as if realising she was deliberately provoking him, he added, 'In any case, there was no need for her to say anything. What happened between us was a mistake. It will not happen again.'

Cassandra absorbed these words with a mixture of relief and resentment. He was so arrogant, she thought. So sure of himself. It would be almost worth the pain it would no doubt cause her to prove to him that he wasn't half as in control as he believed.

But that way lay madness, particularly as she already knew he was involved with another woman. So, putting all thoughts of pursuing that aside, she said, 'So what did you want to talk to me about? Has your mother told you to get me out of here before your father comes home?'

Enrique swore softly. 'Will you stop implying that I am answerable to anyone but myself?' he demanded. 'It may interest you to know that for the past eighteen months I have been in virtual control of both the estate and the winery. That is why I am living in the *palacio* again instead of at my own house.'

Cassandra's eyes widened. 'You have your own house?'

'Is that so surprising? I am thirty-four, Cassandra. I lead my own life.'

'And—your house: is it far from here?'

'Why do you want to know?' Now it was his turn to be sardonic. 'Would you like to see it?'

Cassandra lifted her shoulders in an eloquent gesture. 'Of course not. But your work is here. I'd have thought—'

'It is on the estate,' put in Enrique drily. 'My house is on the estate. Further up the valley. A much more modest dwelling than this, but I like it.'

Cassandra couldn't prevent herself. 'You surprise me,' she said drily. 'I'd have thought Tuarega was much more to your taste.'

'Which just goes to show how little you know me,' he retorted, his eyes dropping with sudden concern to her unprotected shoulders. 'Your arms are getting burned. We should continue this discussion indoors.'

Oh, no! Cassandra moved instinctively away from him, deliberately putting more space between them. She had no intention of inviting him into her living room. Although he'd violated the neutrality of her courtyard, she could still pretend that their apartments were their own.

'I'm all right,' she said, brushing a careless hand over her hot skin. 'Why don't you tell me what you want and then I can get on with what I was doing?'

'Cassandra!' His voice was curiously rough as he followed her across to the pool. 'When are you going to stop fighting me?'

Cassandra shook her head. 'You said yourself that any contact between us was a mistake. Why should it matter to you what I think of you?'

'I do not know.' There was harshness in his tone now. Then, with obvious unwillingness, 'But it does.'

Cassandra's eyes were drawn to him then. His reply had been so unexpected, and although she'd toyed with the thought of baiting him earlier, she hadn't really expected this response.

'I don't think you mean that,' she said at last, her voice not altogether steady. 'Please: I'm sure you've got better things to do than waste my time and yours.'

Enrique's lips twisted. 'You enjoy insulting me, do you not?'

'I just want you to go,' exclaimed Cassandra, driven beyond endurance. 'I'm sure your mother wouldn't approve of this conversation.'

Enrique frowned. 'My mother is not my keeper,' he said,

the intensity of his gaze increasing as he absorbed her words. 'And I did not come here to speak about family matters, as it happens.'

'No?' Cassandra's nails dug into her palms. 'Then what? The woman you deny is your girlfriend, perhaps?'

Enrique pulled his tie away from his collar, exposing the brown column of his throat to her unwilling gaze. 'You persist in provoking me, Cassandra,' he said wryly. 'But, as it happens, I am glad you brought her name up. Sanchia, the woman I explained that Antonio was betrothed to, is coming here this evening. I think it would be a good idea if you joined us for dinner.'

CHAPTER TEN

WHY had she agreed to such a crazy scheme?

As Cassandra prepared for dinner that evening, she berated herself again for agreeing to Enrique's request. She could have refused. She could have ignored his invitation and not laid herself open to possible insult and injury. But curiosity had got the better of her and she was ashamed to say that she wanted to see the woman that both Antonio and Enrique had loved.

Yet, if she was totally honest with herself, she had to admit that that wasn't the only reason. Antonio had told her about Sanchia de Silvestre. He'd said how he suspected she'd really wanted to marry Enrique and, when he'd shown that he wasn't interested, she'd transferred her attentions to his younger brother. Now, it seemed, she was getting her wish, and Cassandra couldn't deny that she was curious to see her and Enrique together.

And how intelligent was that?

Peering at her reflection in the long carved mirror in her bedroom, Cassandra couldn't avoid the sudden anguish in her eyes. She had thought, she'd really *believed*, that nothing Enrique did could hurt her any more. But it wasn't true. He'd always had the power to reduce her defences to ashes and she just kept on letting him do it…

When had she first realised that she was attracted to Enrique? How long before she'd begun to look forward to the time they spent together? Why had she fooled herself that her feelings for Enrique were innocent of any sexual intent?

Because she hadn't wanted to admit it, she acknowledged now. All those days they'd spent together when Antonio was finishing his exams: she'd let Enrique get close, so close, never suspecting that his agenda had been so cruelly different from her own.

Looking back, it was easy to be wise after the event. Easy to tell herself that she should have known that a man like Enrique de Montoya, a man with his background, his prospects, was unlikely to be seriously attracted to a penniless librarian. Yet he'd been so likeable, so charming, so unconsciously sexy that, before she'd known it, she'd been totally fascinated.

Totally *infatuated*, she amended bitterly, remembering with a shameful pang how helpless she'd been against his sensual assault.

But it had begun innocently enough, she remembered. So innocently that she hadn't known what was happening until it was much too late to do anything about it.

Ten years ago, she'd been living in a bedsit just off the Edgware Road. Although her widowed father lived just a few miles away in the suburbs, she'd decided to get her own place when she'd got the job at the Kensington Historical Library. She'd wanted to be independent; she'd wanted to live her own life.

And it was through the library that she'd met Antonio. He'd come into her department to do some research, and until his brother came on the scene she'd never had any doubts that she loved him.

Of course, Antonio hadn't told her he was engaged to a young woman back home in Andalucia. He'd let her think he was as unattached and fancy-free as she was herself. It hadn't been until they'd started talking about getting married that he'd confessed that he hadn't told her the complete truth.

At first, she'd wanted to call the whole thing off. But Antonio had persuaded her that, whatever happened between them, his engagement to the Spanish girl was over. He loved her and if she wouldn't marry him he'd spend the rest of his life alone.

Overly dramatic, perhaps, Cassandra thought now, but she'd wanted to believe him. He'd even shown her the letter he'd written to Sanchia and she'd eventually given in, and they'd arranged to get married as soon as his final exams were over.

She knew he'd doubted that any of his family would turn up for the wedding. He'd written to his father, too, telling him that he was in love with an English girl, but Julio de Montoya hadn't replied. Instead, he'd sent his elder son to accomplish what he'd known his words alone would not achieve, and Cassandra had been thrown into contact with the man who was to have such a fateful influence on her life.

Yet, to begin with, it hadn't seemed that way. Although she herself had been a little anxious when Enrique appeared, Antonio had been so delighted to see him she'd soon buried her own doubts and accepted his presence at face value.

And it hadn't been difficult. Enrique was sufficiently like Antonio to make their rapport with one another seem not only easy but natural, and when he had started showing his attraction for her she had persuaded herself that he was just being kind.

Taking her hand when they were crossing a busy road; a light pressure in the small of her back when he was guiding her into a bar or a restaurant; a careless stroke on her neck; his thigh brushing hers when they shared a sofa or a banquette. These were the things he'd used to make her aware of him, and she, idiot that she was, had been completely overwhelmed by it all. Why hadn't she realised what he was doing? she wondered. Why had she trusted him?

The truth was that she'd been flattered. Flattered that he was paying her so much attention; flattered that he seemed to enjoy being with her. She'd enjoyed being with him, and if she'd sometimes indulged in daydreams about what it would be like to make love with Enrique, she'd excused herself on the grounds that because she was still a virgin she was naturally curious about sex.

Curious!

Cassandra shivered. God, that was such an inadequate word to describe how she'd felt about Enrique. She'd been aware of him with every fibre of her being, and when they were together she'd found it incredibly difficult to think about anyone else. She supposed she'd wanted him—although she hadn't known then what wanting meant.

She decided that that must have been when she'd started noticing the differences between the brothers. Both men had been tall and dark, but Enrique was taller, darker, with a sexual magnetism that Cassandra had begun to find increasingly hard to ignore. What she'd found attractive about Antonio had been accentuated in Enrique, like finding the original of a painting after getting used to a copy. A very appealing copy, she acknowledged wryly, but a copy nonetheless.

A couple of days before the wedding, she and Antonio had arranged to go down to Essex to visit her father. He and her sisters were coming to the ceremony, of course, but Cassandra had wanted to see them, to finalise the details for the following weekend. Perhaps she'd unconsciously been searching for confirmation of her decision, Cassandra reflected now. Her sisters had been so enthusiastic. It had been easier with them to convince herself that she was doing the right thing.

But, at the last minute, Antonio had asked if she'd mind if he didn't accompany her. There was to be a reception for graduating foreign students that evening, he'd explained apologetically, but he'd spoken to Enrique and his brother was more than happy to take his place.

How cruelly right he'd been, thought Cassandra bitterly. And, although she'd insisted she was quite capable of going alone—and had done so—Enrique had been waiting for her when she'd got back to St Pancras Station.

'Railways stations are not the place for single women,' he'd declared, when she'd questioned his presence, and although she'd argued the point she couldn't deny she'd been touched that he should have spent the better part of an hour waiting for her.

They'd taken a taxi to her lodgings and it had seemed only polite to invite him in for a coffee. It was the first time any man but Antonio had entered her bedsit, and almost at once she'd realised her mistake. Enrique's dark masculinity had dominated the modest contours of her room and although she had never felt intimidated by Antonio's presence, Enrique was a whole different ball game.

While she'd added coffee to the filter one of her sisters had bought her as a housewarming present, Enrique had wandered about the room, picking up a picture here, adjusting an ornament there. She'd wished he would sit down, but apart from the two dining chairs that had flanked her folding table there'd been only the divan she'd slept on. And although she'd added a coloured throw for daytime use, it had still been far too personal for her peace of mind.

Eventually he had subsided onto the divan, sitting on the edge, his legs spread wide, his lean wrists hanging between. He'd looked so attractive sitting there, his head bent to expose the unexpectedly vulnerable curve of his nape. She'd found herself wanting to touch his neck, to slide her hand into the darkness of his hair, to feel the thick lustrous strands curling about her fingers. But, of course, she hadn't touched him. Not then. She'd realised—or at least she'd *believed*—that he was as nervous about the situation as she was. And that had made what had happened afterwards so infinitely hard to forgive.

At the time, however, she'd been perfectly willing to accept his behaviour at face value, and when the coffee was ready, she'd carried both cups to the divan and seated herself beside him. He'd been wearing a leather jerkin, she remembered. Black, like the close-fitting jeans he'd worn with it, his dark blue shirt the only trace of colour in his outfit. He'd always worn his clothes well; both men had. But whereas Antonio had merely looked good, Enrique's outfit had moulded his powerful body with loving elegance.

'This is good,' he'd said, indicating the coffee, and Cassandra remembered feeling pleased at the compliment. So pleased that she'd offered to get him a second cup. But, when she'd put down her cup and attempted to get to her feet, Enrique had caught her wrist, drawing her back down beside him. 'Later,' he'd told her huskily, and when she'd looked into his eyes, she'd known exactly what he meant.

She should have stopped him. She should have covered her lips with her hand and prevented his from finding their target.

But she hadn't. She'd lifted her hands, yes, but instead of blocking his searching mouth she'd cupped his neck and given herself up to the union they'd both desired.

Or she'd thought it was what they'd both desired, she amended bitterly. At the time, she'd been too blinded by her own needs to notice his response. It had been enough that he was kissing her at last, that his weight was compelling her back against the cushions behind her. That his hard muscled body was aroused and urgent; that his kiss was full of emotion.

But what those emotions might have portrayed, she hadn't questioned. Why should she have? She'd been so sure that Enrique felt the way she did, and although she'd felt guilty for betraying Antonio, she'd assured herself naïvely that he would understand. Once he realised that she and Enrique loved one another—

How deluded she'd been! How stupid! How pathetic!

Remembering now, Cassandra was appalled anew at her own gullibility. She'd really believed that Enrique cared about her, that he'd been as helpless in the face of such powerful feelings as she'd been.

What a fool!

Nevertheless, however calculated his approach, she was sure he'd been shocked by the passion that had erupted between them. However cynically he'd set out on his plan to discredit her, what had happened had driven all thoughts of revenge out of his head. For a time, anyway. He'd wanted her just as much as she'd wanted him, and perhaps it was that knowledge that had made what had happened so much more significant, so much more devastating.

To begin with she'd thought he'd only meant to kiss her. She'd been innocent, trusting, so used to Antonio, who had always respected her wish to remain a virgin until they were married, that the idea of Enrique abusing that trust hadn't occurred to her.

She should have known better. Now, she realised, she should have known at once that Enrique was nothing like Antonio. The way he'd kissed her, the way he'd crushed her lips, the sensual way he'd pushed his tongue into her mouth;

so many things should have warned her that she was playing with fire.

Perhaps they had. If she was completely honest she would have to admit that she'd never been in any doubt who was making love to her. Enrique had been so much more eager; so much more demanding; so much more *experienced*. Yes, that was the word to describe Enrique's lovemaking: experienced. He'd known exactly what he'd wanted, and he'd had no intention of allowing anything to stand in his way.

Least of all a foolish girl to whom his practised caresses had seemed a natural forerunner to romance. She'd convinced herself that Enrique had fallen in love with her and, although that was no excuse for what had happened, it had been enough to salve her conscience at the time.

And, with Enrique's weight imprisoning her beneath him on the divan, she'd been left in little doubt as to his body's reaction to what they were doing. His breathing had been as ragged as hers, laboured gulps of air snatched between long, soul-drugging kisses, that had stifled any protest and left her weak with longing. The throbbing heat of his arousal had pressed against her stomach, and need, hot and unfamiliar, had poured through her.

Neither before nor since had she felt such powerful emotions. She'd been lost to all sanity, lost to all shame. It had felt so good, so right, and there'd been no way she could have prevented what had happened, however humiliated it made her feel now.

She remembered pushing Enrique's jacket off his shoulders, sliding her hands into the open neck of his shirt, touching the warm flesh at his nape which had inspired such forbidden feelings in her earlier. The moist hair had curled about her fingers and she'd used it to drag his sensual mouth back to hers.

Enrique's hands had found the buttons on her shirt, she recalled, her breathing quickening in remembrance. The tiny pearl studs had been no match for his searching fingers, and her breasts had become hot and heavy beneath the lacy confinement of her bra. She'd wanted him to touch them. She'd actually ached with the need for him to do so. So much so that she'd managed to arch her body so that she could release the catch of her bra herself.

God, she'd been so easy, she fretted unsteadily. So desperate for him not to stop what he was doing that she'd have stripped herself naked if he'd asked her to. But he hadn't. He'd been quite content to attend to that detail himself. Nevertheless, he must have thought she knew what she was doing, she conceded unwillingly. She hadn't behaved as if it had been her first time, that was a fact.

He'd shed his own shirt a few moments later, letting her help him peel the fine fabric from his bronzed skin. His chest had been lightly spread with dark hair, she recollected with a shiver. A sensual covering that had arrowed down into the waistband of his trousers.

Her own skirt had been discarded next, and she remembered the disturbing brush of his chest hair against her bare stomach when he lowered himself to take her breast into his mouth. The sensation of his tongue circling her nipple, sucking on the tender tip, had left her breathless, and her breasts tingled now in protest at the direction of her thoughts.

She remembered unbuckling his belt, drawing down his zip, touching him between his legs with tentative fingers. He'd shuddered at her timid caress, but he hadn't objected, rolling to one side to divest himself of both his trousers and his shorts.

It wasn't until his hands had slid beneath her bottom, drawing her up against him, that she'd experienced any trepidation about what they were doing. When the pulsating heat of his maleness had probed the moist triangle of curls at the apex of her legs, she'd known an instant's sheer panic. She ought to tell him, she'd thought anxiously. She ought to warn him that she was a virgin. But she'd been afraid that if he'd known the truth he might have drawn away.

In any case, that was the last coherent thought she'd had. Enrique's fingers had found the sensitive cleft of her bottom, sliding between to explore the pulsing entrance to her womanhood. She'd been wet. She'd felt it on his hands, she recalled tensely. Her untried senses had swum with her first taste of her own sexuality.

She'd been aroused and eager, she remembered now, so that Enrique had never suspected he'd have any problem achieving his own ends. As it happened, he hadn't become aware of her innocence until he'd thrust into her, and by then it had been much too late. He was inside her, filling her, expanding her tight muscles with his powerful shaft. Cursing her perhaps, she thought now, but needing her, creating a mindless excitement that only complete surrender on both their parts could have assuaged.

And had, she recalled, but without bitterness for once. She supposed she ought to be grateful. Many a woman's first experience of sex was with a vastly inferior partner, whereas Enrique, whatever his private agenda, had made sure she'd stayed with him all the way. She'd spun out into infinite space only seconds before he'd achieved his own climax, when the flooding heat of him spilling into her had reminded her that she hadn't thought of the consequences that might ensue…

Shaking her head now, Cassandra reached for her hairbrush, using it on her newly washed hair with unwarranted violence. But remembering what had happened did that to her. It left her feeling weak and vulnerable even after all this time.

The idea that she might be pregnant hadn't become a reality until much later. At that time, she'd still believed that she and Enrique had a future together. She'd believed they were a couple; that they would tell Antonio the following day that they loved one another. Then, whatever happened, Enrique would stand by her.

Another big mistake.

Despite having taken her innocence, despite the fact that he must have known when he'd left that she'd expected to see him the next morning, he'd told her nothing of his plans. When he'd departed in the early hours, going silently down the stairs so as not to alert Cassandra's landlady, he'd kissed her goodbye with a lingering passion that she'd been convinced was genuine. She'd gone back to bed and spent the rest of the night dreaming about him, never imagining that, as far as Enrique was concerned, he'd achieved his objective. He'd had no intention of ever seeing her again.

Of course, when she'd awakened the next day, she'd faced the prospect of telling Antonio what had happened with some trepidation. And regret. She had loved Antonio. She had cared about him. But compared to the way she'd felt about Enrique, the feelings she'd had for her fiancé just didn't compete.

Learning from Antonio later that morning that Enrique had left to return to Spain had been a shock, but her fiancé had had even worse news to relate. Although Enrique had obviously not told his brother that he'd seduced his fiancée, he had admitted that he'd had reservations about Cassandra's suitability all along. He'd maintained that he couldn't, in all conscience, attend a wedding that he and his father opposed, and his advice had been that Antonio should think again before incurring their father's wrath over a woman who wasn't worthy to bear the de Montoya name.

Cassandra had been stunned. There had been no way she could convince herself that this was Enrique's way of preventing the wedding. Whatever he was—and she'd eventually come to regard him as a monster—she hadn't believed he was a coward. If he'd cared anything for her, he'd have stayed and faced his brother like a man.

She'd eventually had to accept that what had happened between them had been a carefully orchestrated seduction. However emotionally involved he'd seemed, for him she had been just another woman, another body in which to slake his lust. He hadn't loved her. She doubted he could love anyone besides himself. He'd tricked her and he'd used her, and she'd been left to pay the price.

Even so, she'd known that she couldn't marry Antonio now. However despicable Enrique's behaviour had been, it had proved to her that her feelings for her fiancé were not strong enough to stand the test of time. But when she'd tried to convey this to Antonio, he'd refused to listen to her. As far as he'd been concerned, she was only responding to his brother's censure, and he'd begged her not to shame him now and confirm his family's judgement about her.

It seemed that Enrique hadn't confessed his own betrayal. And how could she have told Antonio what Enrique had done? She'd loved him too much to hurt him so badly. He would have been permanently damaged; totally devastated. Whatever her faults, she hadn't been that cruel.

So she had allowed the marriage to go ahead, telling herself that the hatred she had now conceived for Enrique had no part in it. She had loved Antonio, after all. She'd determined to make him a good wife. But she'd been nineteen, and, as Enrique had discovered, totally inexperienced. It was only now she realised that she'd been in a state of shock. She'd been in no way capable of making any rational decisions about her future at that time.

The wedding had gone ahead as planned, and Antonio had been content. He'd been disappointed by his brother's absence, of course. But one of Cassandra's brothers-in-law had stepped in as best man in Enrique's place. The marriage at the local register office had served its purpose. Cassandra's father and sisters had been there to support her, and if they'd thought the bride looked to be in something of a daze, they'd said nothing to mar the event.

It had been raining when they'd left to drive down to Cornwall, she remembered. The roads had been slick and wet and Antonio had been driving an unfamiliar car. It was one he had hired for their honeymoon and he had not been an experienced driver. But, even so, it hadn't been his fault when the huge articulated vehicle ahead of them jack-knifed on the slippery tarmac.

The rear end of the wagon had hit the nearside wing of their car, crushing the steering wheel against the window, so that the airbag, which had inflated, had offered Antonio no protection at all. He'd been killed instantly, and Cassandra, who'd suffered only minor injuries, had regained consciousness in the ambulance. And, when she'd asked about her husband, they'd told her regretfully, but unalterably, that she was a widow.

Expelling an unsteady breath, Cassandra put down the hairbrush now and stared bleakly at her reflection. Antonio's family had been quick enough to come to his funeral, she recalled painfully, despising the fact that it still hurt her to think of it. His mother hadn't attended, but Julio de Montoya and his elder son had been there. Not that either of them had spoken to her, she acknowledged bitterly. Even though she'd agreed, via the Spanish lawyer who had contacted her, to allow Antonio's body to be removed to Spain for burial, she had received no thanks from them. She hadn't even known where he was buried, until Carlos had shown her. When David was born—Enrique's son, of course—she'd told him that his father had died in a car crash just after they were married, and thankfully her son had never questioned why they'd never visited his father's grave.

CHAPTER ELEVEN

ENRIQUE raised his wine glass to his lips, watching with dark hooded eyes as Cassandra responded to something Luis Banderas had said. The Spaniard, a distant cousin whom he'd invited to even the numbers at dinner, was evidently fascinated by the fair-skinned Englishwoman. He'd had eyes for no one else since she appeared and Enrique, who had foolishly imagined that Luis would remove the need for him to spend the whole evening entertaining Sanchia, was left in the unenviable position of having to be nice to the woman for whom he had suddenly acquired a distinct aversion.

Meanwhile, Luis was enjoying himself immensely. The meal was over and for the past fifteen minutes he'd been describing the religious festival that took place on his family's estate when the grapes were harvested. Although Enrique felt sure Cassandra couldn't be that interested, she was gazing at Luis as if every word he spoke was of the utmost importance to her, and it infuriated him.

Enrique's jaw compressed. He knew what she was doing, he thought. As far as she was concerned, Luis was the first person she'd met since she came here who had treated her with any kind of respect. His mother had insulted her, and Sanchia, although she'd been polite, had made no attempt to hide the contempt in her eyes.

But what had he expected? Enrique asked himself impatiently. In Sanchia's eyes, Cassandra was an intruder; an interloper. The woman who had stolen her fiancé and who now had the audacity to come here, bringing an heir to the de Montoya estate with her.

He dragged his eyes away from Cassandra's expressive features and stared down, grim-faced, into the wine in his glass. Thinking about David wasn't conducive to his mood either.

In recent days, as he'd recovered from the shock of learning he had a nephew, he'd discovered that his feelings towards the boy were no less ambivalent. As his unwilling awareness of Cassandra had deepened, he'd found himself disliking the fact that David was Antonio's son and not his. He should have been his son, he brooded, and then was ashamed of the thought. But he had to concede that he resented the idea that Cassandra had turned instantly to Antonio for comfort as soon as he'd deserted her.

Or had she?

His head jerked up and he stared intently at her lightly flushed profile. The sun had already laid its fingers on her and the touch of colour suited her, but Enrique noticed these things without really being conscious of them. His mind was full of the question he had just posed himself, and, while it might sound very intriguing to probe the hypothesis, did he really want to know?

'What are you thinking about, *querido*?' Sanchia spoke softly in Spanish, stretching out her hand to cover his where it lay beside his glass. 'I cannot believe you are enjoying this—this evening any more than I am.'

'You are wrong.' Enrique spoke in English, aware that his words must have been clearly audible to the other couple at the table. His eyes challenged the Spanish woman's. 'But if you are bored...'

Sanchia's lips tightened and for a moment he thought she had taken umbrage at his insensitivity. He half hoped she had. But, with an obvious effort, she gathered herself and regarded him with seductive eyes. 'How could I be bored when I am with you, *querido*?' she asked, using English as he had done, but, judging by the way she included Cassandra in her sweeping gaze, for different reasons. She squeezed his hand. 'Is there any chance of us spending the rest of the evening alone?'

Enrique withdrew his hand with careful deliberation. 'Would you have me neglect my other guests?' he asked smoothly, picking up the wine bottle and offering to refill her glass. 'Shall we have another bottle of this? It is rather good.'

Sanchia covered her glass with her hand, and almost instinctually Enrique was aware that Cassandra's head had turned in their direction. What had she thought Sanchia had been saying when she'd spoken in their own language? he wondered irritably. Certainly not what had been said, judging by what had come after. Did she think he and Sanchia were conducting a flirtation at the table? The idea was distasteful to him.

'Wine?' he asked, his eyes holding Cassandra's even when he knew she wanted to look away, but she shook her head.

'Not for me, thank you,' she said, the two long strands of silky-soft hair that she'd left to curl in front of her ears shining red-gold in the candlelight. She'd wound the rest of her hair into a precariously secured knot on the top of her head this evening and Enrique had to stifle an almost uncontrollable impulse to tear out the pins and bury his face in its vivid beauty.

Whether Cassandra had sensed what he was thinking, he didn't know, but something gave her the will to break that revealing eye contact. And Luis's cheerful intervention at that moment was clearly a relief to her.

'*Por favor*, Enrique,' he said, pushing his glass towards the other man. Then, to his companion, 'My cousin keeps an excellent cellar, do you not think so?'

'I don't know very much about wine,' answered Cassandra honestly. 'I didn't even know that Rioja could be white as well as red until I came here.'

'Miss Scott is not used to drinking wine with every meal, Luis,' said Sanchia, regarding the other woman slightingly. 'The English drink tea, do they not? In great quantities, I believe.'

'Then you must allow me to take you on a tour of my family's vineyard,' said Luis at once, watching Enrique refill his glass. 'I can teach you all there is to know about wine, Cassandra.'

'And about other things, too, no doubt,' put in Sanchia insidiously. 'But I hardly think Miss Scott will be here long enough to have time to visit La Calida, Luis. Is that not so, Miss Scott?'

'Her name is de Montoya,' declared Enrique harshly, before

Luis could answer her, unable to deny the automatic reproof. 'Cassandra de Montoya. Or Señora de Montoya, if you will. But not Miss Scott. I realise this is not easy for you, Sanchia, but she is Antonio's widow. *Entiendes?* Do you understand?'

Sanchia sucked in her breath, but it was Cassandra who saved her from taking offence at his words. 'I'm sure Señora de Romero understands that very well,' she said firmly, although she still avoided looking at him. 'And she's right. I'm sorry, Luis, but I don't think I will be able to accept your invitation.'

'There, you see.' Now, Sanchia arched narrow eyebrows at Enrique. 'Even your guest understands that she and her son will be leaving soon.'

'That depends,' said Enrique, refilling his own glass, aware that Cassandra had reacted to the challenge. He was drinking too much, he thought, and the wine was loosening his tongue.

'That depends?' echoed Sanchia, determined to have her way. 'When your father returns from the hospital, Enrique, he will not want his home to be full of strangers, no?'

'Hardly strangers, Sanchia.' Enrique didn't know why he was pursuing this. It wasn't as if he cared what she thought. 'Cassandra is my father's daughter-in-law; his *nuera*. And David is his grandson. They are family.'

'But strangers, nonetheless,' insisted Sanchia, albeit a little stiffly now. She paused. 'I did not realise you had told your father that—that they are here. When I spoke with your mother, she said that your father was unaware of David's existence.'

'But she is not,' said Enrique grimly, wondering when Sanchia had spoken to his mother. What had Elena de Montoya told her about their unexpected visitors? It infuriated him that his mother might confide her feelings to Sanchia when she'd scarcely spoken a word to Cassandra.

'In any case,' Sanchia continued quickly, as if she'd suddenly realised that allying herself with his mother might not have been the wisest choice, 'I am sure discovering he has a grandson may be exactly what your father needs to implement his recovery.'

Are you? thought Enrique dourly, sure she didn't think any such thing. He scowled. Why was this evening going so badly wrong? Why, when his original intention in inviting Sanchia here had been to prove to himself that he and Cassandra had nothing in common, did he find her so much more appealing than the woman he'd known for half his life? And why was he spending his time defending her when it was towards Sanchia he should feel some remorse?

'I am sure when Julio meets Cassandra, he will be as enchanted with her as I am,' Luis inserted gallantly, evidently deciding the conversation was getting too heavy, and, setting down his glass, Enrique pushed back his chair.

'I think we should all adjourn to the *salón* for coffee,' he said non-committally, and then felt another twinge of irritation at Sanchia's smug expression. He crossed to the sideboard where a bell-cord summoned a waiting manservant. 'Is that agreeable to everyone?'

Cassandra folded her napkin and laid it beside her plate. But it was Luis who answered him. 'It is okay with me, *amigo*,' he said, getting to his feet. 'It will give me time to persuade Cassandra that La Calida is only an hour's drive from here.' He smiled down at her. 'What do you say, *cara*?'

'I think I should go and check on David,' she responded, lifting her head, looking at him, not at Enrique. 'If you'll excuse me...'

'Pero—'

'I will come with you,' said Enrique, pre-empting any offer Luis might have made to accompany her, earning an annoyed look from both his other guests. The arrival of a dark-coated retainer prevented any argument, however, and he ordered coffee to be served in the Salón de Alcazar. Then, before Cassandra could think of any objection, 'Make yourselves comfortable. We will not be long.'

'There's no need for anyone to come with me,' declared Cassandra shortly, as he followed her towards the door, and he heard the tremor in her voice she was trying hard to disguise. She looked up at him now and there were tears of outrage as well as anger in her eyes. 'Really, I would prefer to go alone.'

'And lose your way back?' he suggested in a low voice that only she could hear, and she pressed her hands together as if to the quell the urge to scratch his eyes out.

'I'm not completely stupid,' she said, her lips tight. She looked at the other woman, who was watching them with hard resentful eyes. 'If I don't see you again, Señora de Romero, it's been a—singular pleasure.'

Sanchia was taken aback. Enrique guessed she'd thought Cassandra was too intimidated by her surroundings to notice her veiled hostility, but she'd been wrong. They'd all been wrong about Cassandra, he admitted wryly. Including himself.

But he had the advantage in that this was his father's house and as his guest Cassandra could hardly order him not to go with her. Nevertheless, she set a brisk pace along the corridor that linked the family apartments with the other areas of the house and he was forced to quicken his step to keep up with her.

He didn't know how she walked as fast as she did in the high-heeled sandals she was wearing this evening; high heeled sandals that drew his attention to the slim ankles appearing below the hem of her long skirt. Her stride gave tantalising glimpses of the pale thighs exposed as her long steps parted the wrap-around folds.

He'd wished earlier that she'd worn a shorter skirt until he'd seen the way Luis was looking at her. Sanchia was wearing a short chiffon gown that displayed her silk-covered thighs to advantage, but the sequinned vest Cassandra had teamed with the ankle-length skirt was revealing enough. He'd found he objected to the other man ogling her narrow shoulders and slim arms, and he'd known a quite uncharacteristic desire to behave as his ancestors might have done and shut her away from any male eyes but his own.

Which was not something he wanted to think about at this moment. He tried to convince himself that his only motive in offering to accompany her was, as he'd said, to ensure that she found her way back. But now that they were alone together all he could think about was his own intense attraction to her. His hand went out almost involuntarily to fasten around her upper arm.

'Slow down!'

'I don't want to slow down.' Cassandra glanced scornfully at him. 'If you don't like the way I'm walking, why don't you do us both a favour and stop embarrassing me?'

'Embarrassing you?' Enrique exerted himself and brought her to a halt. 'How am I embarrassing you?'

'By behaving as if I'm not capable of finding my own way about the *palacio*.' Cassandra looked pointedly at his hand gripping her arm. 'I found my way here, didn't I? You have no right to do this.'

'In my culture, escorting a guest to her room is not considered to be embarrassing her,' retorted Enrique stiffly.

'Well, in mine, forcing your company on someone else is considered harassment,' replied Cassandra tersely. 'I wish you would leave me alone.'

Enrique didn't know how to answer that. She had every right to resent his actions and he would find it very hard to explain to himself why he was persisting with this. Far better to let her go and return to the others, to Sanchia, who would welcome him back with open arms. Why was he pursuing Cassandra when he'd already stirred up a storm by kissing her in the courtyard the morning his mother had arrived at the *palacio*? What did he want from her, for God's sake? Why didn't he just put the past behind him and let her go?

The truth was, he didn't want to let her go. And he was finding it far too easy to delude himself that she felt the same. If David *was* his son… But that way lay madness. David was Antonio's child. She'd told him so herself.

Or had she?

He looked down at her flesh beneath his hand and knew a surge of emotion. He liked holding her; he liked the warmth the connection was generating throughout the rest of his body. He liked the sense that she was his prisoner, though that was not a thought he wanted to pursue. But he liked the contrast between his dark tan and her much paler skin, the notion that, like the warp and weft of the tapestries behind him, they belonged together.

Trying not to look at the too-tempting beauty of her mouth, he said, 'I thought you might be glad of my company.' He spread a hand to encompass the long corridor with its high vaulted ceiling and sombre portraits of his ancestors. 'The Galería de los Inocentes can feel intimidating at night. I used to feel ghostly eyes watching me when I was a child.'

'But I'm not a child.' Cassandra glanced indifferently about her and he realised she had been too incensed by his behaviour to notice her surroundings. Now she acknowledged his words with a careless shrug of her shoulders. 'I'd say these paintings are more likely to haunt you than me. I've done nothing to arouse their—disapproval.'

'And I have?'

Her words provoked him. He was attempting to convince her that his motives were genuine, and all she was doing was trying to pick a fight.

'Haven't you?' she countered now, her voice low and scornful. 'Why don't you go back to your guests, Enrique? Whatever you say, Señora de Romero obviously considers she has some prior claim to your affections and I wouldn't like her to suspect that there was anything between us. Except contempt, of course.'

'*Maldita sea!* Damn you!' The words were wrung from him in spite of himself. It was hardly a surprise to learn that she had noticed Sanchia's proprietary attitude towards him but he resented the indifference she displayed. 'There is nothing between Sanchia and myself. Nothing!'

'If you say so.'

Patently she didn't believe him, and Enrique's patience grew close to breaking point. In the name of God, he thought, didn't she realise he had feelings? That when he was with her, he couldn't think about anyone else, let alone admit to a previous liaison?

'It's the truth,' he said, grasping her shoulder with his free hand and forcing her to face him. '*Bien*, perhaps we did turn to one another in the past, but it did not mean anything to either of us.'

'Like when you slept with me? That didn't mean anything to you either, did it?' she asked through suddenly tight lips, and he groaned aloud at the chasm he'd inadvertently dug for himself.

'Not like that, no.'

'Are you sure?'

Her eyes were glistening in the muted illumination from a dozen shaded wall-lights and for a moment he thought she was exulting in her victory. But then he realised that the shimmering between her burnished lashes was caused by tears and with an exclamation of remorse he gathered her into his arms.

'*Querida mia*,' he breathed unsteadily against her lips. Then, capturing her mouth with his, he pushed his tongue greedily into the moist yielding cavern that opened up for him. '*Te deseo*—I want you,' he found himself confessing as he had said once before. '*Tocame, cariña!* Touch me! *Dejame*—Let me—'

He sensed she wanted to resist him. The tears were now spilling down her cheeks. But although her hands came to grip his wrists, as if she would push him away from her, her lips told a different story. When he drew back to take a breath, she made a protesting little sound and sought his mouth again, twining her tongue with his and pressing her slim frame against him.

Enrique swayed back against the wall behind him, uncaring of the chill that shivered his spine. He took her with him, his hands sliding possessively from her shoulders to her hips, caressing the inch of skin that bared her navel. He didn't care that she must be able to feel the hard thrust of his arousal. As he rubbed himself against her he was speculating on the very real possibility that he might have to have her here, in the *galería*, with all the disapproving faces of his ancestors looking down at them. He'd never felt such desire for any woman except Cassandra, and the knowledge that she had been his brother's wife was like a knife that tore him apart.

His mouth captured hers again and he sucked on her lips,

drawing a moan of intense pleasure from deep inside him. She ought to have been his, he thought frustratedly, as the ache between his legs grew ever more insistent. She was his; he wanted her. And if his penance was that he should have recognised that fact sooner, then he was more than ready to pay the price.

His mouth moved from hers, along the silken curve of her cheek and jawline to the scented hollow of her throat. He slid the strap of the sequinned vest aside to taste the luscious skin of her neck, knowing as he did so that he wanted to bite her, to devour her, to make her his woman, his beloved, his *amante*...

'Enrique,' she whispered weakly, but it was hardly a protest. Even when he parted her skirt with his thigh and slipped his fingers into the soft folds, she didn't object. Beneath the hem of her lacy panties, which were all she was wearing under the skirt, a pulse beat against his fingers. Damp curls guarded the quivering core of her womanhood, and when he pressed between, he found her wet and ready for him. 'My God, Enrique,' she gulped. 'What are you doing to me?'

'I think you know what you are doing to me, *querida*,' he countered breathlessly, his lungs labouring for air as his fingertips probed the slick honeycomb of muscles he'd found. He couldn't prevent a groan of satisfaction. '*Dios*, Cassandra, I should never have let you marry Antonio. You were mine before you were his. David should have been my son. Mine! How could I have been such a fool as to let you go?'

He heard her catch her breath, felt the sudden shudder that rippled over her body and for a moment he thought it was a response to his stroking fingers. But then, with an agonised cry, she tore herself away from him.

'Don't say that!' she said on a choking breath. 'Don't dare pretend that what passed between us was anything more than a brutal attempt on your part to break us—Antonio and me—to break us up!'

Enrique muffled an oath. 'You do not understand,' he said roughly, pushing himself away from the wall and making a futile attempt to capture her again. 'Cassandra, listen to me.

Why do you think I left for Spain before the wedding? Because I could not bear to see you with him! As God is my witness, I have not been able to think of you and he together without it tearing me apart.'

Cassandra shook her head, staring at him with wide disbelieving eyes, her cheeks still stained with the tears she had shed earlier. 'Oh, you're good, I'll give you that,' she said bitterly. 'If I didn't know better, I'd almost be prepared to believe that you mean what you say.'

'I do mean it,' protested Enrique harshly. '*Dios*, Cassandra, it is the truth. Ever since I found out about David, I have suffered the pains of Hades! If I had only realised what I had, what I was losing, you would have been my wife! David would have been my son!'

'He is your son.'

The words were spoken so softly, barely audibly in fact, that Enrique thought for a moment that he had imagined them. Yet he was so wired by his emotions he knew he would have heard a pin drop.

He swallowed. 'What did you say?'

Cassandra trembled, and he could tell from her expression that she was already regretting her impulsiveness. 'Nothing,' she said now, her eyes wide and apprehensive. 'I made a mistake.' She glanced fearfully about her. 'I—I have to go—'

'Not yet.' Enrique moved with more speed than he would have thought he was capable of a moment ago and stepped into her path, barring her way. His eyes narrowed incredulously, his desire for her being stifled by raw disbelief. 'What do you mean by saying something like that? David is Antonio's child.' He took a steadying breath. 'He must be.'

'Must he?' Cassandra hesitated, but then it seemed she'd decided to bluff it out. She held up her head with a touching air of dignity. 'Yes, you're probably right.'

Her vulnerability tore at him, but he refused to allow himself to be distracted by the anxiety he could see in her eyes. In God's name, why was she lying? Did she believe David was his son or not?

'Why would you say a thing like that?' he demanded, the

harshness of his tone belying the uncertainty he was feeling. 'Dammit, Cassandra, are you playing with me? Do you not think I have suffered enough for that one mistake?'

'You've suffered?' Her voice broke and she struggled to control herself. 'Oh, Enrique, you have no idea what it means to feel pain. I—I was a virgin when you made love to me,' she reminded him tremulously. 'Did it never occur to you that there might be consequences for what you did?'

Enrique stared at her. 'You are saying he is my son?' He was staggered. 'But how do you know that? What proof do you have?'

'Proof?' Cassandra gazed at him pityingly. 'I don't need any proof,' she told him painfully. 'You know what happened as well as I do. Antonio died on the day we were married. Thank God, he never had the chance to—to discover what you'd done.'

CHAPTER TWELVE

DAVID came into Cassandra's bedroom the next morning with a sullen expression marring his good-looking features. For one awful moment, his mother wondered if Enrique had been talking to him about what had happened the night before, but David's first words were reassuring.

'Tio Enrique's gone,' he muttered, slouching moodily about her room for a few minutes before subsiding onto the end of her bed. 'Carlos says he doesn't know when he'll be back. Do you think he's sick of us? Do you think he's hoping we'll be gone before he comes home?'

Cassandra refrained from pointing out that Tuarega was not strictly Enrique's home. It would be his one day, and telling David that his uncle—his *father*—had a house further up the valley was not wise. He might well decide to go and see if Enrique was there and she had enough to worry about without fretting about her son's whereabouts, too.

She still couldn't quite believe what she'd done. She'd hardly slept, and she'd been lying here for the past few hours trying to understand why she'd been so stupid. Now, hearing that Enrique had left the *palacio*, she knew she ought to feel grateful. He was giving her time to come to terms with the situation, she thought tensely. Or would Enrique be so considerate? Might it not be the case that he had gone away because he didn't believe her? Perhaps he thought she had some idea of using her son to her advantage. By saying he was his son and not Antonio's, she had obviously strengthened David's claim to be Julio de Montoya's heir.

She felt sick. Surely he couldn't think she was as mercenary as that? She hadn't wanted to come here. She'd wanted nothing from the de Montoyas. But, whichever way she looked at it, she had given Enrique unwarranted power over her; over both of them. Dared she wait and see what he chose to do with it?

And this was all because she hadn't been able to control her hormones, she thought bitterly. Because Enrique had kissed her and stroked her, and brought her to the brink of orgasm with his caressing hands, she'd been deluded into thinking that what they were sharing was real, was honest, that it meant the same to him as it did to her.

God, what a fool she'd been!

Enrique had wanted her. He'd wanted to have sex with her, but that was all. All evening, he'd watched her with his dark, hooded eyes, mentally undressing her with his sensual glances. Glances that had brought the hot blood coursing to the surface of her skin and caused liquid heat to pool between her thighs.

How had she known what he was thinking? Because, however much he might resent the fact, he was attracted to her. Physically attracted, she amended. He had desired to bury his hard flesh within hers. And it might have come to that if she hadn't been so reckless; if she hadn't opened her mouth and confessed the secret she'd been guarding all these years.

'Do you know where he's gone?' asked David suddenly, misinterpreting her silence, and Cassandra realised she was in danger of allowing him to see that something was wrong.

'Why would I?' she countered, propping herself up on her elbows and pushing the heavy weight of her hair out of her eyes. She forced a smile. 'Have you had breakfast?'

'I thought he might have said something last night,' persisted David, not interested in her attempt to change the subject, and Cassandra's lips parted.

'Last—night?'

Her voice faltered but David didn't appear to notice her hesitation. 'You had dinner with him and his friends, didn't you?' he demanded impatiently. 'He must have said something.'

'Not about going away,' said Cassandra, throwing back the sheet and sliding her legs out of bed with more determination than enthusiasm.

In fact, Enrique had said nothing after her assertion that she and Antonio had never consummated their marriage. After one stunned look in her direction, he'd turned and walked away, and she'd been left with the cold conviction that she had destroyed any chance of them ever forgiving one another for the past.

'I bet he's gone away with that woman,' grumbled David now, getting up from the bed and dragging his feet across to the open balcony doors. 'Is he going to marry her, do you think?' He hunched his shoulders and rested his arms on the balcony rail, his back to the room. 'I hope not.'

'Why?' Cassandra couldn't prevent the question and David turned to give her an old-fashioned look. 'What?' she protested. 'I don't know what you're talking about.'

'Oh, Mum!' David gave her a pitying look. 'Don't you see? If Tio Enrique marries someone else, he won't care about us any more. He'll have a wife, maybe a family. We'll just be the poor relations.'

Cassandra swallowed. 'If he marries *someone else*?' she echoed faintly. 'I didn't know he'd been married.'

'He hasn't,' exclaimed David impatiently. 'I meant, instead of you. Surely you've thought about it, too?'

'Thought about what?' Cassandra refused to put words to what he was suggesting.

'About marrying Tio Enrique,' replied her son at once. 'It's the ideal solution. Dad's dead and you don't have anyone else. We could be a real family. You and me and—'

'No!' The word was strangled and Cassandra gazed at him with horrified eyes. He was truly his father's child, she thought bleakly. He didn't hesitate. He went straight for the jugular. 'You don't know what you're talking about,' she protested. 'I—Enrique de Montoya would never marry me!'

The fact that she'd entertained such a thought herself last night when he'd been making love to her was not something she cared to share with him. Not that or what had come after. Remembering the way Enrique had looked at her before he strode away, she wondered if she was a fool in thinking he'd ever want to speak to her again.

'Why not?' David wasn't prepared to give up that easily.

He came back into the room. He caught his mother's cold hands in his, pulling her up from the bed and gazing at her as if he'd just solved the secret of the universe. 'You're young. You're quite pretty, even if you are nearly thirty.' He made thirty sound like middle age. 'You need someone to—to look after you.'

'No, David.'

He scowled, and then flung her hands away from him. 'You always say that,' he exclaimed unfairly. 'Whatever I want to do, you always have a better idea.'

'That's not true.' Cassandra was defensive.

'Yes, it is.' He pushed his hands into the pockets of his baggy shorts. 'You didn't want to come here, did you? And if you'd known I'd written that letter to Grandpapa, you'd have stopped me from sending it, too.'

Cassandra sighed. 'David, you don't understand—'

'No, I don't,' he muttered sulkily. 'You like it here. I know you do. All right, maybe Grandmama wasn't very friendly, but you can't blame her.'

'Can't I?' Cassandra's voice was faint with dismay.

'No.' David sniffed. 'I mean, what did you expect? They didn't even know they had a grandson.'

Cassandra's lips parted. 'How do you know that?' she asked, sure Enrique must have told him, but David was nothing if not honest.

'It was Juan, actually,' he said, having the grace to look slightly discomfited now. 'He told me.'

'Juan?' Cassandra shook her head in bewilderment. She'd never imagined that their affairs might be common knowledge among the estate staff. But she supposed she should have known better. She steeled herself for the worst. 'So what did he tell you?'

David hunched his shoulders. 'Not a lot.'

'David!'

He hesitated. 'He said that no one at Tuarega had known that Señor Antonio had a son. He—he said that if they had, Grandpapa would have—would have brought me to live with him.'

'Did he?' Cassandra found she was trembling and she wrapped her arms about her midriff, hugging herself tightly. 'And what was your response to that?'

David shrugged. 'I don't remember.' His mother stared at him, but this time he refused to budge. 'I don't,' he insisted defensively. 'I—I thought at first that he must have made a mistake.'

Cassandra moistened her lips. 'And when did you decide he hadn't?'

'I guess I just worked it out for myself,' muttered David unhappily. 'I think Tio Enrique would have come to see us if he'd known. Why wouldn't he? Juan says that family is really important to the de Montoyas. And we are family.'

'You are,' said Cassandra flatly, unable to continue with this. Her worst fears had been realised. Not only did David believe he knew who he was, but he blamed her for his estrangement from his father's family. Oh, he hadn't said so, not in so many words. But it was just a matter of time and then…

'You're family, too,' protested David, suddenly seeming to realise that this wasn't going at all the way he'd expected. 'Mum!' This as she turned away and began taking clean underwear out of a drawer, preparatory to taking her morning shower. 'Look, I'm sorry if I've upset you. But, honestly, I really think you've got this all wrong.'

'Do you?' With fresh shorts and a sleeveless tanktop draped over her arm, Cassandra paused in the doorway to the bathroom. 'Well, you're entitled to your opinion, of course. But David, believe me, Enrique de Montoya isn't interested in me. In you, yes. As you say, you're—family. As far as I'm concerned the de Montoyas made it very clear ten years ago that they wanted nothing to do with me. Right?'

'But they didn't know about me,' exclaimed David, following her across the room, and Cassandra gave him a disbelieving look.

'Do you think that makes a difference?' she demanded, and once again, he looked shamefaced.

'I—don't know.'

'Well, it doesn't,' said Cassandra tightly, and unable to hide her feelings any longer, she did the unthinkable and slammed the door in his face.

'Mum!'

David was hurt. He wasn't used to being treated this way, but Cassandra didn't give in to his pleas. With the lock secured and her shoulders pressed against the door for good measure, she gave in to the emotions that had been threatening for the past few hours. Ignoring her son's agitated rattling of the handle, she allowed the hot tears to stream unchecked down her cheeks, and not until David had given up and gone away did she make any attempt to do what she'd come into the bathroom for.

Enrique had always thought that Seville was the most Spanish of cities. It was also one of the most beautiful places in Spain, some might say in the world, and he'd always loved it.

But today even the sight of its famous cathedral did little to lift his spirits. The huge Gothic church and the Giralda tower, which was the city's most famous landmark, were just monuments to a way of life that he didn't want to identify with any more.

Cassandra's words had cut deeply into the fabric of his existence. The devastating realisation that for the last ten years he had been living a lie left him feeling sick and bewildered. Although he wanted to deny it, to accuse her of using one mistake to justify her actions, he knew in his heart of hearts that she was telling the truth.

The boy was his. David was his; the child he had so instantly recognised as being his own flesh and blood was in reality so much more. Flesh of his flesh; blood of his blood; fruit of his genes, of his loins. The son he had never expected to have.

And Cassandra's, he added tensely. Though there was no chance of him forgetting that. He gave a snort of disgust. God, and he had blamed her for keeping the child a secret from them! She must have spent the last ten years hating him, hating his father, hating the very name of de Montoya. No wonder she had been so shocked when he had turned up at the *pensión* in Punta del Lobo. He must have been the very last person she wanted to see.

If David hadn't written that letter...

But he couldn't think about that now. He had other, arguably more important, matters to attend to. His father was due to leave the hospital tomorrow and his mother had requested him to come and drive the old man home to Tuarega. She had asked him to come today because she wanted all the formalities dealt with in advance of her husband's release date; or so she'd said. But Enrique suspected that she still hadn't told Julio about David and she wanted him to tell his father before he arrived at the *palacio* and discovered the truth for himself.

It was still early when he arrived at the block of apartments where his mother was staying. Not yet ten o'clock, and already he felt as if he had done a day's work. He hadn't eaten since Cassandra's revelation of the night before; hadn't slept. And now, faced with the prospect of telling his mother who David really was, he felt hopelessly unequal to the task.

Yet strangely elated, too, he realised, parking the Mercedes in the shade of a huge flowering acacia. Its yellow blossoms dripped feathery shadows over the car and as Enrique got out he inhaled the distinctive aromas of heat and vegetation and the unavoidable smell of exhaust fumes that hung in the languid air.

The de Montoya *apartamento* occupied the top floor of the five-storey building that overlooked the formal gardens of one of the city's parks. After exchanging a few words with the doorman, Enrique took one of the old-fashioned elevators up to the penthouse. A padded bench furnished the small panelled cubicle and hand-operated wrought-iron gates replaced the efficient sliding doors he was used to but Enrique scarcely noticed. Everything about the building proclaimed its age and conservatism, but his parents liked it and there was no doubt that, when any of the apartments became vacant, there was always a list of would-be tenants waiting to move in.

Bonita, his mother's housemaid, let him in, her plump face exhibiting her surprise at his early arrival. 'Señora de Montoya is not yet up, *señor*,' she explained, following him into a spacious salon whose long windows gave a magnificent view of the cathedral. 'I will tell her you are here.'

'There's no hurry, Bonita,' he replied, glancing about him at the familiar surroundings of the apartment. Heavy carved furniture, richly coloured upholstery echoed in the thick drapes hanging at the windows: the room was a mirror-image of the apartments his parents occupied at the *palacio* but without its height and space to mitigate the oppressive effect. 'I'll have some coffee while I wait.'

'Yes, *señor*.'

Bonita bustled away to do his bidding and Enrique moved to the windows, standing with his hands pushed into the hip pockets of his black trousers, the collar of his dark green shirt gaping open to expose the hair-roughened skin of his throat. The apartment was air-conditioned and he was grateful for it. He'd begun to feel the heat coming up in the elevator.

'Enrique!'

His mother's voice disturbed him. Turning, he found her standing just inside the door that led to the inner hall of the apartment, a lavender-coloured velvet robe wrapped tightly about her, as if she was cold.

Judging by her expression, Enrique apprehended that she thought his early arrival heralded bad news and he hurried to reassure her. 'Mamá,' he said, going to her and bestowing a kiss on her dry cheek. 'How are you? All ready to return to Tuarega?'

'As I'll ever be,' declared Elena de Montoya shortly. 'I take it you are eager to tell your father what you've done? That is why you are here before breakfast, I assume?'

'You haven't told him?' Enrique knew it was a pointless question. Obviously she hadn't or she would have said so.

'No.' Elena gathered the folds of the robe at her throat and gave him a haughty look. 'You brought that woman and her son to Tuarega, Enrique. It is your duty to tell your father who they are.'

'They are your daughter-in-law and your grandson, Mamá,' retorted Enrique, feeling the nerves coiling tightly in his stomach. 'You cannot dispute that.'

His mother drew a deep breath. 'The boy is a de Montoya,' she agreed. 'Of that there is no doubt.'

'Then?'

'But he has not been brought up as a de Montoya, Enrique,' she exclaimed impatiently. 'As he would have been if he had been your son.'

'He is my son, Mamá.'

It was as easy as that. The words simply formed themselves and before he could consider their impact they had slipped out, as clear and as damning as the conviction behind them.

His mother stared at him blankly for a moment. Her eyes dilated, mirroring the numbing effect of his words, and it was apparent that she was in a state of shock.

He would have gone to her then but she waved him away, moving to the armchair nearest to her and groping for its support. Like a much older woman than she actually was, she lowered herself onto the cushioned seat and sat for several seconds just gazing at him as if she'd never seen him before.

Then, when his own skin was feeling clammily damp with sweat, she spoke again. 'Why didn't you tell me this before?'

'As you told me you had discussed David's future with Sanchia?' Enrique sighed. 'I didn't know before last night.'

His mother avoided his question and asked one of her own. 'You expect me to believe that?'

'It's the truth.'

'But you must have—'

'No.' Enrique's nostrils flared. 'No, I didn't. How could I? You know how Cassandra feels about me, about us. She didn't even want to come here, to Spain. That was David's idea; the letter was David's idea. If he hadn't written to Papá...'

'We would never have known of his existence,' said his mother faintly, and Enrique nodded. 'But why not? Surely she must have known how we would have felt if we'd known she was expecting a child?'

'My child?' suggested Enrique drily, and his mother came unsteadily to her feet.

'Your child,' she said incredulously. Then, with harsh emphasis, 'How could you, Enrique? How could you? Your own brother's wife!'

'She wasn't his wife when—when we—'

'Spare me all the sordid details,' exclaimed Elena, shaking her head in distaste. 'I cannot believe this, Enrique. All the time that I was at Tuarega; all those hours I spent talking with David, believing he was Antonio's child.'

Enrique shrugged. 'I am sorry.'

'Sorry?' His mother looked up at him with bitter eyes. 'Sorry does not even begin to cover it.' She paused. 'But how do you know that woman—Cassandra—is not lying? How can you be sure that David is *your* son?'

'He is,' said Enrique flatly.

'But how—?'

'She was a virgin when I made love to her,' replied Enrique harshly, and his mother winced. 'She and Antonio never had the chance to consummate their marriage. He was killed only hours after the wedding, remember?'

'How could I forget?' asked Elena bleakly, and then glanced round apprehensively when Bonita came back carrying a tray of coffee and freshly squeezed orange juice.

The housemaid greeted her mistress warmly, setting the tray on the table nearest to where she was sitting before turning to Enrique. 'Some toast or a croissant, perhaps, *señor*?' she suggested. 'I have some home-made strawberry conserve.'

'The coffee will do, Bonita,' he replied with a small smile. 'Thank you.'

'And you, *señora*?'

'Nothing, nothing.' Elena waved an agitated hand at the housemaid. 'Leave us.' This as the woman went to pour the coffee. 'My son can take care of it. He seems to think he can handle everything else.'

'Yes, *señora*.'

Bonita withdrew, but not before she had exchanged a startled look with Enrique, and after she had gone he pulled a wry face. 'There's no need to take your feelings out on the staff,' he remarked reprovingly. 'It's not Bonita's fault that you're stressed.'

Elena's lips tightened. 'Nor mine either,' she reminded him tightly. 'And please don't use that language in my presence. You are a de Montoya, Enrique. That should mean something to you.'

'It does,' he said flatly. 'It means arrogance, and pride, and an overwhelming belief in one's own importance in the scheme of things. But do you know what, Mamá? All of a sudden that sounds awfully hollow to me.'

'Because you've just found out that you have a son you never knew?' she demanded contemptuously. 'We all make mistakes, Enrique. Even you.'

'Yes, we do,' he agreed, suddenly wanting to be out of the apartment and away from this dried-up old woman who always believed she was right. 'But you'll never guess what my mistake was. Never in a million years!'

CHAPTER THIRTEEN

ENRIQUE didn't return to Tuarega that evening.

Cassandra had spent the morning in a state of extreme agitation, sure he would want more of an explanation than she had given him the night before and steeling herself to face his anger. But her lunch had been served without any explanation being given for his departure, and she consoled herself with the thought that the longer he stayed away, the shorter time there would be left for them to remain at the *palacio* when he got back.

She was reluctant to consider what he might be thinking. If he had believed her, she didn't want to contemplate what his actions might be. No matter how attractive the proposition, the possibility that he might have dismissed what she'd told him as pure fabrication became more and more unlikely as each hour passed. He'd believed her, she thought sickly, and now she had to ponder how she was going to deal with it.

The most attractive option was to leave Tuarega. The idea of calling a cab, of loading herself and David into it and driving to the airport to catch a flight back to England, was almost irresistible. But she couldn't do that. Apart from anything else, she doubted David would want to go with her, and, while she could override his wishes, sooner or later she was going to have to face the consequences of what she'd done.

Why had she done it? she had asked herself again that afternoon, having left the *palacio* in search of her son and found herself standing at the rail of one of the paddocks where some of Enrique's bulls had been grazing the lush grass. Why had she told him? No one had forced her hand. However loath she might be to admit it, hadn't she secretly just been waiting for a chance to cut the ground out from under him? To wipe the smug smile from his face once and for all?

She had shuddered, wrapping her arms about herself as the cold suspicion took root. She didn't want to admit that she'd found any pleasure in telling him. She hadn't, she assured herself fiercely. But she must have hurt him and that was an emotion she could identify with very well.

'Señora?'

It had been Carlos, his lined face wearing an anxious expression, and Cassandra had wondered if Enrique had confided in him before taking off for God knew where.

'Hi,' she said, forcing a smile. And then, nodding towards the bulls, one or two of whom had lifted their heads and were regarding them with disconcerting interest. 'I was just admiring the stock.'

'Sí, señora.' Although Carlos spoke a little English he understood considerably more and he looked at the powerful herd with a certain amount of pride. Then, with a shrug, 'But you do not like *los toros*, no?'

Cassandra tried to be objective. 'I have nothing against the animals exactly...'

'But you do not like the—um—bullfight, *sí*?'

'Sí,' agreed Cassandra, resting her elbows on the rail and gazing at the bulls with doubtful eyes. 'It's—cruel.'

'Ah, *cruel*.' Carlos used the Spanish pronunciation. 'Many things are *cruel*, *señora*.' He paused. '*El toro* dies a—how would you say?—a death *valeroso*, no?'

'A valiant death? No.' Cassandra was diverted from her own problems by his teasing provocation. 'The bull dies in pain; in agony. It bleeds to death, doesn't it?'

'Ah, no.' Carlos lifted one finger and shook it from side to side. '*El torero*, he kills with *la estocada*. His sword. Into the neck, so!'

'I'd rather not hear the details.' Cassandra shivered and the old man smiled.

'Señor Enrique: he was like you when he was younger.'

'Enrique?' She couldn't believe it.

'Pero, sí.' Carlos watched one of the bulls that was approaching them with wary eyes. 'Even today, he does not attend the *corrida, señora*. These are his bulls; his *toros bravos*.

But he has no wish to know what happens to them after they leave, *entiende usted*?'

Cassandra shook her head, remembering what she had said to Enrique, what she'd accused him of. Dear God, was there no part of their relationship that had not suffered from misunderstandings? Was she always to feel the ignominy of being in the wrong?

'Come, *señora*.' Carlos indicated the bull which was now only a few feet away and was watching them with sharp beady eyes. 'We would not want to offend *nuestros companeros*, no? Let me escort you back to the *palacio*. Señor Enrique would never forgive me if anything happened to you.'

Cassandra went with him, but she doubted Enrique cared what happened to her. From his point of view, it would make his life considerably less complicated if she were to go back to England. Alone, of course. After her revelations, he would have even more reason to want to keep David here.

David himself was another matter. She didn't honestly know how her son would react if he was given the choice. He loved her; of course he did. But he loved being here, at Tuarega. And it was bound to be a temptation if Enrique explained that it would all be his some day.

Depression enveloped her. All this, and she still hadn't taken into account how her son would feel when he learned the truth. Would he blame her for keeping him from his father? Would he ever understand her dilemma after the way the de Montoyas had treated her?

Somehow, she doubted it. In David's world, things were either black or white, bad or good, and telling lies did not come naturally to him. It was one of the things she had always loved about him. His candour, and his honesty; his willingness to take the blame if he was at fault. But he wasn't at fault now. She was. And she didn't know what to do about it.

Then, that evening, she got a call from her father.

She'd left a forwarding address with the proprietor of the *pensión* where they'd stayed in Punta del Lobo, mainly because she hadn't wanted to phone her father and tell him where they were going. She'd known Mr Scott wouldn't approve and it would have taken too long to explain the situation to him. Or that was what she'd told herself. Foolishly, she'd imagined that all explanations could wait until they got home, but now it seemed her father had decided to ring and assure himself that all was well and they hadn't been there.

'What's going on, Cass?' he demanded, as soon as she came on the line. 'I thought you told me you had no intention of contacting Antonio's family.'

'I didn't,' said Cassandra quickly, aware of David standing behind her, listening to every word. 'I—David wanted to meet them.' She glanced over her shoulder. 'He's here. Do you want to have a word with him?'

'No, I want to know why you'd go to Tuarega without telling me where you were,' retorted her father shortly. 'For heaven's sake, Cass! Don't I deserve an explanation?'

'Of course you do.' Cassandra sighed, and David came to stand by her shoulder. 'Look, we can't talk on the phone. We'll be home in a few days. I'll tell you all about it then.'

'Is that Grandad?' asked David, catching on. 'Let me say hello.'

'In a minute.' Cassandra felt as if she was wedged between a rock and a hard place. 'Dad, give me the chance to explain.'

'Explain what?' He was angry. 'You had all this planned, didn't you, Cass? You knew exactly what you were going to do before you left England. All that talk about worrying whether the de Montoyas might find out where you were was all—rubbish, wasn't it?'

'No.' Cassandra was hurt that he should think so. 'I had no idea that David—'

She broke off, not wanting to tell him what her son had done, but her father wouldn't leave it there.

'You had no idea that David—what?' Mr Scott snorted. 'You're not going to tell me that this was his idea?'

'It was.' Cassandra sighed again. 'Here: I'll put him on. He can tell you about it himself.'

David took the phone eagerly, and before his grandfather could speak, he exclaimed, 'You ought to see this place, Grandad! It's fantastic! It's got a gym and a swimming pool, and as well as the horses that Tio Enrique rides there are about a hundred bulls! They're great! A bit scary, sometimes, but Tio Enrique says that so long as you're careful, they won't hurt you.'

'David, David!' Cassandra could hear her father trying to calm him down. 'Let me speak to your mother again, will you, son? I'll hear all about the holiday when you get back.'

David's face dropped. 'But Grandad—'

'Not now, David.' Cassandra knew her father was having difficulty in controlling his temper. 'Put your mother on. This call is costing me a fortune.'

David handed the phone to Cassandra with ill grace. 'Here,' he said, pushing his hands into the pockets of his shorts and staring defiantly at her. 'Why should I speak to him anyway? He's never been interested in what I do.'

'That's not true,' protested Cassandra, horrified, covering the phone with her hand. 'David, your grandfather has always cared about your welfare. Where would we have been without him, that's what I'd like to know? Don't be such a baby. He's worried because we'd left the *pensión* without telling him, that's all.' She paused. 'Go and get your pyjamas on. It's nearly time for bed.'

David left the room without speaking and she hoped she was not going to have to mediate between him and her father. She seemed to be spending her time lurching from one crisis to another, and it seemed to be the pattern at the moment for her to be the scapegoat for everyone's grievances.

Somehow, she managed to placate her father without telling him about David's letter. She sensed that that would infuriate him still more, and, after assuring Mr Scott that in an emergency she would do as he suggested and use her credit card to get an earlier flight home, she managed to end the call. But he wasn't satisfied, she knew that, and he would demand a full explanation when she got back. Someone else, she thought drily. How many more explanations would she have to make?

She awakened the next morning feeling more hungover than she'd done the previous day. She had slept; exhaustion had seen to that. But her sleep had been shallow and punctuated with nightmare scenes of David being pursued by one of Enrique's fighting bulls, its beady eyes red and glittering with malevolence.

She crawled out of bed feeling sick and headachy, her mouth tasting foul, and her skin sticky with the sweat her dreams had generated. Even a shower did little to lift her mood, and when she emerged from her bedroom to find David tucking into butter-slathered rolls and freshly squeezed orange juice, she thought how unfair life was.

'Hi, Mum,' he said, his expression considerably more cheerful than it had been the night before. 'I know where Tio Enrique is. He's in Seville. He's gone to fetch Grandpapa home. Isn't that exciting?'

Cassandra swallowed. Exciting wasn't the word she'd have used to describe her feelings at the thought of seeing Julio de Montoya again. She couldn't even claim to have *met* him before. A stiff black-suited figure at the service Cassandra had held for her late husband, he hadn't so much as exchanged a word with his daughter-in-law. He'd saved all his comments for the priest who'd conducted the service, and her nerves prickled at the thought of his anger when he discovered the secret she'd been keeping from them all these years.

'How do you know?' she asked obliquely, pouring herself a cup of the strong coffee Consuela had provided for them. Carlos had said nothing to her, but then the old man was always excessively discreet where his employer was concerned.

'Consuela told me,' David replied at once, helping himself to another roll. 'They'll be home later today. According to her, Grandpapa is leaving the hospital this morning. He'll be surprised to meet me, won't he?'

'No doubt.' Cassandra tried to keep the anxiety out of her voice. 'Um—just don't expect too much, will you, David? I mean, your grandfather's been very ill. He may need a few days to—to recover from the journey.'

David's eyes darkened with a mixture of doubt and resentment. 'But Tio Enrique said Grandpapa would be pleased to hear he had a grandson,' he protested peevishly. 'Are you sure that's not just you hoping we won't get on? I mean he is my dad's father. I think he'll be rapt when he knows we're here.'

Cassandra couldn't imagine Julio de Montoya being rapt about anything, least of all a grandson who was half her blood. She was still the outsider as far as he was concerned. And nothing that had happened since she arrived in Spain had given her any reason to think that that was likely to change.

Apparently preferring Juan's company to hers, David disappeared after breakfast and, left to herself, Cassandra decided to start packing their belongings. It would give her something to do, and although there were still a few more days before they were due back at Punta del Lobo to catch the bus which would take them to Seville airport, it made her feel as if she was doing something positive for a change.

It was early afternoon when she heard the car. She didn't want to admit that she'd been listening for it, but she had. She found herself going out into the sunlit courtyard and staring out across the wide sweep of the valley, wondering with a shameful sense of apprehension if Julio de Montoya would want to see her. Not today, she assured herself firmly. When he was rested, perhaps. She had no illusions as to who would bear the brunt of her father-in-law's wrath, but he must need time to recover his strength.

In fact it was less than an hour before she heard the sound of footsteps crossing the marble floor of the *salón*. Cassandra was still in her bedroom, pretending to be engrossed in sorting through the contents of her cosmetics bag, when a shadow filled the open doorway and she looked up to find Enrique standing there, watching her.

He was the very last person she had expected to see. Consuela, perhaps? David? But not Enrique. And yet, why not? It was appropriate, she thought bitterly. He was used to doing his father's bidding.

All the same, she couldn't meet his searching gaze for long. His absence had done nothing to damp the leaping fires inside her, and all she could remember was how weak and helpless he'd made her feel.

For his part, Enrique's face was expressionless, and she had no way of knowing what he was thinking. In a more formal shirt than she was used to seeing—ice-blue silk teamed with an Italian-styled suit in navy blue—he looked darkly handsome, disturbingly elegant. Her nemesis, she reflected a little shakily. Her fate and her temptation, and ultimately her destruction.

'If you're looking for David, he's not here,' she said, when the silence between them was beginning to strip her nerves. And Enrique shrugged.

'I can see that,' he replied, with no apparent inflection in his voice. 'What are you doing?'

'Nothing much.' Cassandra had been sitting on the padded stool beside the vanity, but now she got to her feet. There was no need for him to know she'd started packing. 'What do you want?'

Enrique rocked back on his heels. 'What do *I* want?' he queried, an edge of sarcasm colouring his tone. '*Dios*, where do I begin?'

Cassandra held up her head, not answering him. 'I understand you went to Seville to bring your father home,' she said instead, managing somehow to keep her voice cool and controlled. 'How is he? I expect he'll be tired after the journey.'

Enrique swore then. It wasn't in English, but Cassandra had no difficulty in identifying his intent. So much for hoping they could deal amicably with one another, she thought tensely. Like her, Enrique had not forgotten any part of what she'd said.

'Let us not pretend that you care how my father is feeling,' he said at last. 'And I understand perfectly what you are doing; what you are hoping to achieve. But it is not going to work, Cassandra. You and I are going to talk about what happened before I went away. You cannot tear my world apart and then behave as if nothing had changed. Even you are not that thoughtless.'

'Don't you mean stupid?' demanded Cassandra, stung by his accusation. 'And if you are going to talk about worlds being torn apart—'

'I know, I know.' Enrique dragged his hands out of his

pockets to rake long fingers through his hair. 'I have had time to think while I have been away and I realise it must have been—difficult—for you, too.'

'Oh, thanks.'

'Do not be sarcastic, Cassandra. It does not suit you.' He drew a steadying breath. 'In any case, now is not the time to get into this. It will take considerably longer than we have at present to deal with all the repercussions of this situation.'

Cassandra quivered. 'You're going away again?' she enquired tautly, and he uttered another muffled oath.

'No,' he said, leaving the door to cross the room towards her. He halted only when she put out her hand to prevent him from getting too close to her. '*Dios mio*, Cassandra, you must know how I feel. When you told me David was my son, I was shocked, yes. But it does not alter the way I feel about you.'

Cassandra moistened dry lips. 'Am I supposed to understand what that means?'

'You should,' he said roughly, taking the hand she had put out to stop him and raising it to his lips. 'I thought I made the way I felt about you very clear the other evening.'

'That was—that was before—'

'Before you told me that David was my son?' he enquired softly, his tongue devastatingly sensual against her palm. 'Ah, *sí*. And you do not think that that would reinforce those feelings?'

'I—don't know.' Cassandra didn't know what to believe any more.

'Then I will have to—'

But before he could finish what he'd been about to say, a throat was cleared behind them. *'Señor!'* It was Consuela. *'Lo siento, Señor Enrique,'* she murmured with obvious reluctance. *'Pero, señor, su padre—puede—'*

'Mierda!'

There was no mistaking Enrique's irritation now. With his jaw compressed in evident frustration, he dropped Cassandra's hand and turned to confront the red-faced maidservant, giving in to a stream of angry Spanish that was hardly warranted. And, although Cassandra could understand a little of his provocation, she couldn't help feeling sorry for Consuela, too. The Spanish woman wasn't to blame for the interruption. Someone else had sent her here.

Su padre. Your father. Cassandra translated the words without difficulty and her stomach tensed. Who else?

Enrique had apparently come to the same conclusion. He was being unreasonable, and, taking a deep breath, he shook his head. Recovering his temper, he offered the woman a swift apology, and this sudden reversal of blame brought a relieved smile to her lips. His words were eagerly accepted and Consuela hurried away, her rope-soled mules squeaking on the marble floor.

Listening, Cassandra was amazed they hadn't heard her coming. But perhaps that wasn't so surprising. For a few moments Enrique had had all her attention, and she was horrified to find that she was still so easily seduced.

Now, however, she had had time to gather her senses, and when he turned back to her, she was ready for him. 'I think you'd better go,' she said, trying not to show how upset he'd made her. 'I understood a little of what Consuela was saying. Your father is asking for you, isn't he? You'd better not keep him waiting.'

'As a matter of fact, it is you he is asking for, Cassandra,' Enrique declared, and there was an element of resignation in his voice now. 'He sent me here to bring you to him. He is eager to meet his daughter-in-law at last.'

Cassandra took an involuntary step away from him. 'He wants to meet *me*!' she echoed disbelievingly. 'Are you sure?'

'Por supuesto.' Enrique gave a shrug. 'You are David's mother. It is more than time for him to acknowledge your connection to this family.'

Cassandra moved her head from side to side. 'You did this,' she said accusingly. 'You persuaded him to meet me.' She twisted her hands together. 'Did you ever consider my feelings? What if I don't want to meet him?'

Enrique stared at her. 'You would defy him? Knowing that his health is far from good?'

'That's blackmail!'

'No.' Enrique was patient. 'It is—how do you say it?—common sense, no? I thought you would be glad to hear that my father has accepted the situation. It was not easy for me, breaking such news to him.'

Cassandra's breathing felt as if it had been suspended. 'You've told him David is your son?'

'Yes.' Enrique made a dismissive movement with his shoulders. 'But David himself does not know yet. I thought you would prefer it if I did not tell him.'

'You got that right.' Cassandra felt as if her life was moving out of control. 'I—then it's David he wants to see,' she added. 'Why don't you admit it? Julio de Montoya does not want to meet me.'

'He does,' insisted Enrique inflexibly. He paused and then added reluctantly, 'He has already met David. The boy was eager to meet his grandfather,' he continued, before she could make any objection. 'He saw the car arrive and he came to meet us.'

He would, thought Cassandra tightly. So that was where David had been all afternoon. It hurt a little that her son hadn't bothered to ask her permission. But, since coming to Tuarega, David had become a stranger to her in some ways.

'So where is he now?' she asked, and Enrique expelled a weary sigh.

'He is with my father,' he said flatly. And then, 'Why do I get the feeling that you are going to blame me for what David has done?'

'Who else can I blame?' she demanded, not altogether fairly. 'If you'd never come to find us, we wouldn't be having this conversation now.'

Enrique stiffened, his eyes dark and guarded. 'Are you saying you would have preferred it if we'd never met again?'

'Yes! *No!* Oh, I don't know.' Cassandra cupped her hot cheeks in confusion. 'You'd better leave me.' And as he arched an enquiring brow, she indicated her tee shirt and shorts. 'I can't meet your father dressed like this.'

'Cassandra—'

His anguished use of her name was almost her undoing. It

would have been so easy to give in to his persuasive tongue and let him bear the burden of what came after. But she had the awful feeling that Enrique still had his own agenda. She feared that without the knowledge that David was his son, and not Antonio's, he would never have attempted to rekindle emotions that had surely been deeply buried in the past.

CHAPTER FOURTEEN

'SO WHEN is David coming home?'

Henry Skyler, Cassandra's employer at the bookstore, was nothing if not direct and she gave him a determined smile. 'At the end of the summer holidays,' she replied brightly, as if there wasn't a shred of doubt in her mind. 'Do you want me to get rid of this dump bin? We don't have enough copies to fill it any more.'

'Oh, yes.' Henry nodded. 'That thriller did sell rather well, didn't it? People seem to have an insatiable appetite for that kind of book.' He rubbed his hands together. 'Good for business, of course.'

Cassandra nodded and started taking the few copies of the book that were left from the stand, waiting for Henry to return to his office at the back of the shop. But he remained where he was.

'You must miss him,' he said, returning to his earlier topic, and Cassandra's teeth ground together in frustration. 'I don't think I could have abandoned my son with strangers for—what?—three months?'

'Ten weeks, actually,' Cassandra corrected him shortly, but it was a moot point. Counting the two weeks they had been on holiday, David would have been away nearly three months by the time he came home. *If* he came home, she amended tensely. There were no guarantees in the arrangement. So far, she had had one phone call from David, and that was a couple of weeks ago now. Since then, she had heard nothing.

'All the same—'

'Henry, they're not strangers! They're his family!' she protested, desperately wanting to avoid a discussion about the situation. 'Where do you want me to put these books? Shall I stack them with the new fiction or put them back on the shelf?'

'With the new fiction, I think,' said Henry absently, obviously more interested in David's whereabouts than in that of his stock. 'And you say you don't mind? Aren't you afraid David won't want to come home?'

Cassandra heaved a sigh. 'Look, David wanted to stay,' she said tightly. 'His grandfather had just come home from hospital and they needed time to get to know one another. The hardest part was getting his school to agree to giving him the last few weeks of term off.'

Liar!

Cassandra was amazed she could make such a statement without her tongue falling out. God! Contacting the educational authorities and arranging for David to miss school for several weeks had been the least of her worries. Returning home to Luton airport without him: that had been the hard part.

'Well, if you say so,' said Henry now, realising he wasn't going to persuade her to part with any juicy gossip about her in-laws. He grimaced. 'He's a lucky boy. I wish I could discover I had a wealthy Spanish grandfather.'

Cassandra forced another smile and to her relief Henry left her to get on with her work. But she doubted if it would be the last she'd hear of it. He was intensely inquisitive, and learning that they'd accidentally encountered her late husband's family while they were in Spain had certainly aroused his interest. And his suspicions, she conceded ruefully. Even to her ears, it had sounded an unlikely scenario.

But she had no intention of telling him about David's hand in it. As far as Henry was concerned, her son had been as surprised to meet his mother's in-laws as she had, and she intended it to stay that way.

A customer came in as she was stacking the books, and she was glad of the diversion to take her thoughts from her son. She tried not to think about what he was doing or who he was with too often. Or acknowledge the uneasy belief that she might have made a terrible mistake in allowing David to stay with his father.

Yet, after the customer had departed, she wondered for the

umpteenth time what she could have done differently. If she'd insisted on David coming home with her, he'd have been miserable. Besides, it would only have been a matter of time before either Enrique or his father got the European courts involved and obtained a court order allowing the boy to spend time with his Spanish family. And what kind of a future would that have portended for any of them?

No, she had had no choice but to agree to Julio de Montoya's request. Anything else would have created even more bitterness between them, and for her son's sake she had had to swallow her pride. But, oh, it had been a painful decision, and even now she wondered how Julio had persuaded her to do it.

When she'd arrived at her father-in-law's suite of rooms that afternoon nearly three weeks ago, she didn't know what she'd expected of him. Anger, of course; hostility, definitely. However delighted he might have been to learn he had a grandson, she'd been certain that Enrique had exaggerated his father's desire to meet her. To *berate* her, perhaps. To deliver the kind of tirade Enrique had bestowed on the unfortunate Consuela; she'd been prepared for that. What she hadn't been prepared for was Julio's cordiality; his reasonableness; his apparent willingness to accept that she'd had good reasons for keeping David's existence to herself.

Of course, when she'd first been shown into Julio's room, she'd known none of that. In his impressive sitting room, with its deep ochre-tinted walls and heavy furniture, she'd been confronted by all the members of his immediate family, and it had been incredibly daunting.

David had been there, of course, but she hadn't felt she could look to her son for any support. Of all of them, he had had the most to lose, financially at least, and where the de Montoyas were concerned, as she knew to her cost, financial considerations were paramount.

Elena de Montoya had been standing beside her husband's wheelchair. Slim and autocratic, her expression had, as always, been impossible to read, though Cassandra had sensed that she didn't altogether approve of her husband dealing with something so potentially explosive on his first day home.

Enrique had been there, too, she remembered. He had been lounging against the wrought iron grille that framed the windows, his dark eyes narrowed and intent. The rich red curtains had accentuated his sombre countenance, and she had made a determined effort not to look his way.

Julio, himself, had proved to be a mere shadow of the man Cassandra remembered. At Antonio's funeral service, he had appeared so strong, so powerful; a dominant figure whom she had marvelled that Antonio had dared to oppose. But now he was older, frailer, showing the effects of the heart surgery Enrique had told her about. And infinitely less intimidating.

'Cassandra.' Julio had said her name slowly and succinctly, his accent, like his son's, giving her name a foreign sibilance. 'Thank you for coming.'

Cassandra could have said that she hadn't had much choice, but she didn't. Instead, she moved her shoulders in a dismissive gesture, saying politely, 'I hope you're feeling better, *señor.*'

'I have been better,' he agreed, using her term. 'But the news my son has given me has gone a long way towards advancing my recovery.' He held up a veined hand, summoning David to approach him. 'This boy is my passport to health, Cassandra. My hope for the future.' He took David's hand between both of his. '*Sí, hijo?* You agree, do you not?'

David's smile came and went, the look he cast towards his mother mirroring his uncertainty. Cassandra realised that he was still unsure of her reaction, and she was so eager to reassure her son that she inadvertently gave him the go-ahead to say whatever he liked.

'I'm sure he does,' she blurted swiftly, surprising all of them, and David wasted no time in assuring his grandfather that he loved being here at Tuarega.

There was more of the same, with Elena joining in to tell her husband that David was already beginning to speak a little Spanish, which was news to Cassandra. Still, it pleased the old man, and if it wasn't for Enrique, a disturbing presence beside the windows, she might believe that some kind of compromise was possible.

But then, once again, Julio did the unexpected. With infinite courtesy, but with an unmistakable edge of steel in his voice, he asked his wife, his son, and his grandson to leave them. He wanted to speak to his daughter-in-law alone, he said, by way of an explanation. There were misunderstandings between them, long-standing grievances that needed to be cleared up before they could embark on a lasting relationship. He said he hoped they would all understand and give him and Cassandra some breathing space.

Elena protested, saying that he wasn't well enough to conduct any kind of healing process now, but he was adamant, and it was left to Enrique to voice the loudest objections.

'I think I should stay,' he said, which was the first remark he'd made since Cassandra came into the room. And, although his father blustered, Cassandra knew that Julio would be no match for his son.

'I'd prefer it if you left,' she declared then, aware that she might be being a little foolhardy, but persisting with it anyway. She had no desire for Enrique to fight her battles for her. 'I'd like to hear what your father has to say.'

Enrique looked as if he would like to argue with her. The glitter in his eyes was intimidating and promised a certain retribution. But he accepted their decision. With studied deliberation, he left the room with his mother and his son, his only protest the grazing brush of his thumb against Cassandra's bare arm as he passed.

Cassandra shivered now, remembering his touch with every fibre of her being. She hadn't known then that that was the last time Enrique would want to touch her; hadn't comprehended that he'd known exactly what his father was going to say to her.

Julio had been tired. She'd known that. Despite his assertion to the contrary, the day had exhausted him, and Cassandra had wondered since if his choice of time had been deliberate; if he'd known exactly how she would feel, confronted by a man in his condition.

Whatever, at that moment she'd been preparing herself for the kind of reception she'd expected when she'd first entered his rooms, and she'd been taken aback when he'd invited her to sit in the chair nearest to him and asked if she'd like some refreshment.

She'd refused, of course. She'd wanted to get this over with, for him to make his feelings known and allow her to return to the anonymity of her rooms. But now that they were alone, Julio had been in no hurry to get to the point. He'd asked about her father, about her family, assuring himself that they were well before going on to ask about David, about where he went to school, about the life they shared back in England.

Cassandra had been disarmed; she recognised that now. She'd been expecting censure, criticism, and what she'd got had been tolerance and kindness, and an obvious desire to put her at her ease.

'Enrique has told me the whole story,' Julio said at last, when Cassandra was totally at his mercy. 'He is not proud of his part in it. He bitterly regrets being the cause of this estrangement between our families, and it is his wish that you allow us to take some of the strain of raising the boy from now on.'

Cassandra was taken aback. It was news to her that Enrique considered his actions the reason for her cutting herself and David off from the de Montoyas, but who was she to argue with his father? Surely he must know his son better than she did.

Then, before she could express any protest, he went on to ask how she'd feel if he requested that she allow David to stay in Spain for a few more weeks instead of accompanying her home at the end of her holiday. He said he was sure David would take her lead in this, and, although she doubted that premise, she was hard-pressed to find a reason to refuse. When he went on to suggest that he might not get such an opportunity again, Cassandra knew she couldn't say no. Julio's tacit reference to his own mortality was a powerful lever, and David would never forgive her if she denied him possibly his only chance to get to know his Spanish grandfather.

The one condition she insisted on was that David remained in ignorance of his real father's identity. She said she understood their eagerness to integrate him into their family, but she would prefer to wait until he was older before burdening him with that news. She just hoped that when that time came, David would forgive her. As far as she was concerned, he was the innocent victim here.

She slept badly again that night and awoke to the news that, once again, Enrique had left the *palacio*. According to David, who seemed enviably well informed about these things, he'd gone to Cadiz to attend to business matters for his father and wouldn't be back until the following day at the earliest.

To Cassandra, who'd half expected Enrique to come and see her the night before, it was the last straw. It seemed that everything Enrique had done had been to an end, and now that she'd agreed to allow David to stay at Tuarega he had nothing more to gain. He hadn't even had the decency to thank her for her co-operation. She fretted throughout the next seventy-two hours, before deciding to try for an earlier flight home. There was nothing for her here, and she guessed that everyone would feel infinitely happier when she was gone.

David objected, of course. Even though she explained that, since speaking to his English grandfather, she'd been worried about the situation back home, her son wanted her to stay until Enrique got back.

'I'm sure he'll expect you to stay,' he insisted, but Cassandra was equally insistent that he wouldn't.

'I told you,' she assured him gently, 'Enrique and I have nothing in common.' *Except you!* 'He'll be glad not to have to worry about me any more.' *If he ever had!*

She flew back to England the following day, having been driven to the airport in Seville by Julio's chauffeur. She didn't see the old man again, though Elena had the courtesy to come out to bid her farewell.

'We will look after David,' she said, a possessive hand resting on the boy's shoulder, and Cassandra found it incredibly difficult not to snatch her son into her arms and take him with her.

She sighed now, realising that she was wasting time fretting about something over which she had no real control. She'd committed herself to allowing the de Montoyas to play a part in her son's life and if her father thought she was mad: well, so be it.

It was a week later, and Cassandra was serving a group of teenagers who were looking for copies of Virgil's *Aeneid*, when her eyes were drawn to the sight of a gleaming limousine drawing up outside the shop. It wasn't usual for cars to stop outside The Bookworm, and she could only assume that whoever was driving was a stranger to the district.

A stranger!

Her mouth went dry, and she inadvertently gave one of the youths a ten-pound note instead of a five in change. My God, what if it's Enrique? she thought unsteadily. What was he likely to be doing there?

Fortunately, her youthful customer was honest, but her nervous laugh brought Henry to the front of the shop to see what was going on. 'I'm just trying to cut your profits,' she managed lightly as the teenagers left the shop, but her face was burning and she soon realised that Henry wasn't listening to her in any case.

'Nice car,' he remarked instead, as the limousine idled at the kerb. 'But he'll get a parking ticket if he stays there.'

'Hmm.' Cassandra told herself she didn't care what happened to the limousine. It wasn't going to be Enrique. If he'd cared anything about her, he'd never have stayed away as he had. And, so long as it didn't belong to any other de Montoya, she had nothing to worry about. 'Um—is it all right if I go for my lunch now?'

'What?' Henry looked blankly at her. Then, without answering her question, 'Hey, someone's getting out of the car.'

'Henry!' Cassandra tried not to look towards the window. 'Don't be so nosy.' She paused. 'About lunch—'

'My God, he's coming in,' Henry interrupted her quickly. 'He looks foreign, Cass. Are you sure you don't know who it is?'

Cassandra's head jerked up, a mixture of fear and excitement churning in her stomach. Henry was right. A darkly tanned individual was entering the bookstore. But it wasn't Enrique, as she'd imagined; *as she'd hoped*? Nor was it his father. But the man was known to her. It was the chauffeur who had driven her to the airport when she left.

'Señora,' he said, making directly for Cassandra, and Henry's eyes widened as he looked at his assistant. '*Por favor, señora,* Senor de Montoya wishes to speak with you.'

Cassandra quivered. The man—she knew his name was Salvador—was waiting for her response, but she was too shocked to answer him.

'Señora?' echoed Henry admiringly, making a wry face, and Cassandra struggled to pull herself together.

'Señor de Montoya?' she got out at last, hardly daring to voice the words. 'Señor Enrique de—'

'Señor Julio, *señora*,' Salvador interrupted her swiftly, nodding towards the car behind him. 'He is waiting, *señora*. You will come, *sí*?'

Julio!

Cassandra felt sick. For a moment she'd allowed herself the luxury of believing that Enrique hadn't abandoned her, that he cared about her and not about what he wanted from her. But now he had his son! The child he'd never known he had. He didn't need her any more.

Besides, she should have had more sense, she chided herself. A man who'd apparently allowed his father to do what he should have done himself was hardly likely to be having second thoughts now.

And, as her head cleared, she thought she could guess why Julio de Montoya was here. They had given her three weeks to get used to being without David, and now it was time to put the second part of their plan into operation. Julio was going to suggest that her son was happy with them, that they could give him so much more than she could, that perhaps she might consider allowing him to live with them instead of returning him to England at the end of the summer.

No!

'Yes, go along, Cass,' urged Henry, evidently eager to find out what they wanted for himself. 'It is lunch time. I can spare you for—well, for a couple of hours.'

A couple of hours! Cassandra's lips twisted. Usually, she had a struggle to get half an hour in the middle of the day.

'I—I don't know—'

She was shaking her head, wondering how on earth she was going to avoid talking to Julio de Montoya, when another voice spoke from the doorway.

'Cassandra!' It was Julio himself, still pale and drawn, but evidently much recovered from the last time she'd seen him. Even his voice had acquired a little of the imperiousness she remembered from ten years ago. 'Please,' he added, with surprising humility. 'We need to talk.'

'Do we?' She was uneasy, but there was really no contest.

'I believe so,' he asserted heavily, and now she saw that he was leaning on an ebony cane. 'Will you come?'

Henry watched from the doorway as Salvador assisted first his employer and then Cassandra into the back of the limousine. Julio apologised for preceding her, but it had become apparent that he was still far from strong. Cassandra was amazed that Señora de Montoya had allowed her husband to make the journey himself.

But perhaps he'd insisted that his powers of persuasion were superior to hers and those of his son. There was no doubt that he had succeeded before, and the fact that Enrique wasn't with him seemed to point to the fact that he had decided to leave it to his father. Again.

For her part, Cassandra was too tense to worry about protocol. Taking her seat beside Julio in the back of the car, all she could think about was David and how bleak her future would be if he didn't want to come home.

'Por favor, Salvador,' said Julio once she was seated, indicating that the chauffeur should drive on, and Cassandra glanced behind her to see Henry turning rather disappointedly back into the shop.

'Your employer?' asked Enrique's father as she swung round again, and she nodded.

'Henry Skyler,' she conceded. 'It's his shop.'

Julio inclined his head. 'You have worked there long?'

'Several years,' she agreed, her tone sharpening. She wished he would tell her why he was here and stop wasting time. They had nothing in common and pretending he was interested in her life was just a way to get her to let down her guard. 'Where are we going?'

'Ah.' Julio appeared to acknowledge her impatience. 'If you will permit, we will go to the hotel where I usually stay when I am in London.'

Cassandra pressed her lips together. So, it was to be a prolonged encounter. Instead of tea and sympathy, it was to be lunch and sympathy. Whatever way you looked at it, she doubted it was her feelings he was thinking about.

'Is this necessary?' she asked, deciding she would rather know the worst right away. 'I realise you might find it easier to say what you have to say in a restaurant, where I'd be constrained to be polite, but I'd rather you were honest with me.'

'Honest with you, Cassandra?' To her surprise, Julio looked disturbed now. 'You would rather I came right out and told you what has happened *en seguida*? At once? *Que?* You have reason to believe I bring bad news?'

Cassandra swallowed. 'Well, don't you?'

Julio stared at her with troubled eyes. 'Elena,' he said with sudden comprehension. 'Elena has telephoned you. She promised she would not, but I should have known—'

'Señora de Montoya hasn't contacted me,' Cassandra interrupted him shortly. 'But it's obvious you're not here to ask after my health. We don't have that kind of a relationship.'

'No.' Julio conceded the point. 'And you are sure my wife has not been in touch with you? That she hasn't warned you—?'

'Warned me?' Cassandra looked at him. 'Warned me of what? That I shouldn't upset you when you tell me you want to keep David in Spain? That I should just accept the fact that you intend to appropriate my son?'

'Your son?' Julio looked dismayed. 'You think this is about David?'

'Well, isn't it?'

Cassandra wouldn't allow the sudden curl of fear to daunt her. Why else would Julio de Montoya have made this journey? Only something terribly important to him would have persuaded him to come and see her only weeks after such a serious operation. And, aside from his grandson, what else could it be?

His son?

The thought caught Cassandra unawares, although she suspected that that was what she had been suppressing since Enrique's father had denied this was anything to do with David. A feeling of coldness enveloped her. Oh, God, what could possibly have happened to cause this arrogant old autocrat to come to her?

'I—it has to be David,' she insisted, refusing to let him see what she was thinking. 'What else could it be?'

Julio shook his head. 'I—I would prefer it if you could wait until we reach the hotel,' he said stiffly, glancing towards Salvador, and she realised it was against his principles to discuss family matters in front of the chauffeur.

But Cassandra was in no mood to humour him. 'Is it David?' she persisted, still refusing to believe that it could be anything else. 'You might as well tell me. I think I deserve a little time to prepare my defence.'

'Your defence?' Julio was ironic. 'Oh, Cassandra, you are so cold; so suspicious. Does it not occur to you that if I wanted to—what was it you said? Appropriate your son? Yes, that was the term you used—appropriate your son, I would have allowed my lawyer to deal with it?'

'Then—'

'There has been an accident,' said Julio heavily, and not without some reluctance. 'As you insist on—'

'An accident?' Cassandra interrupted him again, her heart in her mouth. 'David?'

'No, Enrique,' said the old man wearily. 'My son. My only son. I have come to beg you to return to Spain with me. If you do not, I fear—I fear the consequences.'

CHAPTER FIFTEEN

APPROACHING Tuarega from the north was different from approaching it from the south. The north was wilder, harsher, the landscape punctuated by dry riverbeds and rocky ravines where prickly pear and spiky agave were the only vegetation.

Sitting in the back of another limousine, Cassandra paid little attention to her surroundings. Darkness had fallen, and it was difficult to think of anything except the reason why she was here. The stark peaks of the *sierra*, briefly glimpsed in the headlights of the car, only accentuated her feelings of isolation, of being far from everything she knew, everything she believed. She still wasn't absolutely convinced that she should have come, and she didn't know if she could take another rejection.

Nonetheless, she had thought of little but Enrique since Julio had delivered the news of his accident. Hearing how he had entered one of the pens where a rogue bull was corralled and been gored for his pains had horrified her. It seemed so unlike him, somehow. David had told her that Enrique had always cautioned him to show great respect for the animals, and, according to Julio, Juan had warned him not to approach the beast.

So why had he? Julio's opinion was that his son had had something on his mind; that he hadn't been thinking when he'd entered the pen and found himself face-to-face with an enraged bull. Whatever, before any of the hands could create a diversion, the animal had charged, its sharp horns ripping Enrique's arm and gouging an ugly gash in his thigh.

Cassandra shivered now, just thinking of it. Flesh wounds always bled profusely and Julio had admitted that the floor of the pen had been soaked with his son's blood. It had taken four men to drag the infuriated beast away from him and, since then, the bull had been destroyed.

Enrique had been unconscious when a helicopter had airlifted him to the hospital in Seville where his father had so recently been a patient. He'd needed a blood transfusion, but fortunately the wound in his leg had just missed the artery. Even so, he'd lost a lot of blood, and for several days his condition had been closely monitored.

Cassandra found it incredible that all this could have been going on while she had been totally ignorant of it. No one had phoned her; no one had told her that the man she was very much afraid she had never stopped loving was fighting for his life. Only now had she been apprised of the situation. Only now had the de Montoyas been forced to humble themselves and contact her. And that only because although Enrique's physical condition was much improved, his mental state was proving a cause for concern.

'He seems—uninterested in everything,' Julio had told her, with evident frustration. 'The accident happened—what? Two weeks ago? At least that. And his wounds are healing well. After all, they are used to such injuries in my country. You English think the bull is such a helpless creature, but I have seen men lose limbs—lose their very lives—in the cause of the *corrida*.'

Cassandra hadn't answered that. The fact was that in the *corrida* the bull was always fighting for its life. But that was their culture. It wasn't up to her to criticise something she really knew nothing about.

'He should be up and about by now,' Julio had continued unhappily. 'He has duties; responsibilities. He knows I am not capable of doing very much and yet he will not listen to me, will not talk to me, will not even talk to David.'

So why did they think he would talk to her? Cassandra wondered uneasily. Julio hadn't offered an explanation. He hadn't even mentioned David's reaction to all this, merely responding to her enquiry by saying the boy was with his grandmother and leaving it at that.

Yet surely Enrique would want to spend time with his son?

But when she'd mentioned as much to Julio, he'd been curiously reticent. 'He sees no one,' he'd insisted shortly and with evident reluctance. 'Apart from Carlos Mendoza, *por supuesto*. You will see for yourself, if you will come.'

As if she'd had any choice, thought Cassandra now, taut with apprehension and anxiety. What if Enrique refused to see her? What then? Would they pack her off back to England again? She doubted they'd have any choice. And, God knew, she wouldn't want to stay in those circumstances…

The limousine was descending into a valley now and, although Cassandra had no real knowledge of where they were, she sensed they were nearing their destination. She could see lamps burning at the gates of a building ahead of them and, below, the clustered lights of a small village. She guessed they were still some distance from Tuarega itself, but perhaps this might be an appropriate time to warn Julio of their imminent arrival.

The old man had dozed on and off for most of their journey and she wasn't surprised. She guessed he was exhausted. This had been a gruelling day for a man in his condition, and she was amazed at his stamina.

She certainly hadn't expected him to suggest that they left for Spain that afternoon. They'd had lunch at his hotel, but, after gaining her consent to his request for her to return to Spain with him, he'd been anxious to get away.

He'd had a private jet waiting for them at Stanstead Airport. Cassandra had only had time to phone her father and give him the briefest of explanations, asking him to relay the news to Henry Skyler, before leaving.

But, before she could do anything, she realised the big car was slowing and Julio opened his eyes as they turned between the stone gateposts she'd glimpsed earlier. Ahead of them, she could see the dark stone walls of a strange building, and her stomach prickled with nerves. What now? she wondered apprehensively. Where were they? Why had Julio brought her here?

He was struggling to sit up now. He had slumped against the squabs since they left Seville, but now he endeavoured to straighten his stiff spine and bring some feeling back into his cramped limbs.

Then he caught Cassandra looking at him, and his dark eyes widened in obvious enquiry. 'Is something wrong?'

'Where are we?' she demanded, aware of the tremor in her voice. 'This isn't Tuarega.'

'*Bien*, it is Tuarega land,' replied Julio, with a lift of his shoulders. 'I thought I told you. Enrique has been—how do you say it?—covered up here at La Hacienda since he came home from the hospital, no? He does not care for any company.'

Cassandra blinked. 'Covered up?' she echoed blankly. Then comprehension dawned. 'Oh, you mean—*holed* up,' she corrected him tensely. Then, glancing up at the forbidding aspect of the dwelling, 'You mean, this is Enrique's house?'

'La Hacienda,' he agreed, a little impatiently. 'With your permission, I will bid you farewell here.'

'What?' Cassandra stared at him. 'You're leaving me here? Alone?'

'You will not be alone,' replied Julio implacably. 'Enrique is here. And Mendoza. Mendoza will see that you have everything you need.'

'But—'

'Cassandra, I am depending on you to save my son's sanity. Believe me, I would not have asked for your help unless—unless there was no other alternative.'

Unless he was desperate, thought Cassandra bitterly. Could he have made it any plainer? She was only here because everything—and everyone—else had failed.

The car had stopped and now a door opened and a shaft of light fell across the bonnet of the limousine. Carlos Mendoza stood in the doorway, clearly expecting them. Like his employer's, his face bore an expression of concern, and Cassandra only paused to cast another doubtful look at Julio before accepting Salvador's hand to help her out of the car.

Carlos came down the steps. '*Bienvenido a La Hacienda, señora,*' he said, his smile warm and sincere. 'Do you have a bag?'

'No bags, Carlos,' replied Cassandra ruefully, turning back to look at the car. '*Adiós, señor.*'

'Hasta mañana, Cassandra,' responded Julio de Montoya, leaning out of the limousine. 'Until tomorrow.'

Salvador slammed the car door and went around to take his seat behind the wheel, and Cassandra waited until the vehicle had started to move away before looking again at the house. She was feeling weak and inadequate, and she had no idea why Enrique's father thought she might have more success with his son than he had.

'Es por aquí, señora,' said Carlos gently, urging her up the steps and into the building. 'This way.' He paused to close the heavy door behind them. 'You had a good journey, no?'

Cassandra shook her head. 'I suppose so,' she said, looking about her a little dazedly. They were in a marble-floored entry, where a curving staircase with a wrought-iron banister wound to the upper floors of the house. Beside the staircase, long mirrors hung opposite one another, and a huge bowl of purple orchids was reflected over and over again in their lamplit depths. 'I—where is Enrique?'

'You wish to eat, *señora*?' asked Carlos, without answering her. 'Maria—she has left you a small—um—*comida, sí*?'

'Maria?'

Cassandra looked at him and he spread his hands. 'Maria is—*la criada, señora*,' he replied awkwardly, and she frowned.

'The—the maid?' she ventured at last, trying to remember the little Spanish she had learned and he nodded in some relief.

'*Sí*, the maid, *señora*.' He paused, gesturing through an archway beyond the curve of the staircase. *'Por aquí.'*

Cassandra hesitated. Then, 'Enrique,' she said firmly, having no interest in the food he was offering. 'I'd like to see him first.'

'Señora—'.

Carlos spoke guardedly, his diffidence revealing a wealth of uncertainty. Cassandra guessed that, although he had been forced to accept Julio's decision to bring her here, he was by no means convinced of its wisdom.

But, before he could say any more, someone else interrupted them. 'Why?' enquired a voice that was both unbearably cold and undeniably familiar and Cassandra lifted her head to find Enrique standing looking down at them from the head of the first flight of stairs.

Cassandra's lips parted in dismay. This was not the way she'd hoped to announce her arrival. It was obvious from the hostility in Enrique's tone that he had known nothing of his father's meddling, and her mouth dried at the realisation that he could just turn around and refuse to speak to her.

And he needed to speak to someone, she thought worriedly. Whatever his motives, Julio hadn't exaggerated his fears for his son's well-being. Enrique looked grey; emaciated. In three short weeks his skin had lost the glow of health, and his loss of weight was evident in the cream knit sweater and draw-string sweats that hung on his lean frame.

'I—how are you?' she got out awkwardly, trying desperately not to show how concerned she was.

Enrique's lips compressed into a thin line. 'What are you doing here, Cassandra?' he asked at last, his long fingers curling and uncurling about the iron balustrade. 'How did you get here? Who told you where I was?'

'Does it matter?' Cassandra caught her lower lip between her teeth and glanced briefly at Carlos. Then, returning her attention to the man at the head of the stairs, 'Um—can we talk?'

'Oh, please!' Enrique's tone was sardonic now. 'I do not think you and I have anything to talk about.' He paused. 'I imagine it must have been my father who brought you here.' His lips twisted. 'I did not realise he was that desperate.'

Cassandra winced at the deliberate insult, but she stood her ground. 'Yes,' she said, looking up at him. 'Your father did bring me here. But if I hadn't wanted to come, I wouldn't have accepted his invitation.'

'How sweet!'

Enrique's voice was cold and Carlos evidently decided that his presence was superfluous. 'If you will excuse me, *señor*,' he murmured, and Enrique made an indifferent gesture of affirmation. The man bowed and disappeared through a door at the end of the hall and Cassandra was left with the unpleasant feeling that Carlos knew she was wasting her time.

'Enrique—' she began again, but before she could say any more he interrupted her.

'No,' he said bleakly. 'We have nothing to say to one another. I do not know what tale my father concocted to persuade you to return to Tuarega, but, whatever it was, he obviously exaggerated. As you can see, I am still—what is it you say?—in one piece, *sí*?'

'Are you?' Cassandra's fingers felt sticky where they were gripping the strap of her haversack. She hesitated. 'I know you've been ill.'

Enrique scowled. 'I am sure you do. My father would use anything to gain his own ends.' He suddenly looked unbearably weary. 'Go away, Cassandra. I do not have the inclination to speak with you now.'

Or the strength, thought Cassandra anxiously, her spirits plummeting when he turned and walked away, out of her sight. Dear God, no wonder Julio was desperate. He must despair of finding any way to reach his son. The amazing thing was that he thought *she* might.

Cassandra set her haversack down on the hall table and looked doubtfully about her. To her right was the room Carlos had indicated where the maid had left her something to eat. But she wasn't hungry. She could always go in search of Carlos, of course. He was probably close at hand, waiting for some sign from her that she either wanted to be taken to Tuarega or back to the airport in Seville. But she couldn't leave. However unlikely, Julio believed she might have a chance of getting through to Enrique. She had to try.

Taking a deep breath, she put her hand on the banister and started up the stairs. Subtle lights set into the ceiling illuminated her way and a broad-based standard lamp occupied a prominent position on the first landing. The stairs continued up to a second floor, but Cassandra knew Enrique hadn't continued upward. He'd crossed the landing and disappeared into one of the twin corridors that confronted her, and, after a moment's hesitation, she took the one to her left.

Here the illumination came from a string of spotlights that highlighted the paintings that adorned the walls. Not gloomy paintings, like she'd seen at Tuarega, but more modern renditions of local scenes, one of which bore a strong resemblance to Tuarega itself.

But Cassandra knew she was only distracting herself by looking at the paintings, that sooner or later she would have to confront her own inadequacies. She was intensely conscious of the sound of her thick-soled boots squeaking on the tiled floor, aware that the ankle-length cotton skirt and tee shirt she'd worn for work that morning were totally unsuitable in these elegant surroundings. She should have insisted on going home to change, she thought pointlessly. But she had allowed Julio to infect her with his concern for his son's recovery.

At the end of the corridor, double doors stood open onto a dimly lit vestibule. Nervously, she stepped across a circular rug, whose vivid colours were muted in the shadowy light, and paused at the entrance to a large sitting room. Pale walls hung with hand-sewn tapestries; overstuffed beige sofas and leather chairs flanking a cream stone fireplace; and cushions everywhere: on the sofas, on the chairs, and in some cases piled in heaps upon the huge fringed rug. It was the cushions that gave the room its colour, its warm ambience, its attractive personality.

But it was the man standing on the balcony beyond open floor-length windows who drew Cassandra's eyes. Like the stairwell, this room was lit by a handful of lamps, but the open windows allowed a glimpse of the starlit sky outside. And of the moon, a sickle of white against that night-dark canopy.

Enrique hadn't seen her. As far as he knew, she was still downstairs, possibly even preparing to leave, and she wondered if the balcony overlooked the entry. But that was wishful thinking, she thought ruefully. And besides, if Enrique was looking for her to leave, it was not because he was hoping she would stay.

She didn't know what to do; what to say. Even coming into his suite of rooms was an unwarranted liberty. He hadn't invited her there. In fact, he'd made it blatantly obvious that she wasn't welcome here. So why didn't she just accept defeat and leave?

Because she couldn't.

Because, no matter how painful this might be for her, she had to try and talk to him. To talk some sense into him, she reflected dubiously. If his depression had something to do with David, to do with the fact that she had kept his existence a secret from him all these years, she had to try and do something about it. Even if it meant leaving David here longer than the limited number of weeks she had agreed to.

Or was that being absurdly ingenuous? What if this was all a clever ploy instigated by Enrique and his father to gain control of her son? She was certainly easily persuaded if that was so.

But she dismissed the idea as soon as it generated itself. This was no ploy, no plan of Julio's to delude her into giving her son away. Enrique looked ill; far more ill than she had expected. How serious had his injuries been, for God's sake? And was there any chance that he'd confide in her?

'Hasta nunca, Carlos.'

While she'd been hovering just inside the door, trying to decide what she could say to attract his attention, Enrique had apparently heard something and assumed it was the manservant. And, realising she would have to identify herself, she found the words to say.

'Hasta nunca?' she echoed softly. 'What does that mean?'

Enrique swung round, swaying a little as he did so, and she longed to go and put her arms around him. 'It means, get lost,' he informed her harshly. 'And it applies to you just as much as to Carlos.'

Cassandra blew out a breath. 'That's not very polite. I always thought Spaniards prided themselves on being excessively polite. Although I suppose your family is a law unto itself.'

Enrique's eyes were hooded, so she couldn't read their expression, but his nostrils flared. 'As you say,' he conceded, after a moment. 'Will you go now?'

Cassandra shook her head. 'I can't.'

'Why not? Carlos will call Salvador for you, if you wish. Or a cab, if you would prefer. We do have telephones at La Hacienda.'

'Enrique—'

He breathed a deep sigh and, leaving the balcony rail, he walked wearily back into the sitting room. 'You are determined to persist with this, are you not?' he said heavily. 'Why? Why are you here? Of what possible interest can it be to you that I have had a minor accident that resulted in a short spell in hospital?'

'It was hardly a minor accident,' exclaimed Cassandra at once, and he shook his head.

'*Sí*, it was.' He rolled back the sleeve of his sweater, exposing a raw scar on his forearm. '*Aquí tiene*, it is healing. Juan has had many such injuries over the years and his family do not panic at the first sight of blood.'

Cassandra felt sick, her stomach twisting at the thought of the pain he must have suffered before the paramedics could get to him. 'That—that wasn't your only injury,' she protested. 'I know you had to have a blood transfusion.'

'Dios!' Enrique propped himself against one of the sofas and Cassandra had the feeling he was in danger of falling without that support. 'I do not intend to show you my other injury, Cassandra.' He snorted. '*El viejo*—the old man—he has certainly laid a—how is it?—a guilt trip on you, no?'

'No.' She couldn't help moving a little closer even though he stiffened when she did so. 'Oh, Enrique, I've been so worried about you.'

'Que?' His lips twisted. 'And this from the woman who ran away rather than face me after confessing her cruel little deception? You must be careful in future, Cassandra. Wine can loosen the sharpest tongue.'

'I didn't run away,' insisted Cassandra indignantly. She took a breath. 'That was you.'

'Me?' Enrique stared at her for a moment and then he shook his head. 'No, Cassandra, I do not run away. I admit that when you told me that I was David's father I was glad to have to go to Seville to bring my father home. I needed a little time to come to terms with what you had told me. I admitted that. But I did not run away.'

Cassandra quivered. 'What about ten years ago?' she countered, unable to prevent herself, and his face contorted with sudden loathing. But whether it was for himself or for her, she had no way of knowing.

'Ten years ago,' he echoed bitterly. 'Ah, you do not intend for me to forget that, do you, *querida*.' He used a term of endearment, but there was no affection in his tone. 'You asked me once what I said to Antonio, *sí*? Would it surprise you to hear that I said nothing? Nothing.' He shook his head. 'I made a mistake, Cassandra. A terrible mistake, I admit it. And I have been paying for it ever since.'

'You don't mean that.'

Cassandra was confused, and he bent his head to run weary hands through his hair. His hair needed cutting, she noticed inconsequentially. It overlapped his collar at the back. Then, lifting his head, he speared her with a tormented stare.

'I do mean it,' he said. 'But I see I am only satisfying whatever twisted thread of your nature brought you here.' His voice was rough. 'If my father had not told you about the accident, you would not be here. What did he tell you? Did he imply I was at death's door? I can think of no other reason why you would agree to see me again.'

'I wanted to see you!' The words were torn from her. 'And you know very well why I went back to England. You might not have been present at the interview I had with your father, but you knew what he was going to say. You wanted David to stay here. It was what you'd wanted all along, even before you knew David was your son. How could I insist on taking him back to England when it might be your father's only chance to get to know his grandson? I'm not that heartless, Enrique. Besides—' she heaved a sigh '—it was what David wanted.'

'So why did you not stay, too?'

'Because I have a job,' exclaimed Cassandra at once. 'I can't just take time off when I feel like it.'

'But your holiday was not over,' retorted Enrique, pushing

himself away from the sofa. 'You left without even having the—the courtesy to tell me goodbye.'

'You weren't there,' exclaimed Cassandra defensively. 'I was told you'd gone to Cadiz, on business for your father. I waited. I did.' This as Enrique pulled a wry face. 'But day followed day and you didn't come back.'

Enrique studied her indignant face. 'I almost believe you.'

'Almost?' she caught her breath. 'It's the truth!'

'Then why did you tell David that you did not want to see me again? That your own father was more important than waiting around for me to come back?'

'I—didn't say that.' But she had said something like it. Something that had persuaded David to intercede on her behalf. With, apparently, disastrous consequences.

'I can see you are having second thoughts,' said Enrique bitterly. 'You did tell David you never wanted to see me again. Why deny it now?'

'Because it wasn't true,' blurted Cassandra impulsively. 'Dear God, Enrique, you can't possibly believe that. Not—not after I'd told you—'

'That David is my son? His tone was harsh. 'That not only had I seduced you but I had also condemned you to spend the last nine years caring for my child? Oh, yes, I can see that that would persuade you to stay.'

'It wasn't like that,' protested Cassandra huskily. 'Why do you think I told you as I did? I didn't have to. I *wanted* to.'

'To torture me?'

'No!' Cassandra stared into his dark tormented face for a long moment and then, coming to a decision, she stepped forward and, reaching up, brushed his lips with hers. 'That's—that's why,' she added, a little breathlessly. 'Do you believe me now?'

Enrique didn't touch her. 'I believe you'll regret your impulsiveness,' he declared roughly. 'And I am forced to accept that you have a conscience. But that is all.'

Cassandra shook her head. 'You're wrong.'

'Am I?' Enrique breathed deeply. 'So what are you saying?

That what happened between us ten years ago meant something to you?'

Cassandra hesitated. 'You know it did.'

'Do I?' But he had the grace to look away as he added in a low hoarse voice, 'Yet you went ahead and married my brother.'

Cassandra nodded. 'Yes.'

Enrique's face contorted. 'How could you?'

Cassandra closed her eyes for a moment. 'I tried to tell him I couldn't marry him,' she insisted dully. 'I did. But he didn't want to hear it. He said that if I let him down, it would shame him; that it would prove to you and to the rest of his family that I really had only wanted to marry him because of who he was.' She lifted her lids again, to find Enrique, watching her with bleak unforgiving eyes. 'It's the truth. Can't you try and understand how I was feeling? I was nineteen years old, Enrique. I was in a state of shock. You—you'd left. I didn't know what to do.'

'You must have hated me,' said Enrique harshly, but it wasn't a vindication and she shivered.

'You don't understand,' she said again. 'Antonio—Antonio loved me. And I cared for him, too. I didn't know I was already carrying the seed of your child. I just wanted to do what was right. I—I swore to myself that I'd make him a good wife, and—and I would have. But then the accident happened. It was an accident, you know? Nothing else. Antonio never knew about us. I suppose I'd hoped he never would. But not in that way. Never in that way.'

'And if we had met again?' suggested Enrique with bitter emphasis, and she turned away.

'I—I—I can't answer that,' she said brokenly, and, unable to take any more, she stumbled towards the door.

She didn't make it. Before she'd gone a dozen yards Enrique caught her, his hands closing about her upper arms from behind and preventing her from going any further. Although his hands were slick with sweat, proving how weak he was, and she could feel the unsteadiness in his body, he somehow managed to drag her back against his shaking frame. Then his head dipped to find the vulnerable curve of her neck and she felt the roughness of his jaw against her skin.

'Lo siento,' he groaned, his lips moving against her flesh. 'I'm sorry. *Lo siento mucho.*' I'm so sorry. 'Will you forgive me?'

Cassandra tipped her head back against his shoulder, her arms crossing her body to capture his hands with hers. 'There—there's nothing to forgive.'

'There is,' he contradicted her huskily, turning her in his arms to cradle her face between his palms. 'I have been such a fool; such an arrogant fool. I have no right to ask for explanations from you when my own behaviour has been so much less than admirable.'

'Oh, Enrique—'

Her eyes were shining with unshed tears, but he wouldn't let her reassure him. 'Let me speak,' he said, and she could feel the tremor of his body through his hands. 'I told you that ten years ago I made a terrible mistake. I did. But the mistake was not in making love with you.' His thumbs brushed her cheeks. 'The mistake was in letting you go.'

Cassandra stared up at him. 'Enrique…'

'It is true. That was what I meant when I said I had been paying for it ever since.' His lips twisted. 'Oh, I have tried to deny it. I have tried to forget and move on with my life, but it has not worked. I am still unmarried, and until I read David's letter I believed I would never get the chance to speak to you again.'

'Enrique…'

'No, listen to me, *querida*. I want to tell you how it was when I saw you in Punta del Lobo. Until then, I had held out some hope that you were not the reason why I have resisted all my father's efforts to find me a wife. But when I saw you, when I saw the fire in your eyes—' He took a shuddering breath. '*Dios*, Cassandra, you must have known how I felt.'

'No.' She shook her head. 'All I saw was the shock you got when you saw David.'

'Ah!' He lowered his head and rested his forehead against

hers. 'That was a shock, *sí*. And a source of some envy on my part.'

'Envy?'

'I thought David was Antonio's child,' he reminded her drily. 'I was selfish enough to resent the fact that he wasn't mine.'

Cassandra lifted her hands to his shoulders. 'He's yours,' she said simply. 'You know that now.'

'Yes, I do.' He paused. 'But when I returned from Cadiz and found you gone—' He turned unsteadily away, as if the emotions his words had generated were too much for him. 'I am sorry. I have got to sit down…'

'Oh, Enrique!'

With sudden understanding, Cassandra put her arm about his waist and guided him to the nearest sofa. Then, when he was seated, she came down beside him, close enough so that her hip and thigh and the whole side of her body was touching his.

'I am sorry,' he said again, when she lifted a hand to stroke his damp forehead. 'You must think I am useless.'

'Just suffering from a surfeit of emotion,' she told him gently, leaning closer and depositing a soft kiss on his mouth. 'Oh, Enrique, why didn't you tell me how you felt?'

'I intended to,' he said, his eyes dark with passion. He was feeling stronger now that he was off his feet, and the arm that came about her shoulders, holding her against his chest, was surprisingly firm. 'But when I got back from Cadiz, you had gone.'

'There are phones,' she reminded him, and he closed his eyes briefly, as if recalling his anguish.

'There are,' he agreed. 'But I regret to say I am a proud man and I preferred not to humiliate myself again.'

'Again?'

'*Por supuesto*. I could not believe that after speaking to you in the gallery, and when I came to your bedroom, you could have any doubts about the way I felt about you. And when I came back and David told me what you had said—' He shrugged. 'I hardly needed my father to tell me what a fool I was.'

Cassandra caught her breath. 'He told you that?'

'As good as.' He sighed. 'He told me he had tried to persuade you to stay until the end of your holiday but that you had been determined to leave.'

'But he didn't.'

'I know that now.' Enrique grimaced. 'I also realise that that was why he insisted I must attend to his affairs before addressing my own. He was a sick man. I knew I needed to speak with you, but I consoled myself with the thought that you'd be here when I returned. You weren't, and that was when my life fell apart.'

Cassandra groaned. 'But he must have relented.'

'Oh, yes.' Enrique was sardonic. 'He would never have gone to the trouble of bringing you here if he hadn't felt some responsibility for what had happened.'

'He said you'd entered one of the pens where a bull was being kept. He made it sound as if you'd gone in there deliberately.'

Enrique touched her cheek. 'It was a crazy thing to do.'

'So why did you do it?'

'I was not thinking,' he told her heavily. 'My mind was occupied with other things. I do not believe I did it deliberately, but it is true that since you went away I have had little interest in anything.'

'Oh, Enrique!'

'There,' he said cynically. 'I have laid a guilt trip on you myself. So what are you going to do about it?'

Cassandra looked at his mouth. She was remembering how sensual his mouth was, how delicious it had felt earlier against her skin. 'What do you want me to do about it?' she asked at last, inviting his response, and, with a groan, Enrique sank onto his back against the cushions, taking her with him.

'I can think of many things,' he said, his accent thickening with emotion, and Cassandra was stunned by the sudden strength of his hand at her nape. His mouth found hers with an urgency that brooked no resistance, and with a little cry she surrendered to the magic of his touch...

EPILOGUE

ENRIQUE married Cassandra three weeks later in the small church at Huerta de Tuarega. The whole village turned out for the wedding of *el patrón's* son, and afterwards there was a *fiesta* in the village square.

Despite her happiness, Cassandra couldn't help but compare this wedding with the civil ceremony she and Antonio had shared. This time there had been no question that all the de Montoyas would attend. And, although she doubted Elena de Montoya was overjoyed at the outcome of her husband's interference in his elder son's life, she had had to accept that Enrique loved Cassandra, and only she could make him happy.

Sanchia had attended, too, of course. Along with representatives from all the foremost families in the district, she would have appeared churlish not to do so. Enrique had told Cassandra all about Sanchia: about how quickly she had transferred her attentions to him after Antonio had broken their engagement. He'd also confessed that he and Sanchia had had a passing relationship in recent months. But that as soon as he'd met Cassandra again, he'd had nothing more to do with the other woman.

'Poor Sanchia,' Cassandra had said one evening, a few days after her return to Spain.

She and Enrique had spent the day at the *palacio*, Enrique speaking to his father freely for the first time since his accident, and Cassandra confiding to David that perhaps the hopes he'd had for the future were not so fanciful after all. She'd told him she'd forgiven him for writing to his grandfather. That without his intervention she might never have found happiness at last.

She and Enrique had already talked of getting married, and her son had been in seventh heaven at the thought of having a surrogate father at last. Not that Enrique was a surrogate anything, Cassandra had reflected. But for the present it was kinder to let events proceed at their own pace.

'Why "poor Sanchia"?' Enrique had demanded, taking great pleasure in watching her brush her hair in front of the mirror in his bedroom at La Hacienda. He'd been lounging on the bed, looking much better than when she'd arrived at La Hacienda. The wound on his thigh still looked ugly, but he had started eating again and there had been a trace of healthy colour in his face.

'Why do you think?' she'd countered, putting down the brush and turning towards him. In a cream silk negligee that Elena had lent her, she'd looked unknowingly provocative. 'To lose Antonio was bad enough. To lose you as well must be devastating.'

'If you come here, I will show you exactly how devastating,' he'd told her huskily, stretching out a hand towards her, and Cassandra had gone to him willingly, as captivated by their love as he was.

The days before the wedding had been a magical time. Although Enrique's parents had expected them to return to the *palacio*, both Enrique and Cassandra had preferred to stay at La Hacienda. Ever afterwards, Cassandra would think of it as a pre-honeymoon, and she had been delighted when Enrique decided that the three of them—including David, of course—would live there after they were married.

Cassandra made a beautiful bride. Her dress—a medieval sheath with a cowl neckline and long pointed sleeves—gave her a touching vulnerability. Enrique insisted that she still looked like the virgin she had been when he first knew her, and Cassandra had to confess that there had been no other men since the night David was conceived.

She knew that pleased him. He was still enough of a chauvinist to be glad that she'd known no other man's touch but his. He would deny it, but he was shamelessly possessive where she was concerned.

Henry Skyler had not been surprised when Cassandra sent him her notice. He'd been disappointed she wouldn't be returning to The Bookworm, but hardly surprised. He'd hoped she'd come to see him when she and her husband visited London, and had been kind enough to wish her well.

They were going to the Seychelles for their honeymoon. Enrique said that the islands, set in the Indian ocean, were an ideal place for lovers, and he was determined that they should have at least three weeks to themselves before returning to Tuarega.

Cassandra's father and sisters attended the wedding, too, although as the sister nearest to her in age was pregnant they had decided not to stay long in Spain. Enrique had expressed his delight at their presence, and had persuaded her father to stay on for several days after the wedding so that David could show him the *palacio* and introduce him to the bulls. Mr Scott had demurred at first, but for once Julio de Montoya had been on his best behaviour, due no doubt to his son's influence, and he had endorsed the invitation.

Cassandra was changing for their departure in the bedroom which had been allocated to her at the *palacio* when her new husband came to find her. He entered the room with a distinct and appealing air of satisfaction, closing the door behind him and leaning back against it with undisguised pleasure.

In a lacy bra and panties, Cassandra looked very alluring, and Enrique was not immune to the sensual attractions of her body.

'You look—beautiful,' he said, advancing towards her across the room. He was still wearing the formal morning suit he had worn for their wedding only hours before, but he shed his jacket on the way, unbuttoning his waistcoat with eager fingers. 'Come here.'

'We can't,' she protested, even as her lips responded to the sensuous brush of his. 'Enrique, we don't have time…'

'We will always have time for this,' he insisted huskily, loosening her bra and filling his hands with her breasts. Then, his mouth muffled against her soft flesh, 'Do you want me to stop?'

'Oh, God—no,' she groaned, giving in completely. With his hands cupping her bottom, letting her feel what the pressure of her body was doing to his, she could think of nothing but him. 'But—what if someone comes to find us?'

'We are married,' he reminded her gently. 'We have a son. I do not think anyone can object if I want to make love to my wife.'

THE ITALIAN MATCH

by

Kay Thorpe

Kay Thorpe was born in Sheffield in 1935. She tried out a variety of jobs after leaving school. Writing began as a hobby, becoming a way of life only after she had her first completed novel accepted for publication in 1968. Since then she's written seventy books, and lives now with her husband, son, German Shepherd dog and lucky black cat on the outskirts of Chesterfield in Derbyshire. Her interests include reading, hiking, and travel.

CHAPTER ONE

STRANGE to think that this could have been her homeland, Gina reflected, viewing the lush Tuscany landscape spread before her as the car breasted the rise. Beautiful as it was, she felt no particular draw to the place.

Pulling into the roadside, she took a look at the map laid open across the passenger seat. If her calculations were correct, the collection of red-slate roofs and single-bell tower some mile or so distant had to be Vernici. Smaller than she had imagined, though big enough to offer some kind of accommodation for the short time she was likely to be spending in the vicinity. This close to her destination, she still had doubts as to the wisdom of what she was planning to do. Twenty-five years was a long time. It could be that the Carandentes no longer even resided in the area.

If that turned out to be the case, she would put the whole thing behind her once and for all, she vowed. If nothing else, she would have seen parts of Europe she had never seen before.

Surrounded by olive groves, the little town had an almost medieval air about it, its narrow streets radiating from a central piazza. The car that burst from one of the narrow streets at breakneck speed would have hit Gina's car head-on if she hadn't taken instant evading action. There was only one way to go, and that was straight through a flimsy barrier protecting some kind of road works, finishing up tilted at a crazy angle with her offside front wheel firmly lodged in the deep hole.

Held by the safety belt, she had suffered no more than a severe shaking up, but the shock alone was enough to keep her sitting there like a dummy for the few moments it took people attracted by the screeching of brakes to put in an appearance.

Her scanty Italian could make neither head nor tail of the voluble comment. All she could do was make helpless gestures. Eventually one man got the passenger door open and helped her clamber out of the vehicle, all the time attempting to make himself understood.

The only word Gina recognised was garage. *'Si, grazie, signor!'* she responded thankfully, trusting to luck that he would take her meaning and call someone out for her. That the car would be in no fit state to be driven when it was pulled out of the hole, she didn't doubt. She simply had to hope that repairs could be effected without too much trouble.

Her helpmate disappeared up a side street, leaving her to lean weakly against the nearest support and wait for succour. It was gone two, the heat scarcely diminished from its midday high; her sleeveless cotton blouse was sticking to her back. An elderly woman addressed her in tones of sympathy. Assuming that she was being asked if she was feeling all right. Gina conjured a smile and another *'Si, grazie. Inglese,'* she tagged on before any further questions could be put to her.

It might have been an idea to learn at least enough of the language to get by on before setting out on this quest of hers, she thought wryly, but it was a little late for if onlys. She was in Vernici, and quite likely going to be stuck here for however long it might take to get her car back on the road.

Straightening, she walked round the vehicle to view the uptilted front end, in no way reassured by what she saw.

The wheel had been crushed inwards by the impact, the whole wing and a corner of the bonnet badly crumpled. It was some small consolation that the car itself was Italian. If new parts were needed that surely had to help.

Hindered more than aided by the all-too-ready helping hands and eager advice, it took the two men who eventually arrived in a battered tow truck almost half an hour to drag the car free. It was, Gina saw with sinking heart, in an even worse state of disrepair than she had thought. The wheel was buckled, the wing a total write-off, the bonnet probably salvageable but unlikely to look pristine again without a lot of expert hammering and filling.

The happy-go-lucky manner employed by both mechanics gave little rise to confidence. One of them, who spoke some English, indicated that it would be necessary to send to Siena, or perhaps even to Florence for a new wheel and wing. When asked how long that might take, he spread his hands in a gesture only too easily recognisable. Perhaps a week, perhaps even longer. Who could tell? And then, of course, there would be the work. Perhaps another week. The possible cost? Once more the hands were spread. The cost would be what the cost would be, Gina gathered, by then in no fit state to press the issue any further.

Declining an offer to squeeze her into a seat between the two of them, she followed the truck on foot to a small backstreet garage, to see her only means of transport tucked away in a corner to await attention. The parts would be ordered at once, the younger man assured her. In the meantime, he could supply a good place for her to stay.

Faced with his overt appraisement of her body, Gina gave the suggestion scant consideration. For the first time she turned her mind to the car that had caused the accident. The driver had been female not male, and young, the car itself big and blue.

With faint hope, she described both car and occupant to her mechanic friend, to be rewarded with a grinning acknowledgement. 'Cotone,' he said. 'You go to San Cotone. Three kilometres,' he added helpfully, and drew a map in the dust. 'Very rich. You make them pay!'

Gina had every intention of trying. She was covered by insurance, of course, but claims for accidents abroad were notoriously difficult to get settled. The more she thought about it the angrier she became, her object in coming to Vernici in the first place temporarily pushed to the back of her mind. She was stuck out here in the back of beyond because of some spoiled teenager with nothing better to do than tear around the roads without regard for life or limb. Recklessness didn't even begin to cover it!

The question was how to reach the place. 'Taxi?' she queried. 'Bus?'

He shook his head. 'You take car.'

'How the devil can I—?' she began, breaking off abruptly when she saw where he was pointing. With almost as much rust as paint on the bodywork, and tyres that looked distinctly worn, the little Fiat's better days were obviously a long way in the past. Beggars, however, couldn't afford to be choosers. If that was the only vehicle available that was the one she would take.

'How much?' she asked.

The shrug was eloquent, the smile even more so. 'You pay later.'

In cash, not kind, she thought drily, reading him only too well. Her bags were locked in the boot of her own car. After a momentary hesitation she decided they would have to stay there for the present. She had to get this other matter settled while the anger still burned good and bright. The question of accommodation could wait.

Despite its appearance, the Fiat started without too much

trouble. Gina headed out along the route by which she had approached the town, to take the turning her adviser's drawing had indicated through the gently rolling landscape.

Olive groves gave way to immense vineyards tended by what appeared to be a regular army of workers. Only then did Gina make the connection with the label she had seen on Chianti wines back home. A rich family indeed, she thought, well able to pay for the damage to her car, for certain.

A pair of wide wrought-iron gates gave open access to a drive that curved through trees to reach a stone-built villa of stunning size and architecture. Gina drew to a stop on the gravelled circle fronting the place, refusing to allow the grandeur to deflect her from her aim. A member of this household had driven her off the road; the onus was on them to reimburse her.

Set into the stone wall beside imposing double doors, the bell was of the old-fashioned pull-type. It emitted a deep, repeated note, clearly audible from where she stood. The elderly man who answered the summons was dressed in dark trousers and matching waistcoat along with a sparkling white shirt. A member of staff rather than family, Gina judged. His appraisement was rapid, taking in her simple cotton skirt and blouse. The disdain increased as his glance went beyond her to the battered vehicle standing on the gravelled forecourt.

'I'm here to see the owner,' she stated before he could speak, wishing she had thought to get a name from her mechanic friend. *'Padrone,'* she tagged on, dredging the depths of her scanty vocabulary.

The man shook his head emphatically, loosed a single, terse sentence, and began to close the door again. Gina stopped the movement by placing her hands flat against the wood and shoving.

'Padrone!' she insisted.

From the look on the man's face, she wasn't getting through. Which left her with only one choice. She slipped past him before he could make any further move, heading for one of the doors leading off the wide, marble-floored hall with no clear idea in mind other than to block any immediate attempt to remove her from the premises.

There was a key in the far side lock. She slammed the heavy dark-wood door to and secured it, leaning her forehead against a panel to regain both her breath and her wits. That had been a really crazy thing to do, she admitted. A move hardly likely to impress the owner of the establishment, whoever he or she was.

A knock on the door was followed by what sounded like a question. Gina froze where she stood as another male voice answered, this time from behind her. She spun round, gaining a hazy impression of a large, book-lined room as her gaze came to rest on the man seated at a vast desk on the far side of it.

Slanting through the window behind him, the sun picked out highlights in the thick sweep of black hair. Dark eyes viewed her from beneath quizzically raised brows, the lack of anger or even annoyance on his leanly sculptured features something of a reassurance.

'Buon pomeriggeo,' he said.

'Parla inglese?' Gina asked hopefully.

'Of course,' he answered in fluent English. 'I apologise for my lack of perception. I was deceived by the blackness of your hair into believing you of the same blood as myself for a moment, but no Italian woman I ever met had so vividly blue a pair of eyes, so wonderfully fair a skin!'

A fairness that right now was more of a curse than an

asset, Gina could have told him, dismayed to feel warmth rising in her cheeks at the sheer extravagance of the observation. She was unaccustomed to such flowery language from a man. But then, how many Latins had she actually met before this?

'It should be me apologising for breaking in on you like this,' she said, taking a firm grip on herself, 'but it was the only way to get past the door guard.'

A smile touched the strongly carved mouth. 'As Guido speaks little English, whilst you obviously speak even less Italian, misunderstandings were certain to arise. Perhaps you might explain to me what it is that you are here for?'

Feeling like a stag at bay with her back braced against the door, Gina eased herself away, conscious of a sudden frisson down her spine as the man rose from his seat. No more than the early thirties, he had a lithe, athletic build beneath the cream silk shirt and deeper-toned trousers. Rolled shirt sleeves revealed muscular forearms, while the casually opened collar laid the strong brown column of his throat open to inspection.

'I need to see the head of the household,' she said, blanking out the involuntary response.

He inclined his head. 'I am Lucius Carandente.'

Shock robbed her of both speech and clarity of thought for a moment or two. She gazed at him with widened eyes. There had to be more than one Carandente family, she told herself confusedly. This couldn't possibly be them!

Yet why not? asked another part of her mind. She knew nothing of the family other than the name. Why assume it more likely that they be of proletarian rather than patrician stock?

The dark brows lifted again, a certain amused speculation in his gaze. 'You appear surprised.'

Gina pulled herself together. 'I was expecting someone

older,' she prevaricated, in no way ready to plumb any further depths as yet. 'The father, perhaps, of a girl who drives a blue tourer.'

Speculation gave way to sudden comprehension, all trace of amusement vanished. 'Donata,' he said flatly. 'My younger sister. What did she do?'

'She caused me to crash my car an hour or so ago. Down in Vernici. It's going to need new parts. The garage down there tells me they'll have to be ordered from Florence, and it's going to take a lot of time—to say nothing of the cost!'

'You carry no insurance?'

'Of course I carry insurance!' she returned with asperity, sensing an attempt to wriggle off the hook. 'Waiting for the go-ahead from my company would take even more time. In any case, it's your sister's insurance that should be responsible for the damage—always providing *she* carries some!'

She paused there, seeing his lips take on a slightly thinner line and aware of allowing her tongue to run away with her. 'I'm sorry,' she tagged on impulsively. 'That was very rude of me.'

'Yes, it was,' he agreed. 'Though perhaps not entirely unmerited. If you will kindly unlock the door behind you and allow Guido entrance, I will take the necessary steps.'

Gina obeyed with some faint reluctance, not at all certain that he wouldn't order Guido to toss her out on her ear. The manservant entered the room without haste, his glance going directly to his master as if she didn't even exist.

Lucius Carandente spoke in rapid Italian, despatching the older man with a final *'Subito!'*

'Please take a seat,' he told Gina, indicating the nearest of the deep club chairs.

He didn't sit down himself, but leaned against the desk edge as she complied, placing her at a distinct and probably intentional disadvantage. No matter, she thought resolutely; she could always stand up again if she felt the need.

'You have yet to give me your name,' he said.

'I'm sorry,' she proffered once more. 'I'm Gina Redman.'

'You are here on vacation?'

It was easier at the moment to say yes, Gina decided, not yet convinced that the name wasn't just a coincidence. Other than the obvious characteristics, this man bore no great resemblance to the photograph in her handbag.

'I'm touring,' she acknowledged. 'I've driven all the way through France and Switzerland without a single mishap. If your sister hadn't been going so fast...'

Lucius held up a hand. 'It would be better that we wait until she is available to speak for herself, I think. She arrived home, I know, so it should not be long before she joins us. Until then,' he added in the same courteous tones, 'we will talk of other matters. The colour of your hair does not suggest the English rose. Is it possible, perhaps, that you have mixed parentage?'

Short of telling him to mind his own business, Gina was left with no choice but to answer. 'My father was Italian.'

'Was?'

'He died before I was born.' She forestalled the next question, hoping he would leave it at that until she had time to consider just how she was going to find out if he was indeed one of the Carandentes she had come so far to find. 'I was adopted by my English stepfather.'

'I see.'

To her relief he refrained from asking the name discarded for Redman. He probably assumed that her mother had never held title to it to start with.

The opening of the door heralded the entry of a girl whose appearance was totally at odds with her surroundings. Multilayered and finger-raked into a rough tumble about her tempestuous young face, her hair looked more like a bird's nest than the crowning glory it must once have been. She was clad in black leather, the trousers skin-tight about rounded hips, the jacket outlining a well-endowed figure.

It was apparent at once that she recognised Gina, though she gave no sign of discomfiture. She addressed her brother in Italian, switching to English with no more effort than he had displayed himself when told to do so—and with even greater fluency.

'The blame wasn't mine,' she declared flatly, without glancing in Gina's direction. 'There's no damage to *my* car.'

'Only because I managed to avoid what would have been a head-on crash!' Gina asserted before Lucius could respond. 'You were going too fast to stop. You didn't even attempt to stop! Even to see if I was all right!' She was sitting bolt upright in the chair, not about to let the girl get away with her denials. 'Leaving the scene of an accident is against the law where I come from—especially where there are possible injuries to either party.'

'If you'd been injured you wouldn't be sitting here,' Donata returned.

Gina kept a tight rein on her temper. 'That's not the point. I'm going to be stuck in Vernici until my car can be repaired—with a hefty bill at the end of it. At the very least, I need your insurance details to pass on to mine.'

'But what you really want is for Lucius to give you money now!' flashed the younger girl.

Her brother said something short and sharp in Italian, increasing the mutinous set of her jaw. When she spoke again it was with sullen intonation. 'I'm sorry.'

Lucius made no attempt to stop her from leaving the room. His mouth tautened as the door slammed in her wake.

'I add my apologies for the way Donata spoke to you,' he said. 'I also apologise for her appearance. She returned last week from her school in Switzerland...' He broke off, shaking his head as if in acknowledgement that whatever he had been about to say was irrelevant to the present matter. 'I believe it best that I take responsibility for the financial affairs,' he said instead. 'You have accommodation already arranged?'

Gina shook her head, the wind taken completely out of her sails.

'So where is your luggage?'

'I left it locked in the boot of the car,' she said. 'My car, not the one I came here in. I hired that from the garage.'

'It will be returned, and your luggage brought here. If you give me your car keys I will make the necessary arrangements.'

'Here?' Gina looked at him in some confusion. 'I don't—'

'You will naturally stay at Cotone until your car is repaired,' he stated. 'That will be done in Siena.'

'I can't let you...' she began again, voice petering out as he lifted a staying hand.

'You must allow me to make what reparation I can for my sister's lack of care. It would be most discourteous of you to reject my hospitality.'

'Then I must of course accept,' she said after a moment. 'Thank you, *signor*.'

His smile sent a further quiver down her spine. 'You will please call me Lucius. And I may address you by your first name?'

'Of course,' she said, bemused by the totally unexpected turn of events. 'You're very kind.'

The dark eyes roved the face upturned to him, coming to rest on the curve of her mouth. 'I find it difficult to be otherwise with a beautiful woman. A weakness, I know.'

Gina gave a laugh, doing her best to ignore the curling stomach muscles. 'I doubt you'd allow anyone, male *or* female, to get the better of you!'

'I said difficult, not impossible,' came the smooth return.

His gaze shifted from her as the door opened again to admit a young maidservant. He must, Gina surmised, have summoned her via some hidden bell press.

'Crispina will show you to your room,' he said, having spoken to the girl. 'Your bags will be brought to you. Until then, you would be advised to rest. An ordeal such as the one you experienced can produce delayed shock.'

Gina didn't doubt it; she felt in the grip of it right now. She got to her feet, vitally aware of his eyes following her as she crossed to the door. Crispina answered her greeting smile with a somewhat tentative one of her own. She shook her head when Gina asked if she spoke English, which left the pair of them with very little to say as they climbed the grand staircase to the upper storey.

The bedroom to which she was shown was every bit as grand as the rest of the house, with glass doors opening onto a balcony that overlooked the magnificent view. The spacious *en suite* bathroom had fittings Gina was pretty sure were solid gold, the walls lined in mirror glass. She eyed her multireflection in wry acknowledgement of a less than pristine appearance. Clambering from a car halfway down a hole in the ground had left its mark in more ways then the one.

Back in the bedroom, she extracted the long envelope from her bag, and sat down on the bed edge to study the photograph afresh. Arms about each other, the young couple portrayed looked so blissfully happy, the girl's fair skin and pale gold hair a total contrast to her partner's Latin looks—both of them scarcely out of their teen years.

Gina had come across the photograph while browsing in the attic one rainy afternoon when she was fifteen. The accompanying marriage licence had tilted her world on its axis, the explanations reluctantly furnished by her mother when confronted with the evidence even more so.

Her mother and Giovanni Carandente had met as students at Oxford and had fallen madly in love. Knowing neither family would approve the match, they had married in secret, planning on taking their degrees before telling them. Her pregnancy had changed everything. Giovanni had set out to face his family with the news in person, only to meet his death in a road accident on the way to the airport. Two months later, with her parents still unaware of the truth, Beth had married her former boyfriend, John Redman, the two of them allowing everyone to believe that the baby was his.

Sitting here now, Gina went over the scene in her mind once again, recalling the anguish. Although she bore no facial resemblance, John Redman's colouring had always lent credence to hers. She would never in a thousand years have suspected the truth.

Asked why she hadn't attempted to contact the Carandentes herself, her mother had made a wry gesture. She knew nothing about them, she admitted, except that they lived in the town of Vernici in Tuscany. They had been the ones informed of Giovanni's death not her. She had found out only on reading about the accident in the following day's newspaper.

'It was a terrible time,' she acknowledged. 'I hardly knew which way to turn. If it hadn't been for your father—'

'But he isn't my father, is he?' Gina said hollowly.

'In every other way he is. He gave you his name—provided us both with a home and a good life. He's a good man. The very best.' Beth's voice was tender. 'I love him dearly.'

'But not the way you loved Giovanni?'

Beth shook her head, her smile wry again. 'No two loves are the same, darling. What Giovanni and I had was wonderful, but whether it would have lasted—well, who can tell?' She hesitated before continuing. 'I know it's a lot to ask, but can we keep it just between ourselves? John regards you as his own child. He'd be terribly upset if he knew that you knew you weren't.'

Loving him the way she did herself, she'd had no inclination to tell him what she knew, either then or since, Gina reflected, but the knowledge couldn't be wiped out. For years she had toyed with the idea of some day coming out here and searching for her forebears, only an idea was all it had been until now. She had three more weeks before she started the new job she hoped would rekindle the interest and ambition so lacking this last year or so. Once into that, her free time would be severely restricted.

It was coming up to six o'clock, she saw, glancing at her watch. She'd been sitting here for more than half an hour thinking about it all. The question of whether these Carandentes were of the same family line as her father still remained to be answered. The most direct way was to ask outright, of course, but she was somehow reluctant to do that.

A knock on the door signalled the arrival of her bags. Dinner, she was advised by Guido in fragmentary English, would be served at nine-thirty in the salon. The master requested that she join the family for prior refreshment on the terrace at nine.

Gina thanked the man, receiving a bare nod by way of return. It was obvious that her presence was not looked on with favour. As an old family retainer, he would naturally take Donata Carandente's side in the matter of who was to blame for the accident, she supposed. It was possible that the rest of the staff would take the same attitude—although Crispina had shown no sign of it.

Whether through the delayed shock Lucius had spoken of, or simply the effects of a long day behind the wheel, the weariness overtaking her was not to be denied. It was doubtful if she'd sleep, but a couple of hours just resting would revive her for the evening to come. She would hate to nod off over the dinner table.

She took off her outer clothing before lying down on the silk bedspread, stretching out luxuriously beneath the spinning fan. So much nicer than functional air-conditioning, she thought, watching the moving blades. The soft, whirring sound was soporific in itself.

Lucius had said Donata was his younger sister. Were there other siblings? For him to be *padrone*, his father must be dead too, but perhaps there was still a mother alive. If these people really did turn out to be her father's kith and kin, then she and Lucius could be cousins. She found the idea oddly displeasing.

Daylight had faded to a dim glimmer when she awoke. It was a relief to see there was still half an hour to go before she was expected to join the family on the terrace.

The sleep had refreshed her, the shower did an even

better job, but no amount of revitalisation could make what was to come any easier. At some point this evening she had to bring up her father's name and learn the truth. For peace of mind alone she needed to know her origins.

Having planned on staying at good hotels throughout her journey, she had packed clothes to suit most circumstances. Cut on the bias in deep blue silk jersey, the dress she picked out to wear to dinner skimmed her figure to finish on the knee. Teamed with a pair of high-heeled sandals, it should fit the bill, Gina reckoned.

A stroke or two of mascara along her lashes, a dash of lipstick, and she was ready to go. There hadn't been time to put her hair up into the French pleat she would have preferred, but it would have to do. Thick and glossy, it fell in soft waves to her shoulders—the bane of her life when it came to drying after washing, but she could never bring herself to have it cut short.

Night was fast encroaching when she reached the wide, stone-balustered terrace, the lamps already lit. Of the five people gathered there, three were female, the family resemblance pronounced.

Lucius came forward to greet her as she hesitated on the threshold of the room through which she had emerged, the look in his eyes as he scanned her shapely length tensing muscle and sinew. He was making no secret of the fact that he found her as much of a draw as she had to admit she found him. A man who might well be her cousin, she reminded herself forcibly. A first cousin, even.

The prospect of a family relationship was hardly enhanced by Donata's open hostility. Her sister, Ottavia, was around twenty-seven or eight and married to a man some few years older named Marcello Brizzi. Their response to the introduction was courteous enough on the surface, but it was apparent that they too regarded her presence as an intrusion.

It was left to the matriarch of the family to show any warmth in her welcome. Skin almost as smooth as Gina's own, the still luxuriant hair untouched by grey, she scarcely looked old enough to have a son Lucius's age.

'My son tells me you are half Italian yourself,' she said. 'I believe you never knew your father?'

Seated in one of the comfortable lounging chairs, the gin and tonic she had asked for to hand, Gina shook her head. 'He died before I was born.'

Signora Carandente expressed her sympathy in a long, drawn sigh. 'Such a terrible thing!' She was silent for a moment, contemplating the girl before her. 'You have older siblings, perhaps?'

Gina shook her head again, eliciting another sigh.

'For a man to die without a son to carry on his name is a sad matter indeed! Should anything happen to Lucius before he produces a son, our own lineage will be finished too. You would think, would you not, that he would recognise such a responsibility?'

'I am not about to die,' he declared calmly.

'Who can tell?' his mother returned. 'You must marry soon. You have a duty. And who better than Livia Marucchi!'

His shrug made light of the moment, but Gina sensed an underlying displeasure that such matters should be discussed in the presence of a stranger. She'd found the episode discomfiting enough herself. From what little she had seen of him, she judged him a man who would make his own decision about whom and when he should marry anyway. His choices, she was sure, would in no way be limited to one woman.

'What was your father's name?' asked Ottavia, jerking

her out of her thoughts and into sudden flaring panic. She wasn't ready! Not yet!

'Barsini,' she said, plucking the name out of some distant memory without pause for consideration. 'Alexander Barsini.'

She regretted the impulse the moment the words left her lips, but it was too late to retract.

'Barsini,' Ottavia repeated. 'Which part of Italy did he come from?'

Having begun it, she was left with no option but to continue, Gina acknowledged ruefully. 'Naples,' she said off the top of her head.

'He has family still living?'

This time Gina opted for at least a partial truth. 'I don't know. I came to Italy to try and find out.'

Ottavia's brows lifted in a manner reminiscent of her brother, though minus any humour. 'Your mother failed to maintain contact?'

Gina returned her gaze with a steadiness she was far from feeling. 'My mother never met his family. They knew nothing of the marriage.'

'I think that enough,' Lucius cut in before his sister could continue the catechism. 'Let the matter rest.'

Ottavia looked as if she found the command unpalatable, but she made no demur. Gina doubted, however, that her curiosity would remain contained. Catching Donata's eye, she tried a smile, receiving a glare in return. There would be no softening of attitude there for certain. She was well and truly in the doghouse!

Dinner proved less of a banquet than anticipated, with no more than four courses. Gina drank sparingly of the free-flowing wines. She loved the reds, but they didn't always love her. The last thing she needed was to waken with a hangover in the morning.

Lucius insisted that all conversation was conducted in English for her sake, which made her feel even more of an outsider. Marcello, she learned, was the estate comptroller, Ottavia a lady of leisure. The latter confined her questions this time to Gina's present background, expressing astonishment on hearing she was a qualified accountant.

'Such an unusual job for a woman!' she exclaimed. 'Do you not think so, Lucius?'

'An admirable achievement for anyone,' he returned, directing a smile that set every nerve in Gina's body tingling. 'Especially at so young an age.'

'I'm twenty-five,' she felt moved to respond. 'Not that much younger than yourself, I imagine.'

The smile came again, accompanied by an unmistakable glint in the dark eyes. 'Eight years is no obstacle, I agree.'

Obstacle to what, Gina didn't need to ask. Neither, she was sure, did anyone else. That his interest in her was purely physical she didn't need telling either. It could hardly be anything more.

Her cool regard served only to increase the glint. Opposition, it appeared, was an enticement in itself. More than ever she regretted the situation she had landed herself with. If she wanted to know the truth, not only was she faced with the prospect of explaining a lie she had no logical reason to have told in the first place, but the possibility of mortifying Lucius with the news that he had been making advances to a relative.

'And what does your stepfather do for a living?' Ottavia persisted, claiming her attention once more.

'He's in textiles,' she acknowledged.

'On his own account?'

'His own business, yes.' A highly successful one, Gina could have added, but saw no reason to go into greater detail—especially when said success was dependent on factors she found rather worrying at times.

Ottavia seemed content to leave it at that for the moment, but Gina sensed that the digging was by no means done. Plain nosiness, she assured herself. There was no way the woman could suspect the truth.

Midnight brought no sign of an end to the evening. Hardly able to keep her eyes open, Gina finally gave in.

'I hope it won't be taken amiss if I go to bed,' she said. 'I was on the road at seven this morning, and didn't have all that good a night's sleep before it.'

'But of course!' Signora Carandente responded. 'You must feel free to do whatever you wish while you are our guest. Perhaps you would prefer to have breakfast served in your room?'

'Not at all,' Gina assured her. 'I'll be fine.' She added impulsively, 'Your hospitality is second to none, *signora*.'

'Contessa,' corrected Ottavia with some sharpness of tone.

'You may call me Cornelia,' her mother told Gina graciously.

Still grappling with the implications, Gina inclined her head. 'Thank you.'

She took her leave with a general 'Goodnight,' avoiding any clash of glances with Lucius himself. If his mother was a Contessa, his father obviously had to have been a Count, which meant the title must have been handed down. It made the likelihood of her father having any connection seem even more remote. What would a son of such a family have been doing attending an English university as an ordinary student?

On the other hand, it was surely unlikely that either now or in the past another, entirely unconnected, Carandente family resided in Vernici.

She was going around in circles, Gina acknowledged. The only way to be sure was to do what she should have done several hours ago and tell the whole story. Concealing the name had been an idiotic gesture all round. Tomorrow, she promised herself, she would come clean. It was hardly as if she was after feathering her nest in any fashion. All she wanted was to know who her father had really been.

CHAPTER TWO

DESPITE her tiredness, Gina was wide awake at six. The early morning sunlight beckoned her out onto the balcony to view the beautifully landscaped gardens stretching to all sides. The vistas beyond were shrouded in early morning haze.

There was no one about that she could see from here. On impulse, she returned to the bedroom to don a pair of light cotton trousers and a shirt. Half an hour or so's exploration would still leave her plenty of time to get ready for the day proper.

She could hear the muted sound of voices coming from somewhere towards the rear of the premises as she descended to the lower floor, but no one appeared to question her purpose. Not that any member of staff would do that in any case, Gina supposed. As a guest of the house she was, as Cornelia had assured her, entitled to do as she wished.

All the same she reduced the chances of running into anyone by using the front entrance. The Fiat was gone, the driveway clear of vehicles of any kind. There would be garages around the back somewhere, she assumed.

She headed left, away from the house, dropping down stone steps between white marble pillars to terraces overhung with luxuriant plant life and strewn with classical statues. Gina revelled in the beauty of it all against the clean, clear blue of the sky.

On one level lay a pond laced with water lilies of every hue, the carved stone bench at its edge positioned to take full advantage of the harmonious view across the valley. She slowed her steps on sight of the man already seated there.

'I didn't realise anyone else was up and about yet,' she said a little awkwardly. 'I thought I'd take a look around before breakfast.'

'I saw you from my window,' Lucius admitted. 'It seemed probable that you would eventually reach this spot.' His regard this morning was fathomless. 'So, how do you find our home?'

'It's truly beautiful,' she acknowledged. 'A dream of a place! Why didn't you tell me you were a Count?' she tagged on.

He gave a brief shrug. 'I have no use for status symbols.'

'Ottavia doesn't appear to share the aversion.'

'My sister clings to an order long gone.' He patted the seat at his side. 'Come sit with me.'

'I have to get back,' she said hurriedly. 'It must be getting on for breakfast time.'

'Food will be served whenever and wherever required,' he advised. A hint of amusement in his eyes now, he added, 'You are afraid of me, perhaps?'

'Of course not!' she denied.

'Then, of what I make you feel?' he continued imperturbably.

Pretending not to know what he was talking about would be a waste of time and breath, Gina knew. 'You take a great deal too much for granted,' she retorted.

The amusement grew. 'That is your English half speaking. Your Barsini blood responds to mine.'

The time to tell him the truth was now, but the words wouldn't form themselves.

'Grateful as I am to you for what you're doing with my

car, I'm not about to become your playmate for the week,' she said coolly instead.

'Playmates are for children,' he returned, not in the least rebuffed. 'We are neither of us that.'

'But we *are* strangers,' she replied with deliberation. 'You don't really know anything about me.'

'Then, tell me,' he invited.

The moment was there again, but Gina still couldn't bring herself to take advantage of it.

'I should be getting back,' she repeated.

'Then, I will come with you,' he said.

He got to his feet, lean and lithe as a panther in the black trousers and shirt. Gina steeled herself as he moved to where she stood, but he made no attempt to touch her, falling into step at her side as she turned back the way she had come. Catching the faint scent of aftershave, she was supremely conscious of the fact that she had yet to shower, yet to put a brush to her hair.

'Are you always up this early of a morning?' she asked.

'I rise when I awaken,' he said easily. 'No later than six, sometimes as much as an hour before that.'

'Even when you don't get to bed until the early hours?'

'A matter of custom. If I tire in the day I may take siesta. It depends on my commitments.'

'I imagine those are extensive.'

'Not too much so.'

Doing her best to keep the conversational ball rolling, she said, 'You speak excellent English.'

'But somewhat structured compared with the way you speak, yes?'

Gina cast a glance at the chiselled profile, responding to the curve of his lips. 'My old English teacher would approve every word. It's usually tourists who introduce bad habits.'

'Few tourists find Vernici,' he said. 'It is off the regular routes.'

'I know. I had some difficulty finding it myself.'

It was Lucius's turn to slant a glance, expression curious. 'Why were you looking for Vernici at all if your father came from Naples.'

Do it now! an inner voice urged her, even as she mentally cursed the slip-up. 'Latterly,' she heard herself saying regardless. 'But he was apparently born in Vernici, so I thought it worth taking a look there too.'

'I see.' From his tone, it was obvious that he was wondering why she hadn't mentioned that fact last night. 'The name is unfamiliar to me,' he went on after a moment, 'but the older townsfolk will surely recall the family. I will have enquiries made.'

She was getting deeper and deeper into the mire, thought Gina unhappily. What the devil was wrong with her that she kept on fabricating things?

They had reached the front of the house. Lucius preceded her up the steps to open a door for her to pass through, too close by far for comfort as he followed her in. Soles wet from their passage across the grass, her sandals had no purchase on the terrazzo. Lucius shot out an arm as she skidded, hauling her up against him, his hand warm at her waist.

'You must take more care,' he said, making no immediate attempt to let her go again.

'I will,' Gina assured him. 'I'm fine now, thanks.'

His laugh was low, the brief pressure of his lips at her nape where the curtain of hair had parted stirring her blood in a manner she deplored.

'I'd prefer you didn't do that,' she got out.

He laughed again, but this time released her. Gina made herself meet the dark eyes. 'I realise you probably won't be used to it, but I'm telling you again that I'm not…available.'

'Do you not think that you might be the one now taking too much for granted?' Lucius returned with mock gravity.

'Am I?' she challenged, and saw the glint return.

'No. I would be only half a man if I could look at you and not want you in the instant, *cara.*' He gave her no time to reply—if she could have come up with a reply at all. 'I will begin enquiries about the Barsini family this very morning. I would hope to have news of them before the day is over.'

A forlorn hope, Gina reflected ruefully. The longer this charade of hers continued, the harder it became to revoke.

'There's something I—' she began, breaking off as Guido heaved into view.

'Something you…?' Lucius prompted.

She shook her head, courage lost. 'Forget it.'

Leaving him standing there, she ran lightly up the stairs to head for her room. The situation was becoming increasingly difficult. If it weren't for her lack of transport, she would be tempted to abandon the whole idea and return home. She was vitally attracted to a man who might just be a close blood relation, a man who was making no effort to conceal *his* objective. Even if there should prove to be no connection, she wasn't into the kind of casual, ships that pass in the night, relationship that was all Lucius would have in mind.

Despite last night's refusal, breakfast was brought to her at eight o'clock. Gina ate it out on the balcony, enjoying both the view and the warmth. The sky was so blue, the quality of light a joy in itself. It was possible that her father had viewed the same scene—perhaps even from this very room. Could she really bear, Gina asked herself, not to know for certain?

She went downstairs again with no notion of how she was going to spend the day. Wandering out to the terrace, she found Ottavia stretched out on a lounger beneath an opened umbrella. She was wearing a gold-lamé bikini that barely covered her voluptuous curves, her eyes shielded by designer sunglasses. Her toenails, Gina noted, were painted the same shade of scarlet as her fingernails and lips, the whole effect more reminiscent of the film world, she thought, than Italian aristocracy.

'Buon giorno,' she proffered tentatively.

Ottavia pulled down the sunglasses a fraction to run a disparaging eye over the cotton dress Gina had elected to wear. 'You are quite recovered from your weariness, I trust?' she enquired, without bothering to respond to the greeting.

'Quite, thank you,' Gina confirmed. She felt it necessary to add, 'The breakfast was very good, but I really don't expect to be waited on while I'm here.'

'As you are here at my brother's invitation, you are entitled to be treated as any other guest,' came the smooth reply. 'You realise, of course, how fortunate you are to have gained his support in this affair.' She didn't wait for any answer. 'A word of warning, however. Lucius may pay you some attentions because he is a man and you are attractive to look at, but it means nothing.'

'In other words, don't run away with the idea that he might be about to offer marriage,' Gina returned. 'I'll certainly bear it in mind.'

The irony left no visible impression. 'Good,' was the only comment.

Her presence wasn't exactly welcome, Gina gathered, as the glasses were replaced and the head returned to the supporting cushion. She was tempted to stay anyway, just for the hell of it, but there was little to be gained from keeping company with someone who so obviously didn't want her there.

She had only covered a small part of the immediate grounds earlier. Now would be the right time to take a turn round the other side of the house before the heat became too great for comfort. With several days to fill, and nowhere else to go, she was probably going to be spending a lot of time out of doors. Which in this climate would be no great hardship, she had to admit.

She was crossing the drive when a low-slung sports car came roaring round the bend. Gina leapt instinctively for safety, missed her footing and went down on one knee in the gravel, steeling herself for the impact she was sure was to come. The car screeched to a halt with its front bumper bare inches from her. Spouting Italian at a rate of knots, the driver leapt out without bothering to turn off the engine, a look of concern on his handsome face as he came to lift her to her feet.

'Inglese,' Gina said for what seemed like the millionth time in response to what she took to be a spate of solicitous enquiry. *'Non capisco.'*

'English!' he exclaimed on a note of surprise.

'That's right.' Gina gave a wry grimace as she eased her knee. 'Does everybody round here drive like bats out of hell?'

His brows drew together in puzzlement. 'Bats?'

'It's just a saying,' she explained, regretting the use of it. 'It means fast, that's all.'

The frown cleared. 'Ah, fast!' Concern leapt once more in his eyes as he caught sight of the trickle of blood running down her leg. 'You are hurt! Why did you not tell me you were hurt?'

'I hadn't realised it was grazed,' Gina admitted, lifting the edge of her skirt to view the not inconsiderable damage. 'I thought I'd just knocked it.'

'It must be cleaned and dressed,' he declared. 'Before it becomes infected.'

'It will be,' she assured him. 'Just as soon as I get back to the house. I'm a guest there,' she added, in case he was in any doubt. 'Gina Redman.'

'A friend of the family?' He sounded intrigued.

'Not exactly. There was an accident. My car was badly damaged. Lu—Signor Carandente very generously invited me to stay until it's repaired.'

His lips curved. 'But of course. Lucius is the most generous of men. I am Cesare Traetta. You must allow me to drive you to the villa.'

'It's hardly any distance,' Gina protested. 'I might get blood on the upholstery.'

'If so it will be cleaned.' He went to open the passenger door. 'Please to get in.'

Gina wiped away the trickle of blood with her handkerchief before doing so. The soft leather seat cocooned her, its contours designed to hold the body in position. Definitely needed, she thought, as Cesare set the car into motion again with a force that caused the rear wheels to spin. She judged him around Lucius's age, which made him Donata's senior by fifteen years, yet the two of them appeared to be on a par when it came to road sense.

They rounded the final bend to come to a further screeching stop outside the house. Switching off the engine, Cesare got swiftly from the car to help Gina from the seat she was struggling to vacate without having her skirt ride up any further than it already had.

'I think I can manage, thanks,' she said drily when he

made to assist her up the steps. 'A damp flannel, and I'll be as good as new!'

'You are bleeding!' exclaimed Lucius from the doorway, startling her because she hadn't seen him arrive. 'What happened to you?'

'I slipped and fell on the drive.' Gina saw no reason to go into greater detail. 'Signor Traetta was kind enough to give me a lift.'

'Cesare,' urged the man at her back. 'You must call me Cesare.'

She gave him a brief smile. 'Cesare, then.' To Lucius she said, 'I'll go and clean myself up.'

'The necessary materials will be brought to you.' he said. 'We must be sure no foreign substances remain in the wound.'

'Of course.' Gina was fast tiring of the fuss. 'I can cope.'

'I am sure of it.' His tone was dry. 'Your self-sufficiency does you credit. You will, however, wait for assistance in this matter.'

He took her agreement for granted, indicating that she precede him into the house. Gina battened down her instincts and meekly obeyed. 'I'm sure you know best,' she murmured in passing, tongue tucked firmly in cheek.

The dress was not only dirty but torn at the hem, she found on reaching her room. Not beyond repair, she supposed, examining the rip, though she was no expert needlewoman. At any rate, she had plenty of other things to change into, so it could wait until she got home.

Despite instructions, she ran hot water in the bathroom basin and began cleaning off the worst of the mess. The graze was quite extensive, with tiny pieces of gravel embedded in the shredded flesh. Concentrating on extracting them, she was taken unawares when Lucius entered the room bearing a first-aid box.

'You were to wait until I brought this!' he exclaimed.

Seated on a padded stool, her foot raised on the bath edge to enable her to see what she was doing, Gina resisted the urge to pull down the skirt she had raised to mid thigh.

'I hardly expected you to bring it up yourself,' she said lamely.

Dark brows rose. 'You think such a task beneath me?'

'Well, no, not exactly. I just took it...' She left the sentence unfinished, holding out her hand for the box. 'It's very good of you, anyway.'

Lucius made no attempt to hand it over. Placing it on the long marble surface into which the double basins were set, he seized soap from the dish and washed his hands. Gina watched in silence, reminded that she should have done the same before attempting to touch the graze at all.

His presence in the confines of the bathroom—spacious though it was—made her nervous. She found it difficult to control the quivering in her limbs when he took a pair of tweezers from the box and sat down on the bath edge to start work on the gravel.

The hand he slid about the back of her calf to hold her leg still was warm and firm against her skin, his fingers long and supple, the nails smoothly trimmed; she could imagine the way they would feel on her body—the sensual caresses. Her nipples were peaking at the very notion.

Stop it! she told herself harshly, ashamed of the sheer carnality of her thoughts. It might be a long-established fact that women were as capable as men of enjoying sex without love, but she had never followed the trend. From her mid teens she had determined not to settle for anything less than the real thing: the kind of love her mother had known for Giovanni Carandente. The possibility that

Lucius could be her father's nephew was enough on its own to prohibit any notion she might have of relaxing her ideals.

'I am sorry if I hurt you,' Lucius apologised as her leg jumped beneath his hands. 'There are only a few more small pieces to come, and then we are finished but for the antiseptic.'

'No problem,' she assured him. 'You're being very gentle. It's quite a mess, isn't it? I didn't realise how deep some of the bits had gone.'

'Thankfully, there should be no lasting scars,' he said without looking up from his task. 'It would be a pity to mar such a lovely leg.'

'Don't you ever stop?' she asked with a sharpness she hadn't intended.

This time he did look up, expression quizzical. 'You find my admiration irksome?'

Gina drew a steadying breath. 'I find it a little too...practised, that's all.'

'Ah, I see. You think I express the same sentiments to all women.' The dancing light was in his eyes again. 'Not so.'

He was hardly going to admit it, Gina told herself as he turned his attention once more to her knee. Not that it made any difference.

The antiseptic stung like crazy, but Lucius made no concessions. He finished the dressing with an expertly applied bandage.

'You may remove the dressing tomorrow to allow the healing tissue to form,' he said, relinquishing his hold on her at last.

Gina got to her feet to try a somewhat stiff-legged step, pulling a face at her reflection in the mirrored wall. 'I haven't had a bandaged knee since I was eight!'

'Long skirts, or the trousers women everywhere appear to have adopted, will cover your embarrassment.'

The dry tone drew her eyes to the olive-skinned face reflected in the mirror. 'You disapprove of the trend?' she asked lightly.

'I prefer a woman to dress as a woman,' he confirmed. 'As most men would say if asked.'

'Donata wears them,' Gina felt bound to point out, stung a little by the implied criticism. 'With that attitude, I'm surprised you allow it—to say nothing of the rest!'

'I said preference not outright rule,' came the steady response. 'Assuming that by the ''rest'' you refer to the state of my sister's hair, no amount of castigation can hasten the regrowth.'

Gina turned impulsively to face him, ashamed of the dig. 'I spoke out of turn. You said yesterday that she'd recently returned from school?'

The smile was brief and lacking in humour. 'She was despatched from her school for behaviour no reputable establishment could tolerate.'

'Not just for a haircut, surely!'

'A minor transgression compared with breaking out of the school in order to attend a nightclub in the nearby town. Not for the first time it appears. This time she was caught by the police when they raided the place in search of drugs.'

Gina gazed at him in dismay. 'You're not saying Donata was actually taking them?'

'She assures me not.'

'You do believe her?'

Lucius lifted his shoulders, mouth wry. 'I hardly know what to believe. I bitterly regret allowing her to persuade me into sending her to Switzerland at all. Her education was complete enough without this ''finishing'' she was so anxious to acquire.'

'She can't have been the only one to kick over the traces,' Gina ventured.

'If by that you mean was she alone on the night in question, the answer is no. There were two others caught with her. One American girl, one English. They too were despatched to their respective homes.'

'I see.' Silly as it seemed, Gina felt like apologising for the part the English girl had played. 'I don't suppose it helps much.'

'No,' Lucius agreed. 'I am still left with the problem of a sister turned insurgent. While she resides here at Cotone I can demand that she obeys certain rules of conduct, but there are limits to the penalties I can impose should she choose to defy me.'

'I can appreciate that,' Gina said carefully. 'It isn't as if she's a child any more.'

'She is eighteen years of age,' he advised on a harder note. 'By now she should be looking towards marriage and children of her own!'

'Marriage isn't the be all and end all of every woman's ambition.' Gina felt moved to protest, turning a deaf ear to the faint, dissenting voice at the back of her mind.

The dark eyes regarded her with a certain scepticism in their depths. 'You intend to stay single all your life?'

'I didn't say that. It depends whether I meet a man I want to marry.'

'And whom, of course, also wishes to marry you.'

'Well, obviously.' The mockery, mild though it was, stirred her to like response. 'Two hearts entwined for all eternity! Worth waiting for, wouldn't you say?'

'The heart has only a part to play,' he said. 'The body

and mind also have need of sustenance. The woman I myself marry must be capable of satisfying every part of me.'

'Typical male arrogance!' She exploded, driven beyond endurance by the sheer complacency of the statement. 'It would serve you right if…' She broke off, seeing the sparkle of laughter dawn and realising she'd been deliberately goaded. 'Serve you right if you were left high and dry!' she finished ruefully. 'Not that it's likely, I admit.'

The sparkle grew. 'You acknowledge me a man difficult for any woman to resist?'

'I acknowledge you a man with a lot more than just looks going for him, Count Carandente,' she said with delicate emphasis.

If she had been aiming to fetch him down a peg or two, she failed dismally. His shrug made light of the dig. 'Despite Ottavia's claim, the woman I marry will not carry the title of Contessa because she will be no more entitled to do so in reality than anyone in the last few hundred years. As I told you this morning, it is simply a status symbol. One for which I have little use myself.

'Which leaves me,' he went on with a wicked gleam, 'with just the looks you spoke of going for me. The looks that warm both your English and your Italian blood to a point where the differences no longer have bearing. Or would you still try to deny what lies between us, *cara*?'

The pithy response that trembled on her lips as he moved purposefully towards her was rejected as more likely to inflame than defuse the situation. What was she doing indulging in the kind of repartee scheduled to bring this very situation about to start with? she asked herself.

'Whatever you have in mind, you can forget it!' she said with what certainty she could muster, resisting any urge to try fighting him off physically as he drew her to him. 'I already told you, I'm not playing!'

'Words! Just words!' He put a forefinger beneath her chin to lift it, bending his head to touch his lips to hers with a delicacy that robbed her of any will to resist.

She was conscious of nothing but sensation as he kissed her: the pounding of her blood in her ears, the warmth spreading from the very centre of her body, the growing weakness in her lower limbs urging her to give way to the need rising so suddenly and fiercely in her. He drew her closer, moulding her to the contours of his masculine shape—making her aware of his own arousal in a manner that inflamed her even further. The words he murmured against her lips transcended all language barriers.

This man might be a close relative, came the desperate reminder, pulling her up as nothing else could have done right then.

'That's enough,' she got out, jerking away from him. 'In fact, it's more than enough!'

Anticipating at the very least a show of frustrated anger at her withdrawal from what must have appeared a near foregone conclusion, she was taken totally aback when Lucius simply laughed and shook his head.

'I think not, for either of us, but there is no haste. You will find Cesare and myself on the terrace should you care to join us for refreshment. He will be anxious to know that you suffered no long-lasting injury.'

He gathered the items he had taken from the first-aid box, and departed, leaving Gina standing there feeling all kinds of an idiot. Aroused he might have been, but he was obviously more than capable of controlling it. He certainly wouldn't demean himself by insisting on satisfaction, however encouraged to believe it forthcoming.

Telling him the truth now, and discovering that there was indeed a close blood relationship, could only prove embarrassing for them both. Probably the best thing she could do was forget the whole affair and head for home as soon as her car was repaired.

And spend the rest of her life wondering, came the thought. She was Giovanni Carandente's daughter. Having finally started on the quest, she had to see it through to the end, no matter what. There must be some way of finding out if this really was his place of origin that didn't involve giving herself away.

Her inclination was to spend the rest of the morning right here in her room, but that was no way for a guest to behave. With the bandage in mind, she donned a long, sarong-type skirt along with a silky vest, and slid her feet into a pair of thonged sandals. Not exactly haute couture, but it served the purpose.

Hair loose about her shoulders, face free of make-up apart from a dash of lipstick, she hid behind a pair of tortoiseshell sunglasses on going out to the terrace. Not just Lucius and Cesare to face, she saw, but Ottavia and Donata into the bargain, the former now fully and beautifully dressed.

Wearing a pair of deck trousers and a T-shirt, her hair raked through with a careless hand, Donata looked hardly less of the teenage rebel than she had in the leather outfit yesterday. She viewed Gina's arrival with a marked lack of enthusiasm.

Not so, Cesare, who leapt to see her seated with a solicitude that went down like a lead balloon with both sisters.

'Your leg must be supported,' he urged, raising the chair's built-in foot rest for her. 'You are in much pain?'

'None at all,' Gina assured him, submitting to his ministrations only because it was marginally less awkward than asking him to desist.

'I ordered fresh orange juice for you,' said Lucius as

one of the younger male staff members came from the house bearing a loaded tray. 'It can, of course, be replaced by something stronger if you prefer.'

'Thanks, but this is just what I need,' Gina assured him as the tall, ice-cool glass was set before her. She seized on it gratefully, sending a good quarter of the contents down her throat in one gulp.

'Iced drinks should be sipped so that the stomach suffers no sudden shock,' commented Donata with a certain malice. 'Isn't that so, Lucius?'

'Advisable, perhaps,' he agreed easily. 'If you are finding the heat overpowering we can move to a cooler part of the terrace,' he said to Gina herself.

The only heat she found overpowering was the kind he generated, came the fleeting thought. 'I find it no problem at all,' she assured him. 'I always did enjoy the sun.'

'What little you see of it in England.'

'Oh, we have our good days,' she returned lightly. 'Sometimes several together. You've visited my country?'

'Never for any length of time.'

'Tomorrow is the Palio,' Cesare put in with an air of being left too long on the sidelines. 'I have grandstand seats long-reserved should anyone care to share them.'

'Si!' declared Donata before anyone else could speak. *'Vorrei andare!'*

Lucius said something in the same language, wiping the sudden animation from her face. Pushing back her chair, she got jerkily to her feet and stalked off, mutiny in every line of her body.

'What exactly is the Palio?' asked Gina in the following pause, feeling a need for someone to say something.

It was Cesare who answered. 'A horse race run twice a year between Siena's *contrade*. Riders must circuit the

Piazza del Campo three times without the benefit of saddles.'

'A bareback race!' Gina did her best to sound enthused.

'A little more than just that,' said Lucius. 'The city's seventeen districts compete for a silk banner in honour of the Virgin. A tradition begun many centuries ago. The race itself lasts no more than a minute or two, but the pageantry is day long. You might enjoy it.'

'You were only there the one time yourself that I recall,' said Cesare. 'Why do we not all of us attend together?'

'It has become a tourist spectacle,' declared Ottavia disdainfully. 'I have no desire to be part of it. Nor, I am sure, will Marcello.'

'Then, perhaps the three of us,' he suggested, undeterred. 'Gina cannot be allowed to miss such an event.'

If Lucius refused too, it would be down to the two of them next, Gina surmised, not at all sure she would want to spend a whole day in Cesare's company. Equal though he appeared to be in age to her host, he lacked the maturity that was an intrinsic part of Lucius's appeal.

'The three of us, then,' Lucius agreed, to her relief. 'Providing that I drive us there. I would prefer that we arrive without mishap.'

Cesare laughed, not in the least put out. 'You have so little faith in me, *amico*, but I accept your offer.'

It had been an ultimatum not an offer, but Lucius obviously wasn't about to start splitting hairs. Gina found herself wishing it was just going to be the two of *them* taking the trip. Safer this way though, she acknowledged ruefully. With Cesare around to act as chaperon, there would be no repeat of this morning's assault on her senses. Whichever way things might turn out, she was in no position to risk that kind of involvement.

CHAPTER THREE

CESARE took his departure shortly afterwards, accompanied by Lucius who wished to discuss some obviously private matter with him. Left alone with Ottavia, Gina made an effort to open a conversation, but soon gave up when her overtures failed to draw more than the briefest of replies.

'I think I'll go and find that cooler spot Lucius mentioned,' she said at length, getting to her feet. 'It's too hot to even think straight out here.'

The older woman made no reply at all to that; Gina hadn't really expected one. She could understand Donata's attitude regarding her presence in the house, but what axe did Ottavia have to grind?

There had been neither sight nor mention of Cornelia so far this morning. Either she was a late riser, or had gone out, Gina surmised. It still needed half an hour or so to noon. Lunch, she imagined, wouldn't be served much before one-thirty or even two. Not that she was hungry yet, but there was a lot of day still to get through.

The coolest place at this hour was going to be indoors. She went in via the glass doors to the *salotto*, welcoming the immediate flow of cooler air from the overhead fans. Reaching the hall, she stood for a moment wondering in which direction to head. Of the rooms that opened off it, she had so far only seen the one she had just come through and the library where she had first run into Lucius.

Feeling a bit of an intruder still, she opened a door under the right wing of the staircase, looking in on a small room that appeared at first glance to be something of a depository for unwanted items of furniture, with little in the way of style about it.

About to close the door again, she paused as her eye caught a reflection in the mirror almost directly opposite. Eyes closed, Donata was seated in a high-backed chair that concealed her from casual observation. From the look of her, she had been crying.

It was likely that her company would be far from welcome, Gina reckoned, but she found herself stepping quietly into the room and easing the door to again regardless. What she was going to say or do she had no clear idea.

The floor in here was laid in parquetry, the design largely obscured by the heavy pieces of furniture. Donata opened her eyes at the sound of footsteps, coming jerkily to her feet as she registered the identity of the intruder.

'Leave me alone!' she urged. 'You have no right to be here!'

Still not at all certain just what it was she hoped to achieve, Gina halted a short distance away. 'I know I haven't' she said, 'but, as I am, supposing we bury the hatchet?'

Distracted by the unfamiliar phrase, Donata drew her brows together. 'Bury the hatchet?'

'It means we forget about the accident and start again. I'd rather be your friend than your enemy.'

A variety of expressions chased across the younger girl's face as she gazed in silence for a moment or two. When she did finally speak, the belligerence seemed almost forced. 'Why should *you* wish to be my friend?'

Why indeed? Gina asked herself, answering the question in the same breath: because in all probability they shared the same genes—or some of them, at any rate.

'I suppose I just don't like being disliked by anyone,'

she said on a semi-jocular note. 'Not that I'm having much success where your sister's concerned either.'

'Ottavia has little concern for anyone but herself,' declared Donata with unconcealed animosity. 'What *she* would most like is to be in Lucius's place.'

Gina could imagine. As *padrone*, Lucius would have total control of all Carandente affairs. Playing second fiddle wouldn't come easy to a woman of Ottavia's temperament. She wondered fleetingly what had prompted her to marry a man who appeared to be little more than an employee of the estate. It could hardly have been for lack of any other choice.

'You must miss your father,' she said softly, changing tack. 'How long is it since you lost him?'

The question took Donata by surprise; her response was automatic. '*Padre* died six years ago.'

'He can't have been all that old.'

'He was forty-eight.'

Which meant there had been just seven years between him and Giovanni Carandente, Gina calculated. Not that the knowledge brought her any closer to either proving or disproving a family connection.

'A big responsibility for your brother to take on so young,' she said. 'Especially as the last in line. It must put a lot of pressure on him.'

Donata eyed her suspiciously. 'Why should it matter to you?'

'It doesn't,' Gina hastened to assure her. 'I was just musing, that's all. It was very rude of me to make any comment at all on your family affairs.' She made a wry gesture. 'I'd better go. I shouldn't have intruded on you in the first place.'

'Then, why did you?'

'I could see you were upset.' Gina hedged. 'I couldn't just leave you like that.'

'You thought your offer of friendship all the comfort needed?'

Gina paid no heed to a sarcasm that had little real bite to it. 'Not all, but perhaps a little.' She hesitated before taking the plunge, aware of treading on delicate ground. 'Lucius told me what happened to you. It must have been a dreadful experience.'

The sympathy had an unexpected effect. Donata's face suddenly crumpled. 'He believes I took drugs!'

'I'm sure he doesn't.' Gina resisted the urge to go and put her arms about the girl. 'You just happened to be caught in the wrong place at the wrong time. It's only been a few days. He'll get over being angry about it.'

'No, he won't.' The tears were threatening to spill again, all trace of insurgency vanished. 'He can't bear even to look at me! No one can!'

And therein, thought Gina in swift understanding, lay the true source of misery. She kept her tone calm and level. 'Because of your hair, you mean?'

'Yes. It was like yours before I allowed Meryl to take scissors to it. She told me it would look so much smarter cut short.'

'Meryl is a hairdresser?'

'No, she was my friend.'

Some friend! Gina reflected. 'A very jealous one, I'd say,' she observed. 'It's going to take time to grow back,' she went on, seeing no point in pretending otherwise, 'but it could be made to look much better than it does.'

Faint hope dawned in the girl's eyes. 'You could do this?'

It wasn't exactly what Gina had had in mind, but she could scarcely make a worse job of it, she decided. 'I can try,' she said. 'You should really have a properly qualified stylist take a look at it.'

'Now is the most important,' declared Donata with growing eagerness. 'If I look less like the scarecrow Lucius called me, he might allow me to accompany you to the Palio tomorrow. He likes you very much, I can tell. He would listen if you asked him.'

Gina very much doubted it, but she couldn't find it in herself to refuse the request out of hand. 'I can but try,' she said again.

'Thank you.' The smile was radiant. 'And I'm truly sorry about your car. It *was* all my fault. I was driving recklessly.'

'Don't worry about it.' Gina could hardly credit the change in the girl. 'I'm sure it will come back as good as new. Anyway, we'd better get to it if we're to be through before lunch.

'Luncheon is at two o'clock,' Donata confirmed. 'Almost two hours away yet.'

Almost two hours to effect a make-over that would persuade Lucius to relent; Gina only hoped she was up to it.

It took every minute, and some judicious snipping, to achieve anything of a success. By the time she'd finished blow-drying the thick dark mass, she was beginning to regret ever having got involved.

She drew a breath of cautious relief on viewing the finished product. With the layers given some shape and lift, and shorter fronds framing the face, it was no salon creation, but it was certainly a vast improvement. Donata seemed pleased enough with it, at any rate.

At Gina's suggestion, she exchanged the deck trousers for a cream linen skirt, the T-shirt for a pale green blouse. She was, she declared extravagantly, happy to accept any advice from someone she now regarded as the only true friend she had ever known.

Something of an achievement in less than twenty-four hours, Gina supposed. She hoped Lucius wouldn't see it as presumption on her part.

Lunch was served on a side terrace beneath a projecting canopy. Ottavia viewed her sister's transformation with limited interest. Better than no effort at all, she said, though hardly a cause for celebration.

It was left to Lucius to express a more complimentary opinion. All the same, Gina had the feeling that he didn't really like the idea of her pitching in on a family affair. In which case, he should have kept his mouth shut about the whole thing, she told herself stoutly.

With Donata urging her in every way without actually saying anything, Gina collared him straight after the meal before she could lose courage.

'About tomorrow,' she began.

'You no longer wish to see the Palio?' Lucius asked.

'Yes, of course I do.' She paused, sidetracking for the moment. 'Although I'd hate to feel I was dragging you away from more important matters. I'm grateful for what you're already doing. I certainly don't expect you to provide entertainment too.'

'I have no other commitment,' he assured her. 'Unless you would prefer to spend the day with Cesare alone?'

'Oh, no!'

The denial was quick—too quick—drawing a smile to his lips. 'Then, where is the problem?'

'Donata hopes to come with us.'

'Commendable though your efforts to improve her appearance are,' he said on a suddenly curious note, 'I find myself asking why you would go to such lengths for someone who has given you nothing but aggravation?'

'I can't help feeling some sympathy for her,' Gina admitted truthfully. 'She's young for her age, and impressionable. I'd say this friend of hers—Meryl—has a lot to answer for. She was the one who persuaded her to have a hair cut. She was probably the one who instigated the break-out in the first place. Some people get a lot of pleasure out of leading others astray.'

'You appear to speak with some authority,' he said.

'I went through a bad phase myself in my teen years through mixing with the wrong kind of people—' she forbore from mentioning that she had been just fourteen at the time '—so I do have some insight into what's been driving Donata since she came home.' Gina had the bit too firmly between her teeth to consider letting go now. 'She's simply living up to the image she believes everyone has of her. What she needs is a little compassion. Did you never get yourself into unfortunate situations when you were a boy?'

'Nothing of any great note.' There was no telling what Lucius was thinking or feeling. 'You consider me lacking in humanity, then?'

Gina eyed him uncertainly, aware of having rather overstepped the mark as a mere guest in the house. 'I think you're probably finding it a difficult situation to deal with all round,' she said at length, feeling it a bit late to start apologising. 'Your mother, or Ottavia, would surely be better equipped.'

'Not all women are necessarily attuned to others,' came the dry return. 'You are certainly the most outspoken I have met.'

'I never did know when to mind my own business,' she

admitted, going for a lighter note. 'Forget I spoke, will you?'

The strong mouth slanted. 'I would find that difficult indeed. You may tell Donata you succeeded in convincing me of my harshness in refusing her request to attend the Palio.'

'Thank you.' Gina was taken aback by the sudden capitulation. 'I'm sure she'll really appreciate it.'

'I doubt that Cesare will share the feeling.'

'Oh?' She searched the olive features. 'Why not?'

Lucius lifted expressive shoulders. 'Donata has had what I believe is termed a crush on him since she was sixteen. She counted, I think, on this year in Switzerland turning her into the kind of woman he would want for a wife.'

'Cesare knows how she feels?'

'Of course. He used to find it amusing, but not so much now.'

'You should have said.'

'And have you accuse me of putting Cesare's feelings before those of my own sister?' he responded with irony. 'No, he must find it in himself to bear with the situation. Unless, of course, you can make use of this rapport the two of you appear to have formed to persuade her of her foolishness in pursuing a man so many years her senior.'

'I really did jump in with both feet, didn't I?' Gina said wryly. 'I don't imagine anything I could say would change the way she feels.'

'It can do no harm to try.'

Gina regarded him in some doubt. 'You seriously want me to talk to her?'

'It can do no harm,' Lucius repeated. 'She has somehow to be convinced that Cesare will never see her in the way she wants him to see her.'

'She'd have to accept it if he married someone else,' she said. 'Is that likely to be happening in the near future?'

'Not that I am aware of.'

'I suppose, like you, he's looking for an ideal.' Gina kept her tone light. 'I saw a film not so long ago where women were turned into robots programmed to satisfy a man's every desire.'

Amusement sparkled in the dark eyes. 'An on-off switch might have its uses at times, but my needs would be far from satisfied by programmed compliance.'

They were still seated at table. Gina resisted the urge to snatch her hands away as he reached across to take them in his.

'So smooth and lovely!' he murmured.

'I thought we were discussing your sister,' she said, willing herself to reveal no hint of the turbulence his very touch aroused in her. 'I'm no agony aunt, but I'll give it a go.'

Lucius raised a brow. 'Agony aunt?'

'They give advice to people who write in with problems. I imagine magazines over here have them too.' Gina could no longer contain her quivering reaction to the gentle circling of his fingertip in the centre of her palm. 'Don't!' she said huskily.

Lucius complied at once, sitting back in his seat to regard her with a quizzical expression. 'What is it that you fear about me, *cara*? That I may pass on some dread disease?'

'It hadn't even occurred to me.' She could say that in all honesty. She made herself look him in the eye. 'I just don't like being taken for granted, that's all.'

'I take nothing for granted, if by that you mean you believe me convinced of my ability to conquer,' he responded equably. 'I make no secret of the fact that I find you desirable because I see no point in pretending otherwise, but there is little pleasure to be gained from a foregone conclusion. Would you deny your own desires?' he continued when she made no reply. 'Are you telling me that your response to my touch is a figment of my imagination?'

Gina lifted her shoulders, fighting to stay on top of her warring emotions. 'I find you physically attractive, yes. That doesn't necessarily mean I want to jump into the nearest bed with you.'

'It doesn't mean that you *have* to jump into bed with me,' Lucius amended. 'Could it be that you fear being thought a woman of easy virtue if you give way to your urges?'

'Isn't that the way a lot of men still secretly feel about women who do?' she challenged.

'I can speak only for myself. I find nothing wrong with a woman indulging her needs.'

'Even the one you eventually marry?'

'Ah!' The exclamation was soft. 'That would be a different matter.'

'That's sheer hypocrisy!' Gina accused.

'Perhaps,' he returned. 'I make no claim to faultlessness. The mother of my children will have known no other man but me.'

He meant it, she realised. Every word! 'If you're planning on a family, you're leaving it rather late to get started, aren't you?' she said with a tartness that fired a sudden spark in his eyes.

'I doubt that my ability to father a child is much impaired. As to the woman I do take to wife, she will obviously be young enough to bear as many babies as it takes to produce a son who will carry on the name of Carandente.'

'It's all so damned clinical!' Gina could scarcely contain her repugnance. 'I pity whoever you do marry. I really do!'

This time he showed no visible reaction. 'There are many who will envy her the life she will lead. Many who would all too willingly take her place.'

'Fine.' Gina pushed back her chair to get to her feet, the scorn in her voice reflected in her eyes. 'Gives you plenty of choice, then. I'm going to take siesta, if that's all right?'

'But of course,' Lucius said smoothly, having risen to his feet with her. 'Perhaps we may talk again later when you are rested. There are matters we should have clear between us.'

Gina gave a brief nod, unable to trust her voice. She had gone beyond the boundaries again, and this time a little too far for comfort. Lucius might not show it, but she could sense the anger in him at her unequivocal condemnation. Distasteful as she found his attitude, it was hardly her place to revile him for it. He would no doubt be pointing that out to her.

She made it to her room without running into Donata. Kicking off her sandals, she lay down on the bed, welcoming the airflow from above. This was only her second day at the villa, and already she had managed to alienate her host. She couldn't possibly stay on here now. She must find accommodation in town until repairs to her car were completed. No Palio trip for certain.

She hadn't expected to sleep, but she did, waking to the sound of a tentative knock on the door an hour or so later.

'Am I disturbing you?' asked Donata, hovering on the threshold.

The obvious answer was yes, but Gina hadn't the heart to say it. 'I was about to get up anyway,' she said instead, suiting her actions to her words. She pulled a wry face. 'I'm getting into bad habits sleeping in the middle of the day!'

'*Madre* always takes siesta,' rejoined the younger girl. 'She considers it essential for her well-being.'

'A matter of what you're used to, I suppose. Is your mother not at home today?' Gina added casually.

'She went to visit with friends in Umbria. She won't be at home for three more days.' The pause was brief, the anxiety spilling over. 'You asked Lucius about my accompanying you to the Palio?'

Gina hesitated, wondering how best to say what she had to say. 'I did,' she responded. 'But—'

'He said no!' Donata's face set into lines recognisable from the day before, her eyes glittering with resentment. 'I hate him!'

'As a matter of fact, he said yes. You didn't give me chance to finish. It will be just the three of you. I shan't be coming.'

Her fury dying as swiftly as it had arisen, Donata looked flatteringly disappointed. 'But why?'

'Because I've decided to move to Vernici first thing in the morning.'

Disappointment gave way to perplexity. 'But your car won't be ready for several more days at least.'

'I know. I just feel it too much of an imposition to stay here all that time. The car can be delivered straight to the garage in Vernici.'

'Lucius won't allow you to go,' Donata declared with confidence. 'He'll insist that you stay.'

Lucius, Gina reflected drily, would probably be happy to see the back of her. She'd blotted her copybook with a vengeance.

* * *

Dinner was an uncomfortable meal. Lucius treated her with no less courtesy than before, though there was precious little humour in the gaze he rested on her from time to time.

Donata waited until halfway through the meal before announcing Gina's intention of leaving the villa in the morning.

'She feels she is imposing,' she said. 'But she must stay, must she not, Lucius?'

'There can be no question of it,' he returned levelly. 'Vernici has no suitable hotel.'

'My standards aren't that high,' Gina interposed.

'Mine,' he declared, 'are very high. You will please not insult me by refusing to accept my hospitality.'

Gina met his eyes, flushing a little. 'I didn't mean to insult you.'

'Then, the matter is settled.'

Ottavia kept her own counsel, although Gina suspected that she for one would have been more than ready to see her depart. Short of simply walking out on the household, she really had little choice. Lucius might not be feeling too friendly towards her after her diatribe earlier, but his breeding prevailed. Like it or not, she was here for the duration.

Anticipating some eventual move on his part to take her aside for the clarification he had spoken of, she was on tenterhooks for the rest of evening. By the time they retired for the night she had come to the conclusion that he'd decided to let silence speak for itself. One thing did appear clear: there would be no further flirtation on his part. A relief, she told herself.

Morning brought a fresh dilemma. With no way of knowing whether the Palio trip was still on, she was uncertain of how to dress. Her now unbandaged but scabby knee ruled out any short skirts for certain. She settled in the end on the bottom half of a white linen-mix trouser suit, to which she could easily add the jacket if necessary, along with a sleeveless blue top for coolness.

She was just about ready to venture downstairs when Crispina arrived with breakfast. The note she brought with her was short and to the point. Cesare would be here at nine. There was no indication as to whether Lucius would be accompanying the party, but Gina believed it unlikely. Having breakfast sent to her room was probably his way of expressing his lack of desire to see her at all. She considered developing a sudden headache and crying off herself, but that was too much like crawling into a hole.

Convinced by the time she did go down at five minutes to the hour that Lucius would not be around, she was torn between conflicting emotions on finding him waiting with Donata and Cesare in the hall. Like the latter, he was wearing a lightweight suit in a neutral colour, both jacket and shirt collar left open. Two equally devastating males, Gina acknowledged, yet it was only the one who could make her heart beat faster.

Cesare greeted her with an admiration that was more than a little overdone in her estimation.

'Bella!' he exclaimed. *'Sfarzosa!* Your injury?' he added solicitously in English. 'It gives you no pain this morning?'

'None at all,' she assured him. 'It looked a lot worse than it actually was.'

'I thank the heavens that I caused you no greater hurt!'

Gina looked away from him to give Donata a smile, unsurprised to receive a somewhat strained response. Having the man of one's dreams show interest of any kind in another woman was bad enough; having him lay it on as thickly as he'd just done was too much altogether. Donata was, Gina suspected, already beginning to regret last night's eagerness to have her remain.

'Shall we go?' said Lucius crisply.

The car awaiting them out front was an opulent saloon that looked as if it had just been fetched from the showroom.

'Gina must sit up front with Lucius,' declared Donata, and made sure of it by sliding into a rear seat herself.

Looking resigned, Cesare saw Gina into the car while Lucius went round to get behind the wheel, then took his seat at Donata's side.

Gina did her best to relax as Lucius put the vehicle into motion, but it was impossible while the atmosphere between them remained so cool. If she was going to be here for several more days, then steps had to be taken to restore at least a measure of harmony. And it was up to her to make the move.

CHAPTER FOUR

DOMINATED by the sparkling white fantasy of its cathedral, Siena was a maze of narrow streets lined with Gothic mansions. Reaching the Campo to see the throng crushed into the centre where viewing was free of charge, Gina could only be thankful for the shade and relative comfort of their grandstand seats.

She took advantage of the first opportunity that arose to speak with Lucius out of earshot of the other two.

'I owe you an apology for what I said to you yesterday,' she tendered frankly. 'I was out of order.'

Expression enigmatic, he inclined his head. 'You are entitled to an opinion.'

'But not to express it in such a manner.' She made a rueful gesture. 'I really am sorry.'

A reassuring glimmer of humour lit the dark eyes. 'The humility is appreciated. So we are friends again, yes?'

Gina smiled back a little tentatively, wondering how he would react to the news that they possibly shared the same blood-line. 'Friends,' she agreed.

As promised, the day was full of spectacular pageantry, with costumed processions, flag-hurling and drumming. Gina enjoyed that far more than the race itself. A hectic, three-lap circuit with few holds barred, it left several horses and riders with injuries.

There would be another race in August, Lucius advised, with practice races and qualifying heats held between. By then this whole episode would be just a memory, Gina reflected dispiritedly.

Retracing their steps to the place where they had left the car proved no easy task in the milling throngs. Having paused for a moment to watch a puppet show in the belief that the others were at her back, she was surprised and a little perturbed to find herself apparently abandoned when she turned. She pushed on through the crowd in the direction she thought they had been taking, expecting to come on the three of them waiting for her to catch up at any moment.

It was a relief to see Cesare's face through the sea of heads, although he appeared to be approaching from a different direction altogether.

'I came back to find you,' he said on reaching her side. 'Lucius and Donata are waiting up ahead. To where did you vanish?'

'I stopped to look at a sideshow,' Gina admitted. 'I thought you'd all done the same. I was just about to start panicking,' she added with a laugh.

'There is no need now that I am with you,' Cesare assured her. He took her arm. 'We must go this way.'

Totally disorientated, Gina stuck to his side as he forged a passage through the crowds. Hard as she looked, she could catch no glimpse of either of the Carandentes.

'We must be going in the wrong direction!' she exclaimed after several fruitless minutes had elapsed. 'We'll never find them now!'

'We will all of us meet back at the car in due course,' Cesare consoled. 'At the moment you look very much in need of refreshment. A cool drink would be welcome, yes?'

Gina hesitated, torn between the urge to keep on searching, and the thirst she couldn't deny. It was so hot here in the midst of the surging throng, the humidity oppressive. Thirst won the battle. As Cesare had said, they would all meet at the car in due course. Meanwhile, a few minutes respite over a drink was surely going to make little difference.

They were lucky enough to slide into seats just vacated on the terrace of a nearby bar. Gina asked for a lager as the drink most likely to settle the dust in her throat, closing her eyes in near ecstasy as the icy cold liquid slid down.

'That,' she declared, setting her empty glass on the table, 'was pure nectar!'

'You would like another?' asked Cesare.

She shook her head. 'One's quite enough thanks. I'd hate to turn up at the car tipsy.' She eyed his own glass, which was still half full. 'How long do you think it will take us to get to where we left it?'

'It will depend,' he said, 'on whether I can accurately recall the exact street. Did you take note of the name yourself, by any chance?'

Gina shook her head again, this time in some alarm. 'It never occurred to me.'

'Nor to me. My mind was on other matters.' He made a wry gesture. 'I find it difficult to know how to deal with Donata's feelings for me. She is little more than a child!'

Gina hesitated before responding to the unspoken plea. 'In your estimation, perhaps, because you've probably known her all her life, but not in hers.'

'But I am almost twice her age!'

'Some girls go for older men. Especially those who've lacked a father figure, I've read.'

Cesare looked anything but flattered. 'Lucius has been a father to her these past six years since Paulo died.'

'Lucius is her brother. It's a totally different thing.'

'I have given her no cause to think of *me* in such a role!'

'It's only a suggestion,' Gina assured him. 'You don't exactly fit the image, I have to admit.'

A smile lit the handsome features. 'I would hope not indeed!' He viewed her with frank appreciation, gaze travelling from her face down the firm line of her throat to linger for a second or two on the thrust of her breasts. 'Lucius tells me you are half Italian yourself, with a father *you* never knew at all. Shall you continue to search for his family when your car is ready to drive again?'

'It depends how much time I have left,' she said. 'I'm due to start a new job in a couple of weeks.'

'You should stay here in Italy,' he returned caressingly. 'You belong in the sunlight, *cara*.'

Odd, thought Gina, how the same endearment could have such little impact when used by another man. Not that Lucius employed the word in any really meaningful sense either. It was just a term of address that came all too easily to male lips in this part of the world.

'I belong where I'm accustomed to being,' she said on a light note. 'I can't even speak the language.'

'The language of love is universal. We could speak it together, you and I.'

'We could, but we won't.' Gina was taking him no more seriously than his sparkling eyes indicated. 'Are you going to finish your drink?'

He gave a mock sigh. 'You will never know what you miss!'

'What I don't know can't be missed.' She let a moment or two pass while he took another pull at his glass before saying casually, 'How long *have* you known the Carandentes?'

'Since they first came to Tuscany seventeen years ago,' he acknowledged.

Gina felt her heart give a sudden lurch. 'So who owned San Cotone before they arrived?'

'Cotone has been in the family for many generations. As a distant cousin, Paulo was not in the direct line of inheritance, but he was the only one left to carry on the name.'

'What happened to the rest of them?'

'The son who should have been the next in line was killed some years before his father passed on. There was no other issue.' Cesare gave her a quizzical look. 'Lucius is the person to ask about the family history if it interests you.'

Grappling with the implications of what she'd just been told, Gina raised a smile and a shrug. 'Just plain old curiosity. I think it's time we went in search of the car, don't you?'

With the crowds still thick, and lacking a definite location, it took them more than half an hour to find the vehicle, and only then because Gina happened to recognise an ornate building on the corner of the street where they had parked. Donata was already seated inside the car, which was within shade; Lucius greeted the pair of them in mingled relief and annoyance.

'We,' he declared, 'have been waiting here for almost an hour! I was on the verge of calling for assistance in finding the two of you!'

'My fault,' claimed Cesare. 'I forgot to take note of the location. But for Gina's better senses, we could have wandered the streets for ever!'

'Sheer luck,' Gina disclaimed. 'It was my fault we got separated in the first place. I'd have been in real trouble without Cesare. I wouldn't even know how to say "I'm lost" in Italian!'

'A few basic phrases should be simple enough for even

the English to learn,' came the unsympathetic retort. Lucius opened the rear door, indicating that she should get into the car. 'We had best be on our way before the roads from the city become blocked with traffic, as will begin to happen very shortly.'

As was starting to happen already, if the route she and Cesare had just traversed was any example, Gina reflected. She weathered a glowering look from Donata as she slid into the seat at her side. The younger girl had nothing at all to worry about so far as she was concerned, but this was hardly the time or the place to tell her so. It was up to Cesare to put her straight with regard to his feelings—or lack of them. And the sooner the better.

There had been little opportunity up to now to go over the information Cesare had supplied. With Donata in no mood for conversation, she was able to put her mind to it at last. The coincidences were too many for there to be any mistake. The son who had been killed must have been her father. If Paulo Carandente hadn't been in the direct line of inheritance, then the blood connection between her and Lucius was too remote to be of any account.

So what now? she asked herself, thrusting that latter thought aside. If she told the truth she would not only be faced with the problem of explaining the fabrications, which would be difficult enough, but all the questions, the probing—the possible assumption that she was after financial gain. All she'd ever really wanted was to know where her father had come from. Why cause unnecessary disruption?

Cesare took off in his own car almost immediately on reaching the villa, leaving Donata to make what she would of his excuses for not staying longer. Now wasn't the time to try talking to her either, Gina reckoned, as the girl headed indoors without so much as a glance in her direction. Whatever rapport they had developed yesterday was right out of the window at present.

'I think she believes I'm interested in Cesare myself,' she remarked to Lucius as they followed her inside.

'And are you?' he asked.

Gina glanced his way uncertainly. 'Is that meant to be a joke?'

His mouth slanted. 'Why should I joke about such matters? Cesare has many admirers.'

'I don't doubt it,' she said. 'But I'm not one of them. Not in the way you mean, at any rate.'

Suit jacket slung casually over a shoulder, Lucius paused in the hall to view her with a certain cynicism. 'How many ways are there?'

'More than one, for certain,' she returned, not altogether sure where this was going. 'I like Cesare as a person, and he is very good-looking, but he doesn't attract me as a man.'

'But *I* do?'

Gina kept a tight rein on her impulses, lifting her shoulders in a brief shrug. 'In some respects.'

This time his smile was genuine. 'I would be interested to hear what you find disfavourable in me. Apart from the matters we discussed yesterday, that is.'

'Your arrogance, for one thing,' she said with purpose.

'You prefer a man who is unsure of himself?'

'Of himself, no. Of me, yes.'

'You believe me incapable of knowing what you are thinking, what you are feeling?' His voice had softened, his eyes acquiring an expression that set every nerve aquiver. He brought up a hand to trace the tip of a finger down the side of her face and across her lips. 'You feel the same desire I feel for you, *mi tesoro*. The desire we must both of us satisfy before too long.'

'I'm going to get a shower,' she said with what composure she could rally. 'I'd suggest you take a very cold one.'

His laughter followed her as she turned away to mount the stairs. Gina fought to stop herself from looking down on reaching the gallery, though her senses told her he was still standing there. Staying celibate was easy enough when there was no real temptation to do otherwise, but the whole idea of saving herself for Mr Right held little sway right now, she had to admit.

If the day had been long, the evening seemed to stretch to infinity. Donata was subdued, picking at her food with little interest. Nothing anyone could say was going to help, Gina judged. The girl had to come to terms with the unlikelihood of Cesare returning her feelings.

Used to eating no later than seven-thirty at home, unless being taken out to dinner, she found it difficult to accustom herself to a mealtime that not only started when she would normally be long finished, but could last into the small hours if the diners were of a mind. As always, wine flowed freely, with the house Chianti readily available.

'Would it be possible for me to see the vineyards?' she asked over coffee. 'I've never visited one before.'

'By all means,' Lucius said easily. 'I will show you them myself tomorrow.'

Gina met his eyes, unable to penetrate the dark depths. 'Thank you.'

'You will find it all very boring,' Ottavia advised. 'To see one grape is to see them all!'

'Gina will make her own assessment,' her brother responded. 'Perhaps you might like to take a walk around the gardens before we retire for the night?' he added on the same easy note.

Was there just the slightest emphasis on the 'we', Gina wondered, or was she reading too much into too little? She knew a sudden reckless surge. There was only one way to find out.

'I would, yes,' she said.

Lucius got to his feet, the coffee left in his cup ignored. 'Then, we will go now, while the mood is on us.'

Gina rose from the table to join him, keeping her expression under strict control as she sensed Ottavia's gaze. '*Buona sera,*' she murmured.

'*Sera* is evening, *notte* is night,' came the tart reply. 'Enjoy your stroll. The night air will, I am sure, aid restful sleep.'

Gina refused to let the suspected innuendo affect her. So what if Ottavia did have a notion of what was in her mind? Why should she care *what* the woman thought of her? Once she left here she would never see her again.

Lucius neither, came the thought, bringing a momentary despondency before her spirit reasserted itself. Forget next week. Concentrate on now.

The night was warm, the skies cloudless, the stars so much bigger and brighter than they ever appeared back home. Lucius made no immediate attempt to touch her in any fashion, strolling at her side much as he had done the previous morning, hands thrust into trouser pockets.

'There is a difference about you tonight,' he remarked shrewdly after a moment or two. 'Would I be wrong in thinking you ready to acknowledge what lies between us?'

'I decided it was time to start being honest with myself, yes,' she said, fighting the urge to run for safety while she still had the chance.

'You admit that you want me in the same way that I want you.' It was a statement not a question. 'What was it that made this decision for you?'

Gina gave a light shrug. 'I just saw no point in further pretence. After all, we're both adults.'

'True.' There was just the faintest trace of irony in his tone. 'So we waste no more time.'

Blood hammering in her ears as he drew her to him, nerves jumping all over the place, Gina met his lips, every last doubt vanishing at the first spine-tingling contact. The arms he slid about her were already possessive, drawing her close, making her feel his strength, his heat. She clung to him, lips opening to the silky pressure of his tongue, tasting him the way he was tasting her. There was no room for anything else in her mind but what was happening this very minute. She wanted what he wanted. *Everything* he wanted.

'Not here,' he murmured roughly. 'Come.'

They made it to her room without running into anyone, although by that time Gina was past caring.

Aroused though he was, Lucius refused to hurry, kissing her into a state where she hardly knew whether she was standing on her head or her heels before removing a single garment.

Nude, he was magnificent: a bronze statue come to full and vibrant life. Her skin looked almost translucent in contrast. She trembled to the feel of his hands as he slowly traced a passage down over her slender curves, breath catching in her throat when he slid a gentle finger between her thighs to penetrate her most intimate depths. She moved instinctively in rhythm with the motion, the tumult gathering until she could no longer contain it, overcome by wave after wave of overwhelming sensation.

Only then did he lower her onto the bed, supporting

himself on his forearms as he nuzzled her breasts. Gina opened her thighs to accommodate the burgeoning pressure, thrilling to the sheer weight of him, the size of him—moving her body in urgent seeking of even closer encounter.

It took her a moment to realise what was happening when he lifted himself away for a brief period. She hadn't even thought about protection until now, she realised. She forgot about it again almost instantly as he lowered himself back to her. The feeling as he slid inside her was indescribable. Flesh to flesh, spirit to spirit, came the hazy thought before everything merged into one great spinning Catherine wheel.

He was still there when she awoke at first light. For a moment or two she just lay studying his face, committing every wonderful, masculine line to memory. He had taken her to a place no amount of imagination could have painted for her, with little of the half anticipated pain to mar the moment of merging. Not that it wouldn't have been worth any amount of pain.

No regrets, she told herself firmly. And no backsliding on the decision previously made either. There was nothing to be gained from the truth.

She became suddenly aware that Lucius was awake, his eyes fired by the same memories as he looked back at her. His smile was a caress in itself.

'You,' he said softly, 'are a beautiful, warm and passionate woman, *cara mia*!'

'It must be the Italian in me,' she murmured, and saw the embers flare into vibrant life again.

The first time had been wonderful enough, but this surpassed it. If there had been any restraint left in her at all, she shed it in those tumultuous minutes, wrapping slender limbs about him as he came into her once more; loving his power, his passion, his very dominance.

They lay together in drowned repletion for some time afterwards. Gina was the first to stir, albeit with reluctance.

'I have to visit the bathroom,' she whispered.

Lucius kissed the tip of her nose before releasing her. 'I must leave you,' he said with obvious reluctance. 'The sun is already well-risen.'

He sat up as she slid from the bed, watching in some amusement as she pulled on a cotton wrap. 'A little late, I think, for such modesty. You have no secrets from me now.'

She had one, she thought wryly. 'Call it a foible,' she said. 'I'm not used to flaunting myself.'

'There is no shame in showing so beautiful a body. But the choice, of course, is your own.' He threw back the covers and rose to his feet, totally at ease with his own nudity. 'We will go to the winery immediately after breakfast,' he said, reaching for the clothing he had discarded in such haste a few hours ago.

Gina tore her eyes away from him with an effort, and headed for the bathroom. So far as Lucius knew, she had done nothing with him that she hadn't done with other men before him. All this talk about a man being able to tell when it was the first time for a woman was obviously rubbish. True, he'd made sure she was thoroughly aroused—which perhaps many men neglected to do.

The euphoria of a few minutes ago had diminished. While she couldn't bring herself to regret giving herself to him, he had probably set a precedent it was going to be difficult to match. It was also possible that having achieved his aim with so little effort, he would have no interest in pursuing it any further himself.

Expecting him to be gone when she returned to the bedroom to look out something to wear, she was surprised to find him standing fully dressed by the bed. The expression on his face unnerved her.

'Why did you make yourself out to be what you are not?' he asked softly.

For a fleeting moment she thought he was talking about the lie she had told, but he would hardly have waited until now to face her with it if he'd somehow learned the truth. Which left only one thing he could possibly mean.

There was no point in prevarication, but she found herself doing it anyway. 'What are you talking about?'

He stretched a finger to indicate a point on the bed. 'That.'

Gina moved forward reluctantly to view the exposed sheet, biting her lip on seeing the smear of blood. It hadn't occurred to her to even consider the possibility of such evidence appearing. Further denial was obviously useless. Lucius was fully aware of what the stain signified.

'Does it really matter?' she got out. 'I had to lose it sometime.'

'But why now, and to me?'

Gina tried a smile, a hint of irony. 'I hardly need to tell you what you're already well aware of.'

'You found me impossible to resist.'

'That's right.'

Lucius studied her hardily. 'If you waited this long, it can only be because you intended saving yourself for the man you marry.'

'I waited this long,' she said, 'because I never met anyone else who made me want it enough.'

'Or who could perhaps offer you sufficient return?'

Gina pushed a distracted hand through her hair, leaving it standing out in a dark cloud from her head. 'You can't possibly think—'

'I think it possible that our conversation the other afternoon may have led you to believe I would consider an offer of marriage obligatory in the circumstances.'

'That's ridiculous!' She could still scarcely credit the suggestion. 'I'm not looking for marriage with anyone!'

'You would refuse me, then?'

'You can count on it!' She was too furious to care what she said, or how she said it. 'You may consider yourself the catch of the century, but I'd be looking for a great deal more in a husband than *anything* you could offer! If you—'

'I take your word,' he interrupted drily. 'Although I would dispute the *anything*.'

Gina caught herself up, eyeing him in sudden confusion. 'If this is your idea of a joke, it certainly isn't mine!'

'No joke,' he assured her. 'Just a means of discovering the truth.' He paused, his expression difficult to read. 'If you had no thought of entering into a relationship before we met, I assume that you use no form of protection?'

'Does it matter?' she said again. 'You did.'

'A habit to be cultivated in this day and age. But supposing I had neglected to do so. You would have been running the very real risk of becoming pregnant.'

'I assumed you'd be careful,' she lied.

His lips twisted. 'A dangerous assumption indeed.' He seemed about to say something else, then apparently changed his mind. 'We will talk again later,' he declared.

He left her standing there, closing the outer door quietly behind him. 'A means of discovering the truth,' he'd said, but he didn't know the half of it, thought Gina hollowly. She hesitated to think what his reaction might be if he made *that* discovery.

With Ottavia watching for any sign that her suspicions had foundation, breakfast was an ordeal. Not that Lucius appeared to be aware of the interest his sister was taking in the pair of them. Men being men, he probably wouldn't be in the least bit fazed by it anyway, Gina reflected with a cynical edge.

Donata hadn't put in an appearance at all this morning. As no one had commented on her absence, she could only assume that it wasn't an unusual occurrence. She resolved to have a word with the girl at the first opportunity. It might not do any good, but at least she would have tried.

At dinner last night her mind had been on other matters; thinking about it now, she realised that if her father hadn't been killed, none of these people seated at table would have been here, while she herself might well have been. While she regretted never having known her natural father, it was the only thing she did regret. She'd certainly suffered no deprivation.

Contrary to Ottavia's prediction, the visit to the vineyards proved anything but boring. Lucius took her through the whole process from the harvesting of the grapes to the finished product in its distinctively shaped, dark blue bottle. Marcello left him to it.

Gina found the man a difficult character to fathom all round: part of the family, yet aloof from it too. She had tried once or twice to draw him into conversation, but his responses had been so monosyllabic she had given up.

She hadn't called home for several days, she recalled guiltily in the car returning to the villa. While her parents were accustomed to her living her own life in her own flat, they did like to stay in regular contact. So far as they knew, she was touring in Europe with no set itinerary. They would be starting to worry about her by now.

She had already decided that there was no question of

telling her mother about finding the Carandentes. Why rake up a past that for her was over and done with long ago? All she need say was that she'd had an accident with the car and was waiting for repairs to be completed.

Right now, the car was the least of her problems. She stole a glance at the man at her side, wishing she could tell what was really going on behind the impassive profile. There had been little indication of intimacy between them during the past few hours; she suspected he'd come to the conclusion that the affair was best left to die a natural death. He was probably right, but it still left an aching sense of loss.

'You still have to tell me why you pretended to be a woman of experience,' he said unexpectedly, as if sensing something of her thoughts.

'I pretended nothing,' Gina denied, gathering herself. 'You simply took it for granted.'

'You had the opportunity to correct me.'

'It would have made a difference?'

'It would have caused me hesitation, yes. Virginity is a precious commodity, not to be taken lightly. I have robbed your future husband of the gift.'

'I may not get married at all,' Gina replied with careful control. 'If I do, few Englishmen would expect an untouched bride—especially one my age, or more—so you needn't feel guilty about it.'

Lucius was silent for a moment or two. When he spoke again it was in neutral tones. 'So there is no reason why we should not continue to enjoy what we feel for each other?'

Every reason, came the thought, if she was to avoid even deeper involvement. 'None at all,' she heard herself saying regardless. 'You do realise that Ottavia already suspects what's going on?' she added, blotting out the consequences. 'She was watching us like a hawk at breakfast.'

'It concerns you?' he asked.

'I thought it might concern you.'

The sculptured face took on a certain austerity. 'I am not accountable to anyone but myself for my actions. If Ottavia utters one word out of place to you, you will tell me at once.'

If this morning was anything to go by, words were unnecessary, Gina could have told him. Something she was going to have to put up with because it was beyond her to forgo any further contact while she was here.

They had reached the villa. Lucius drew the car to a stop, putting out a hand to detain her when she made an automatic move to open the door.

'There are matters we must discuss,' he said with serious expression. 'First and foremost—'

He broke off as Ottavia emerged from the villa, her face like a thundercloud. She descended the steps to the open-topped car, thrusting the long white envelope she was carrying at Gina, her eyes glittering with anger.

'What kind of trickery is this?' she demanded.

CHAPTER FIVE

GINA found her voice with an effort. 'You had no right to search my things!'

'What is it?' Lucius sounded bewildered. 'Ottavia?'

His sister lapsed into rapid Italian, from which Gina was able only to recognise the words Giovanni and *conjugali*. She didn't dare look at Lucius, sensing his growing confusion.

'I think this would be best discussed indoors,' he said at length, cutting through Ottavia's continuing tirade. He slid from his seat to come round and open Gina's door as she sat in frozen silence, eyes penetrating her defences. 'Come.'

She got out of the car and accompanied him up the steps into the villa, Ottavia following on behind. Lucius made for the library where they had first met, ushering both women through ahead of him, and closing the door.

'First,' he said in English, 'I will see for myself what is contained in the envelope.'

Ottavia handed it over, the look she gave Gina as she did so like a knife stab. 'A fake, of course,' she stated.

'I'm afraid it isn't,' Gina felt moved to retort. 'It's only too real.'

Lucius quelled her with a glance. Extracting the contents of the envelope, he studied first the photograph and then the licence, the muscles about his mouth tautening ominously as he read. Gina was unsurprised by the icy quality of his regard when he finally looked up.

'Who are you?' he demanded.

'Giovanni was my father,' she admitted.

'You told us your father was named Barsini,' Ottavia chimed in. 'Alexander Barsini!'

Gina lifted her shoulders in a helpless little shrug. 'I lied.'

'Why?' Lucius's voice was clipped, his whole demeanour the antithesis of the man she had known to date.

'It just seemed...easier, at the time.'

'Easier?'

'I wasn't sure you were the same Carandentes I was looking for.'

'You could have asked.'

She searched for the words to explain. 'I didn't feel able. I thought you might think I was looking for handouts. Money,' she translated, seeing his brows draw together afresh. 'All I wanted was to know who my father really was.'

'This is all lies!' Ottavia burst out. 'There was never any marriage!'

'Yes, there was!' Gina flashed. 'They fell in love at university. They didn't tell anyone about the wedding because they knew it wouldn't meet with approval—from either side. Giovanni was on his way home to tell his family when he was killed. My mother knew nothing of his background, except that he came from Vernici.'

Ottavia made a repudiative gesture. 'All lies!'

'Why would she make no effort to seek out his family herself?' asked Lucius.

Gina shrugged again. 'Perhaps because she was afraid of some claim being made to the baby she was carrying.'

'The child being yourself.'

'Yes.' She put up a somewhat shaky hand to her hair. 'This, and my mother's word, is the only real proof I have, of course.'

'You were conceived before the marriage took place.'

Her cheeks burned at the assumptive tone of the question. 'No, damn you!'

Lucius held up a staying hand. 'Anger alters nothing. If this licence is valid, you are a Carandente by right, regardless of the circumstances under which the marriage took place.'

'No!' Ottavia looked and sounded outraged. 'There can be no question of it!'

'You don't have to concern yourself,' Gina told her shortly. 'I want nothing from you.'

Lucius made an abrupt movement. 'Your requirements have no bearing on the matter. If you are Giovanni's child, you have more right to be here than we ourselves.'

'No!' Ottavia cried again.

Gina ignored her, her whole attention on Lucius. 'I'm not interested in rights. I told you, all I wanted was to know something about my father.'

The pause was lengthy, the eyes resting on her face, shorn of all expression. 'We will talk again when I have considered what is to be done,' he said.

Further protestations would be a waste of time and effort, Gina judged. For the moment, at any rate. Short of renouncing all claim to San Cotone in her favour, which was hardly likely, there was little enough he could do.

Ottavia burst into furious Italian again, answered by her brother in equally vehement tones. Gina left them to it. Clear of the room, she stood for an indecisive moment or two wondering what to do. With no transport available, she couldn't even ditch the whole problem and head for home. She had to stay and front it out: to somehow convince Lucius that she had no ulterior motives.

With memories of the night before hanging in the air, her bedroom proved no retreat. She had rinsed out the blood stain in the bathroom before going down to breakfast, with the intention of replacing the sheet on the bed when it was dry. It was gone now, the bed remade with fresh linen. Probably a daily happening, Gina thought wryly, wondering what conclusion the person given the task might have reached. One thing was certain: there would be no more nights like the last.

It still needed more than an hour to lunch. Not that food held any great appeal. She didn't give a damn about Ottavia, but she dreaded seeing Lucius again. And Donata. How was she likely to react? It was such a mess, and all her own fault. If only she'd left things alone!

Barely half an hour had passed when Lucius came to find her. He looked, Gina thought, as if weighty decisions had been made.

'We have much to discuss,' he stated.

'There's nothing *to* discuss,' she responded staunchly. 'I'm here under false pretences, and I'm sorry, but the way I feel is genuine enough. So far as I'm concerned, San Cotone is all yours. I want no part of it.'

Lucius eyed her with open scepticism. 'So why did you sleep with me last night?'

'Because I wanted to,' she said. 'Because you made me want to.'

'I was unaware of our relationship then. You were not.'

'We're hardly close relations.' Gina protested weakly. 'From what Cesare told me, we're no more than distant cousins.'

Lucius curled a lip. 'So you drew Cesare into your web too.'

'It wasn't like that. I wasn't sure I even had the right Carandente family until I spoke with him.'

'Which was when exactly?'

'Yesterday, when we were separated in Siena.'

'After which, you decided the time was right to surrender your virginity to me.'

'No!' Gina could see where this was leading. 'Not the way you mean. I felt…attraction towards you the moment we met, but I couldn't let myself give way to it until I was sure we weren't closely related. If Ottavia hadn't taken it on herself to search my room for some reason, you'd none of you ever been any the wiser.'

'You planned to leave the moment your car was ready for use again?'

'Yes.'

'Having spent several irresistible nights in my arms between times.' The scepticism had increased to searing proportions.

Gina passed the tip of her tongue over dry lips, trying to keep a level head. 'Having been there once, I daresay I might have succumbed to temptation again, but I'd still have gone when the time came. If I'd intended otherwise, why keep the photograph and licence concealed? I could hardly count on Ottavia coming across them.'

'How can I be sure of that? How can I be sure of anything where you are concerned?' Face set, eyes like black coals, Lucius wasn't giving an inch. 'Whatever your intentions, you leave me little choice. The obligation now is twofold.'

Gina gazed at him uncertainly. 'Obligation?'

'We must marry.'

Shock held her rigid for a several seconds, her mind blanked of all rational thought. 'That's quite ridiculous!' she managed at length.

'Other than relinquishing title to everything my family has known these past seventeen years, it is the only way I have of restoring honour.'

Gina searched her mind for the words needed to counteract the preposterous proposal, finding nothing of sufficient note. 'You said twofold?' she queried, playing for time to come up with *some*thing.

'A matter of honour once more.'

Blue eyes widened anew as his meaning went home. 'Because of last night? But it was my own choice.'

'It makes no difference. It is *my* duty to make reparation.' He was speaking now with a clipped quietness more telling than any amount of ranting and raving. 'Arrangements will be made immediately.'

'They most certainly will not!' Her voice had gathered strength, spurred by an anger that overwhelmed all other emotions. 'I've absolutely no desire to marry you! To marry anyone, if it comes to that!'

There was no hint of relief in his eyes at the pronouncement; if anything it served to firm their purpose even further. 'You would deny me the means of righting the wrong done to you?'

'You've done no wrong,' Gina insisted. 'This is the twenty-first century, for heaven's sake, not the Middle Ages!'

For all the impression she made she may as well have saved her breath. Lucius was already turning away. 'Arrangements will be made,' he repeated.

This was getting more and more incredible by the minute, thought Gina dazedly as he departed. Four days ago she had arrived in Vernici with just the one thought in mind. Never in a thousand years could she have imagined finding herself in a situation like this. She had a mental image of Ottavia's face when Lucius informed her of his intentions, and knew a sudden insane desire to laugh. Hysteria, she told herself, taking a firmer grip. Hardly surprising in the circumstances.

It wasn't going to happen, of course. She could hardly be forced into a marriage she didn't want. Lucius couldn't possibly want it himself. Not in any way that mattered.

She was still standing there in a daze when the door was flung open without ceremony. Ottavia looked ready to kill.

'You think yourself so clever!' she snapped. 'But I am not so easy to deceive! *You* are no Carandente!'

Much as she might wish at the moment that she had never come near the place, Gina took exception to the accusation. 'If I'm not,' she said with control, 'how would you explain the photograph and marriage licence?'

'You had them forged in the hope of making claim to San Cotone for yourself! It is a simple matter to join two photographs together!'

'And how would I have got hold of a photograph of Giovanni to do that?'

'It is quite possible that your mother and he were at the university at the same time. Possible too that they had a relationship, of which you were the result.' The last comment was on a contemptuous note that brought Gina's blood to near boiling point. 'But no Carandente would marry beneath their class!'

'Including yourself?' The words were out before Gina could stop them—immediately regretted.

Ottavia's olive skin had visibly paled. When she answered it was with venom. 'Marcello's ancestry is no less than my own. How dare you suggest otherwise!'

'How dare *you* come bursting in here accusing me of deception?' Gina retorted, abandoning the apology trembling on her lips. 'Like it or not, the marriage took place. If you don't believe the licence is real, you can have it checked quite easily. Not,' she added with deliberation, 'that your brother appears to doubt it.'

'Lucius is a fool!'

Gina raised a meaningful eyebrow. 'You're prepared to tell him that?'

The older woman looked as if she'd bitten into a bitter lemon. *'Vacca!'* she spat out.

Whatever the word meant, it was far from complimentary, Gina gathered from the tone. She checked the inclination to reply in kind, forcing a conciliatory note instead. 'There's no point in this. Ottavia. I no more want to be here than you want me to be.'

'Then, why come at all?'

Gina sat down on the bed, her legs too shaky to support her any longer. 'I already told you downstairs. I just wanted to trace my father's background. I had no idea of all this. Neither, I'm sure, did my mother.'

'You believe an English university within reach of the lower classes here?'

She had a point, Gina had to admit. The cost alone would have been prohibitive. 'I didn't consider that angle,' she confessed.

Ottavia still looked far from convinced. 'If it was so important to you to know Giovanni's background, then why have you waited so long?'

'I was fifteen before I knew anything at all about it. With school, university and then work, there hasn't been time to think about it before this. I'm between jobs at present, so I decided to take advantage of the break.' Gina spread her hands in a gesture meant to convey her own confusion. 'I never anticipated anything like this happening.'

'Including spending the night with a man you had known only a few days?'

Biting her lip, Gina said hollowly, 'He told you that?'

'That and more.' The antagonism was muted though by no means extinguished. 'My brother is a man to whom family honour is of great importance. To restore it he would make whatever sacrifice he considered necessary. You, he tells me, were a virgin before he unbeknowingly took you. In his view he would have no choice but to offer marriage, even without this other matter.'

'An offer I already turned down on both counts,' Gina stated, hating the thought of Ottavia being privy to the intimate detail, hating Lucius for making free with it. 'If you want to put a stop to it all, you can help me get away.'

Ottavia regarded her narrowly for a lengthy moment or two. When she did finally answer, it was on a rather more amenable note. 'Your own car has yet to be returned. If I drove you to Vernici you would still be without transport.'

'Then, drive me to Siena. If you can discover where my car is being repaired, there's a chance it might be ready.'

'And if it is not?'

'I'll deal with that if and when,' Gina answered with a confidence she was far from feeling. 'Just get me there.'

'If I did, it would have to be at night,' Ottavia said after a brief consideration. 'If we left after everyone is asleep, I could be back in my own bed before morning—able to deny any knowledge of your departure.'

'What about Marcello?' Gina asked.

'Marcello would say whatever was required.' Ottavia's voice had softened just a fraction. 'I believe I may have done you an injustice.'

As apologies went, it left something to be desired, but it was, Gina guessed, all she was going to get. She couldn't really blame the woman for feeling the way she did. She was hardly going to welcome the news that Giovanni Carandente had not after all died without issue.

'Think nothing of it,' she said.

If Ottavia noted any trace of satire, she gave no indication of it. 'That leaves us with the rest of today to get through. We must act naturally, the two of us, so that Lucius has no suspicion.'

Gina gave a brief, wry smile. 'Like enemies, you mean.'

There was no trace of regret in the other eyes. 'It should not be difficult.'

For her, perhaps not, Gina reflected. For herself, it was going to be the most difficult day she had ever spent. She still found it hard to believe it wasn't all some stupid dream she was going to waken from any minute. Except that dreams tended to have little consistency.

'You have fifteen minutes to prepare for lunch,' the other woman advised, glancing at her watch. 'I would suggest a change of clothing. The trousers you have on are stained. Tonight, we will meet at the garage compound. Two o'clock.'

She departed at that, leaving Gina to get stiffly to her feet to view herself in the cheval mirror. Her trousers were indeed stained, although the mark was small enough to go unnoticed by all but the most critical eyes. She exchanged them for a long skirt nevertheless. The grazes on her knee were healing fast but still needed covering. The memory of Lucius pressing his lips to the injury last night brought a painful tightness to her chest. He would take some forgetting for certain.

She turned her mind to the planned escape, forced to acknowledge the flaws. If, as was likely, her car wasn't ready, she could hardly abandon it and fly home, which meant she would have to sit it out in Siena hoping that Lucius would see fit to let the whole affair drop. In either case, she would probably have the repair bill to pay herself, with all the subsequent problems entailed in claiming on insurance, although that was a relatively minor detail in comparison.

* * *

It was three women to the one man at lunch, Marcello not in evidence. She found Donata already in possession of developments. Any ill-feeling over Cesare apparently forgotten for now, the girl seemed to view the whole situation in a totally different light from her sister.

'So you're actually a cousin!' she exclaimed. 'And soon to be a sister too!'

Blue eyes met impassive black ones across the width of the table. 'I'd doubt it,' Gina said levelly.

Donata looked from one to the other in sudden confusion. 'But Lucius told me—'

'It takes two to tango.' The flippancy was deliberative. 'I already said I wasn't interested.'

'Your lack of interest is duly noted,' he responded drily.

Donata looked even more confused. 'I don't understand. Did you not come to claim the inheritance that should have been yours?'

'No.'

'Then...why?'

'Curiosity.' Gina was tired of repeating the same thing over and over. 'It killed the cat.' She took pity on Donata's obvious incomprehension. 'Finding out who my father was seemed important once. I realise now it would have been better to let things alone.'

Lucius made an abrupt gesture. 'Too late for regrets. What must be must be.'

Catching Ottavia's eye, Gina refrained from comment. It was easier for now to let him believe her resigned to the prospect. By this time tomorrow she would be long gone. He might not be willing to acknowledge it, but he could only be relieved to find the onus removed.

She had little appetite for food, beautifully prepared and served though it was. Try as she might, she couldn't close out the memories evoked by every movement of the masculine hands. Last night those same hands had roved her whole body—had discovered her every intimate secret. It was going to be a long time before she could bring herself to make love with any other man.

He left them the moment the meal was over. To do what, he didn't say. Ottavia vanished too. Reluctant to be on her own with her thoughts, Gina was happy to settle for Donata's company on the terrace, even if it did involve answering more questions.

'It will be good to have a sister I can talk with,' declared the girl when her curiosity regarding Gina's life up to now was at last satisfied.

'Even one you believe was making up to Cesare only yesterday?' Gina asked steadily.

'I had reason then to be jealous,' she said. 'Now that you're to be married to Lucius, I have no more.'

Gina hesitated before making the attempt. 'I appreciate how you feel about Cesare, but he's almost twice your age.'

'Older men have so much more to offer than younger ones,' came the unconcerned reply. 'Cesare is not only the most handsome man I know, but the richest too. If I marry him I will be a marchioness.'

'Does everyone in this country have a title?' Gina queried only half in jest.

Donata took the question quite seriously. 'In our society there are few with no claim at all. Lucius is an exception in declining to use his own entitlement. You realise he won't allow you to take title yourself?'

'I wouldn't want to.' Gina could say that with truth.

'*Madre* is going to have such a surprise when she returns!' Donata declared. 'You'll be expected to produce a son to carry on the family name as soon as possible.'

One member of this family she wouldn't have to lie to,

thought Gina thankfully. 'Who is this Livia Marucchi she spoke of the other night?' she asked, surprising herself because she hadn't realised she even remembered the name.

'No one of any importance,' Donata assured her. 'Not now.'

'But Lucius has considered her as a prospective wife?'

'She would be suitable.'

Gina kept her tone casual. 'Is she attractive?'

'She is beautiful, but I have never seen Lucius look at her in the same way that he looks at you. I overheard him telling *Madre* once that he needed more than suitability in a wife. I know now that he meant he wanted someone who could also stir his blood.'

She'd done that all right, thought Gina ruefully. But it was still no basis for marriage.

The day wore on. Lucius was still absent when she went to change for the evening. Emerging from the bathroom some twenty minutes later to find him seated on one of the elegant chairs was a total shock. Motionless in the doorway, only too well aware of the emotions just the mere sight of that patrician face and lean, lithe body aroused, she took refuge in belligerence.

'What the devil do you think you're doing just walking in here?'

He studied her in turn before answering, eyes travelling her slender, shapely length in the short towelling robe all the way up from her bare toes to her flushed cheeks and sparking eyes, his expression unrevealing. 'The arrangements are made,' he said without apology.

'Like hell they are!' Hands clenched, Gina fought the small, treacherous part of her that leapt at the thought. 'There's no way I'm going to marry you!'

'You would betray your father by turning your back on the inheritance that should have been his before you?'

'That's utter rot!' she exclaimed.

'It is a fact,' he stated, still without raising his voice. 'Your mother and stepfather will, of course, be welcome to visit you.'

Gina felt hysteria welling up again. 'Will you get it through your head that it isn't going to happen,' she said through gritted teeth. 'So far as I'm concerned, your honour can go take a running jump!'

'It would be difficult, I think, for an abstract to perform such a feat.'

She made an abrupt gesture. 'There's nothing in the least bit funny about this!'

'I agree,' he said. 'It is a very serious matter.'

The pause was lengthy, the growing purposefulness in his regard increasing Gina's pulse rate by the second. Her heart leapt into her throat when he rose from the chair.

'It seems there is only one way to convince you,' he affirmed.

Gina's first thought as he moved towards her was to step back into the bathroom and close the door in his face. But there was no key, she recalled, no means of locking it at all, in fact.

'Whatever you have in mind, you can forget it!' she flung at him.

He paid no heed. Pulling her into his arms, he quietened her protests with his mouth, his hands sliding the length of her back to draw her up close against him.

Gina felt no sense of violation in the embrace; his hold on her was light enough to allow her to pull away from him again if she wanted to. Only, while her mind was saying one thing, her body was saying quite another, pressing instinctively closer to his heat and hardness. There was no doubting his desire for her—no denying her own for him. Conquering the urge to give way to it called for a strength of mind beyond her to summon right now. Did the whys and wherefores really matter? asked the fading voice of reason.

He lifted her without effort and carried her across to the bed. Gina made one last effort to drag herself out of it as he parted the towelling robe, but the feel of his lips at her breast was too much for her. Her legs parted on their own accord to his gently insistent urging, body arching as he found the tiny bud. All thought of resistance had flown. She wanted, needed, had to have the whole of him again!

The sensation when they came together was even more incredible than before: warm, vibrant velvet wrapped around a steel core. It was only on feeling the final hot rush of his release that she realised why he felt so different, and by then it was too late. Far, far too late!

'You did that purposely,' she whispered when he finally rolled away from her to sit up and adjust his clothing.

'True,' he agreed. 'I saw no other course.'

Gina sat up herself, pulling the robe jerkily around her. 'There's no certainty of pregnancy!'

'The chance alone should be enough,' he said.

She gazed at him in confounded silence for a moment or two, unable to come to terms with the sheer ruthlessness of his action. He met her gaze without a flicker of remorse.

'There are compensations for the loss of freedom for each of us.'

'If you mean, what we just did, I wouldn't let you near me again for a fortune!' she retorted.

A spark momentarily lit the dark eyes. 'I think you might be persuaded.'

He gave her no time to form a reply. Feeling totally at a loss, Gina made no move for several minutes after he'd left the room. Conception wasn't guaranteed, but it was a very real possibility. It would be another couple of weeks before she knew for certain.

One thing *was* certain, she told herself forcefully: whatever the outcome, there could be no marriage. She had planned to leave tonight, and leave she would. If she had to hang around in Siena waiting for her car to be ready, then so be it. Any attempt on Lucius's part to fetch her back would be dealt with by the police.

The question of what she would do if she did turn out to be pregnant she pushed to the back of her mind. There was nothing to be gained from dwelling on things that might not happen.

The others were already gathered in the *salotto* when she eventually geared herself into going down. Lucius poured the gin and lime she asked for and brought it across to where she sat, lifting a sardonic eyebrow in response to the black look she gave him. Little more than half an hour ago they had been together in the most intimate sense. It was hard, Gina thought hollowly, to equate the man who had held her then with the one who faced her now. They were two different people.

She refrained from drawing away when he took a seat at her side, although every instinct in her prompted the action. She could feel his body heat, smell his masculine scent. Casting around for some distraction, she caught Ottavia's meaningful glance, assuming it meant that tonight's venture was still very much on. Lucius would be bound to suspect his sister of having a hand in it, but that was her problem. She had enough to worry about on her own account.

If Donata sensed any untoward atmosphere, she showed no sign of it. Gina was sorry to deceive her—especially after what she had said earlier about having a sister she could talk with. She would need someone to turn to for solace when Cesare finally plucked up the guts to tell her where she stood with him, and she almost certainly wasn't going to get it from Ottavia.

As anticipated, it proved to be one of the longest, most fraught evenings Gina had ever spent. She stood it as long as she reasonably could before pleading tiredness. It was only on taking her leave that the possibility of Lucius planning a further visit to her room tonight occurred to her, although there was nothing in his attitude to suggest that he might have it in mind. Something else to be dealt with if and when, she thought wearily.

She felt safe enough, when no approach had been made by one-thirty, to get dressed again, having packed her suitcase earlier. Silence reigned when she left the bedroom. The suitcase was heavy. She regretted not ditching at least some of its contents; clothes could always be replaced. It was too late now, anyway. She would just have to manage. Once at the car there would be no problem.

There were lights still lit on the stairs and down in the hall, but no tell-tale strips beneath the doors. Glad of the flat pumps she had chosen as the most practical wear, Gina descended as quietly as she could.

Her elbow felt as though it was being pulled out of joint by the time she reached the hall. She set the suitcase down for a moment in order to ease the muscle. All this could have been hers, came the thought as she viewed the superb decor. This, and more. If only…

She stopped herself right there, unwilling to acknowledge the particular if only that had crossed her mind.

Traversing the whole of the ground floor to reach the rear of the house took longer than she had allowed for, escaping via the bolted doors even longer. It was well gone two when she finally reached the compound, to find Ottavia waiting in a fever of impatience.

'I was beginning to think you had changed your mind,' she snapped. She flung open the door of the car she had already brought from the garage. 'We must go at once!'

Gina slung her suitcase in the back, then got into the front passenger seat. It was too late now to change her mind, even if she wanted to. And she didn't want to. Quite definitely she didn't. There was nothing here for her.

The morning light did nothing to enhance the room's bare white walls and sparse furnishings. Rising without reluctance from the bed that had afforded her little sleep, Gina consoled herself with the thought that it was at least clean.

Best that she stay somewhere Lucius would never think of looking for her, Ottavia had said on dropping her at the door of the small backstreet hotel. The name and location of the company handling the car repairs had completed her contribution.

Gina hoped to be heading north before the day was done, but until she could be sure she had to keep the room on. Breakfast could wait. First and foremost she had to check on the car.

Last night's desk clerk had shown a lively curiosity at her late arrival. It was a relief to find him replaced by a woman who called a taxi for her without showing any interest whatsoever.

Ottavia had written the details down, enabling her to simply show the paper to the driver with the minimum of verbal exchange. The repair shop was no backstreet business. Not that Gina would have expected it. She was relieved to find the receptionist in the impressive front office bilingual.

'My car is here for repair,' she advised. 'I'd like to know if it's ready yet, please.'

Armed with the registration number, the man brought up the details on computer screen, a frown creasing his brow as he studied them.

'There must be a mistake. This vehicle is to be returned to the Villa San Cotone when repairs are completed.'

'I'm staying there,' Gina said quickly. 'I thought I'd just check on it while I was in town.'

The frown gave way to apology as he once more scanned the screen. 'I'm afraid the work is not yet complete. A difficulty in obtaining a part.'

'How much longer might it take?' she asked, doing her best to mask the disappointment.

'If the part arrives today, the car will be ready tomorrow.'

If the part arrived today. Gina conquered the urge to demand some better assurance, doubting if it would do any good to get stroppy. Considering what she'd said about taking the chance while she was in town, it might look a little odd if she called in again tomorrow, but it was all she could do.

She spent the whole day exploring parts of the city not already seen, returning to the hotel to spend another night tossing and turning. By morning she was almost ready to abandon the car altogether rather than spend any more time hanging around.

She couldn't, of course. Cars didn't grow on trees. If it still wasn't ready, the best she could do was find somewhere a little more upmarket to stay until it was.

The hotel had neither lift nor porter to help with the transportation of luggage, but it was at least a little easier carrying her suitcase down three flights of stairs than it had been lugging it up. This was the very last time, she vowed, that she travelled with anything but a capsule wardrobe. Her arm sockets were never going to be the same again.

She reached the shabby lobby at last, with a sigh of relief. The same sullen woman who had been on duty yesterday watched without batting an eyelid as she dragged the case across to the desk.

'I'd like to check out please,' she said.

'Non capisco,' declared the receptionist without expression.

Gina gazed at her in rapidly mounting impatience. It had to be obvious to anyone but a total moron that she would hardly be touting a heavy bag all the way down here for any other purpose but to leave.

'Terminare,' she tried, reminding herself that she was the foreigner here. *'Quanto costa?'*

'Adesso!' ordered a crisp voice.

The woman went without haste to leaf through one of the card files on the desk, leaving Gina to turn and face the man at her back.

'How did you find me?' It was all she could think of to say.

Lucius regarded her dispassionately. 'Ottavia was persuaded to tell me where you were.'

'A few minutes more and I wouldn't have been.'

'So it appears. Fortunate then that I arrived when I did.'

He reached past her to take the slip from the woman behind the desk and give it a cursory glance. Gina made a small sound of protest as he took a billfold from an inner pocket of his jacket and extracted a clutch of notes, but he ignored her, tossing them down on the desk and bending to swing the suitcase up without effort.

'I have a car outside,' he said.

Gina had little choice but to go with him—for the moment, at any rate. The open-topped Lancia had already created a jam in the narrow, one-way street. Lucius turned a deaf ear to the irate shouts from those unable to proceed, slinging the suitcase in the boot and making sure Gina was secure in her seat before going round to get behind the wheel.

'I'm not coming back to San Cotone with you,' she stated as he put the vehicle into motion.

'How do you intend stopping me from taking you there?' he asked.

A good question, she acknowledged wryly. Jumping from a moving car was not to be recommended.

'You don't really want this,' she appealed. 'You can't possibly want it!'

'Do not,' he returned, 'tell me what I do or do not want. I make my own decisions.'

'A very bad one in this case.'

'The only one open to me.'

'But not to me.' Gina was doing her best to stay on top of her emotions. 'As I already told you, I want nothing from you.'

Expression unyielding, he said, 'You may have no choice in the matter.'

He meant the possibility of her being pregnant, Gina surmised. 'A chance I'm prepared to take,' she claimed with a great deal more certainty than she actually felt.

Lucius concentrated on extracting the car from a three-lane confluence before answering, 'You consider it no more than a chance?'

'No slur on your virility, but yes.'

The taunt made no visible impression. 'And if that chance became reality?'

She swallowed on the sudden lump in her throat. 'I'd deal with it.'

'In what manner?' His tone had sharpened.

She took his meaning immediately, with no need to consider her reply. 'It certainly wouldn't be abortion!'

'So you would bring up the child alone.'

'I wouldn't be alone. I'd have—' She broke off abruptly, shaking her head. 'There's no point in thinking about something that might not even happen! That definitely *wouldn't* be happening if you hadn't...done what you did!'

'As you yourself were unprotected the first time, it may still have happened,' came the brusque reply. 'There is no such thing as a hundred per cent guarantee.'

There was a pause while he negotiated a busy junction. When he spoke again it was on a moderated note. 'I make no excuses for my actions. It was wrong of me. I have no right to stop you from leaving, if that is what you wish, but you must promise me one thing.'

Gina swallowed again on the same lump. 'What?'

'That if there is to be a child, you will allow me to take responsibility for the welfare.' He winged a swift glance when she failed to reply right away, mouth tautening anew. 'On this I *must* insist.'

'All right.' It was the only reply she could make in the circumstances. Eyes fixed on the traffic ahead, she added tonelessly, 'So where now?'

'We go to pick up your car,' he said. 'The readiness was confirmed to me late yesterday afternoon. You can be on your way home before noon.'

Gina felt her chest constrict. 'You intended that all along?' she got out.

'Only if you made it quite clear to me that you have no interest in becoming my wife, whatever the incentive.' His tone was as flat as hers. 'My conscience must, it seems, remain unappeased.'

'You don't have anything to feel guilty about,' she reiterated. 'If I'd left well alone, you'd never have known about me.'

'But you did come, and I do know. And I must learn to live with the knowledge that San Cotone is mine only by default.'

Gina had no reply to that. None, at any rate, that would help him come to terms with the situation. She should be feeling relieved that he'd seen sense regarding the marriage idea, but all she did feel was despondency.

Washed and gleaming, the Fiat looked fresh from the showroom. Lucius hoisted Gina's suitcase into the boot, and locked it, handing over the keys without further delay.

'You have your route planned?' he asked.

'I'll just reverse the one I took coming down.' She hesitated, searching the incisive features, reluctant now that the moment was here to make the final move. 'I'm really sorry for putting you in this position.'

The dark eyes concealed whatever thoughts were going on behind them. 'I am the one who should apologise for attempting to force you into a union that would benefit only myself. Just remember your promise.'

She murmured some assurance, unwilling to acknowledge the possibility that she might be called upon to keep her word. With no more reason to linger, she got into the car and started the engine, taking a moment to fasten her seat belt before releasing the handbrake. The last glimpse she had of Lucius was through the driving mirror as she turned out onto the road: an image that was to stay with her throughout the long journey home.

CHAPTER SIX

COMING three days after starting her new job, the evidence that she wasn't pregnant should have proved a source of relief not despondency. Gina contemplated putting Lucius's mind at rest on that front at least, but shrank from making contact again.

The one visit she had paid home since her return from the European trip had been difficult. Her parents had naturally wanted to hear all about it. If she had turned out to be pregnant they would have had to know the truth, of course, but with that particular pressure removed there was no need for them to know anything.

She left it till the end of the month before making another trip, travelling up on the Friday evening in order to have a lengthier stay. Her mother's greeting was unusually subdued.

'I suppose you have to know sometime,' she said. 'Hayes and Harlow have cancelled their contract.' She made a wry gesture. 'Turning over the whole production line to one company was a big mistake.'

With Redman's not the only one to make it, Gina reflected. Not that knowing it was any solace. She had entertained doubts herself over the contract set up five years ago, but hadn't felt qualified at the time to express them. Now her worst fears had been realised.

'What's the outlook?' she asked, already knowing the answer.

'Bankruptcy, if substantial new orders aren't forthcoming inside the next month or so,' Beth confirmed. 'John borrowed to the limit again to renew the machinery last year. The bank will foreclose if he can't prove his viability. We could lose the house too.'

Gina let out her breath on a faint sigh. It was worse even than she had imagined. 'Where's Dad now?'

'In the study, trying to make the figures add up differently. He's spent the whole week looking for new business. Without very much success, I'm afraid.'

Not really to be wondered at after five years, Gina thought. Even if orders could be gleaned it wouldn't help the immediate problems. What was needed was an injection of capital to keep things going until the company was in profit again—fortune allowing.

Only how? She could probably manage to scrape ten thousand or so together, but it was going to take a great deal more than that.

'Is it all right if I go in to him?' she asked, shying away from the thought that sneaked into mind.

'He'll welcome the interruption,' her mother assured her. 'He's very depressed, although he tries hard not to show it.'

Gina didn't wonder. It would be very hard to be anything else but depressed over a situation like this one.

She left her mother in the sitting room, and went through to the front of the house where the study was. Compared to San Cotone, a four-bed detached set in a bare acre was no big deal, but she had spent an idyllic childhood here, and still regarded it as home.

San Cotone. She closed her mind to the images—and to the suggestion still hovering. There had to be some other way!

Her tap on the door elicited no response. She opened it to find her father seated at his paper-strewn desk under the window with his head in his hands and a look of defeat about his bowed shoulders.

'Hallo, sweetheart!' he said, making a visible effort to lift his mood along with his head. 'When did you get in?'

'About twenty minutes ago,' Gina confirmed. 'You didn't hear the car?'

'I didn't notice. How are things with you?'

'Fine.' She went on impulse to slide her arms about his neck and press a kiss to the bald spot developing at his crown. 'Mom told me about H. and H. I'm so sorry.'

'My own fault for putting my faith in long-term assurances,' he said. 'I'm just sorry that your mother has to suffer the consequences too. It will break her heart to lose the house. She's put so much into it over the years.'

'Will it really come to that?' Gina asked.

'Unless a miracle happens, very probably. I've managed to secure a couple of one-off orders, but it takes time to build up a reliable customer list again, and time is in pretty short supply. I'll have to start laying people off, which means I'm not going to be in a position to accept substantial work if and when it becomes available.' He broke off, shaking his head in self-recrimination. 'I shouldn't be burdening you with it all!'

'Who else but family?' She paused, unable this time to turn a deaf ear to the inner voice. 'I might be able to provide some time.'

Her father gave a faint smile. 'It's a nice offer, darling, only the amount I'd need to have any chance at all of sticking it out would be more than you could possibly hope to raise.'

'I'm not talking about raising a loan,' she said. 'It would be more of an investment.'

His brow puckered. 'Just who do you think would be

prepared to invest in a company that's so close to going to the wall?'

'Someone I recently met might.' Gina straightened purposefully. 'I'll need to make a phone call. In private, if you don't mind.'

John Redman made no protest as she left the room. She went upstairs to use the extension in the master bedroom. It would be around ten-thirty Italian time, which would probably mean dragging Lucius away from the dinner table, but it had to be now, before she had time to think too deeply about it.

It took the international operator several minutes to make the connection. Guido answered, his voice instantly recognisable.

'It's Signorina Redman,' Gina said slowly and clearly. 'I want to speak with Signor Carandente. *Urgente*,' she tagged on.

Whatever the man's thoughts, he made no protest. Gina drew an unsteady breath when the familiar, sensual voice came on the line bare moments later.

'Gina? Where are you?'

'At my parents' home.' She hurried on before he could comment. 'I'm in need of help.'

There was a pause before he answered. 'Of what kind?'

'Money.' She made the statement deliberately bald. 'What else?'

'What else indeed?' His tone had hardened. 'For what reason do you need money?'

'Not what you're thinking,' she denied. 'My father's business is under threat of bankruptcy. Given a little time he can bring it round—' she hoped that was true '—but he doesn't have the capital available to see him through. I thought you might care to make an investment on the strength of our…relationship.'

The pause this time was even lengthier. 'And the sum in question?' he said at last.

'I'm not sure,' she confessed, having focused only on the actual request up to now. 'You'd have to speak to my father about that.'

'He knows you are making this call?'

'No. As a matter of fact, he doesn't even know you exist yet. Neither does my mother. I only found out about this whole mess half an hour or so ago. If you're going to say no,' she burst out, 'just say it!'

'My answer will very much depend on the return offered,' he said. 'I think it a subject best discussed in person. I can be with you by tomorrow afternoon. That will give you a whole night and morning to explain to your parents who exactly I am.'

So what had she expected? Gina asked herself hollowly: that he'd simply write out a cheque and post it to her? The last thing she wanted was to see him again, but she didn't have a great deal of choice if she was to secure the rescue package her father so desperately needed.

'I suppose,' she said, 'I'd better tell you where to come.'

'No need,' came the smooth return. 'I had both you and your family traced.'

'How?' she asked blankly.

'The information you gave me when you were here was sufficient. I had no trust in your promise.' He paused briefly. 'You must know by now.'

'I'm not pregnant,' she said.

The silence was weighty. 'Until tomorrow, then,' he said at length.

Gina replaced the receiver, wondering whether it was relief or disappointment she had sensed in his voice. His failure would probably weigh heaviest with him, she decided with irony. Men took such pride in their virility.

She had the task now of explaining things to her parents. Of the two of them, it was going to come as the greatest shock to her father, who wasn't even aware that she knew about Giovanni Carandente.

It seemed best to put her mother in the picture first. She found her in the kitchen, making coffee. Beth listened in stunned silence to the carefully edited story.

'I never realised quite how deeply you felt about it all,' she confessed ruefully. 'I knew Giovanni came from a good background, but he never said very much about his home life.' She paused, her brow puckering as she went over the detail in her mind again. 'What I can't understand is what interest this Lucius could possibly have in John's business problems.'

'He feels he owes me for what should by rights be mine.' That much Gina could say with truth.

'Which very likely would have been yours if I'd had the courage to go and find his family myself.'

'And robbed us both of the life we've had here with Dad. I wouldn't exchange that for *any* fortune!'

'Bless you,' Beth responded gratefully. She shook her head. 'It's still hard to take in. Lucius Carandente sounds a very upright and principled man.'

Gina wondered if she would say the same of the man who had made purposely unprotected love to her.

'He'll be relieved to unload some of the burden,' she said. 'I'm only sorry that Dad has to know where the money's coming from.'

Beth sighed. 'I shouldn't have asked you to keep it from him that you knew about Giovanni in the first place. He'll be reluctant to accept help from such a source, but he can hardly afford to turn it down.' She made a decisive movement. 'I'll tell him the story myself if you don't mind.'

Gina didn't mind at all. It had been difficult enough

telling it the once. The bits she had left out weighed heavily on her mind, but at least she didn't have pregnancy to add to the score.

Lucius arrived as promised the following afternoon, in a car hired from the airport. Opening the door to him, Gina composed her features into what she hoped was an inscrutable expression, the tightness in her chest increasing painfully on sight of the arresting face. He was wearing a superbly tailored suit in mid blue, with a darker toned shirt and tie, the whole effect stunning.

'Good journey?' she asked huskily.

'As to be expected,' he said. He dropped the suitcase he was carrying on the floor next to the umbrella stand, studying her narrowly. 'You look drained. Were you telling me the truth last night?'

'Yes,' she confirmed. 'My parents are waiting to meet you in the drawing room, but perhaps you'd like to go up to your room first?'

The expression that flickered across the dark eyes was come and gone too swiftly for analysis. He shook his head. 'I see no reason to delay matters.'

Gina had expected no less. He wouldn't want to be here any longer than absolutely necessary. She paused with her hand on the doorknob to say levelly, 'You realise, of course, that there'll be little chance of capital repayment? The best Dad could offer is a partnership.'

The lean features acquired a sudden austerity. 'There will be no question of either. Whatever sum I invest, it can only be a small part of your entitlement.'

Both Beth and John Redman came to their feet as they entered the room, the former advancing with a somewhat strained smile.

'It's so good of you to come all this way, Signor Carandente.'

'The very least I could do,' he assured her. He took the hand she offered in greeting and raised it briefly to his lips, his own smile as he lowered it again totally at ease. 'Please call me Lucius.'

From her expression, her mother was as bowled over by him as she herself had been on first acquaintance, Gina thought. Shades of Giovanni, perhaps.

John Redman had also come forward, his reticence apparent from the tension in his jaw line. 'It's been shock on shock this last couple of days,' he said. 'I hope you'll forgive me if I seem a bit dazed by it all.'

'I understand your feelings,' Lucius assured him, shaking hands. 'I felt the same sense of shock on first discovering the truth. Gina tells me you have business problems. Perhaps we might discuss them together.'

Meaning in private, Gina assumed. She opened her mouth to dispute the idea, closing it again on catching her mother's eye. She was right, of course. This was between the two men now.

'Have you had lunch?' she asked.

'On the flight,' Lucius confirmed. 'But I would welcome a coffee while your father and I talk.'

'I'll bring it through,' she said. 'Dad?'

'I'll have the same, please.' He was obviously finding it difficult to adjust to the younger man's direct approach. 'If you'd like to come to the study, I can show you the books.'

Lucius inclined his head. 'That would be a good start.'

Gina looked at him sharply, but there was nothing in his expression to suggest sarcasm. He wouldn't stoop that low, anyway, she assured herself. He was here to right what he considered a wrong in any way that he could.

She gave her mother a faint smile as the two men left the room. 'And that, as they say, is that! Or it will be by the time he's finished. I'll go make the coffee.'

They were already well into it when she took the tray through some ten minutes later. Neither man paid her more than a passing attention, leaving her feeling distinctly miffed. She, after all, was the catalyst in all this.

It was well over an hour before they emerged from the study. Her father, Gina thought, looked considerably better than he had earlier, if not altogether his usual self.

'Everything okay?' she asked.

Lucius answered for them both. 'It will be. If you would show me where I am to sleep, I would like to change into something a little more casual.'

'Of course,' she said.

She made an attempt to pick up his suitcase from the hall, to find it taken firmly from her hand. 'I will do my own carrying,' he declared. 'Just lead the way.'

Gina did so, vibrantly conscious of his presence at her back as they mounted the stairs. So far he had shown no inclination to touch her in any fashion at all. Hopefully, he would continue to observe the same rule.

She was lying through her teeth, and she knew it. She *ached* for him to touch her! Had done since the moment she'd laid eyes on him again. And not just touch either. She wanted him the way she had always wanted him.

The guest bedroom was next door to the one still regarded as hers. 'No *en suite* bathroom, I'm afraid,' she said with forced lightness, pausing in the doorway as Lucius moved forward to swing his suitcase up onto the blanket chest at the foot of the double bed. 'It's right opposite though, and there is a shower, if you want one.'

'I am sure I shall be very comfortable.' He looked back

to where she stood, raising an ironic eyebrow. 'You fear my actions?'

Not so much his as her own, she could have told him. 'Not in the least,' she denied. 'I just want to say how much I appreciate what you're doing. If there had been any other way...'

'You would have taken it.' The pause was brief, his expression resolute. 'There is a condition attached.'

Gina gazed at him in slowly dawning realisation, heart beginning an irregular tattoo against her ribcage. 'You're saying you'll only advance the money to my father if I agree to marry you?'

There was no element of apology in his regard. 'Exactly that. It is the only course I have left to me.'

'You're putting me in an impossible position!' she protested thickly.

'You would prefer to see your father made insolvent?' He gave her no time to answer, jaw firming afresh. 'Nothing you can say or do will change my mind this time. I will know no peace until your rights are restored.'

He meant it, she knew. Throat constricting, Gina closed the door on him, leaning against the jamb for a moment to try and calm herself down. None of this would be happening, she thought wretchedly, if she'd left well alone to start with!

Except that there'd be no rescue package for Redman's at all if she had, of course. If nothing else, she could be thankful for that.

She found her mother in the kitchen preparing a special dinner in celebration.

'We have a lot to be thankful for,' Beth acknowledged. 'Although John is still having trouble coming to terms. Talk to him, will you?'

No amount of talking could alter the fact that he was

having to rely on a member of her real father's family for aid, Gina reflected, but she kept the thought to herself. There was a whole lot she was keeping to herself. For as long as she could, at any rate.

The guest room door was closed when she went up for a shower and change of clothing, with no sound of movement from within. She wondered if Lucius had seen fit to inform his family of his renewed intentions. Their reactions if he had were fairly predictable. While Donata might be willing to accept it, Ottavia certainly wouldn't. Neither could his mother be expected to look on the union with any favour.

The whole thing was impossible, she thought desperately. One way or another, Lucius had to be made to see sense!

In her own room, she undressed and put on a cotton wrap, laying out clean underwear and a blue silk tunic in readiness for her return. There was still no sound from Lucius when she got to the bathroom. She flicked the catch on the door handle before sliding out of the wrap and starting the water running in the cabinet.

Soothed by the warm flow, she lingered longer than usual. The shock when Lucius opened the cabinet door and stepped inside with her rendered her speechless for several vital seconds.

He wasted no breath on words himself, turning off the water and sliding a hand beneath the dripping black mass of her hair to draw her to him. Her protest died beneath the pressure of his lips, her response instantaneous and uncontrollable. She tremored at the feel of him, nipples peaking as they rubbed against his chest hair, thighs parting to the lordly demand—no thought in mind other than the breathtaking sensation when he lifted her to receive him.

She stood with eyes closed when he finally set her down again, trying to regain control of herself.

'The door was locked,' she got out. 'How—?'

'The door was not locked,' Lucius denied softly. 'Although it is now. I came to take a shower myself, not realising you were already here.'

'You could have left again.'

'I could,' he agreed. 'But the flesh was weak. As was your own.'

She opened her eyes to view the water-beaded face, her body reacting even now to his closeness. 'Don't do it,' she pleaded. 'Don't force me into marrying you!'

'I have no choice,' he said. 'There is no other way.'

He stepped from the cubicle, unself-conscious in his nudity as he seized a towel and held it up for her, expression relentless. 'You have had your shower. I still need mine.'

Gina took the towel from him and wrapped it about herself before stepping from the cubicle. He took her place, closing the door between them before turning on the water flow again, body clearly outlined through the glass.

The short silk robe tossed carelessly on the floor was mute testimony to his claim, but she didn't believe for a moment that what had just happened between them was any spur-of-the-moment idea. His failure to impregnate her struck right at the heart of his manhood. Other matters apart, he would know no rest until he proved himself.

He was still showering when she left the bathroom, having made certain that neither of her parents were in the vicinity first. If she couldn't convince Lucius to abandon his stance they were in for another shock anyway, but she would hate them to know just how far things had already gone.

Beth had prepared a meal fit for a king, though Gina scarcely tasted any of it. Dressed casually now in trousers and light cotton sweater, Lucius appeared completely at ease with himself. When he made the announcement over coffee it took her every ounce of self-control she possessed to conceal her reactions.

John Redman was the first to recover his power of speech. 'Isn't this a little sudden?' he said with admirable restraint. 'You barely know one another!'

'It is not without precedent,' Lucius answered smoothly. 'History often repeats itself.'

The intimation was lost on neither one of the older couple. Seeing the expression that flickered across her mother's face, Gina could have choked at the cause of it.

'Why didn't you tell us about this yesterday?' asked her father. 'You gave no indication.'

'It hardly seemed the right time,' she prevaricated. 'You had too much on your mind already.'

'Matters which will be taken care of tomorrow,' said Lucius.

There was discomfiture in the older man's response. 'Grateful as I am for what you're doing, I can't pretend to be happy about it.'

'Your daughter is *my* only concern,' Lucius returned. 'San Cotone is where she belongs.'

'Just how soon are you planning on making the wedding?' asked Beth with constraint. 'It isn't something that can be arranged overnight.'

'We would prefer an informal ceremony,' Lucius answered, once again before Gina could speak—had she had a reply ready anyway. 'And as soon as is possible.'

'What about your family? They'll surely want to attend?'

This time Gina got in first. 'I'd doubt it. We don't have their approval.'

'That applies only to my elder sister,' Lucius advised calmly. 'My mother and younger sister are very much in approval. My mother unfortunately broke a bone in her foot, so she would find it difficult to travel. And Donata would be reluctant to come alone.'

Like hell she would! Gina thought. What he meant was she wouldn't be offered the chance.

'I'm sorry to hear about your mother's accident,' she said, not believing a word of it. 'How did it happen?'

'She fell getting out of the car on her return from Umbria,' he answered without batting an eyelid. 'She has it in a plaster cast.'

'Poor Cornelia!' Gina laid on the sympathy with a ladle. 'She must hate being incapacitated!'

There was a growing spark in the dark eyes, but his tone remained easy. 'Very much so.' He glanced over to the window where the evening sun slanted through. 'Perhaps we might take a walk in the garden while the light lasts?'

'Yes, do,' Beth urged, obviously desperate for breathing space. 'It's at its best right now.'

Hardly to be compared with what he was used to, Gina reflected, but that wasn't the point of the exercise.

It was pleasantly warm outside, the flower beds aglow with colour, the lawns immaculate as always.

'This all your stepfather's work?' Lucius asked.

'His and my mother's,' Gina confirmed. 'I never think of him as my stepfather,' she added. 'He gave me his name.'

'Soon to be exchanged for the one to which you were always entitled.'

She slanted a glance at the hard-edged profile outlined

against the setting sun, unable to deny the stirring deep inside her at the thought of being married to this man. A bare month ago she hadn't even known of his existence.

'There's still time to change your mind,' she said.

He turned his head to look at her, expression difficult to decipher. 'I already told you, I have no intention of changing my mind. Tomorrow, after your father's affairs are dealt with, we make the arrangements.'

'Is it really necessary to do it in such a hurry?'

'In the possible circumstances, yes.' Lucius shook his head as she started to speak. 'Whether or not, it makes no difference.'

'It does to me.' Gina made every effort to keep her tone level. 'I have a job for one thing. I can't just walk out on it.'

The shrug was eloquent. 'The matter will be taken care of.'

'There's a limit to the things money can buy!' she flashed, losing what tenuous control she still possessed. 'There are women, I'm sure, who would think a loveless marriage was no big deal in such circumstances, but I'm not one of them!'

Something flickered deep down in the dark eyes. 'We are hardly indifferent towards each other.'

'I'm not talking about sex! You could get that anywhere. We both could.'

This time there was no mistaking the expression in his eyes. 'There will be no other man in your life,' he stated brusquely. 'I will make sure of that!'

Gina lifted her chin. 'And no other woman in yours?'

'Of course.'

She didn't believe him for a moment. He might desire her now but, with nothing else to sustain it, the appetite would wither. The same, she imagined, for herself—eventually.

'It's impossible!' she burst out desperately. 'Please, Lucius, don't carry this through!'

'I have no choice,' he repeated. 'We neither of us have a choice. As to sex not being enough...' his lips slanted with slow sensuality '...then we must make it so.'

'Not here,' Gina whispered as he drew her to him. 'It isn't even dark yet!'

He stilled her protests with a kiss so passionate it blotted out everything but the feel of it. He slid his hands into the thickness of her hair to caress the tender skin behind her ears with his fingertips, starting a burn that spread rapidly throughout her body. Gina moved instinctively closer to him, the need to be closer still overwhelming in its force. The desolation when he put her suddenly and firmly away from him was almost too much to bear.

'Is love really so vital to you?' he asked softly. 'Can you not be content with what I make you feel?'

Contentment was the last thing she felt at the moment, she could have told him, fighting to contain the emotions coursing through her. He had her hog-tied in every direction.

'It seems I have to be,' she got out.

'There will be other compensations,' he said.

He meant motherhood, Gina surmised. She felt a sudden, spreading warmth at the thought. Marriage and children might not be every woman's ultimate aim in life, but it held infinitely more appeal for her than the career she had been pursuing so half-heartedly these last years, she had to admit.

'I suppose I owe it to Giovanni,' she murmured, giving way to the growing urge, and saw the unreadable expression flicker once more in his eyes.

'I also.' For a brief moment as he studied her he seemed about to say something else, then he made an abrupt movement. 'It grows cool. We should return to the house.'

By English standards it was a balmy evening, but the temperature was a whole lot lower than it would be in Tuscany right now, Gina knew. She would be a liar if she tried to pretend that the idea of living in such surroundings had no bearing. If only…

She cut the thought off before it could come to fruition.

It was a fraught evening all round, although the older couple did their best to put a good face on things. Most of all, Gina regretted the deception being practised on them, but knew her father would rather the business went down than allow her to marry Lucius against her will. Which it wasn't anyway. Not any more.

All the same, it took everything she had to restrain herself when Lucius suggested they visit the register office to make the necessary arrangements first thing on Monday.

'I have business in Rome on the seventh,' he said. 'We can continue from there to wherever you would like to spend the following days.'

Gina eyed him uncertainly. 'You mean a honeymoon?'

'Of course.' His smile was devoid of mockery. 'All newlyweds have need of a little time alone together.'

'The seventh is little more than a week away,' Beth pointed out. 'Isn't that rushing things a bit too much?'

Lucius turned the smile her way. 'Had it not been for Gina's insistence on returning to England to break the news to you in person, the wedding would have taken place three weeks ago—with your attendance, of course. Now that I am here myself, there seems no further reason to delay.'

'There's your job,' John Redman appealed to Gina. 'You can't just up and leave!'

'If some financial adjustment has to be made, it will be done,' Lucius answered before she could respond.

'But what about your career?' the older man insisted. 'The work you put in to get where you are? Are you going to throw all that away?'

Gina conjured a smile of her own. 'A career isn't everything, Dad.'

He made a resigned gesture. 'If that's the way you see it, there's nothing more to say.'

'Just so long as you're happy,' said Beth.

'I am.' Gina could only hope she sounded confident of it. She caught Lucius's eye, wishing she could tell what was really going on in that arrogant dark head of his. 'We both are.'

'Very much so,' he agreed. 'Your daughter will want for nothing, I assure you. I will take the greatest care of her always. As soon as you have your business affairs under control, you must come and visit with us.'

The thought must have crossed Beth's mind that, had Giovanni not been killed, San Cotone could well have been her own home, but her response gave no hint of it. 'We'll look forward to that.'

She stirred herself, looking at Gina with obvious intent. 'Come and help me with coffee.'

'If all this was arranged while you were over there, why didn't you tell us as soon as you got back?' she asked when the two of them were alone together.

Gina made a wry face. 'It was difficult to find a way. Especially when I hadn't even told you I was planning to look the Carandentes up in the first place. I was going to come clean about the whole thing this weekend anyway. It just worked out a little differently.'

'It's all happened so fast!' her mother exclaimed. 'You can't have known Lucius more than a few days!'

'How long did it take you to know how you felt about Giovanni?' Gina asked softly.

It was Beth's turn to pull a wry face. 'Point taken. I was head over heels on first sight of him. He was very much like Lucius,' she added reminiscently. 'Not all that much in looks, perhaps, but definitely in manner. He knew exactly what he wanted, and wouldn't take no for an answer.' She gave a little laugh, her colour rising. 'As you might have gathered. At least you're not...' She broke off, eyes asking the unvoiced question.

Gina shook her head. After this afternoon, she couldn't be wholly sure, but that was something to be thought about later.

'But you do love him? I mean, you're not marrying him for...other reasons?'

'Money, you mean?' Gina shook her head again, able to say that much with total truth. 'I don't feel any sense of being done down that way. There's no certainty that San Cotone would ever have been mine even if Giovanni had lived.'

'But you told me yesterday that Lucius considered himself under obligation to you.'

'That's the kind of man he is.' Gina kept her tone light. 'Nothing to do with the way we feel about each other. One look was enough for us both, just the way you said.'

'As *he* said, history repeats itself.' Her mother's eyes were misty. 'I'm sure you'll have a wonderful life together!'

Gina made the appropriate response, hoping she was right. Love could grow between two people, she supposed. Of a kind, at any rate. If she wasn't pregnant already, it was odds on that she would be before too long. Lucius needed a son if the Carandente name was to survive. Children could cement a shaky marriage.

Contrary to her expectations, Lucius made no attempt to invade her room that night. Considering what had happened in the shower earlier, it was a bit late for courteous gestures on the grounds of this being her parents' home, leaving her to conclude that his desire for her was far from irresistible. It was a long time before sleep overcame the hunger churning her own insides.

CHAPTER SEVEN

EVENTS moved quickly over the following week. With Redman's safeguarded, and the wedding booked for the sixth, it left just five days in which to settle personal affairs. The company Gina worked for proved surprisingly amenable to her leaving at a moment's notice—causing her to suspect that Lucius had already made an approach behind her back. Certainly, his offer of six months' rent on the flat in lieu of notice settled any protests her landlord might have made.

Apart from her clothes and a few bits and pieces, there was nothing she wanted. Definitely nothing she needed, considering where she was going to be living. She still found it difficult to take in that her whole life could change so radically in the space of a few weeks.

The one London friend she considered close enough to be put in the picture viewed the whole situation from a purely romantic aspect. A fairy tale come true, was her summing up.

'Drop-dead gorgeous, *and* superrich!' she commented when Lucius left the two of them alone for few minutes in the restaurant where they'd met for lunch. 'What more could anyone want!'

Some deeper emotion than duty alone, perhaps, thought Gina wryly. They had made love at the flat last night—she felt her stomach muscles contract at the very memory of it—but she was no closer to knowing the man within.

* * *

'I'm leaving my whole life behind,' she said in the car on the way back north that afternoon. 'Family, friends, career...'

'You can visit family and friends whenever you wish to,' Lucius answered steadily. 'Or have them visit you. If you fear becoming bored with no job of work to attend, you might like to join Marcello in the winery offices on occasion.'

Gina stole a glance at the clean-cut profile, suspecting satire. 'Oh, I'm sure he'd go for that!'

'It would not be his place to refuse.'

She hesitated before voicing the thought. 'It seems odd that your sister's husband should work for the company at all. Especially when she told me he shares the same kind of ancestry as the Carandentes.'

'His forebears held title, yes,' Lucius agreed. 'Unfortunately, he made some extremely bad investments after he and Ottavia were married, and lost what was left of the family fortune—including their home. He became comptroller as a means of salvaging his pride on being forced to take up residence at San Cotone.'

'I see.' Gina felt a pang of sympathy for the man. 'Well, I daresay I'll find plenty to occupy me without forcing myself on him. It's going to be bad enough as it is.'

'Ottavia will not be making life difficult for you,' Lucius stated authoritatively.

Maybe not while he was around, came the thought. She shrugged it off. There were far more important things to think about.

The wedding day was hot and sunny, the ceremony brief. Gina wore a cream dress a few shades lighter than Lucius's suit, her wide-brimmed coral hat a last-minute impulse buy she was only too glad to abandon on changing into something a little more practical for the journey to Rome.

Their flight to Heathrow was at a quarter to four, with a connection at five-thirty. They took their leave of her parents at the house. Whatever reservations John Redman might still harbour deep down, he had given the two of them his wholehearted support this past week. Gina turned her face resolutely forward as the car pulled away. She was a Carandente in name now, with a whole new life to live. There was no going back.

The domestic flight was uneventful, the connection on time, landing in Rome just before nine. The hotel where they were to spend the next two nights before travelling south to Capri was set in a square off the Via Claudia, its interior decor a symphony in gilt and crystal and silk-screened walls. Their suite was sheer luxury.

No more so than San Cotone, Gina reflected, taking it in. Something she was going to have to get used to—though hopefully never become complacent about.

'Tired?' asked Lucius softly as she turned from the window with its superb views over the illuminated city.

If she had been, the look in the dark eyes would have roused her. Make the most of it while it lasted, she told herself.

He undressed her slowly, sensually, somehow managing to rid himself of his own clothing at the same time. The smooth olive skin felt wonderful, the muscle rippling beneath as she traced a passage down the length of his body with her fingertips to claim the vibrant manhood. His mouth was a flame searing her breast, the curl of his tongue about her tingling nipple a pleasure close to pain.

He turned back the silk covers on the wide bed before lowering her to it, his lips creating mayhem in their intimate seeking. Gina writhed beneath him in an onslaught of sensation. She could live without love, came her last, fading thought as he slid inside her, but she couldn't live without this. Not ever!

Lucius was gone from the bed when she awoke to morning light. He came through from the sitting room already fully dressed in a formal dark blue suit, bending to press a brief kiss to her lips as she raised herself.

'I have to go,' he said. 'I cannot say for certain how long I will be gone. You only have to ring room service for anything you require. Full English breakfast, if you like,' he added with a smile. 'The staff all speak your language.'

Gina stilled the urge to ask him not to go. Business obviously took precedence this morning. 'What do I do with myself while you're out?' she said instead.

'Whatever you wish,' he rejoined. 'The Colosseum is close by, although I would recommend that you take a taxi if you decide to go there. A woman walking the street alone is apt to attract the kind of attention best not experienced.'

'You mean I might get my bottom pinched?' she said flippantly.

'That could be the least of it.' He didn't look particularly amused. 'Promise me you will take no foolish risks.'

'I won't,' she assured him. 'I'll probably stay around the hotel anyway.'

'It might be best,' he agreed. 'Tonight we will eat at one of Rome's finest restaurants.'

'Can't wait,' Gina murmured, her mind more on the sustenance that would hopefully come later. 'See you later, then.'

She watched him cross the room, appraising the broad-shouldered, narrow-hipped physique. All man, and all hers: in bed if not out of it. This marriage might be missing an ingredient, but what they had was enough to carry it through—for now, at least. It had to be enough.

Breakfast was brought to the suite by a young and handsome waiter who made it clear that he was open to any suggestion the 'lovely *signorina*' might have in mind. More amused than annoyed, Gina despatched him with a few well-chosen words—a joke she doubted Lucius would appreciate. Some things were best not shared.

By mid morning she had had enough of being on her own. She should have plumped for at least a couple of days in Rome when Lucius had asked where she would like to spend the honeymoon, she thought ruefully. By the time he returned it would probably be too late to see anything, and tomorrow they would be motoring south. Providing she stuck to the main thoroughfares, she could hardly come to much harm.

She put on a pair of beige linen trousers and a short-sleeved white blouse as the least likely outfit to attract undue attention. The air outside was hot and humid, the Via Claudia thronged with traffic. As Lucius had said, the Colosseum was close enough to walk to.

As he had also said, a woman on her own tended to draw attention of a less than welcome nature. Gina studiously ignored the whistles and ribald invitations—as she assumed the latter were from the leers accompanying them—niftily sidestepping two grinning youths who attempted to bar her way. A bit like running the gauntlet, she admitted, glad to reach the Colosseum entrance at last.

Despite the crowds, she was overcome by the timeless spell of the place. Looking down from the terraces on the crumbling arena, it was all too easy to imagine an age long gone, when the exposed cells would be filled with wild animals and slaves to be sacrificed for the entertainment of the masses. A cruel age, Gina reflected, thankful not to have lived in those times herself.

She took a taxi from there to St Peter's Square, marvelling along with countless others at the wonders of the Sistine Chapel, then another to see the Trevi Fountain. Hunger finally drew her attention to the time. She was dismayed to see it was already almost three o'clock. Lucius probably wouldn't have returned yet, she assured herself, heading back to the hotel.

She was wrong. Lucius had not only returned, but had been there for the last two hours. He was furious with her. So much so that she was drawn to retaliate with equal ferocity.

'I'm not some chattel to be told what to do and when to do it!' she stormed. 'You left me to twiddle my thumbs with no idea of when you might be back, so you've no room to complain!'

Eyes like black coals, Lucius drew in a harsh breath. 'I will not be spoken to in that manner!' he said in a clipped tone. 'If I have nothing else, I will have your respect!'

About to lash out with further invective, Gina took a hold on herself. Little more than twenty-four hours married and already at loggerheads, she thought dispiritedly. What price the future if this was all it took?

'I apologise,' she said, although it cost her to do it. 'I owe you a great deal, I know.'

'You think I look for gratitude?' he demanded. 'The debt is mine.'

'You think *my* only interest is financial compensation?' she rejoined. 'So far as I'm concerned, the investment you've made in Redman's wipes the slate clean.'

'The investment we both made,' he said. 'Everything I have is now yours too.'

Gina searched the chiselled features in dawning comprehension, mind reeling. 'Was that the business you had to take care of this morning?' she asked faintly.

The dark head inclined. 'My lawyers had the matter already in hand but there was still a great deal to be gone through. As of this day we are partners in every sense.'

Gina sank into the nearest chair, legs suddenly too weak to support her. A fairy tale Isabel had called it, but this went far beyond that.

'There was no need,' she got out. 'I never wanted—'

'It was necessary.' His tone was level, his gaze steady. 'Should anything happen to me, San Cotone will be yours alone, as it would have been had Giovanni lived.'

Alarm leapt in her eyes. 'What do you mean, should anything happen to you? There's nothing wrong with you, is there?'

A smile touched the firm mouth. 'It would pain you to lose me?'

The very thought was a stab in the heart. 'Of course it would!' she said thickly. 'Lucius, what—?'

'So far as I am aware, my health is excellent,' he assured her. 'I spoke only of contingencies. All I ask is that you would care for my family in the event.'

'It goes without saying.' Gina didn't even want to think about such an event. 'I'm sorry about taking off the way I did without even leaving you a note,' she added impulsively. 'It was totally inconsiderate.'

'I will put the blame on your independent English half,' he returned on a lighter note. 'You had no problems?'

She made an effort to match his mood. 'Nothing I couldn't handle. I saw the Colosseum and St Peter's. Oh, and the Trevi Fountain too.'

'You made a wish?'

'No,' she admitted. 'The crowds were too thick to get near enough to toss a coin.'

'Then we must return this evening. Those who visit the Fountain must complete the ritual, or bad luck may befall them. For now, however…' he paused, the smile this time sending her pulse rate soaring '…you wish to continue with your sightseeing?'

Food took second place in the hunger stakes, Gina acknowledged. Would there ever come a time when she failed to want this? she wondered as he took his cue from the shake of her head to draw her into his arms. Right now it seemed impossible.

Capri was as beautiful as Gina had anticipated, although the summer crowds proved something of a drawback. She readily agreed to Lucius's suggestion after a couple of days that they move on, not really caring where they were providing it was together.

The little village in the mainland mountains where they'd spent several precious days and nights was a memory to be treasured. Totally lacking in all but the most basic facilities, though clean as a whistle, the one hotel had boasted just two rooms. Gina had loved every moment of their time there.

Knowing it all had to come to an end eventually made it no easier to accept when the time came. San Cotone might be her home now, but it didn't feel like it. She hated the thought of facing Ottavia's enmity again—and wasn't yet convinced that Cornelia's feelings were any different. Donata was the only one she looked forward to seeing.

They took the train from Naples. Gina grew more despondent with the passing of each mile. She summoned a smile on catching Lucius's eye, reluctant to have him guess her feelings.

'I suppose you already made arrangements for us to be met?'

'Of course,' he confirmed. 'Pietro is to bring a car.'

'Pietro?'

'*Madre's* chauffeur. Tonight we sleep in the suite your grandmother and grandfather would have occupied in their time. The suite your mother and Giovanni would have shared in their turn had he ever completed his journey home.'

'You can't really know what would have happened if he had,' Gina returned. 'His father might not have been prepared to recognise the marriage.'

Lucius gave a brief shrug. 'It would have been up to Giovanni to make him recognise it, but there is little use, I agree, in speculation. It is our place now to extend the Carandente line.'

Towards which end they'd already made serious efforts, Gina reflected, with a familiar stirring in the pit of her stomach at the very thought. She was back to waiting a couple of weeks again before she could be sure, but some inner sense told her it was already an established fact. In nine months she would hold Lucius's child in her arms. Boy or girl didn't matter to her, but it would to him.

The car was already waiting at the station. Pietro greeted the two of them with deference. Gina sat through the journey in growing dread of the ordeal to come. Six short weeks, that was all it had taken to bring her to this point. It hardly seemed possible.

Lit by the evening sun, San Cotone was even more beautiful than she remembered. Stepping from the car, she stood for a moment just gazing at it, unable still to believe it was all hers.

'Welcome home,' said Lucius softly at her back.

Cornelia's appearance in the open doorway cut off any reply Gina might have made. Aided by a walking stick, the older woman limped to the top of the stone steps, her smile a reassurance in itself.

'I have waited so long for this!' she exclaimed. 'Come, *nuora*, let me embrace you!'

Gina went willingly, moved beyond words by the warmth of the greeting. Donata came rushing out to join them, flinging her arms about Gina's neck to hug her with unbridled enthusiasm.

'I'm so happy to have you return to us!' she exclaimed. 'I've had no one to talk with these past weeks!'

Gina made the appropriate responses, wishing she could hope for the same attitude from Ottavia. The latter's absence from the welcome party underlined the unlikelihood.

Donata led the way indoors chattering nineteen to the dozen, Cornelia and Lucius following on. Gina heard her mother-in-law say something in Italian, recognising one word with a sudden dampening of the spirits raised. Livia was the name of the woman Cornelia had proclaimed the ideal wife for her son. Was it possible that the welcome just extended had been no more than a front after all?

Her spirits sank even lower on reaching the salon to see the two people awaiting them. Perhaps a year or so older than herself, Livia Marucchi was one of the most beautiful women she had ever clapped eyes on, her smoothly swathed, blue-black hair drawn back from the perfect oval of her face. There was no warmth in the smile that touched her lips as she looked from Gina to the man at her back.

'I offer my congratulations,' she said in heavily accented English.

There was no telling anything from Lucius's voice when he thanked her. Gina refrained from glancing his way as he moved to her side to perform the unnecessary introduction, summoning a smile of her own. 'Nice to meet you,' she lied.

The curl of Livia's lip was slight enough to go unnoted by most. 'And you also,' she said.

Silent so far, Ottavia came forward to take Gina by the shoulders and place a kiss to both cheeks, the glitter in her eyes the only indication of her true feelings. 'So we are sisters now!'

If Lucius had any inkling of his sister's frame of mind he wasn't allowing it to affect him. 'You will excuse us if we leave you so soon,' he said evenly. 'We are both in need of a shower and change of clothing after our journey.'

Gina accompanied him from the room feeling anything but happy. She longed to be back in the village they had left that morning.

'I didn't ask if the things I had sent from home had arrived,' she said as they mounted the stairs.

'This is your home now,' Lucius responded a little curtly. 'You must begin thinking of it as such.'

She gave him a swift glance, noting the set of his jaw. There was a difference in him since their arrival: a change of mood attributable to Livia Marucchi, if she was any judge at all. Donata had given the impression that her brother had had no intention of marrying the woman, but what would she have really known of his plans?

The suite they were to occupy was on the far side of the villa from the room that had been hers before. Her mind on other matters, Gina viewed the spacious, beautifully furnished rooms with scant interest. Her things had indeed arrived, she saw on opening one of the vast wardrobes in the dressing area. It was going to take a great deal more clothing than she possessed in total to fill even one of them.

There were two bathrooms, each superbly equipped. Lucius was already in the shower, the closed door a barrier she wouldn't have thought twice about breaching only yesterday. It was ridiculous feeling this way on the strength of one short meeting, she told herself hardily. If Lucius had wanted to marry Livia he would have done it before she ever came on the scene. She had to put the whole thing from mind.

He was fully dressed when she emerged from the other bathroom some fifteen minutes later.

'Useful when time presses, perhaps,' he said drily when she commented on the advantages of the arrangement. 'Did you not wish to join me?'

'I wasn't sure you'd want me to,' Gina admitted, drawing a line between the dark brows.

'You consider the home no place for such behaviour?'

'Of course not.' She tried to make light of the situation. 'I suppose I just feel a bit inhibited with all the family here.'

'It is most unlikely that any of them would intrude on our privacy.'

'I'm sure. It's not—' She broke off, spreading her hands with a wry little smile. 'Getting used to being here on a permanent basis at all is going to take time. It was never part of the plan.' She hesitated before putting the question. 'Do they know…everything?'

The shrug was brief. 'I keep no secrets.'

'How did they take it?'

'My mother is already well-provided for, and Donata will no doubt marry well in time.'

His tone discouraged further enquiry, but Gina refused to leave it there. 'And Ottavia?'

'She and Marcello would be reliant on your charity for a time should the need arise.'

'Is that fair?' Gina protested. 'Surely provision can be made!'

'That decision is no longer mine alone,' Lucius returned. 'As I told you, everything I have is now yours too. If I die before you, it will all be yours.'

A sudden little shudder ran through her. To never see him again, never feel his arms about her again…

'If I have a say in things, then I'd like Ottavia and Marcello to be provided for now,' she declared. 'Enough for them to make a new life for themselves without having to rely on family charity.'

'You think Marcello so lacking in pride that he would accept such a gift?' Lucius asked on a note of anger. 'You believe *me* so devoid in humanity that I offered him no other choice than to become comptroller? He chose to draw a salary. One sufficient—if properly invested—to enable him to achieve independence again in the not-too-distant future by his own efforts.'

Gina bit her lip. 'I'm sorry. I should have known better.'

'We have a great deal to learn about each other.' The anger had gone from his voice, replaced by a flatness of tone that was even less desirable. 'It will, as you said, take time.'

Uncertain of his response, Gina quelled the impulse to reach out to him as he turned away. He was right, of course, she thought depressedly. Outside of bed, they were still almost total strangers.

CHAPTER EIGHT

IT WAS a relief not to see Livia when they went down to join the family on the terrace at nine. Gina wouldn't have put it past Ottavia to insist that the woman stayed to dinner. Knowing what she knew, she could understand something of her sister-in-law's feelings. To be ousted from inheritance by someone she hadn't even known existed a couple of months ago took some getting over. It was improbable that they could ever become friends.

If Donata felt done down in any way herself, she gave no sign of it. Her hair had grown considerably in the last month, although it was going to take a year or more for it to achieve any real length.

'I've grown used to it,' she acknowledged cheerfully when Gina commented on the difference. 'I may even keep it short. It's so much cooler in summer!'

'You will never find a husband looking the way you do,' declared Ottavia. 'A woman's hair is her crowning glory! Providing, of course, that she puts both the time and the effort into keeping it so.'

A dig at her, Gina gathered, catching the sly, sideways glance. One she could ignore in the knowledge that her own hair was in no way neglected. For a moment she found herself wishing she was blonde like her mother, just to be different, but the feeling soon passed. She was a Carandente in looks as well as name.

'With a face and figure like Donata's, I'd doubt any man is going to bemoan the lack of a little hair length,' she said with purpose. 'Where I come from, she'd cause riots in the streets!'

'When can I go?' asked Donata promptly, eyes sparkling.

'I think it can be safely said that you caused enough mayhem already in your life,' commented her brother with a sternness belied by the twitching of his lips. 'I shall have a great deal of sympathy for the man who is foolish enough to make you his wife. He will never know a moment's peace of mind again.'

'Cesare has sadly neglected us these past weeks,' observed Ottavia with a malice Gina could have hit her for. 'Perhaps he found himself more pressing interests.'

The sparkle died from Donata's eyes, though she kept her head high. 'I no longer have feelings for Cesare,' she declared, 'so your spitefulness goes unrewarded.'

So put that in your pipe and smoke it! thought Gina, delighted with if not entirely convinced by the response. Ottavia's sisterly empathies left a whole lot to be desired. She looked distinctly put out by her failure to gain a rise.

She answered in rapid Italian, the tone alone enough to convey the meaning of the words spilling from her lips. Lucius put a stop to it with a tersely spoken sentence in the same language. Master of the household in every sense, Gina reflected as Ottavia lapsed into silence.

She felt sympathy for Marcello who was obviously discomfited by the episode. Hopefully for him, it wouldn't be too long before he gained that independence. Not that having Ottavia for a wife could be any picnic. It was surprising that she'd stuck by him at all.

Of them all, Cornelia seemed the least affected by the altercation. Gina doubted if anything ever really upset her. With Lucius married, and likely to produce a grandson to secure the future, she could live out her life however it suited her. In many ways she could be envied.

Tired from the journey, Gina found herself nodding off over coffee, but hesitated to take her departure before Lucius was ready to retire for the night. By the time he did make a move she was almost dead on her feet.

For the very first time she was unable to summon a response when he turned to her in bed, try as she might to keep her mind focused.

'I'm just so tired,' she murmured apologetically. 'If I could just have an hour or two's sleep.'

'There is no compulsion,' Lucius answered drily. 'We have a lifetime ahead. The rest will benefit us both.'

Weary as she was, Gina couldn't deny the pang as he settled himself for sleep. The least he could do was put an arm about her—make her feel wanted for more than just conscience and sex alone. Was he thinking about Livia Marucchi? she wondered dully. Did he wish it was she who shared his bed?

It was just coming light when she awoke. Less than three-and-a-half hours' sleep, she calculated, stretching a cautious arm to turn the bedside clock, yet she felt fully revitalised.

Lying on his back, Lucius was still in the land of nod, his breathing deep and even. He had thrown back the covering sheet in the night, revealing the full length of his body. In the past week, Gina had grown accustomed to sleeping in the nude herself, delighting in the freedom from restraint. Looking at him now, outlined against the pale grey of the window, she felt the familiar stirring in the centre of her body, the quickening of her pulses.

It took everything she had to stop herself from reaching out to waken him with a caress usually guaranteed to create instant arousal. She had refused him last night; why should she expect him to respond to her this morning?

She turned away from him, gazing sightlessly at the far wall. One thing she had learned these last weeks was that real love didn't have to come as a blinding flash, but could grow from a far greater depth through knowledge of a person. Lucius was a man infinitely worthy of love, a man any woman would find it difficult not to love. She might rebel at times against his masculine dominance, yet that in itself was an intrinsic part of his attraction.

What she didn't, and might never have, was his love in return. Not the kind she wanted from him anyway.

Getting through those first days of residence at the villa proved far from easy. There were times when Gina would have given almost anything to turn back the clock. She'd been happy enough in ignorance of all this. Sooner or later she would have met a man she could feel enough for to marry and have children by. A man whose lovemaking would have laboured under no comparison because there would have been none to make.

Where the latter was concerned, she certainly had no cause for complaint. Lucius kept her fully indulged. It was so simple for a man, she often reflected in the darkness when she lay listening to his even breathing and envying him the ability to sleep: the deeper emotions held so much less significance. She was the one who longed to hear the words themselves. Only it wasn't the way he felt about her, and he was no hypocrite.

Suspicion hardened into certainty as the days passed. The thought of the life growing inside her gave rise to a whole new set of emotions. The first of at least three, she decided, having yearned all her life for a brother or sister.

For Lucius's sake, she hoped this one was a boy; so far as she was concerned, good health would be enough.

It was only through Donata that she discovered Lucius had a birthday coming up. Ottavia, she was sure, would have allowed her to continue in ignorance until the day itself, while Cornelia would have probably taken it for granted that she already knew. She resolved to save the news of her pregnancy until then as an extra special present to be given in private, in the meantime racking her brain for some idea on the public front.

In the end she settled on a modernistic Tuscany landscape by an artist she had heard Lucius mention in approving terms, signing the considerable cheque with a sense of burning the final bridge behind her. She not only bore the Carandente blood and name, but was now a fully fledged member of the money-no-object brigade.

Lucius received the painting with gratifying expressions of pleasure. It would, he declared, take pride of place in the study. Gina hugged the knowledge of the present still to come to herself as she watched him open gifts from the rest of the family. Cornelia had arranged a luncheon party in celebration of the event, though not with her son's approval. He would, Gina gathered, prefer to spend the day like any other.

'I grew out of birthday parties long ago,' he said when she commented on his lack of enthusiasm. '*Madre*, unfortunately, refuses to accept it. If this occasion follows the pattern of previous years, there will be champagne in which to toast my continuing health and prosperity.'

'I'll drink to that,' Gina rejoined. 'The health part anyway.'

Lucius raised a quizzical eyebrow. 'You have no interest in prosperity?'

'Money isn't everything.'

'You told me that once before,' he said. 'But you have to admit that it has its uses. Without it, San Cotone would not exist.'

They were in the study, where he had insisted on coming to hang the painting himself. Looking at him as he leaned against the desk edge to admire the landscape, Gina was reminded of the very first time she had set eyes on him. The attraction that had flared in her that day bore no comparison with what she felt for him now.

'I have something to tell you,' she said softly, unable to wait any longer. 'You're going to be a father.'

He came slowly upright from the desk, the dark eyes meeting hers holding an expression that lifted her spirits even further.

'You are certain?' he asked.

'As much as I can be without confirmation from other sources.'

Lucius came over to where she stood, taking her in his arms to deliver a heart-stirring kiss. '*Madre* will be delighted.'

'Providing it's a boy.'

Dark brows lifted quizzically. 'You believe she would look on a girl with disfavour?'

'I believe she might regard *me* with disfavour for producing one.'

Lucius smiled and shook his head. 'The gender is decided by the particular sperm that first reaches the egg, so if anyone is to be held responsible it would be the father. She will, I assure you, receive whatever we produce with open arms.'

Blue eyes bored into his, doing their utmost to penetrate the impenetrable. 'You don't care about carrying on the Carandente name?'

'Naturally I care. The three hundred years of our ancestry makes it imperative that I make every effort to extend it. But if I fail…' he lifted his shoulders '…then, I fail. The world will carry on without us.'

'We don't have to stop at the one in any case,' said Gina impulsively. 'Children need companionship.'

Lucius reached out a hand to smooth the hair back from her face in a gesture so tender it moved her immeasurably. 'You felt the lack of siblings yourself?'

'Yes,' she admitted.

'Your parents had no desire for a family?'

'I think it was more a case of it simply not happening for them.' Gina lightened her voice, bearing down on the urge to declare her love for him there and then. 'The Carandente virility isn't given to every man.'

'I knew failure myself not long ago,' Lucius reminded her. 'Your stepfather is no exception.'

He drew her to him, his kiss this time stimulating a passionate response. Gina knew real regret when he released her again, wishing now that she had waited to tell him about the baby until later when they were unlikely to be interrupted by anyone.

If Lucius suffered the same degree of frustration, his smile as he touched her lips with a fingertip was steady enough.

'With all respect to your instincts, I think it best that we keep the news to ourselves until we have the confirmation you spoke of. I'll make an arrangement for you to see a physician.'

It made sense, Gina supposed. 'That's the first contraction I ever heard you use,' she remarked brightly.

He laughed. 'My English improves by leaps and bounds, as you would say! Soon I'll be speaking it like a native!'

'Not with that accent,' she teased. 'You sound like an

Italian film star all the girls in school used to be crazy about.'

Amusement curved the strong mouth. 'Including yourself?'

'Oh, definitely! He was a real hunk! A bit old, I suppose, thinking about it. He must have been all of thirty-four or five.'

The amusement deepened. 'Tonight,' he promised, 'I will show you what an old man of thirty-four is capable of!'

Gina pulled a face at him, wishing it was tonight already. 'I tremble at the thought!'

'Our guests will soon begin arriving,' declared Cornelia from the open doorway. 'Do you not think it time to prepare for their reception?'

'Of course,' Gina said hurriedly. 'I hadn't realised it was that late.' She hesitated, mindful of the decision already made, yet yearning to tell her mother-in-law the news she knew for certain to be a fact not a fancy. 'Is it to be a very dressy affair?' was all she could think of to say instead.

'No more than you care to make it,' said Lucius. 'Go on ahead. I'll follow in a moment or two.'

Gina would rather he accompanied her now, but with Cornelia there, hardly felt able to make the request. She left the two of them, and headed upstairs, still not at all sure what she should wear for this luncheon party. The buffet was to be served on the terrace, which suggested a certain informality. The white linen tunic she had bought last week and not yet worn should be suitable.

She was already changed when Lucius came up. He closeted himself immediately in his bathroom. As he had made no comment on her choice of dress, Gina could only assume it was suitable to the occasion. Considering the price of it, it darn well should be, she thought, viewing her slender curves in the cheval mirror.

With her legs tanned golden brown, she had deemed the wearing of stockings unnecessary. The kitten-heeled sandals were designed for comfort as well as style; if she was going to be on her feet for two or three hours, the former was essential. Her only jewellery was the single strand of cultured pearls given her by her parents on her eighteenth birthday, along with the filigree silver watch Lucius had bought her in Rome.

Plus her engagement ring, of course. She held up her hand so that the stone caught the light from the window, wishing now that she hadn't allowed Lucius to talk her out of the simple hoop she would have chosen for herself. The solitaire could hardly be called ostentatious, she had to admit, but it was still too much of a statement of worth for her tastes.

She was still standing there watching the colours dance when Lucius emerged from the bathroom. He was nude but for the black silk boxer shorts he had taken in with him, his skin gleaming with health and vitality.

'I thought you would have gone down by now,' he commented.

'It's your birthday not mine,' Gina returned lightly. 'You're the one people will want to see.'

'On the contrary, *you* will be the main attraction. Some will be attending only in order to meet the woman of my choice.'

Except that he'd had no choice, Gina reflected. Not in his estimation, at any rate.

'We call it vetting in my country,' she said, trying for a jocular note.

Pulling on a cream silk shirt, Lucius gave her a slightly sharpened glance. '*This* is your country now.'

'It's where I live,' she responded. 'I still hold a British passport.'

'Born of an Italian father, you will have little difficulty obtaining full citizenship.'

'Always providing I want to become an Italian citizen.'

Lucius stopped buttoning buttons to gaze at her in some exasperation. 'With an Italian father and husband, why would you wish otherwise?'

Up until that moment, Gina had to confess, she had given the matter little if any consideration. Now, she found herself struggling for words to convey what she felt.

'My mother is English. I was brought up to English ways. I can't turn my back on twenty-five years of my life.'

'You think I would ask it of you?'

'Isn't that just what you are doing?' she said. 'I don't *feel* Italian. Not in any sense. Why should it be taken for granted that I'll be prepared to become one?'

'If for no other reason, to honour your father's memory. Had he lived, you would have known no other life.'

'There's no certainty of that even if he had lived.'

Lucius shook his head emphatically. 'With a child on the way the marriage would have been accepted.' He held up a staying hand as she opened her mouth to dispute the statement. 'You have no basis for disagreement. I knew my cousin. You did not.'

Gina had to give best on that score. What she couldn't do was let the rest pass. 'I'm staying British,' she stated flatly.

The dark eyes acquired a sudden steely core. 'You must do as you wish, of course, but our children will take their father's nationality as is customary.'

He turned away to finish his dressing. Gina looked on silently as he donned one of the pale-shaded suits that sat his lithe frame so well, wishing now that she'd tackled the subject in a less confrontational manner. Not that she'd any intention of changing her mind. Her own feelings apart, it would be like a kick in the face for her mother.

When it came to their children, she didn't have much of a leg to stand on. They would learn to speak English as a matter of course, but it would be Italy they regarded as their homeland. She had to accept that.

'It seems like it might be a dressier occasion than I thought,' she commented as Lucius finished fastening gold cuff-links. 'Should I choose something else?'

He ran a cursory glance over her, expression unrevealing. 'I see no reason for it. Your taste, as always, is impeccable. We must go.'

People were already beginning to arrive when they got downstairs. Over the course of the next half hour, Gina was kissed on both cheeks so many times she lost count. Speculation was rife among both male and female alike. She wondered just how much was known of her background.

Thankful to see someone she already knew, she greeted Cesare with pleasure.

'Why have you left it this long to come over?' she asked, drawing him aside. 'We've been back almost two weeks!'

'I was out of the country myself until yesterday,' he acknowledged. 'I was given the news only last night.'

'It must have been quite a shock for you,' Gina said softly.

His smile was a reassurance in itself. 'Lucius had already acquainted me with the fact of your birthright—and with his intention to right the wrong done to you. Giovanni can now rest easy in his grave.' He studied her for a moment. 'You are happy, yes?'

'Of course,' she said. 'Who wouldn't be happy to have all this?'

Cesare looked a little uncertain. 'But you have some regard for Lucius too, I trust?'

'Of course,' she said again, wishing she could tell him—tell anyone—just how much. 'I couldn't have married a man I didn't have any feeling for at all. And what about you?' she went on, eager to change the subject. 'Did you find the girl of your dreams yet?'

The wicked sparkle she remembered leapt in his eyes. 'The girl of my dreams has been taken from me by another, so I must look afresh.'

'You could do worse than Donata,' Gina murmured.

'I could indeed,' he agreed surprisingly. 'I thought about her much these past weeks.' He cast a glance around. 'She is here today?'

'Somewhere, yes.' Gina tried not to let her hopes for her younger sister-in-law rise too high. 'Look for a scarlet dress. Not that she's likely to stand out at a glance,' she added on a humorous note. 'I seem to be the only bird around with dull plumage!'

Cesare made a slow and lingering scrutiny of her arresting face with its wide-spaced, vivid eyes and full-lipped rosy mouth, the glossy cascade of black hair. 'Your plumage,' he declared, 'could never be anything but dazzling! Lucius is a fortunate man.'

But did he know it? she thought, spirits taking an abrupt dive as her gaze went beyond Cesare to the couple seemingly engrossed in conversation a short distance away. Livia Marucchi looked divine in a form-fitting dress the colour of ripe apricots, her feet clad in a mere whisper of light tan leather. From the way Lucius was looking into the eyes fixed on his, no one else existed.

She should have known, of course, that the woman

would be invited. As a long-standing friend of Ottavia's—to say nothing of Lucius himself—she would hardly have been left out. The question uppermost in her mind right now was just how close that latter relationship had been.

'Was there anything between Lucius and Livia before I came on the scene?' she heard herself asking.

Cesare looked disconcerted. 'That is a question only Lucius can answer.'

'I know.' Gina already regretted the unstudied enquiry. 'I'm sorry, Cesare. I shouldn't have asked.'

'Livia is not a woman I would have chosen to relate with myself, if that is of any help,' he proffered after a moment.

Meaning what? she itched to know. It was unlikely that she left him physically unstirred: it would be against nature for any hot-blooded Italian male to look at a woman of Livia Marucchi's undoubted beauty and feel no effect in his loins. It was obvious however that he'd said all he was going to say on the subject.

When she looked again, both Lucius and Livia had disappeared. To where, and for what, she didn't care to consider.

Donata came weaving through the throng, the scarlet dress emphasising every line of her supple young body. The flower in her hair was scarlet too, perfectly matched by the colour of her lips. Flamboyant, perhaps, Gina thought fondly, but it suited her.

She greeted Cesare in Italian, her manner easy. He responded in the same vein. An act on both parts, Gina judged, watching the two of them as they chatted. Her Italian was still too limited to understand more than a few words, especially at the pace in which they were speaking, but the nuances came through loud and clear.

It was Donata who called a halt, apologising in English for her discourtesy.

'I'm hardly going to improve my grasp if everyone speaks English all the time for my benefit,' Gina reassured her. 'I hope to be bilingual by this time next year.'

This time next year she would be a mother too, came the thought. Whether she would be any closer to knowing the man she had married was something else.

She had been aware for some time of a man on the periphery of her vision who appeared to be watching her. Murmuring something about circulating, she moved on, donning a social smile as the man stepped smoothly into her path. She couldn't recall having seen him prior to this moment.

'Mario Lanciani,' he supplied. 'I have waited so long to speak with you alone.'

'About what?' Gina asked.

The good-looking if somewhat dissipated features creased in a smile. 'To speak is perhaps the wrong word. I wish only to tell you that your beauty outshines that of every other woman here today!'

As a line, Gina reflected, she'd heard better. She kept a straight face with an effort. 'You're very flattering, Signor Lanciani.'

'Mario,' he said. 'You must call me Mario if we are going to be friends.'

The straight face was even harder to maintain this time. '*Are* we going to be friends?'

'But of course,' he said. 'You feel what I feel myself. I see it in your eyes.'

It was reprehensible to play him along, but Gina found the temptation too much to resist. He was so utterly confident of his charms. She infused a note of regret in her voice. 'Some things we must fight against.'

Outside of lovemaking, she had never seen a man smoulder before, but she was seeing it now, feigned though she took the emotion to be. 'Why must we?' he demanded softly.

Enough was enough, Gina told herself: in fact, more than enough in this case. 'I have a husband,' she said, letting him down more gently than he merited.

The shrug was dismissive. 'He has liaisons outside of the marital bed, so why should you not?'

She should treat the suggestion with contempt, Gina knew, but her better judgement had gone for a walk. 'With whom?' She jerked the words out.

'Why, Livia Marucchi, of course.' He made it sound as if she shouldn't have needed to ask. 'It is no secret. Doubtless there are others too. Lucius is the kind of man for whom one woman could never be enough.'

Gina bit back the instinctive retort. It was no more than she had thought herself on more than one occasion. 'I think you'd better leave,' she managed with a fair degree of control.

'A pity.' He sighed. 'I believed you a woman of the world.'

She turned on her heel and left him there, not trusting her tongue to stay cleaved to the roof of her mouth for much longer. They had been under surveillance by people in the vicinity, she realised, catching a glance or two in passing. She donned a smile. However bad she might feel inside, she was dammed if anyone else was going to know about it.

CHAPTER NINE

AS LUCIUS had predicted, Cornelia called for a toast to be drunk. What Gina had not anticipated was her own inclusion in the pledge, although she should have realised that the party served a dual purpose in celebrating both birthday and marriage. She set herself to show no resistance when Lucius drew her to him to kiss her first on each cheek, and then on the lips, to smile into his eyes despite her conviction that hers wasn't the only mouth he'd kissed in the last hour.

'Long life and happiness,' she echoed in English, careful to iron out any hint of sarcasm from her tone.

Not quite careful enough though, if the sudden narrowing of the dark eyes was anything to go by. Lucius was all too capable of seeing through the dissimulation.

He kept her by his side for the following half hour or so, an arm about her waist, his hand resting lightly on her hip-bone. There was no sign of Livia. Not that it made any difference, Gina admitted. The woman was here in spirit if not in actual presence.

It was almost five o'clock before the last guest drifted away. With several hours to fill until dinner, and reluctant to spend them alone with Lucius, Gina took herself off into the gardens. The weather had turned sultry, with a heavy build-up of cloud gradually blotting out the blue. They were probably in for a storm, the first she'd have known in this neck of the woods.

Despite the lower heels, her sandals weren't all that

comfortable when it came to extended walking. She took them off in the end and continued in bare feet, sticking to the grass as much as possible and enjoying the feel of it between her toes. She still found it difficult to realise that all this splendour was her home. She doubted she would ever learn to take it for granted, the way her children would in time to come.

Children? Right now, she could conjure little enthusiasm for the one already on the way. There was still a possibility that she was wrong anyway.

Unlikely, she was bound to admit. She'd always been regular as clockwork. In nine months, minus a week or two, she would be giving birth to a son or daughter who would never go short of anything money could provide.

She had wandered out of the formal gardens and into one of the old olive groves edging them, she realised, coming down to earth again. The sudden, startling lightning flash was followed by a clap of thunder right overhead, deafening her for a moment or two as it rolled around the heavens.

Gina sought shelter under a tree as the rain came pelting down with the force of a sledgehammer, but the protection was minimal. There was a tumbledown hut some short distance away. Too wet already to care over-much, she made her way across to it, sinking to a seat on the rough bench running around three sides to view the unremitting downpour through the doorless doorway with unthrilled eyes. It was obviously going to be some time before she could make her way back to the villa, and no one would know where she was. The thought that Lucius might be concerned was somewhat satisfying.

She could hardly believe it when the next flash of lightning revealed the figure dashing through the trees towards the hut. The thunder this time was a little further away, but still loud enough to drown out the words spilling from Lucius's lips as he gained shelter. He was furious, that much she could tell, furious and soaked, his suit a sodden ruin.

'How did you find me?' was all she could think of to say for the moment.

'You were seen heading in this direction,' he snapped. 'What possessed you to come so far with a storm about to break?'

'I didn't notice the cloud coming up until the sun disappeared,' she prevaricated. 'Anyway, you didn't need to come looking for me. I'm a big girl. Storms don't scare me.'

The anger suffusing his face in no way diminished. '*I* will scare you if you ever do this to me again!' he threatened. 'You could have been struck by the lightning and killed—along with the child you are carrying!'

'Which would concern you most?' The question was out before she could stop it, wiping his face clear of all expression as he gazed at her.

'You think me capable of such a choice?' he said at length.

Gina would have given a great deal to turn back the clock just a few minutes. She would rather face his anger, she reflected wryly, than this total blanking out of emotion.

'No,' she said. 'Of course not. I was being…' She broke off, spreading her hands in a helpless little gesture. 'I'm not sure what I was being. Can we forget it?'

'You must have had reason to ask such a question,' Lucius persisted. 'Why should such a thought even cross your mind?'

'I *wasn't* thinking. It was a stupid thing to say at all.'

He studied her a moment longer, then abruptly inclined his head. 'Very well, it's forgotten.'

It wasn't, and wouldn't be, she was certain, but at least she was off the hook for now. She sought a safer topic. 'Is it going to be a long storm, do you think?'

'Long enough for alarm to be raised when we fail to make our appearance,' he said.

'You mean *you* neglected to tell anyone where you were going too?'

The sarcasm lit fresh sparks in the dark eyes. 'My tolerance is stretched very fine,' he warned.

'It must be my hormones,' she claimed, seeking refuge in humour. 'Indulge me, will you?'

His smile was brief. 'It appears I must.'

He slid off his jacket, hanging it on a jutting edge of the rough stone wall. The rain had penetrated through to the shirt beneath in huge damp patches. He took that off too.

'You should remove your outer clothing,' he advised, viewing her saturated dress. 'Better by far than sitting in it until the rain ceases.' He was unzipping his trousers as he spoke, sliding the clinging material down his legs and kicking off his shoes in order to remove the garment and hang it to join the other items. 'We're fortunate here in retaining the warmth when it storms.'

Gina put her tongue to lips gone suddenly dry as she contemplated the superb physique. The black silk shorts he favoured did little to conceal the swell of his manhood. Despite all Mario had said, she wanted him so badly it was like a fire lit inside her, spreading rapidly into every part of her.

He knew it too. It was there in his eyes as he looked at her—in the slow, sensual widening of his lips. He came over to where she sat and drew her unprotestingly to her feet, turning her about to slide the long back-zip of her dress and ease it from her shoulders. Despite the heat, she shivered to his touch, limbs quivering, insides turning to molten lava as he unclipped the flimsy lace bra and slid both hands beneath to cup the firm curves.

'Bella!' he murmured.

The dress fell unheeded to the dry earth floor. Gina leaned against him, eyes closed, relishing the feel of the warm bare flesh at her back, the possessiveness in his touch. It didn't have to be true, she told herself. None of it was true!

He lowered his head to kiss the side of her neck, his lips leaving a trail of fire as they moved slowly upwards. The sensation when he ran the tip of his tongue over the rim of her ear to nuzzle the sensitive lobe was indescribable. Shuddering, she twisted in his arms to press her lips into the coating of hair on his chest, tasting the faint, salty tang of a dampness that had nothing to do with the rain.

The silk shorts were no obstacle. Gina followed them down the muscular length of his legs to remove them completely. It was Lucius's turn to shudder, his whole body tensing to the exquisite embrace. He stood it for no more than a few seconds before drawing her upright again to kiss her with a passion that fired her to even greater heights, murmuring guttural, indistinguishable words against her lips.

There was no softness in the earth floor, but she was past caring about such creature comforts. She lifted her head to look down the length of her body as he poised himself above her, thrilling to the size of him, the leashed power. He entered her slowly, purposefully, watching her face contort as he began the movement she craved. Gina wrapped her legs about the hard, masculine hips as the world came crashing in on them.

It took the sight of her dirt-streaked arms cradling the dark head against her breast to bring her back to reality again. The floor had been dry, her skin and hair hadn't; she must, she thought, look as if she'd taken a mud bath!

'I'm a mess!' she exclaimed. 'How on earth am I going to get cleaned up?'

Lucius lifted himself up to survey her, lips twitching. 'A little less impeccable than before, I agree.'

'Not just me!' she pointed out, eyes seeking the white dress crumpled where it had fallen. 'How can I put that back on?'

'One problem at a time.' He pressed himself to his feet, reaching a hand to pull her to hers. 'The rain is still heavy enough.'

They were outside in it before Gina could find breath to protest. Not that she could come up with a better idea, she acknowledged as the water sluiced over her. She gave in to it, laughing as she raked her hands through her hair to cleanse it of the clinging earth, the streaks running down her body.

Lucius had picked up comparatively little himself. Standing there, body glistening, he exemplified physical perfection: a Michelangelo masterpiece come to vibrant life. She wanted him again, right there and then. Sheer gluttony, she admonished herself.

His damp shirt was little help in drying themselves, although they did the best they could. Gina grimaced as she donned the scraps of underwear and pulled on the badly soiled and crumpled dress.

'I don't suppose there's a secret passage we can get back indoors by?'

Lucius laughed and shook his head. 'Unfortunately no.'

'It's all right for you,' she complained. 'You took care to keep *your* things out of the dirt. What's going to be thought when I turn up like this!'

'That you had a fall,' he said without undue concern.

'It would be probable enough in such a torrent. It will cease shortly now that the storm centre has passed over us. We may even see blue skies again before nightfall.'

The rain was certainly lessening. Gina glanced at her watch, surprised in the circumstances to find it still going—even more surprised to find that barely an hour had passed since her departure from the villa.

'Are they likely to send search parties out for us?' she asked.

'After several more hours perhaps. As we are already so wet, there seems little point in lingering further. You should put on your shoes,' he added. 'They will afford some protection for your feet.'

The state they were in, Gina doubted it, but she complied anyway. Worms liked the wet, and she hated the thought of stepping on one.

Even with the rain letting up, it was hard going through the long grass. Gina was relieved to reach the narrow path she had been following when the storm had begun. Lucius supported her with a hand under her elbow until they were back in the cultivated grounds where the way was smoother.

They entered the villa by a side door. Thinking they'd got away with it when they reached the main staircase without running into anyone, Gina froze with her foot on the first step as the *salotto* door opened.

It had to be Ottavia, of course. And she wasn't alone. Livia looked equally dumbfounded on sight of them.

'We were caught in the storm,' said Lucius before either woman could speak. 'You will excuse us if we go straight away to find dry clothing.'

He urged Gina on up the stairs with a hand in the small of her back, a direction she wasn't loath to take. If it had been Ottavia on her own it wouldn't have mattered as much, but to appear in this state before the woman she still believed was something more to Lucius than a mere friend of the family—even if not to the extent Mario had intimated—was unbearably humiliating.

They reached their suite without a further word passing between them. Lucius strode directly across to his bathroom, leaving Gina to strip off the ruined dress and step under her own shower.

She washed her hair first, rinsing it thoroughly before soaping her body. The euphoria she had felt back there in the hut had vanished completely. She'd given him nothing he wouldn't have experienced before, and no doubt with a great deal more expertise. She was a pure beginner when it came to sexual stimulation, while he knew every move in the book. If not already seeking other outlets, how long would it be before he became bored enough to do it?

Wearing a bathrobe much like her own, he was lounging on the bed when she finally emerged.

'I was beginning to think you had fallen asleep,' he remarked. 'What could have taken so long when the dirt was all but removed already?'

'I felt like a good long soak, that's all,' she said.

'Then, you should have run a bath.' He allowed his gaze to drift the length of her body and back again, his slow smile starting the all too familiar strumming on her heart strings. 'Come here to me,' he invited softly.

Something in her refused to give way to the urge. 'I need to dry my hair,' she said. 'It takes hours!'

'Something of an exaggeration, I think.' His tone was dry. 'Perhaps I can help speed the process.'

He got up from the bed and walked over to the dressing table to take her dryer from its drawer. Plugging it into the nearby socket, he switched it on and picked up a brush, turning to look at her with lifted brows.

'The sooner we begin, the sooner we finish.'

Short of telling him to get lost, Gina was left with little choice but to let him have his way. She took a seat on the padded stool, watching through the mirror as he lifted the first thick strands and got to work.

It felt good, she had to admit. He showed a rare dexterity in his use of both brush and dryer.

'It isn't the first time you've done this, is it?' she felt moved to ask.

'The first time in practice,' he acknowledged. 'I used to watch my mother dry her hair when I was a boy. It always fascinated me to see the difference emerge.'

'You might have been a hairdresser in a previous life,' she said lightly. 'Did you ever try regressing?'

'A waste of both time and energy,' he returned. 'We have the one life to make the best of.'

The one life into which to pack as much as possible was what he meant, Gina surmised, unable to keep the doubts at bay any longer. Why should a wife curtail that aim?

'Might you have married Livia Marucchi?' she heard herself asking without conscious intention, and saw the face in the mirror acquire an indecipherable expression.

'At no time,' he said.

'Why not?' she insisted. 'She's surely everything any man could want?'

'In the purely physical sense, perhaps. I had other requirements in a wife.'

Gina swallowed on the hard lump in her throat. There was no point in feeling hurt by the admission that he found the woman physically desirable when she'd already suggested as much.

'You mean she wasn't a virgin,' she said flatly. 'Didn't she know how you felt about that?'

'I never discussed it with her.'

'But you have slept with her?'

The reply was a moment or two coming, his expression still giving little away. 'Nothing that happened before you came into my life has any relevance,' he said at length. 'It's the future that matters not the past.'

Gina said softly, 'You see us growing old together?'

'The fates providing. Marriage, in my mind, is for life.'

How about marital fidelity? she yearned to ask, but doubted that she would get an honest reply.

'Mine too,' she returned, and saw a smile widen the firm mouth.

'It had better be.'

Her hair was dry enough by now to be brushed into order. Lucius switched off the dryer and unplugged it, rolling the flex around the handle before putting it back in the drawer he'd taken it from.

'We have an hour to spare before we need dress for dinner,' he observed, watching her smooth the shining tresses.

'So read a book,' she suggested, stifling her involuntary response. 'Improve your mind.'

The smile came again. 'You think my mind in need of improvement?'

'I think it's possible to have too much of a good thing,' she said with purpose, needing to get at him in some way. '"Surfeiting, the appetite may sicken, and so die."'

His shrug made light of the intimation. 'Your Shakespeare was a man of many words.'

Regret came swift and sharp as he turned away. If she wanted him to go looking elsewhere for sex, she was going the right way about it. It was hardly as if she found his appetite for lovemaking any hardship. She was usually of the same mind.

* * *

Livia, it turned out, was not only staying on to dinner, but had been invited to spend the night—by whom, it wasn't clear. Gina found herself analysing every word and glance that passed between Lucius and the other woman. Ridiculous, she knew, but she couldn't help herself.

It was Ottavia who brought the conversation round to the luncheon party.

'I saw you talking with Mario Lanciani,' she said to Gina. 'You should be cautious in your dealings with a man of his kind.'

'What kind is that?' Gina asked.

'Why was he here at all?' Lucius demanded of his mother before his sister could answer.

Cornelia shook her head in obvious bafflement. 'He was not invited.'

Lucius turned his attention to Gina, his expression no encouragement. 'What was it you spoke of with him?'

'We just passed the time of day,' she claimed, not about to admit the truth.

Livia gave a laugh. 'Then, he is indeed changed!'

'You know him so well?' Gina challenged.

'His reputation is known to everyone,' came the smooth reply. 'Many women find him captivating.'

Looking at her, Gina wondered if anyone else saw the malice glistening in her eyes. She had a sudden notion that Mario Lanciani's gatecrashing this afternoon had been orchestrated for him; he certainly hadn't put up much of a struggle to retain her company once the message had been delivered, and she'd seen nothing of him afterwards. What Livia might hope to gain by it, she wasn't sure. It might be satisfaction enough to her just to plant the seeds of doubt.

'I'm not all that easily impressed,' she answered with equal smoothness.

Seemingly about to make some further comment, Lucius apparently thought better of it. Conversation moved on—as did the clock. Stifling a yawn, Gina wondered if she would ever become accustomed to the order of things. Apart from when she'd been out somewhere for the evening back home, she'd been used to going to bed around eleven at the latest.

Back home. It wasn't the first time she had felt the longing to be there. For all its grandeur, San Cotone could never mean as much to her as the house where she had been born and done her growing up. She missed so much about her life previous to the one she was leading now.

There had been times when she had felt just being with Lucius at all was enough, but it wasn't. She needed to be loved the way she loved him. She stole a glance at him as he listened to something his mother was saying, remembering the way he had looked that afternoon in the hut—the things he had done to her. If lovemaking was an art, then he was master of it, but it was no substitute for the real thing.

She caught Marcello's eye as she looked away again, surprised for a moment by the empathy she saw there. She had had so little to do with him up to now. He tended to keep himself very much to himself—in public, at any rate. They had something in common by virtue of the fact that both of them were newcomers to the Carandente clan, but his position, reliant on what he probably considered little better than charity, was a great deal harder than hers to bear.

She gave him a tentative smile, rewarded by a glimmer in return. From now on, she resolved, she would make an effort to get to know him a bit better.

For the first time since their marriage, Lucius contented himself with no more than a kiss on retiring. Quid pro quo for her refusal earlier? Gina wondered hollowly as he settled himself for sleep.

Unlikely, she was bound to acknowledge. Lucius wasn't a man to play that kind of game. Which left a lack of desire as the only explanation—with Livia very much to the forefront as the possible reason for it.

She slept eventually, coming half awake again some time later to stretch out an instinctive arm to the warm, male body at her side. Except that there was no body, and hadn't been for some considerable time if the coolness of the sheets was anything to go by.

Rolling onto her back again, Gina lay like a log, trying not to think the worst. No matter how great the temptation, Lucius would surely hesitate to give way to it in such a manner. Yet he wasn't in either of the bathrooms because no light showed beneath the doors, so where the devil *had* he gone?

An age seemed to pass before the bedroom door was softly opened. Gina stifled the urge to demand to know where he'd been, controlling her breathing to appear asleep as he slid into the bed. The silence was heavy, then she heard a long, drawn sigh. If he'd touched her in any way at that moment she would have been physically sick.

Awake half the night, she was late surfacing from a sleep that had held a quality of emotional if not physical exhaustion. It was no surprise to find Lucius already gone. As he'd told her that very first morning, he was an inveterate early riser.

She'd know nothing of this if she'd been content to leave the past alone to start with, she thought wretchedly as she got herself ready to go down and face the woman she was pretty sure had seen a great deal more of her husband than she had herself last night. Running a wife *and* mistress might be common practice for a man out here for all she knew, but in the same house was surely beyond the pale!

Breakfast was long over by the time she reached the terrace, the family dispersed. Gina drank the fresh coffee Crispina brought out to her, and nibbled a croissant without appetite. She felt listless, movement of any kind an effort. It took the sight of Lucius approaching from the lower gardens with Livia by his side to rouse her from her lethargy.

'Buon giorno!' greeted the other woman as they mounted the terrace steps. The derisive gleam in her eyes belied the solicitation in her voice as she added in English, 'You must have been very weary last night to sleep for so long!'

Gina took care to keep her own voice level. 'I suppose I must. I take it you've been up and about for hours!'

Livia laughed and lifted her shoulders. 'Perhaps two, no more. Even so, I found Lucius was before me.'

'Two early birds!' This time Gina couldn't quite eradicate the sarcasm, drawing a narrowed glance from Lucius. 'A big help when it comes to worm-gathering.'

It was Livia's turn to frown. 'Worm?'

Lucius answered in Italian, turning the frown to a comprehensive nod.

'So true,' she said.

Gina would have loved to know just what translation he'd given. One thing she did know: *he* was fully aware of her meaning.

'The coffee's fresh if you fancy some more,' she said.

Lucius shook his head. 'I have things I must do.'

'I will join you,' declared Livia. She turned an intimate

smile on her host. 'Perhaps you would ask Crispina to bring me out a cup?'

There was a bell connected to the table by which to summon the staff, but he didn't point it out. 'Of course,' he said.

He gave Gina a penetrating look in passing. She returned it unblinkingly. Let him wonder just how much she guessed of his night-time activities.

Livia took a seat, her whole manner proprietary. 'You must find our world very different from your own,' she remarked.

'Not all that much,' Gina responded. 'We have women like you where I come from too.'

The well-shaped brows lifted in sardonic enquiry. 'Women like me?'

'Who can't leave any man alone.'

Livia looked amused. 'It takes two of the same mind. Lucius and I have been…friends for many moons.'

'But he married *me*.'

'He was bound by a code no *Inglese* could ever understand,' came the unmoved reply.

She was half Italian, Gina could have pointed out. She didn't because it was a futile exercise.

Crispina's arrival with fresh crockery afforded her breathing space. It was unlikely that the girl would understand a word, but she waited until she had departed before voicing the declaration already formed in her mind.

'This will be your last visit to San Cotone, so make the most of what's left of it.'

All trace of derision suddenly flown, Livia looked ready to explode. 'Who are you,' she demanded, 'to tell me that?'

'Owner of everything you see, for one thing.' Gina regretted the retort the moment the words were out of her mouth, but there was no going back on them now. 'That gives me the right to say who is and who isn't welcome,' she added, thinking she may as well go the whole hog. 'So I'd be grateful if you'd pack your bag and leave as soon as possible.'

'If you think that Lucius will allow you to do this, you have little knowledge of him.' Livia spat the words at her. 'When I tell him what you have said to me—'

'You can tell him whatever you like,' Gina cut in, losing what little tolerance she had left. 'He's my husband, not my controller! If you—'

She broke off as a sudden wave of nausea gripped her by the throat. She fought to keep her face from reflecting what was going on inside her—glad of the lack of comprehension in Livia's expression.

'I'll leave you to finish your coffee,' she said, getting carefully to her feet.

Another wave of nausea made further speech impossible. She headed indoors, only just making it to a lavatory. If confirmation was needed, she thought weakly when it was over, then this had to be it. Right now, it was the last thing she wanted to think about.

Emerging from the room with the intention of going upstairs, she was dismayed to run into Cornelia. Her mother-in-law took one look at her wan face and jumped to an immediate and delighted conclusion.

'Why have you not said you were with child?' she exclaimed.

Gina attempted a smile. 'We thought we'd wait until it was official.'

'I would say there is little doubt of it. I too suffered the malaise. It only lasts the first weeks. After that, all is well.'

With the baby perhaps, Gina thought hollowly.

'You must take care not to overexert yourself,' her

mother-in-law advised. 'And you must see a physician at once!'

'Lucius is going to arrange it,' Gina assured her, anxious to escape any further catechism. 'I think I'll go and lie down for a few minutes until it passes.

'Yes, do that,' Cornelia urged. 'I am so very happy! A grandchild at last!'

'It may not be a boy,' Gina felt bound to point out, and received an expansive gesture.

'If not this time, then the next.'

Gina gave a weak smile, and made her escape. It was difficult enough dealing with the here and now.

Just how difficult was brought home to her some fifteen minutes later when Lucius came to find her. The words he was about to utter faded on his lips when he saw her lying on the bed, replaced by concerned ones.

'You are feeling ill?'

'No more than is normal, according to your mother,' she said.

'You told her?'

Sitting up now, Gina shook her head, wishing she hadn't, as nausea stirred once more. 'I didn't need to tell her. She guessed. Apparently she went through the same thing during the first few weeks. She's delighted, by the way.'

'I would hope so,' he returned. 'We are to see the gynaecologist tomorrow at eleven.'

'We?' Gina queried softly.

'You think I would allow you to go alone?' Lucius paused, expression clouding again. 'I spoke with Livia a few moments ago. She tells me you have forbidden her to visit San Cotone.'

'True.' Gina saw no point in beating about the bush.

'I'm exercising my right as mistress of the house...' she gave the term subtle emphasis '...to choose who is and isn't welcome.'

'As Ottavia's closest and dearest friend, Livia has always been welcome here.'

'As Ottavia's friend, I've no objection to her.'

A spark sprang to life deep down in the dark eyes, though his tone remained level. 'What is it you are saying?'

Gina knew a sudden flicker of doubt, but she gave it no time to grow. 'I'm saying that whatever the custom in this country, I don't have to go along with it. I gave up a whole way of life to salve your conscience, but turning a blind eye while you console yourself with old friends wasn't part of the bargain!'

The silence that followed was weighty. All expression had been wiped from Lucius's face. When he did speak it was with control. 'You believe that is what I am doing?'

'Well, isn't it?' She shot the words at him. 'Where else did you go last night if it wasn't to...her?'

'Where indeed?' The dark eyes were shuttered, the lines of his face etched in sharp relief. 'Denials would obviously be a waste of time and breath. Of course, there will be nothing to stop me from seeing Livia away from here.'

He was turning as he spoke, with the obvious intention of leaving the room. Gina's chest hurt from the pressure building within. So now she knew for sure. For what good it had done her.

'Don't you dare ever touch me again!' She flung the words after him. 'Not in any way! Do you hear me?'

The broad shoulders stiffened, but he made no answer. Gina sank back into the pillows as the door closed in his wake, misery swamping her. This time yesterday she had been so happy. Why had she had to go and spoil it all?

Because there was no way she could live with suspicion locked away inside her, came the answer. What she had to decide now was where she went from here. Home, was her immediate inclination. Her parents would welcome her with open arms.

Except that it wasn't only herself she had to consider. The child she was carrying had rights too.

The knock on the door some time later jerked her out of it. She sat up and swung her legs to the floor before inviting the knocker to enter. Cornelia regarded her in some concern.

'If you are still suffering the nausea I will have the doctor sent for,' she said.

'I'm not,' Gina assured her. 'Not any more. I must have fallen asleep.' She got to her feet, summoning a smile. 'I'll be right down.'

'There is no hurry,' her mother-in-law returned. 'Lucius said you were to be left alone, but what would a man know about such matters? He should have stayed with you to soothe your brow.' The last she said with a twinkle. 'Why should we have to bear all the crosses?'

'All part and parcel of being a woman, I suppose,' Gina answered in like vein. She made a show of examining the skirt she was wearing. 'This is all creased. I'd better change.'

'Then, I will leave you to do so,' said Cornelia. 'You will find me on the terrace should you wish for company. You knew Lucius had gone to Siena, of course?'

'Of course,' Gina echoed, doubting if it was true. He would be with Livia.

Knowing Lucius's opinion of the garment, she more often than not refrained from wearing trousers of any kind. Today, she donned a pair of loose silky ones in place of the skirt. No more kowtowing to his likes and dislikes. From now on she pleased herself.

A furious Ottavia cornered her on her way downstairs.

'I grew tired of waiting for you to appear!' she declared. 'How dare you tell Livia she cannot come here again!'

'How dare *you* tell *me* what I should or shouldn't do?' Gina countered, losing what self-possession she had managed to gather in face of this fresh attack. 'I'll make whatever decision I choose to make. If you object, you can always find somewhere else to live!'

The fury died as swiftly as it had arisen before the look on her sister-in-law's face. She knew instant shame that she could have stooped so low. 'I didn't mean that,' she said gruffly. 'I really didn't!'

'Why would you say it unless it was in your mind?' Ottavia retorted. 'I have known from the beginning that you resented both my own and Marcello's presence. No doubt you would prefer that my mother was also gone!'

'Not true.' Gina searched her mind for some way of undoing the harm she had done—finding nothing of any great help. 'The only one whose presence I resent is Livia Marucchi,' she appealed. 'You can surely understand that?'

Ottavia curled a lip. 'I understand your jealousy of her beauty, but banning her from San Cotone will not make Lucius more attentive towards you. My brother did what he considered his duty in marrying you. Why should he sacrifice everything?'

'He had the opportunity to marry Livia before ever I came along,' Gina responded, trying to keep a level head. 'Why didn't he take it, I wonder?'

'Because Livia herself was not yet ready to make the commitment.'

'I don't believe that.'

The shrug was expressive. 'You must believe what comforts you. I shall, of course, be telling Lucius of your wish for Marcello and myself to find other accommodation.'

Hopeless trying any further appeal, Gina accepted despondently as the older woman turned away. It would normally be against her nature to say what she had, but what about this whole situation was normal? She was married to and carrying the child of a man who not only didn't love her, but was at present very probably in the arms of the woman he had wanted to marry.

She avoided contact with any other member of the family by returning to the bedroom. The nausea had passed, for what difference it made to her mood. Lying on the bed, she went over the happenings of the last weeks. There had been good times—wonderful times, in fact—but how real had they been? How often when making love to her had Lucius imagined she was Livia? How often had he compared her responses with those of the other woman?

How did she go on living this life knowing what she knew?

CHAPTER TEN

SHE must have dozed off at some point, waking with a start to find Donata standing by the bedside.

'I was concerned when you made no answer to my knock,' said the girl. 'Are you still feeling ill?'

Gina raised herself up, forcing a smile. 'Not any more, thanks.' She glanced at the bedside clock, dismayed to find it approaching twelve-thirty. 'I can't believe it!' she exclaimed. 'Where did the time go?'

'You need whatever rest your body tells you you need now,' declared Donata with some authority. '*Madre* says she slept a great deal when she was with child.'

Gina's head jerked round. 'She told you!'

'But of course.' Donata looked momentarily nonplussed. 'Was she not meant to?'

'No. I mean, it hasn't been properly confirmed yet.'

'But you know yourself?'

'Well...yes.' Gina summoned another smile, a lighter note. 'I suppose I'm being overcautious.'

Dark eyes sparkled. 'It's so exciting! Lucius must be joyful!' She sobered to add sternly, 'He should have stayed with you while you were feeling ill.'

'I'm best dealing with it on my own.' Gina kept her tone easy.

'Do you wish me to leave you?' queried her sister-in-law with obvious reluctance.

'Not at all,' Gina assured her. 'You can find me something uncreased to wear to lunch while I take a quick shower to freshen up, if you like, then we'll go down together.'

Her multireflection in the bathroom was no confidence booster. She looked thoroughly washed out, her hair limp and lifeless. It was far too early yet, of course, to detect any change in her slender shape, but it was going to come. Whether she would still be here at San Cotone when the child came into the world was another matter.

Donata had picked out a sleeveless tunic in muted greens, along with a pair of low-heeled sandals.

'High heels are no longer suitable,' she advised. 'You must take no risks with your balance.' She eyed Gina's figure in the brief lace bra and panties. 'You'll need maternal clothing for when you begin to gain weight.'

'Maternity,' Gina corrected, unable to stay sombre in the face of such knowledgeable pronouncements. 'Maternal means mother.'

'Which is what you're to be.' Donata sounded as if the distinction was too slight to be of any great importance. 'And *I* am to be an aunt! Practice,' she added, 'for when I have children of my own.'

'You plan on Cesare becoming the father?' Gina asked, sliding the tunic over her head.

'Of course.' There was certainty in both voice and expression. 'He knows it too, even if the words themselves are still to be spoken between us.'

Recalling what he'd said yesterday, Gina felt it quite possible. She only hoped Donata wouldn't suffer the same disillusionment she was suffering in time to come.

Not looking forward to seeing Ottavia again, she was relieved, if only temporarily, to find Cornelia seated alone on the terrace.

'You look far from your usual self,' remarked the latter

candidly, viewing her. 'Would you not prefer to have a tray brought to you?'

'I'm fine now,' Gina assured her. 'Really I am. I was just a bit tired, that's all.'

'You perhaps have need of an iron supplement.'

'If I do, I'm sure it will all be sorted out tomorrow when I see the gynaecologist.' Gina sought a change of subject. 'The air feels heavy again. Do you think we're in for another storm?'

'There is a likelihood at this time of the year.' Cornelia sounded amused. 'It must be your English blood that makes you so concerned with the weather.'

Gina laughed. 'It's so rarely the same from one day to another back home!'

The older woman looked at her oddly. 'You still think of England as your home?'

She was saved from answering by Ottavia's emergence from the villa, closely followed by Lucius. There was little to be gleaned from his expression, but Gina had no doubt at all that he'd been fully apprised of her transgressions.

'Business concluded?' she heard herself asking.

'Whatever is left will be dealt with another time,' he returned without particular inflection. 'How are you feeling now?'

She stretched her lips in a smile she hoped didn't look as stiff as it felt. 'I'll live.'

Ottavia looked from one to the other in some obvious perplexity. It was left to her mother to put her in the picture.

'Did Lucius not tell you yet? You are to be a *zietta*!'

The expression in Ottavia's eyes was hardly one of pleasure at the news. 'You must forgive me,' she said with satire to Gina, 'for my failure to appreciate your condition earlier. My attention was on other matters.'

'I already told you I didn't mean what I said,' Gina responded on as steady a note as she could manage. 'I apologise for it.'

'Once said, such things cannot be easily forgotten,' came the brittle reply.

'But they can be put aside,' said Lucius crisply. 'Gina has apologised. Let that be an end to it.'

Ottavia lifted her shoulders in a gesture meant to express a reluctant acquiescence. Bursting though they obviously were with curiosity, neither Cornelia nor Donata voiced a question. Meeting her husband's hard eyes, Gina did her best to keep the desolation she felt from showing in hers. No way was he ever going to know her true feelings.

Reluctant to face the questions she was sure Donata for one would be asking, she escaped into the gardens after lunch. There was to be no escape from Lucius however. He found her down by the lily pond where they had met that first morning.

'There are matters we have to have clear between us,' he said.

Gina kept her gaze fixed on the dragonfly flitting from lily pad to lily pad. 'They're clear enough already. Unlike with Ottavia, I meant what I told *you* this morning. I don't want you anywhere near me again!'

'You expect me to accept such an edict?'

He had halted to the side and a little behind the stone seat where she was sitting, right on the periphery of her vision. Her heart was hammering so loudly he must have been able to hear it, but her voice was rock steady. 'You don't have a choice.'

'As your husband, I have certain rights!'

Her head jerked round, eyes blazing into his. 'Like hell

you do! I'm not your property to be used as and when you see fit!'

Dark eyes glittered back at her, the thrust of his hands into trouser pockets indicative of a barely controlled anger. 'I recall no complaints.'

'*I've* no basis for comparison,' she retorted. 'Yet.'

The glitter became a flame, searing her where she sat. He reached her in a couple of steps, jerking her upright. 'There will be no other man in your life!' he said in a clipped voice. 'Should you ever…'

A muscle in his jaw line contracted as his teeth came together. He released her abruptly, striding away without a backward glance. Gina sank back to her seat. She couldn't continue with this, she thought bleakly.

There was no sign of Lucius when she eventually forced herself to return to the villa. Neither was Ottavia nor her mother in evidence. Which left only Donata.

'I saw Lucius follow you to the gardens, and again when he returned,' the girl declared. 'He was angrier than I have seen him since I was sent home from school!'

'We had a disagreement,' Gina acknowledged.

It was apparent that her sister-in-law wanted to ask about what, but she refrained. 'Unlike Ottavia's, his anger doesn't last long,' she advised. 'He will have forgotten it when he returns.'

Not in this instance, reflected Gina hollowly.

Hot and sultry, the afternoon crept to a close. It needed another storm to bring relief. Lucius, it turned out, had gone to the vineyard. He returned with Marcello at six, seemingly bearing out Donata's prediction. Surface only, Gina judged, wondering if she was the only one to see the fiery flicker in the dark eyes whenever he glanced her way.

Taking it for granted that Ottavia would have filled him in on the day's happenings, she sought a few minutes with Marcello before going to change for dinner.

'I was in a bad mood this morning and let my tongue run away with me,' she said frankly. 'I'd hate for you to think I didn't want you here.'

His smile was wry. 'It would be understandable.'

'It's not the way I really feel,' Gina insisted. About you, at any rate, she tagged on mentally. 'San Cotone is as much your home as it is mine.'

'That can never be,' he returned. 'I am deeply indebted to Lucius for providing a roof over my head, but the time must come when I seek a home of my own again.'

The problem being that Ottavia was unlikely to settle for what she would regard as an impoverished standard of living, Gina reflected, feeling genuine sympathy for the man.

'Please try to excuse my wife if she appears resentful of you,' he went on. 'The realisation of who you were was a devastation to her.'

If Ottavia hadn't searched her things that day, in all likelihood there would have been no realisation, Gina could have told him.

'I suppose I can appreciate her feelings,' she said instead. 'Especially considering…'

'Considering my position,' Marcello finished for her as she let the words trail away. 'You must wonder that we are together still.'

'It's crossed my mind,' she admitted.

'As with most who have little knowledge of her. Her loyalty to me is steadfast. Never once has she berated me for my mistakes. To Ottavia, the marriage vows are sacred.'

Providing she wasn't called on to suffer the 'poorer' element, came the sneaking thought.

'You must love her a great deal,' she murmured.

'A very great deal,' he confirmed. 'She is everything to me.'

Gina had never envied anyone in her life before, but she felt a pang right now. One thing she could be certain of, Lucius was never going to say the same of her.

He was already in the shower when she went up. Reluctant to be drawn into any further altercations, she lingered as long as possible under the water herself, hoping he would have gone by the time she emerged. Finding her hope granted when she did eventually regain the bedroom brought only a temporary relief, of course. She had to be alone with him again at some point; while they still shared a bed, she could hardly avoid it. Just let him try exercising the rights he had claimed this afternoon, she thought fiercely, and the whole house would know about it!

It was a long evening, made even longer by Ottavia's unabated hostility. Apart from not having a great deal to say, Lucius gave no indication that anything was amiss. Gina put on a show herself, but was aware of Cornelia's thoughtful regard from time to time.

Donata was too wrapped up in her own affairs to sense any discord. 'Tomorrow,' she announced at dinner, 'Cesare is to take me to Firenze to meet with his grandmother. She will disapprove of me, of course, but I will win her over.'

Gina didn't doubt it. Shorn of the rebel outlook she had first displayed, her sister-in-law was capable of winning anyone over. She had certainly succeeded with Cesare, for all his protestations.

By midnight she had had enough. Cornelia nodded sagely when she announced her intention of going to bed.

'You must learn to take siesta,' she said. 'Rest is good for you.'

'I'll be with you shortly,' said Lucius. His tone was devoid of any undercurrents, but to Gina it still sounded like a threat.

She prepared for bed swiftly, sliding between the cool silk sheets to lie wide awake and tense. Only when the outer door finally opened did she close her eyes, turning her face into the pillow and deepening her breathing.

Every sound, every movement Lucius made over the following minutes seemed magnified. When he got into the bed, she could barely restrain the tremoring in her limbs.

'We must talk,' he said.

Gina gave up on the pretence. 'There's nothing left to say. If it weren't for the baby, I'd be out of here by now!'

He drew in a harsh breath. 'This has gone far enough! What proof do you have of your accusations?'

'Proof?' She rolled onto her back to direct a blazing gaze. 'You admitted it!'

Supported on an elbow, Lucius regarded her with held-in anger. 'I admitted nothing!'

'You didn't deny it.'

'You would have believed me if I had?'

She hesitated, searching his taut, olive-skinned features for some assurance—finding none because the dark eyes gave so little away. 'If you weren't with Livia last night,' she said at length, 'then where were you?'

His expression underwent an indefinable alteration. 'I was walking the gardens.'

'For two hours or more?'

'If that was how long I was gone, then yes.'

'You really expect me to believe *that*!'

The moments stretched interminably as he studied her, the muscles around his mouth showing white beneath his skin from the pressure applied. When he spoke at last it was with iron control. 'If you doubt it still, then you were right. There *is* nothing left to say.'

Gina lay like a stone as he switched out the bedside light and settled himself for sleep, his turned back a barrier. Even if she disregarded what Mario Lanciani had told her yesterday, Ottavia had made the situation clear enough this morning, she defended herself. What else could she believe?

Scarcely needed, the confirmation that she was indeed pregnant brought little immediate cheer. Driving back from Siena with a silent Lucius at the wheel, Gina contemplated a future devoid of even physical closeness, much less love.

She stole a glance at the finely carved profile outlined against a sky still heavy with cloud, wondering what was really going on inside the proud dark head. Even if she could extract a promise from him not to see Livia again, could she trust him to keep it?

'I have business in Rome tomorrow,' he said shortly. 'I must leave this afternoon.'

Gina made no answer, her despondency reaching new depths. Lucius tautened his jaw.

'I hope to find you in a more receptive frame of mind on my return.'

'Receptive to what?' she asked. 'More lies?'

This time it was Lucius who made no answer, knuckles paling as he gripped the wheel. Gina felt suddenly sick. As he had said last night, what actual proof did she have of his involvement with Livia Marucchi? The word of a man she'd never met before yesterday? Of a woman who hated her? Not so much the actual word in the latter case even. Ottavia had only insinuated.

'I'm sorry,' she said thickly. 'I think I might be on the way to paranoia!'

Lucius was a moment or two responding, his profile still austere. 'Are you saying you believe what I tell you after all?'

She made a wry gesture, turning a deaf ear to the misgivings still hovering at the back of her mind. 'Yes.'

He said no more on the subject, but the atmosphere remained heavy. Gina put her head back against the seat rest and closed her eyes. She felt so utterly dispirited.

Lucius left for Rome immediately after lunch. Gina saw him off, aware when he kissed her goodbye of constraint in his embrace. Telling him she believed him innocent of any double-dealing was only half the battle she had with herself, she acknowledged wearily. To do the job properly, she had to reinstate Livia's visiting privileges. That was going to be one of the hardest things she had ever done.

At Cornelia's urging, she retired to the bedroom for siesta, but found little rest. It was no use putting off the evil moment until tomorrow, she decided in the end. If it was going to be done at all, it had to be now.

There was only one Marucchi listed in the telephone book. She dialled the number, struggling against the urge to abandon the whole idea. The call was answered by a man whose manner indicated a member of the family rather than a servant. Gina asked in Italian to speak with Signorina Marucchi, but was forced to request a translation of the fast-spoken response.

She sat for several moments fighting a new inner battle after replacing the receiver—without success. It was too much of a coincidence that Livia should be away from home for a few days at the very same time as Lucius. If Rome was his destination, then it was hers too without doubt.

Like an automaton, she got up and made for the dressing room, selecting a lightweight skirt and jacket from the wardrobe and putting them on, then sliding her feet into a pair of shoes. With no suitcase to hand, she could take little with her, but she was going regardless. Home to England where she belonged. Back to those whose love she could count on.

Her face looked pale in the mirror, her eyes bruised. She closed her mind to everything other than the here and now, considering her options for getting away. Keys for all the cars in the garages were looked after by the man who tended the vehicles. All she had to do was request one. From Florence, she could fly home.

She made it to the garages without running into anyone at all, to find the off-shot room, where the keys were kept, unattended. Gina unhooked a set from the numbered pegs at random, only realising she had chosen the Ferarri when she reached the appropriate stall. She'd driven it only the once, and then with Lucius along, but she didn't hesitate. It would get her where she wanted to go.

Converted from stables, the garaging block had an individual door for every car. It slid open on oiled runners. There was plenty of fuel she saw on switching on the ignition. More than enough to get her to Florence.

The engine started at the first pull. Gina bit her lip at the powerful sound, expecting it to bring immediate attention. Not that it was anyone's business but her own if she chose to take the vehicle out.

A couple of the groundsmen were the only people to see her leave. She reached the Vernici road without mishap, turning north away from the town to head for the highway that would take her to Florence. It seemed more like years than mere months since she had traversed these same roads on the way here, she thought bleakly. If only she'd never bothered!

The rain started when she had gone barely five kilometres, so heavy the windscreen wipers could barely cope. She should stop and wait it out, Gina knew, but that would give her too much time to think about what she was doing. She didn't want to think about anything other than getting away.

The truck looming suddenly through the murk was right on the crown of the road. A sense of *déjà vu* swept over her as she took instinctive avoiding action. There was a timeless moment when the car skidded out of control as the tyres failed to grip, then a huge bang, and darkness.

She drifted up from the depths to the sound of voices, faint and far away at first, but becoming stronger. They were speaking in Italian, of course, and far too rapidly for her to follow. *'Non capisco,'* she murmured before drifting off again.

Her first clear recollection found her lying on her back with a white ceiling filling her line of vision. Her neck felt stiff. She lifted a nerveless hand to touch the collar encircling it, the pieces coming together slowly. Apart from the headache throbbing at her temples, there was no pain.

'You must lie still until they can be sure there is no further damage,' said Lucius from somewhere off to the side.

The anguish that swept her was like a sword thrust. 'The baby.' she whispered. 'I lost the baby?'

'No.' Lucius came into view, the strain evident in both face and voice. 'You still have the child. The seat belt saved you from being thrown around the car when it rolled.'

'Is it a write-off?' she murmured. 'The car, I mean.'

'You think I care about the car?' he demanded with force. 'Why were you driving at all in such weather?'

Gina gazed at the ceiling, in no fit state for the confrontation that would eventually have to come. 'It wasn't raining when I set off.'

'That is not—' Lucius broke off abruptly. When he spoke again it was on a more level note. 'You were drifting in and out of consciousness for several hours. That means you have concussion at the very least. The doctor will examine you now you're fully awake.'

He moved away, his place taken by an older man in a white coat. Gina submitted to his ministrations, responding to the questions translated for her by Lucius. Her relief at the removal of the neck collar, indicating that there was no spinal injury, was tempered by the headache still pounding at her temples. She sat up gingerly when asked, wincing a little as pressure came to bear on bruises she hadn't felt until then, but thankful to have no greater injuries to cope with.

The two men spoke together for a few moments, then the doctor left.

'You're to stay here at least for tonight to make sure there are no delayed repercussions,' Lucius declared. 'Sleep is the best medicine for you. A nurse will be in shortly to make you comfortable.'

'Where *is* here?' Gina asked, more because she felt it expected of her than through any great desire to know.

'The Emanuele Clinic. The accident happened less than a kilometre away.'

'You were on your way to Rome,' she said.

'I naturally turned back on receiving the news.' Tone

steady, eyes impenetrable, he added, '*Madre* was distraught. She was unaware of your departure from the villa at all. Where were you going?'

This was neither the time nor the place for confrontation, Gina acknowledged wearily. 'I just felt like a drive,' she said. 'I'm sorry to have given your mother concern.'

Fire flashed in the dark depths. 'You think her the only one to be concerned? If you could but—' He broke off once again, shaking his head as if in repudiation of what he'd been about to say, face set. 'Tomorrow will be time enough. You have need of sleep.'

Gina reached out an involuntary hand to grasp the bare, bronzed forearm as he began turning away, unable to hold out any longer against the emotions choking her.

'Don't go,' she said huskily. 'I need you, *mi amore*!'

His jaw contracted, the muscles in the arm she held taut beneath the skin. 'Do not use that term without true meaning!'

'I don't.' Gina was past caring about giving herself away. Her voice gathered strength along with her spirit. 'I know you don't feel as deeply for me as I feel for you, but you'd better start learning because I'm not letting go! I'll give any woman who fancies her chances with you a battle royal!'

It was a moment or two before Lucius responded, the expression dawning in his eyes as he gazed at her increasing her already galloping pulse rate to ungovernable proportions.

'From where,' he said at last, 'did you gather the impression that I had no depth of feeling for you?'

Gina lifted her shoulders uncertainly. 'You've never used the word love.'

The faintest of smiles touched his mouth. 'Would words of love have persuaded you to marry me?'

'It would have helped.'

'I doubt it. You were drawn to me physically, but no more than that.'

Gina searched the handsome face. 'You're saying the marriage wasn't *just* a matter of conscience on your part?'

His smile widened a little. 'I fell in love with the girl who gave herself so unreservedly to me that night. The girl I had every intention of making my wife, both before and after I discovered her true identity. Reprehensible of me though it was to take advantage of your father's financial problems, I saw no other means of persuading you.'

He took one of her hands in his, raising it to his lips. 'My love for you knows no limits, *mi tesoro*. You must believe me when I tell you that Livia Marucchi has never, nor ever could, hold a place in my heart. I was angry when you banned her from visiting San Cotone again, yes, but only because you accepted my guilt without question. I walked in the gardens two nights ago in an agony of mind, believing you would never come to love me the way I yearned for you to love me. To have you accuse me of spending those hours with Livia—'

'I was too eaten up with jealousy to see straight,' Gina cut in wryly. 'She's so beautiful!'

'Her beauty bears no comparison with yours!' Lucius declared. 'To look into her eyes is to look into soulless depths! A man may use a woman of her kind for release, but few could countenance any closer relationship.'

'Might you not find a need for that kind of release in future?' Gina murmured, and saw the dark eyes flare again.

'You still think me so devoid of integrity?'

'Love doesn't automatically instil total trust,' she defended. 'You've been used to a full and free sex life. Is one woman going to be enough for you?'

Lucius let go of her hand to place both of his about her

throat, lifting her face to meet his descending mouth. The tenderness in his kiss was more convincing than any words.

'*This* one woman, yes,' he avowed when he lifted his head again. 'You satisfy every craving in me—and always will.'

He released her with reluctance. 'Enough for now. You must rest. I'll return in the morning to—'

'No!' Gina ignored the ache in her head as she shook it emphatically. 'I'm coming home with you now!'

'The doctor said—' he began.

'I don't care what the doctor said! You can keep an eye on me yourself. If you try leaving me here I'll walk out and thumb a lift!' she threatened as he hesitated. 'I mean it, Lucius!'

'I knew you were going to be a trouble to me the first moment I saw you,' he remarked with humour. 'What I failed to foresee was the extent of it. If I removed your clothing from the wardrobe you would have no choice but to stay.'

'Don't count on it. I'd wrap myself in a sheet if necessary!'

Laughter creased the sculptured face. 'A risk I am not prepared to take! Do you feel capable of dressing yourself while I go and speak with the doctor?'

'Perfectly,' she assured him. 'I'll be ready and waiting.'

He kissed her again, long and passionately, before departing, leaving her with a brimming heart. She could deal with anything and anyone knowing he loved her—including Ottavia. San Cotone was her home, as it had been her father's before her. She finally felt she belonged.

EPILOGUE

EXTENDED along the length of the terrace to seat the laughing, chattering throng, the table groaned beneath the weight of dishes still nowhere near empty. Crystal and silver glinted in the sunlight, while myriad scents spilled from the massed blooms festooning the stone balustrades.

Gina turned her gaze from the distant views she never tired of to the infinitely dearer one closer to hand, tears of pure happiness prickling her lids as she surveyed each familiar face. It was wonderful to have everyone together like this: an occasion to be cherished in memory for all time. And all down to her mother-in-law, who had moved heaven and earth to make it happen.

Catching the latter's eye, she mouthed her gratitude, finishing off with a blown kiss, and receiving one in return. This meant so much more to her than any formal celebration, as Cornelia had known it would.

Secure in the knowledge of their own status in her affections, her parents watched the exchange without rancour. They were regular visitors to San Cotone, and would be welcomed as permanent residents if and when they finally chose. As Lucius himself often said, there was room enough and to spare.

Even more so these days, came the thought, bringing a momentary downswing in spirits, just as swiftly conquered. She had flown the coop herself at an earlier age than either Vittorio or Giovanni. Anyway, Doria was still within easy reach, and soon to give birth to a brother or sister for Pietro and Portia. They helped make up for the lack of day-to-day contact with the other grandchildren.

Sitting here now, it still scarcely seemed possible that so much time had passed. The silver in Lucius's hair served only to enhance the sculptured bone structure, the fine cotton T-shirt he was wearing outlining a body still as lean and lithe as when they had first met. Husband and lover without equal, Gina thought mistily, senses stirring as always to the sheer impact of those looks. There would never come a time when she failed to want him, never come a time when her love for him burned any less intense.

Her whole life here in Tuscany had been a joy. Not once had she known regret for the career she had given up to become a wife and mother. She and Ottavia had long ago reached an understanding—helped by Marcello's regaining of independence—and were now the best of friends. The two remained childless themselves, but took great delight in all their nieces and nephews. Donata and Cesare were the proud parents of no less than five children, all of whom were here today too, along with their respective families, making a grand total of thirty-eight. What might be called a typical Italian family gathering.

Lucius was getting to his feet, clinking a spoon against his glass to draw attention.

'I wish to propose a toast of my own,' he said. He looked down at the lovely, unlined face at his side, dark eyes filled with an emotion that brought a lump to Gina's throat. 'To my beautiful, incomparable wife, for twenty-five wonderful years! And for all those yet to come!'

THE UNFORGETTABLE HUSBAND

by

Michelle Reid

Michelle Reid grew up on the southern edges of Manchester, the youngest in a family of five lively children. But now she lives in the beautiful county of Cheshire with her busy executive husband and two grown-up daughters. She loves reading, the ballet, and playing tennis when she gets the chance. She hates cooking, cleaning, and despises ironing! Sleep she can do without, and produces some of her best written work during the early hours of the morning.

CHAPTER ONE

BLACK bow-tie hanging loose around his neck and the top two buttons on his snowy white dress shirt tugged open at his darkly tanned throat, André Visconte sat sprawled in the chair behind his desk, with his feet propped up on the top and the blunt-ended fingers of one beautifully shaped hand lightly clasping a squat crystal glass half full of his favourite whisky.

It was late and he was tired so his eyes were shut, the grooves around his thirty-four-year-old, life-toughened mouth seeming more harshly etched than usual. He should have gone straight home from the gala opening of a friend's new downtown restaurant but instead he had come back here to his office. He was expecting a call from Paris and it seemed more sensible to wait for it here than at his home since the office was closer.

And anyway, home held no welcome for him any more.

Some bright spark somewhere had once made the classic remark that home was where the heart was. Well, André no longer believed he had a heart, so home, these days, tended to be any place he could lay his head. And, depending on where he was, that usually meant one of the plush city residences he possessed in most capitals of the world.

Not that he had used many of them recently, if you didn't count his apartment right here in New York, of course. Though all of his homes were maintained to his expected high standards—just in case he decided to drop in.

Or in case Samantha did.

Samantha… The fingers around the whisky glass tightened fractionally. His tough mouth straightened into a line of such grim cynicism that if anyone had been there to see it happen, they would have been backing right off in alarm by now.

Because André Visconte wasn't known for his good temper these days—hadn't been known for it for twelve long months now.

Not since Samantha had walked out of his life never to be seen or heard from again. Nowadays, only a fool would dare to say her name out loud in his presence and, since fools were not suffered gladly in the Visconte empire, none ever said it.

But he couldn't stop the cursed name from creeping into his own head now and then. And when it did, it was difficult to it to unravel the gamut of different emotions that came buzzing along with it. Pain was one of them, plus a dark, bloody anger aimed entirely at himself for letting her get away from him.

Then there were the moments of real guilt-ridden anguish to contend with, or the bouts of gut-wrenching concern as to what had become of her. And, to top it all off, there was a hard-to-take sense of personal bitterness in knowing that she *could* leave him that made him wish he had never met her in the first place!

But most of all there was an ache. An ache of such muscle-clenching proportions that sometimes he had to fight not to groan at the power of it.

Why—? Because he missed her. No matter what, no matter when, no matter why—sometimes he missed her so badly that he could barely cope with what missing her did to him.

Tonight had been like that. One of those all-too-rare moments when he had caught himself laughing quite easily—actually managing to enjoy himself! Then a beautiful woman with flame-red hair had walked past him. She had reminded him of Samantha and his mood had flipped over. Light to dark. Warm to cold. Laughter to lousy misery…

After that, it had been better to escape here and brood where no one could see him doing it. But, God, he hated her for making him feel like this.

Empty. The word was empty.

The glass went to his mouth, hard lips parting so he could attack the whisky as if it was his enemy. Then, with a sigh that came from somewhere deep down inside of him, he leaned further back into the soft leather chair and waited for the whisky to attack him back by burning Samantha's name right out of his system.

It didn't happen for, being the beautiful red-haired witch that she was, she held her ground and simply paid him back for trying to get rid of her by imprinting her image on the back of his eyelids, then smiling at him provocatively.

His gut wrenched. His loins stung. His heart began to pound. 'Witch,' he breathed.

Twelve months—twelve long, miserable months—with no word from her, no sign that she was even alive. She had, in effect, simply dropped off the face of the earth as if she had never lived on it.

Cruel, heartless—*ruthless* witch.

The phone on his desk suddenly burst into life. With a reluctance that suggested he might actually be enjoying sitting here wallowing in his own misery, André let go of the glass and, without even bothering to open his eyes, reached out to hook up the receiver with a couple of long fingers, then tucked it lazily beneath his chin.

'Visconte,' he announced, voice tinged with a seductive hint of a husky drawl even though it had meant to rasp.

Expecting to hear a barrage of French come back down the line at him, he was shocked to hear the crisp clean tones of his UK-based manager assailing his ears, instead of his man in Paris.

'Nathan?' He frowned. 'What the hell—?'

Whatever Nathan Payne said to him then brought André alive as nothing else could. His eyes flicked open, revealing dark brown irises with a flash of fire. His hand snaked up to grab at the phone and his feet hit the floor with a resounding thud as he launched his lean body out of the chair.

'What—?' he raked out. 'Where—?' he barked. *'When—?'*

From the other side of the Atlantic, Nathan Payne began talking in quick, precise sentences, each one of which sent André paler until his satin gold tan had almost disappeared.

'You're sure it's her?' he asked, when his manager eventually fell into silence.

Confirmation had him sitting down again slowly—carefully, as though he needed to gauge each move he made precisely, in case he used up what was left of his suddenly depleted strength.

'No, I'm sure you couldn't,' he responded to something Nathan said to him. The hand he'd lifted up to cover his eyes was trembling slightly. 'How did it happen?'

Explanation had him raking up the whisky glass and

swallowing its contents in one tense gulp. 'And you saw this in a newspaper?' He couldn't believe it. Couldn't believe any of it.

Samantha... His dark head wrenched to one side as a very familiar pain went slicing through him.

'No!' he ground out at whatever the other man had suggested. 'Just watch her, but don't, for God's sake, do anything else!' And suddenly he was on his feet again. 'I'm on my way,' he announced. 'Just don't so much as let her out of your sight until I get there!'

The phone hit its cradle with a resounding crash. The hard sound was still echoing around the room when he thrust his body into movement. Then he was grimly striding towards the door with his face still showing the kind of reeling shock that would have rendered most people immobile...

He was there again, Samantha noticed. Sitting at the same table he had been sitting at last night, and watching her in a kind of half surreptitious way that said he didn't want her to know he was doing it.

Why, she had no idea.

She didn't recognise him. His clean-shaven fair-skinned face sounded no chords in her memory to offer a hint that she might have known him once, in a different setting or another life maybe.

Another life.

Having to smother the desire to heave out a sigh, she turned away to begin making up the order for drinks Carla had just given her. With a deftness of hand she fed two glasses under the gin optic while the other hand hooked up two small bottles of tonic and neatly knocked off the clamp tops.

'You do that like a professional,' Carla remarked dryly, watching all of this from the other side of the bar.

Do I? Samantha mused as she placed the items down on Carla's tray. Well, there's something else that could belong to that other life I can't remember. 'Do you want draught beer or the bottled stuff?'

'The bottled—are you feeling all right?' Carla asked, frowning, because it wasn't like Samantha not to rise to a bit of pleasant banter when she was given the chance to.

'Just tired,' she said, and limped off down the bar to get the two bottled beers from the chiller, reassured that her answer had some justification since neither she nor Carla should be working in the hotel lounge bar tonight. Officially, their job was looking after Reception. But the hotel was teetering on its very last legs. Business was poor, and the hotel was being run with the minimum of staff, which therefore meant that people had to chip in wherever they happened to be needed.

Like this week, for instance, when the two of them were doubling up shifts by running the bar in the evening and the reception during the day.

But that didn't mean she was feeling so tired that she was imagining a pair of eyes burning into her every time she turned her back. Limping back down the bar with the two requested beers, she took a glance sideways and just caught the stranger's eyes on her before he looked away.

'The man sitting on his own,' she murmured to Carla. 'Any idea who he is?'

'You mean the well-scrubbed, good-looking one in the Savile Row suit?' she quizzed, adding at Samantha's nod, 'Nathan Payne. Room two-one-two, if his charge slips are to be believed. He booked in last night when

Freddie was on duty. And here on business—which doesn't surprise me, because I can't believe a man like him would actually *choose* this place for a holiday.'

Her derision was clear, and Samantha didn't dispute it. Though the Tremount Hotel's setting was outstandingly good, sitting right on the edge of its own headland in a beautiful part of Devon, it had been let go so badly that Carla hadn't been joking when she'd suggested the stranger would not choose it for a holiday. Few people did.

'Rumour has it that he works for one of the huge hotel conglomerates,' Carla went on. 'The ones which buy up run-down monstrosities like this place and turn them into super-modern, ultra-select holiday complexes like the ones you see further down the coast.'

Was that what he was doing—just checking out the whole hotel in general, and not just watching her? Relief quivered through her. Her face relaxed. 'Well, not before time, I suppose,' she opined, feeling much better now she had a solid reason for the man's presence here. 'The old place could certainly do with a major face-lift.'

'But at the expense of all our jobs?' Carla quizzed. 'The hotel will have to close to renovate, and where will that leave us?'

On that decidedly now sombre note, she picked up her tray and walked away, leaving Samantha alone with her words to chew upon. For what was she going to do if the hotel closed? The Tremount might be suffering from age and neglect, but it had thrown her a lifeline when she'd desperately needed one. She didn't just work here, she also *lived* here. The Tremount was her home.

The stranger left quite early. Around nine o'clock he glanced at his watch, stood up and threw some money down on the table for Carla, then moved quickly out of the room. There was something very purposeful in the way he did it. As though he was going somewhere special and was running late.

A suspicion Freddie confirmed when he strolled into the lounge a few minutes later. 'That guy from the Visconte Group left in a hurry,' he remarked. 'He strode out the hotel, gunned up his Porsche, then shot off up the driveway like a bat out of hell.'

'Maybe he couldn't stand the thought of spending another night sharing a bathroom with eight other guest rooms,' Carla suggested. 'No *ensuites* at the Tremount,' she mocked. 'Here, you learn to tough it out or run!'

'If he was running, he went without paying his bill,' Freddie said. 'More like he was meeting someone,' he decided. 'The London train was due in Exeter around—Sam?' he cut in suddenly. 'Are you feeling all right? You've gone a bit pale.'

Had she? Funnily enough she felt quite pale—which was a very strange sensation in itself. It was the name, *Visconte*. For a brief moment there, she'd thought she knew it.

Which was a novelty in itself, because names never usually meant anything to her.

Names, faces, places, dates…

'I'm fine,' she said, and tossed out a smile for the benefit of the other two. 'Are you here for your usual, Freddie?' she asked, lightly passing off the moment.

But the name remained with her for the rest of the evening. And every so often she would think, *Visconte*, and find herself going off into a strange blank trance. A memory? she wondered. A brief flash from her past that had disappeared as quickly as it had come?

If it was, she couldn't afford to let it go by without checking it out, she decided. And, since the Visconte name was linked with the stranger, she resolved to ask him about it at the first opportunity, because what other hope did she have of ever knowing who she was, unless she attempted to do it herself? With twelve long months behind her of waiting for someone else to do it for her, she had to start accepting that it just wasn't going to happen.

Only last week the local paper had run yet another full-page spread on her plight, then pleaded for anyone who might recognise her to come forward. No one had. The police had finally come to the conclusion that she must have been alone in the world and on holiday here in Devon when the accident had happened. The car she had been driving was completely burned out—to the extent that they could only tell it had once been a red Alfa Romeo. They'd had no reports of a missing red Alfa Romeo. No reports of a woman gone missing *driving* a red Alfa Romeo.

Sometimes it felt as if she had died out there on that lonely road the night the petrol tanker had hit her, only to come back to life again many weeks later as a completely different human being.

But she wasn't a different human being, she told herself firmly. She was simply a lost one who needed to find herself. If she hung onto nothing else then she had to hang on tight to that belief.

Eleven o'clock saw the lounge bar empty. Samantha rubbed her aching knee and finished tidying behind the bar. An hour later she was safely tucked up in bed, and by eight-thirty the next morning, after a restless night dreaming about dark demons and roaring dragons, both she and Carla were back on duty behind Reception, doing the job they were officially paid to do.

It was changeover day so the foyer was busy, but

Samantha kept an eye out for Mr Payne, determined to speak to him if she was given the opportunity.

That opportunity arrived around lunch-time. The reception area had just cleared for the first time that morning, and only a few stragglers now hung around the foyer waiting for taxis to take them to the station. She and Carla were busy working out room allocations for the new guests that would be arriving throughout the afternoon when Samantha happened to glance up as the old-fashioned entrance doors begin to rotate and none other than Mr Payne strode in.

He paused just inside the foyer, and Samantha made the quick decision to take her chance while she had it. Murmuring, 'Excuse me for a minute,' to Carla, she opened the lift-top section in their workstation and stepped quickly through it—only to go still when she saw another man walk in and pause at Mr Payne's side.

Both men were tall, both lean, both dressed in the kind of needle-sharp suits you wouldn't find anywhere but at a top-notch tailors. But the newcomer was taller and a lot darker, and just that bit more...forbidding because of it, she observed with a cold little quiver that stopped her from approaching them.

As she watched, she saw his dark brown eyes make an impatient scan of their surroundings. There was a tension about him, a restlessness so severely contained that it flicked along his chiselled jawline as if he was clenching and unclenching his teeth behind his rather cold-looking mouth. Then the mouth suddenly twisted, and Samantha didn't need to be clairvoyant to know what he was thinking right then.

The decor in here was a horrendous mix of pre-First World War splendour and 1960s grot. Originally built to grand Victorian specifications, the Tremount had been revamped in the 1960s, and everything tasteful had been pulled out or hidden behind sheets of flat plasterboard. Even the carpet on the floor was a gruesome spread of royal purple with large splashes of sunshine-gold to complete the horror. There wasn't a stick of furniture in the place that said grace and style; instead it said teak and vinyl rubbish, and even the rubbish had seen better days.

Much like herself, she likened wryly, absently rubbing her knee while watching his gaze go slashing right past her. Then it stopped, sharpened, and came swinging swiftly back again.

Their eyes locked. The hard line of his mouth slackened on a short, sharp intake of air. He looked horrified. And suddenly she didn't like what was happening here. She didn't like *him*, she realised, as a tight constriction completely closed her throat. She couldn't breathe, couldn't swallow. Even her heart stopped beating with a violent thump, then set going like a hammer drill against her right temple.

As if he could see it happen, his eyes flicked up to her temple. She saw him flinch—remembered the fine pink pucker of scar tissue there, and instinctively put up a hand to cover it.

The fact that she'd managed to move seemed to prompt him to do the same. He began walking straight towards her in a strange, slow, measured way that made her want to start backing. Sweat began to break out all over her. The room began to fade, tunnelling inwards in ever-decreasing circles until the only the two people left in the foyer seemed to be herself and him. And the closer he came, the more tight and airless the tunnel began to feel, until she was almost suffocating by the time he came to a halt two short feet away.

And he was big—too big. Too dark, too handsome, too—everything, she finished on a fine, tight shudder. Overpowering her with his presence, with that compelling look burning in his eyes.

No, she protested, though she had no idea what it was she was protesting against.

Maybe she'd said the word out loud, because he suddenly went quite pale, and his eyes were so dark she actually felt as if she was being drawn right into them.

Crazy, she told herself. Don't be crazy.

'Samantha,' he breathed very thickly. 'Oh, dear God...'

She fainted. With her name still sounding in her head, she simply closed her eyes and sank like a stone to the purple and gold carpet.

CHAPTER TWO

IN ALL of the long days and weeks she had spent in pain in hospital, she hadn't fainted. In all of the long, dreadfully frightening weeks and months which had accompanied her slow recovery, she had never fainted. Of all the things she had ever wished and hoped and prayed for during the last twelve empty months, it had been for someone to come in through those revolving doors and say her name to her.

Yet, when someone had done exactly that, she'd fainted.

Samantha came round thinking all of that, in a mad and bewildering jumble of confusion, to find herself lying on one of the reception sofas with Carla squatting beside her, urgently chafing one of her hands, and the sounds of other people talking in hushed voices just beyond her vision.

'Are you all right?' Carla said anxiously the moment she saw Samantha open her eyes.

'He knows me,' she whispered. 'He knows who I am.'

'I know,' Carla murmured gently.

The stranger suddenly appeared over Carla's shoulder. Still too big, still too dark, too—

'I'm sorry,' he rasped out. 'Seeing you was such a shock that I just didn't think before I acted.' He stopped, swallowed tensely, then added. 'Are you okay, *cara*?'

She didn't answer. Her mind was too busy trying to grapple with the frightening fact that this man actually seemed to know her, while she looked at him and saw a total stranger! It wasn't fair—it wasn't! The doctors had suggested that a shock like this might be all that was needed to bring her memory back.

But it hadn't. Sheer disappointment had her eyes fluttering shut again.

'No.' His thick voice pleaded roughly. 'Samantha—don't pass out again. I'm not here to—'

His hand touched her shoulder. Her senses went haywire, crawling through her body like scattering spiders and flinging her into a whirling mad panic that jolted her into a sitting position to violently thrust his hand away.

'Don't touch me…' she gasped out in shuddering reaction. 'I don't know you. *I don't!*'

There was a muttered expletive, then Mr Payne appeared. His fair-skinned face was lined with concern as he murmured something soothing in Italian to the other man. He answered in the same language then, quite suddenly, spun on his heel and sat down abruptly on a nearby chair, as if the strength had just been wrenched out of him. And only then did it occur to Samantha that if he did really know her then he too must be suffering from shock.

'Here…' Carla pushed a glass of water at her. 'Drink some of this,' she urged. 'You look dreadful.'

The stranger's head came up, shock-darkened eyes honing directly onto her own, and for a moment Samantha felt herself sinking into those blackened depths again, as if drawn there by something more powerful than logic.

Oh, God. Confused, she wrenched her gaze away, pushing the glass aside so she could cover her face with a hand while she at least attempted to get a hold of herself.

'Is she all right?'

'What's the matter with her?'

'Has that man upset her?'

Hearing the jumble of questions coming from all directions reminded her that there were other people present. 'Get me away from this,' she whispered to Carla.

'Of course,' Carla murmured understandingly, and straightened up before taking hold of Samantha's arm to help her to stand. It was a well-timed offer of help, because the moment she tried to put any weight on her right leg the knee reacted with a crack of pain that made her gasp out loud.

'I wondered when I saw you fall if that would happen.' Carla frowned. 'You hit your bad knee against the corner of the desk as you fainted,' she explained, looking down at the place where Samantha's uniform-straight navy blue skirt finished, just above the injury. 'I hope you've not done it any further damage.'

Gritting her teeth and clinging to Carla, she began to limp across the reception area towards a door marked 'Staff Only'.

The stranger came towering to his feet. 'Where are you going?' he said sharply, staring at her as though he was expecting her to make a sudden run for it.

Samantha smiled wanly at the prospect. She couldn't run if she tried. 'Staffroom,' she said, then added very reluctantly, 'You can come if you want.'

'I have every intention of doing so,' he replied, and moved to follow them—only to pause and turn to make a flashing inventory of the crowded foyer. 'Are you the only two people running this place?' he questioned.

American. His accent contained the deep velvet drawl of a cultured American, Samantha noticed, then began frowning in confusion, because he and Nathan Payne had been speaking in Italian to each other only a minute ago.

'The manager is away on business today.' Carla did the explaining. 'I'll just help Samantha in here, then I'll come back and—'

'No!' Samantha protested, her hand closing convulsively over Carla's. 'Don't leave me alone with him!' she whispered shrilly, not caring if the stranger had heard what she'd said and was offended by it.

'Okay,' Carla said soothingly, but her expression was looking a little hunted. It was the busiest time of the week on Reception and both of them couldn't just walk off duty.

'Nathan.' Even Samantha, in her state of shock, heard the voice of authority when it spoke like that. 'Take over here,' the stranger instructed—then, at Carla's uncertain look, 'Don't worry. He knows what he's doing. It's his job to know. We are going in here, I presume?' he then prompted smoothly, indicating the door next to the reception desk.

Samantha nodded, having to bite down on her bottom lip now because her knee was hurting so badly. So, leaning more heavily on Carla while trying hard not to show it, she limped slowly through the staffroom door with him following so close behind her that she could actually feel his breath on her neck.

She shuddered, wishing he would just back off a little and give her time to recover and think. She didn't want him here. She didn't like him. She didn't *want* to like him. Which was just stupid when she remembered that this man would be the link to her past she had been praying for.

It was relief to sit down in one of the chairs. At Samantha's mumbled request Carla hurried off to collect her painkillers from her room, and the stranger pulled up another chair right beside her own, then sank down heavily on it. It brought him too close. She could feel his body heat and smell his subtle, masculine scent. Fighting hard not to edge right away from him, she leaned forward slightly to rub at her throbbing knee.

'How bad is it?' he rasped.

'Not too bad,' she lied. In fact it was very painful. 'I just need to rest it for a few minutes.'

'I meant, how badly did you injure your knee in the accident?' he grimly corrected her mistake.

'You know about that?' she responded in surprise.

'How the hell else do you think I found you?' he bit out angrily.

She flinched at his tone; he let out a sigh and suddenly sat forward to lean his elbows on his spread knees, bringing their heads disturbingly close.

'Sorry.' He sighed. 'I didn't mean to bite your head off.'

Samantha didn't say anything, and after a moment he said more levelly, 'Nathan was surveying a couple of properties around here. He saw the article about you in the local newspaper and recognised your photograph. He couldn't believe it!' he ground out. 'Neither could I when he rang me in New York to—' The words dried up, seeming to block in his throat so he had to swallow, and his hands clenched very tightly together between his spread thighs.

'Who is Nathan?' she asked huskily.

His head swivelled round to look at her, dark brown eyes lancing her a bitter hard look. 'Don't you think it's time you asked me who *I* am?' he suggested.

But oddly, even to herself, Samantha shook her head.

She didn't know why, but she just wasn't ready to hear who he was yet.

'This man...Nathan,' she persisted instead. 'He's been staying here over the last few days to keep an eye on me, hasn't he?'

He took her refusal to take him up on his challenge with a tensing of his jaw. He answered her question though. 'Yes. After he rang me and told me about your accident and the—the—God—' He choked, had to stop to swallow thickly, lifting a decidedly shaky hand to press at his mouth. 'I don't want to think about that,' he muttered after a moment. 'I can't cope with thinking about that right now...'

'I'm sorry,' she murmured, accepting that if he had read the article the newspaper had run on her accident, then he had a right to feel this bad about it. It made horrendous reading.

But she didn't accept the cruel way he lashed back at her. 'For surviving when six other people didn't?'

The harsh words sent her jerking back in her seat in reaction, her green eyes spitting ice as a cold anger suddenly took her over. 'I feel no sense of pleasure in being the lucky one,' she informed him frigidly. 'Six people died. I survived. But if you think I've spent the last year counting my blessings at their expense then you couldn't be more wrong!'

'And I've spent the last year wishing you in hell,' he sliced back at her. 'Only to discover that you were already living there and I didn't know a damned thing about it!'

True, so true, she grimly acknowledged, for living hell was exactly where she had been. But it made her wonder why he had wished her in hell. What had she done to him to make him wish something as cruel as that upon her?

Whatever the reason, his harsh words hurt, and did nothing to make her feel more comfortable with him. In fact she was scared.

Maybe he realised it, because he launched himself back to his feet, then just stood there literally pulsing with a sizzling tension. He was tall—over six feet—and the room suddenly grew smaller. He seemed to dwarf everything—and not just with his physical presence. The man possessed a raw kind of energy that seemed to be sucking up all the oxygen.

Then he let out a harsh sigh and muttered something that sounded like a curse beneath his breath. As he did so, some of the tension eased out of the atmosphere.

'I'm not managing this very well,' he admitted finally.

No, he wasn't, Samantha agreed. But then, neither was she.

It was perhaps a good point for Carla to reappear. Glancing warily from one tense face to the other, she came to squat down in front of Samantha, then silently handed her the foil slide containing her prescription painkillers, followed by a second glass of water.

'Thanks,' she murmured, and flipped two of the tablets out into her palm, swallowed them down with the help of the water then, on a sigh, sat back in the chair and closed her eyes to wait for the tablets to take effect. The knee was throbbing quite badly, and hot to the touch, which told her she must have knocked it pretty hard.

But that was not the real reason why she was sitting with her eyes closed like this, she had to admit. It was really a means of escape from what was beginning to develop here—not that closing her eyes was going to make it all go away again, she acknowledged heavily.

He was here, and she was too acutely aware of him standing across the room like a dark shadow threatening to completely envelop her.

And on top of that it was just too quiet. Quiet enough for her to sense that he and Carla were swapping silent messages, which had to involve her, though she didn't bother to open her eyes to see exactly what it was they were plotting.

As it was, she soon found out.

'Sam…' Carla's voice sounded anxious to say the least '…do you think you will be all right now? Only I really must go and see if everything is okay out there…'

A clammy sense of dismay went trickling through her when she realised they had been silently plotting her isolation. She didn't want to be left alone with him. But she also saw that there was no sense in putting off the inevitable. And besides, she understood Carla's predicament. They were paid to do a job here, and this hotel had a poor enough reputation without the staff walking off duty.

So she gave a short nod of understanding, then forced herself to open her eyes and smile. 'Thanks. I'll be fine now.'

With another concerned scan of her pale face, then an even more concerned one of the man who was standing on the other side of the room, Carla stood up and, with a final glance at their two pale faces, left the two of them to it.

And the new silence was cloying.

Samantha didn't move a single muscle and neither did he. His attention was fixed on the view outside the staff-room window which, since it looked directly onto the hotel kitchens, was not a pretty sight. *She* kept her eyes fixed on the empty water glass she was so very carefully turning in her hands.

'What now?' she asked when she could stand the tension no longer.

'It's truth time, I suppose,' he said, sounding as reluctant about it as she felt.

Turning slowly to face her, he stood watching her for a few more tense seconds. Then he seemed to come to some kind of decision and strode over to sit himself down again—and gently reached for the glass.

His fingers brushed lightly across hers and a fine frisson set her pulse racing. Sliding the glass away, he further disturbed her by taking hold of one of her hands as he set the glass aside then turned back to her.

'Look at me,' he urged.

Her eyes lowered and fixed fiercely on their clasped hands; the command locked her teeth together. And for the life of her she couldn't move a muscle. The frisson became a deep inner tremor that vibrated so strongly she knew he could feel it.

'I know I've come as a shock, but you have to start facing this, Samantha…' he told her quietly.

He was right, and she did. But she still didn't want to.

'So begin by at least looking at me while we talk…'

Oh, dear God, she thought and tried to swallow. It took every bit of courage she had in her to lift her eyes and look directly at him.

He's so beautiful, was the first unbidden thought to filter through her like a lonely sigh. His neatly styled hair was straight and black; his skin was warmed by a tan that she'd seemed to know from the moment she'd set eyes on him was natural to him. Sleek black eyebrows, long black eyelashes, eyes the colour of dark bitter chocolate. A regular-shaped nose, she saw as her gaze drifted downward to pause at his firm but inherently sensual mouth. It was a strong face, a deeply attractive well-balanced face.

But it was still the face of a total stranger, she concluded.

A stranger who was about to insist he was no stranger and, indeed, she added frowningly to that, already he did not *feel* like a stranger, because his touch felt familiar. There was an intimacy in the way he was looking at her that told her that this man knew her only too well. Probably knew her better than she knew herself.

'Samantha,' he prompted. 'You know your name is Samantha.'

Glad of the excuse to claim her hand back, she lifted her fingers to part the collar of her blouse, revealing the necklace she wore around her throat.

A necklace spelling out her name in gold lettering. Sweet but childish though it was. 'It's all I had left,' she explained. 'Everything else was lost in the fire.'

The eyes flashed again. 'Were you burned?' he asked harshly.

Her body became shrouded in a clammy coat of perspiration. 'No.' She shook her head. 'Someone dragged me out before the car blew.' Then the trembling fingers left the necklace to quiver up to the small pink scar at her temple. 'I injured my head,' she said huskily, 'my arm…' she gave her right arm a tense little jerk '…and m-my right leg…'

His eyes dropped to her knee, where even the sensible, high-denier thickness of her stockings could not hide the scarring beneath. Then with a slow raising of his oh-too-sensual long black lashes, he looked at the scar at her temple. 'Your lovely face...' he breathed, lifting a hand up to touch the scar.

She flinched back in rejection. And for the first time in months of just being too glad to be alive to want to feel any kind of revulsion for the physically obvious damage she had survived with, Samantha experienced a terrible, terrible urge to hide herself away.

This man's fault! She blamed him wretchedly. He was so obviously one of those very rare people who was blessed with physical perfection himself and no doubt surrounded himself with the same that she suddenly knew, knew that whoever he was and whatever he once had been to her, she no longer fitted into his selective criteria!

It was her turn to get up, move away, though she didn't do it with the same grace he did! 'Who are you?' She turned to launch at him wretchedly.

He stood up. 'My name is *Visconte*,' he told her huskily. '*André* Visconte.'

There it was, 'Visconte.' She breathed the name softly. 'Of the Visconte Hotel Group?'

He nodded slowly, watching her intently for a sign that the name might begin to mean something else to her. But other than the same odd sensation she'd experienced the night before, when Freddie had said the name, it still meant nothing.

'And me?' She then forced herself to whisper. 'Who am I?'

His eyes went black again, nerve ends began to sing. 'Your name is also Visconte,' he informed her carefully, then extended very gently, 'You are my wife...'

CHAPTER THREE

FACE white, body stiff, eyes pressed tightly shut, Samantha simply stood there waiting—waiting to discover if this latest shock, coming hard upon all the other shocks she had suffered today, would manage to crash through the thick wall closing off her memory.

I am Samantha Visconte, she silently chanted. His wife. This man's wife. A man I must have loved enough to marry. A man who must have loved me enough to do the same. It should mean something. She stood there *willing* it to mean something!

But it didn't. 'No,' she said on a release of pent-up air, and opened her eyes to look at him with the same perfectly blank expression. 'The name means nothing to me.'

She might as well have slapped him. He looked away, then sat down, his lean body hunching over again as he dipped his dark head and pressed his elbows into his spread knees—but not before Samantha had seen the flash of pain in his eyes and realised that her ill-chosen words had managed to hurt him. 'I'm sorry,' she murmured uncomfortably. 'I didn't mean it to come out sounding so…'

'Flat?' he incised when she hesitated.

She ran her dry tongue around her even drier lips. 'Y-you don't understand.' She pushed out an unsteady explanation. 'The doctors have been suggesting to me for months that a shock meeting like this might be all that was needed to jolt me into…'

'I need a drink,' he cut in, then stood up and began striding quickly for the door.

Samantha watched him go—relieved he was going because she needed time alone to try to come to terms with all of this. But it didn't stop her gaze from following him, eyes feeding on his tall, lean framework as if she still couldn't quite believe that he was real.

Maybe he wasn't, she then told herself with a rueful little smile that mocked the turmoil her mind was in. Maybe this was going to turn out to be just another nightmare in a long line of nightmares where tall dark strangers visited her and claimed to know who she was.

'Have we been married long?'

Why she stopped him at the door when she'd been glad he was going, she didn't know. But the question blurted out anyway, bringing him to a halt with his hand on the door handle, and stopping her breath as she waited for him to turn.

'Two years,' he replied and there was a strangeness about his voice that bothered her slightly. 'It will be our second wedding anniversary in two days' time,' he tagged on—then left the room.

Staring at the closed door through which he had disappeared, Samantha found herself incapable of feeling anything at all now, as a different kind of numbness overcame her.

Two days, she was thinking. Which made it the twelfth. They hadn't even celebrated their first wedding anniversary together.

Her accident had occurred on the twelfth. Where had she been going on her first wedding anniversary? Had she been rushing back to be with him when the accident had happened? Had that been why she'd—?

No. She mustn't allow herself to think like that. The

police had assured her it had not been her fault. A petrol tanker had jackknifed on the wet road and ploughed into three other cars besides her own before it had burst into a ball of fire. She had been lucky because the tanker had hit her car first then left it behind, a twisted wreck as it careered on. The people in the cars behind her hadn't stood a chance because they'd caught the brunt of the explosion when everything had gone up. Other drivers had had time to pull Samantha free before her car had joined in the inferno. But her body had had to pay the price for the urgency with which they had got her out. Her head, already split and bleeding from the impact, had luckily rendered her unconscious, but they had told her the man who had pulled her free had had no choice but to wrench her crushed knee through splintered metal if he was to get her clear in time. And her arm, already fractured in three places, had been made worse because it had been the only limb the man had been able to use to tug her out.

The arm had healed now, thankfully. And the knee was getting stronger every day with the help of a lot of physiotherapy. But the scar on her face was a reminder she saw every time she looked into a mirror.

And why was she hashing over all of this right now, when she had far more important things to think about? It was crazy!

So what's new? She mocked herself, then with a sigh sat back down again.

She hadn't even considered yet whether André Visconte was lying or not, she realised. Though why someone like him would want to claim someone in her physical and psychological state unless he felt duty-bound to answer the question for her.

Because no one in their right mind would.

No one *had* for twelve long months. So why hadn't he found her before now?

He said he'd wished her in hell, she remembered. Did that mean that their marriage had already been over before their first wedding anniversary? Was that why he hadn't bothered to look for her? And had he only done so now because someone had recognised her in that newspaper as the woman who was his wife?

Agitation began to rise. Her head began to throb, bringing her fingers up to rub at her temple. I want to remember. *Please* let me remember! she pleaded silently. He'd said something about being in New York. Was that where he lived? Was that where they'd met? Yet her accent was so obviously English that even she—who had learned to question everything about herself over the last twelve, empty months—had not once questioned her nationality.

Had they met here in England? Did they have a home in this area? Was he wealthy enough to own homes in two places? Of course he was wealthy enough, she told herself crossly. He owned a string of prestigious hotels. He *looked* wealthy. His clothes positively shrieked of wealth.

So what did that make her? A wealthy woman in her own right for her to have moved in the same social circles as he?

She didn't feel wealthy. She felt poor—impoverished, in fact.

Impoverished from the inside, never mind the outer evidence, with her sensible flat-heeled black leather shoes that had been bought for comfort and practicality rather than because she could really afford them. For months her clothes had been charitable handouts, ill-fitting, drab-looking garments other people no longer wanted to wear but which had been good enough for an impoverished woman who had lost everything including her mind! It had only been since she'd landed this job here that she had been able to afford to replace them with something more respectable—cheap, chain store stuff, but at least they were new and belonged to her—only to her.

What did Visconte see when he looked at this woman he claimed was his wife?

Getting up, she went to stand by the tarnished old mirror that hung on the staffroom wall. If she ignored the scar at her temple, the reflection told her that she was quite passably attractive. The combination of long red wavy hair teamed with creamy white skin must have once looked quite startling—especially before too many long months of constant strain had hollowed out her cheeks and put dark bruises under her eyes. But some inner sense that hadn't quite been blanked off with the rest of her memory told her she had always been slender, and the physiotherapists had been impressed with what they'd called her 'athletic muscle structure'.

'Could have been a dancer,' one of them had said in a wry, teasing way meant to offset the agony he'd been putting her through as he'd manipulated her injured knee. 'Your muscles are strong, but supple with it.'

Supple, slender dancer worthy of a second look once upon a time. Not any more, though, she accepted. She thought of the stranger and how physically perfect he was, and wanted to sit down and cry.

I don't want this, she thought on a sudden surge of panic. I don't want any of it!

He can't want me. How can he want me? If I am his wife why has it taken him twelve months to find me? If he'd loved me wouldn't a man like him have been scouring the whole countryside looking for me?

I would have done for him, she acknowledged with an odd pain that said her feelings for him were not entirely indifferent, no matter what her brain was refusing to uncover.

'Oh, God.' She dropped back into the chair to bury her face in her hands as the throbbing in her head became unbearable.

Pull yourself together! she tried to tell herself. You have to pull yourself together and start thinking about what happens next, before—

The door came open. He stepped inside and closed it again, his eyes narrowing on the way she quickly lifted her face from her hands.

His jacket had gone; that was the first totally incomprehensible thing her eyes focused on. The dark silk tie with the slender knot had been tugged down a little and the top button of his shirt was undone, as if he'd found the constriction of his clothes annoying and needed to feel fresh air around that taut tanned throat.

Her mind did a dizzy whirl on a hot, slick spurt of sudden sensual awareness. 'Here…' He was walking towards her with a glass of something golden in his hand. 'I think you need one of these as much as I do.'

'No.' She shook her head. 'I can't, not on top of the painkillers—thank you all the same.'

If nothing else, the remark stopped him, mere inches away from touching her. She didn't want him to touch her—why, again she didn't know. Except—

Stranger. The word kept on playing itself over and over like some dreadful, dreadful warning. This man who said he was her husband was a total stranger to her. And the worst of it was she kept on getting this weird idea that him being a stranger to her was not a new feeling.

He discarded the glass, then stood in front of her with his hands thrust into his trouser pockets. He seemed to be waiting for something, but Samantha didn't know what, so she looked at the garish carpet between their feet and waited for whatever was supposed to come next.

What could come next? she then thought tensely. There were questions to ask. Things to know. This was the beginning of her problems, not the end of them.

'How's the knee?'

'What—?' She blinked up at him, then away again. 'Oh.' A hand automatically went down to touch the knee. 'Better now, thank you.'

Silence. Her nerves began to fray. Teeth gritted together behind clenched lips. God, she wished he would just do something! Say something cruel and trite like, Well, nice to have seen you again, sorry you don't remember me, but I have to go now!

She wished he would pull her up into his big arms and hold her, hold her tightly, until all these terrible feelings of confusion and fear went away!

He released a sigh. It sounded raw. She glanced at him warily. He bit out harshly, 'This place is the pits!'

He was right and it was. Small and shabby and way, way beneath his dignity. 'I l-love this place.' She heard herself whisper. 'It gave me a home and a life when I no longer had either.'

Her words sent his face white again—maybe he thought she was taking a shot at him. He threw himself back into the chair beside her—close to her again, his shoulder only a hair's breadth away from rubbing against her shoulder again.

Move away from me, she wanted to say.

'Listen,' he said. And she could feel him fighting something, fighting it so fiercely that his tension straightened her spine and held it so stiff it tingled like a live wire. 'We need to get away from here,' he gritted. 'Find more—private surroundings where we can—relax—'

Even he made the word sound dubious. For who could relax in a situation like this? She certainly couldn't.

'Talk,' he went on. 'Have time for you to ask the kind of questions I know you must be burning to ask, and for me to do the same.'

He looked at her for a reaction. Samantha stared straight ahead.

'We can do that better at my own hotel in Exeter than we can here,' he suggested.

'Your hotel,' she repeated, remembering the big, new hotel that had opened its doors only last year.

'Will you come?'

'I...' She wasn't at all sure about that. She wasn't sure she wanted to go anywhere with him, or leave what had become over the last year the only place where she felt safe and secure in her bewildered little world.

'It's either you come with me or I move in here,' he declared, and so flatly that she didn't for one moment think he was bluffing. 'I would prefer it to be the other way round simply because my place is about a hundred times more comfortable than this. But—' The pause brought her eyes up to look warily into his. It was what he had been aiming for. The chocolate-brown turned to cold black marble slabs of grim determination. 'I am not letting you out of my sight again—ever—do you understand that?'

Understand? She almost choked on it. 'I want proof,' she whispered.

'Proof of what?' He frowned.

'That you are who you say you are and I am who you say I am before I'll make any decisions about anything.'

She expected him to be affronted but oddly he wasn't—which in itself was proof enough that he was indeed telling her the truth about them.

Without a word he stood up, left the room again, coming back mere seconds later carrying the jacket to his suit. His hand was already fishing in the inside pocket when he came to stand over her.

'My passport,' he said, dropping the thick, bulky document onto her lap. 'Your passport—an old one, I admit, but it can still give you your *proof*.' That too landed on her knee. 'Our marriage certificate.' It landed on top of the two passports. 'And…' this came less arrogantly '…a photo…' it fluttered down onto her lap, landing face down. 'Of you and me on our wedding day.'

He'd come prepared for this, she realised, staring down at the small heap of items now sitting on her lap without attempting to touch them.

Because she was afraid to.

But why was she afraid? He had already told her who he was and who she was and what they were to each other. She was even already convinced that every word he'd said was the truth, or why else would he be standing here in this scruffy back room of a scruffy hotel in a scruffy corner of Devon saying all of these things?

So why, *why* was she feeling so afraid to actually look at the physical proof of all of that?

The answer came at her hard and cold, and frightened her more than everything else put together. She didn't want to look for the same reason she'd lost her memory in the first place. The doctors had told her it had had little to do with the car crash. The accident might have helped to cause the amnesia, but the real reason for it lay deeply rooted in some other trauma she'd found she could not face on top of all the pain she had been suffering at that time. So her mind had done the kindest thing and had locked up the personal trauma so all she had to do was to deal with the physical trauma.

Looking at these documents was going to be like squeezing open the door on that trauma, whatever it was.

'You never were a coward, Samantha,' he told her quietly, at the same time letting her know that he knew exactly what was going on inside her head.

Well, I am now,' she whispered, and her body began to tremble.

Instantly he was dropping down into the chair again, his hands coming out, covering hers where they lay pleated tightly together on her stomach, safely away from his proof. And this time she did not flinch away from his touch. This time she actually needed it.

'Then we'll do it together,' he decided gently.

With one hand still covering her two hands, he used the other to slide his passport out from the bottom of the pile and flicked it open at the small photograph that showed his beautiful features set in a sternly arrogant pose.

'Visconte', it said. 'André Fabrizio'. 'American citizen'.

'I look like a gangster,' he said, trying to lighten the moment. Closing the book, he then selected the other one.

You weren't supposed to smile on passport photographs. But the face looking back up her from her own lap told her that this person did not know how to turn that provocative little smile off. And her face wore no evidence of strain. She simply looked lively and lovely and—

'Visconte', it said. 'Samantha Jane'. 'British citizen'.

'You lost this particular passport about six months after we were married and had to apply for a new one,' he explained. 'But I happened to turn this up when I was—' He stopped, then went on. 'When I was searching through some old papers.' He finally concluded. But they both knew he had been about to say something else.

When his hand moved to pick up the marriage certificate, she stopped him. 'No.' She breathed out thickly. 'Not that. Th-the other…'

Slowly, reluctantly almost, his fingers moved to pick up the photograph, hesitated a moment, then flipped it over.

Samantha's heart flipped over with it. Because staring back at her in full Technicolor was herself, dressed up in frothy bridal-white.

Laughing. She was laughing up into the face of her handsome groom. Laughing up at *him*—this man dressed in a dark suit with a white rose in his lapel and confetti lying on his broad shoulders. He was laughing too, but there was more—so much more to his laughter than just mere amusement. There was—

Abruptly she closed her eyes, shutting it out, shutting everything out as her body began to shake violently, a clammy sweat breaking out across her chilled flesh. She couldn't breathe again, couldn't move. And a dark mist was closing round her.

Someone hissed out a muffled curse. It wasn't her so she had to presume it must be him, though she was way too distressed to be absolutely sure of that. The next moment two hands were grasping her shoulders and lifting her to her feet. The stack of documents slid to the floor forgotten as he wrapped her tightly in his arms.

And suddenly she felt as if she was under attack from

a completely different source. Attack—why attack? she asked herself as her head became filled with the warm solid strength of him.

'Oh, my God.' She groaned.

'What's happening?' he muttered thickly.

'I d-don't know,' she said tremulously, and tried sucking in a deep breath of air in an effort to compose herself. That deep breath of air went permeating through her system, taking the spicy scent of him along with it, and in the next moment her brain cells went utterly haywire.

Familiar. That scent was familiar. And so wretchedly familiar that—

Once again she fainted. No more warning than that. She just went limp in his arms and knew nothing for long seconds.

This time when she came round she wasn't lying but sitting, with him standing over her pressing her head down between her knees with a very determined hand.

'Stay there,' he gritted when she tried to sit up. 'Just wait a moment until the blood has had a chance to make it back to your head.'

She stayed, limp and utterly exhausted, taking in some carefully controlled breaths of air while she waited, waited for…

Nothing, she realised. No bright blinding flood of beautiful memories. Not even ugly ones. Nothing.

Carefully she tried to move, and this time he allowed her to, his dark face decidedly guarded as she sat back and looked at him.

'What?' he demanded jerkily when she didn't say a word.

Empty-eyed, she shook her head. She knew what he

was thinking, knew what he was expecting. She had been expecting the same thing herself.

His dark eyes glinted, a white line of tension imprinting itself around his mouth. Then he sucked in a deep lungful of air and held onto it for a long time before he let it out again.

'Well, we aren't going to try that again,' he decided. 'Not until we've consulted an expert to find out why you faint every time you're confronted with yourself.'

Not myself, she wanted to correct him. *You.*

But she didn't, didn't want to get into that one. Not now, when it felt as if her whole world was balancing precariously on the edge of a great, yawning precipice.

'So that settles it,' he declared in the same determined tone. 'You're coming with me.' He bent down to pick up the scattered papers, his lean body lithe and graceful even while it was clearly tense. 'I'm going to need to make a few phone calls,' he said as he straightened, then really surprised her by dropping the photograph back onto her lap. 'While I do that, you can go and pack your things. By then I should be finished and we can get on our way—'

'Do I have any say in this at all?' she asked cuttingly.

'No.' He swung round to show her a look of grim resolve. 'Not a damned thing. I've spent the last twelve months alternately thinking you were dead and wishing you were dead. But you aren't either, are you, Samantha?' he challenged bluntly. 'You're existing in some kind of limbo land to which I know for a fact that only I have the key to set you free. And until you are set free, I won't know which of my alternatives I really prefer, and you won't know why you prefer to stay in limbo. The newspaper report on you said they took you to a hospital in Exeter after the accident, which I presume means you received all your treatment there?'

She nodded.

So did he. 'Then, since Exeter is where we are going, we don't mention the past or anything to do with the past until we've received some advice from someone who knows what they're talking about.' He settled the matter decisively. 'All you have to do is accept that I am your husband and you are my wife. The rest will have to wait.'

CHAPTER FOUR

WAIT...

Carla certainly did think she should *wait* for answers before trotting meekly off with him. 'But you don't know him from Adam!' she protested as Samantha moved around her room gathering her few possessions together. 'How do you know if he's telling the truth?'

'Why should he lie?' Samantha countered, turning the question round on itself.

'I don't know.' Carla sighed in frustration. 'It just doesn't *feel* right to me that you are willing to go off with him without knowing what it is you're going to!'

Samantha's only answer was to silently hand Carla the wedding photograph.

She stared at it, then at Samantha, then back at the photo again. And suddenly her mood changed. 'What can have happened to you to make you forget something as beautiful as this?' she murmured painfully.

Samantha wished she had the answer to that one. The story that photo was telling might be bringing tears to Carla's eyes, but she couldn't even begin to describe how it made her feel.

Nothing, she named it. But it was a strange, pained nothing, which was, in itself, something terribly saddening. 'Do you know who he is?' she asked quietly.

'Nathan Payne told me.' Carla nodded. 'But just because he's the great Visconte himself doesn't absolve him from having to explain why it's taken him twelve months to come and get you!'

True, Samantha conceded, and sat down on the bed as the heavy weight of all her own uncertainties came thundering down on her again.

'I mean…' Carla went on, determined to push her point home now that she had Samantha wavering '…you were famous for a week or two in these parts when the accident happened. Your predicament was reported in all the local papers. If you were missing and he was worried about you, wouldn't you expect a man like him to pull out all the stops in an effort to find you? At the very least he could have checked out the police stations and hospitals. Your looks are pretty damned distinctive, Sam,' she pointed out. 'Even without you knowing who you are, for someone to be searching for a tall, slender redhead going by the name Samantha would surely be enough to make the necessary link?'

'Maybe he was away—out of the country or something,' she suggested, thinking of New York.

'You mean, you haven't bothered to ask him?' Carla sounded dismayed.

Samantha was a little dismayed herself at how little she had asked him to explain. But the truth of it was, she didn't want to ask. In some incomprehensible way, it felt safer not to ask.

'The trouble is,' she admitted with a rueful grimace, 'every time we discuss anything even vaguely personal, I faint.'

'Even more reason, surely, for you to think carefully before putting yourself in his care. Don't you see that?'

See it? Of course she did. But…

Easing herself back to her feet, she gently took back the photograph, then looked at Carla with disturbingly bleak yet resolute green eyes. 'If I am ever to discover why I've ended up like this,' she said quietly, 'then I have to go with him.'

To her, it was as simple and as final as that.

Where was she? André flicked a hard glance at his watch then stuffed his hand back into his pocket. She was taking an age!

'Damn,' he muttered, feeling the hellish anger he had been keeping banked down take another step closer to exploding. 'Look at this place,' he growled out contemptuously. 'If it fell down right now, no one would miss it.'

Nathan Payne looked up, and André suddenly saw himself as his manager was seeing him—like a prowling panther pacing up and down on the awful carpet in front of the reception desk, as if in need of a good fight.

Hell, he thought. Ten rounds with the best boxer in the world wouldn't knock out the ugly stuff churning up his system right now.

Samantha, residing in these miserable surroundings. It was enough to snuff the living light out of anyone! And the sooner he got her away from here the better as far as he was concerned.

Where was she? 'Ring her room,' he instructed Nathan.

'No,' the other man refused. 'She will come when she's ready.'

'She's already been an hour.'

And that other girl was with her. She didn't like him. He'd seen it in her face when she'd heard what Samantha was going to do. She thought he was being too pushy and that Samantha was in too deep a state of shock to be going anywhere with anyone. Damn it, she was right, he grimly conceded.

'Don't you think you are being a bit hasty, taking her away from the only secure environment she knows?' Nathan posed levelly.

Don't you start, André thought. 'I can give her a secure environment,' he insisted.

'She's in shock, André.'

'So am I,' he tossed back.

'And she's frightened.'

Did Nathan think he didn't know that? 'I'm not into S&M, Nathan,' he rounded angrily on the other man. 'I'm not going to chain her up in a cage and put a whip to her rear end every hour on the hour!'

'I'm so very relieved to hear that,' another voice inserted.

Spinning round, he saw her standing in the mouth of the corridor which led to the staff quarters. She was wearing a simple blue shift dress and her hair was still fixed in a dreadful, priggish bun, which was in itself a defiance of what the real Samantha was. Deliberate, or a subconscious act? he mused grimly, and felt his senses grind together. Deliberate or not, it was there. Her chin was up, her mouth small, and her eyes were tossing out the kind of cold green sparks that had always declared war—old Samantha style.

He had never been able to resist it, and didn't even try. Relaxing the tension out of his body, he let his eyes send back a counter-declaration, and he taunted lazily, 'Submission is not your forte, *mia dolce amante*. You demand equality in all aspects of your life.'

He threw in the 'my sweet lover' in Italian just to see if she would remember it; he saw her face grow pink and was very, very pleased that she did indeed understand what he'd said. Standing beside her, he also saw her friend shift uncomfortably. Behind him he felt his manager do the same. He didn't actually blame either of them, because sexual tension was suddenly rife in the dull and dingy foyer.

But it was Samantha's response that mattered to him, and as the first truly healthy one he'd managed to rouse in her it did his bad temper the world of good.

'Are you ready to come with me?' he tagged on silkily, deciding to build on his sensual success—a building that crumbled the moment she moved forward and he saw that she was using a walking stick.

Anger roared back to life, making him turn on Nathan like a rattlesnake with poison dripping from its fangs. He snapped out orders which Nathan took in his stride with a kind of silent sympathy that only helped to make him feel worse. But he couldn't even begin to describe what it did to him seeing his beautiful, vibrant Samantha in so much pain that she needed help just to walk!

Samantha left him to it and went outside, hurt by the flare of dismay she had seen on his face when he'd caught sight of her walking stick. Nor did she like the autocratic way he'd spoken to Nathan Payne, whom it seemed was going to remain here and cover for Samantha until the hotel manager returned.

'He's a bully,' Carla said.

Samantha couldn't deny it so she remained silent instead.

'And he fancies the hell out of you,' Carla added.

Static electricity suddenly shivered through her, setting almost every hair she possessed on end. 'Not this girl,' she denied, giving the walking stick a deriding kick.

'What was the Italian seduction scene about, then?'

'You said it.' Samantha shrugged. 'The words ''Italian''

and ''seduction'' always go together. In fact I don't think they can function without each other.'

'So he's an Italian-American.' Carla assumed.

Samantha shrugged again, because she didn't actually know. Certainly the Visconte name was Italian. The accent was most definitely American, but the first name was surely French? she mused frowningly.

'Are you going to be all right?' From being argumentative, Carla had seen the frown and was now sounding anxious again.

No, I don't think I am going to be all right, she thought, staring bleakly out across the potholed car park to where two cars in particular stood out like the symbols of success they obviously were. One was a natty black Porsche, the other a racing-green Jaguar.

'Samantha—?' Carla prompted her for an answer.

She gave one. 'I'm not *all right* as I am now,' she pointed out. There didn't seem anything left to say after that.

André came striding out of the hotel, and the atmosphere suddenly took on a distinct change. Reaching out, Samantha took her suitcase from Carla, who had insisted on carrying it for her this far.

The two girls hugged while he looked on—or 'glared' would have been a better word—a set of keys jingling impatiently in his hands as he did so.

'Take care of yourself,' she murmured to Carla as she drew away.

'No, you take care of you,' Carla returned.

'Let's go,' his hard voice said.

Samantha felt the old panic erupt inside her and had to work very hard at damping it back down. As he set off down the hotel steps the sun came out, giving his skin an extra warmth that added a luxurious sheen to it.

'Call me,' Carla begged as a final farewell.

'I promise.' She nodded, and felt a burn begin behind her eyes as she took that first mammoth step to follow him.

Maybe he sensed the tears. Certainly something made him pause and look back. Eyes like black marble lanced over her. Samantha lowered her own eyes and bit down on her bottom lip, fought hard to concentrate on negotiating the steps instead of the wave of anguish that was trying to overwhelm her.

His hand snaked out. She hadn't even realised he'd moved back towards her until she felt the suitcase being taken from her. Then, without another glance at anyone, he strode off towards the Jaguar, opened the boot, threw the case in, then went round to open the passenger door to stand beside it like a jailer waiting to lock his latest prisoner in.

Which made her think of cages and chains, which in turn almost caused a hysterical bubble of laughter to burst in her throat. Swallowing both tears and laughter, she kept her face turned away as she reached the car and lowered herself into it.

Without a by-your-leave, her stick was taken from her. The door shut with a very expensive thud, and she found herself experiencing a different kind of luxury, made up of soft cream leather and walnut veneer. Five seconds later his door came open and he was bending inside to toss her stick onto the car's rear seat. She caught the tantalising scent of his skin as he folded his long body in the seat beside her. He had put his jacket back on but his tie still hung loose around his throat. He looked lean and mean and decidedly alien.

Without a single word being spoken between them, he pulled his seat belt across his wide chest and locked it in place, glanced briefly her way to check that she had already done the same. Then, with a final settling of his long frame, he started the engine, shoved it into 'drive', and swept them away.

It was all so swift, she decided, so final. As she caught her last glimpse of the hotel, she felt the tears burning the backs of her eyes once again. Goodbye, she lamented silently—then wondered why she felt as if she'd said goodbye like this to some other run-down, dearly loved building?

'Why the stick?' he bit out suddenly.

'If my limp offends you,' she flashed at him coldly, 'then maybe you should turn around and put me back where you found me. Because the limp it isn't going to go away just because you don't like it!'

'It doesn't offend me,' he denied. 'It makes me bloody angry, but it does not offend me.'

She wished she believed him but she didn't, and it didn't help that it had to be her scarred profile he saw every time he flicked a brief glance at her!

'Tell me about it,' he persisted stubbornly.

Does he never give up? Taking a deep breath, she gave him what he wanted. 'The knee was crushed in the accident but the injury was made worse by the urgency with which they had to pull me from my car before it went up in flames.' He winced, but she didn't care; he'd asked for this! 'I've since had four operations on it and, believe it or not, the limp is not half as obvious as it was two months ago.'

With sarcasm abounding in that last comment, still he didn't give up. 'Any more operations to come?'

'No,' she replied. 'What you see now is what you get. So if you were hoping to recover the same person you see in that photograph you gave me, then let me tell you now, before this thing goes any further, that you won't be getting her!'

'I'll be getting the temper, though, I notice,' he drawled, and was suddenly smiling, smiling in a way that made her heart flip over. Smiling with his eyes and a genuine amusement that completely altered his face. He was smiling at her as if she'd just given him some special present instead of yelling at him like a harridan.

'Keep your eyes on the road!' she cried as a desperate diversion away from the emotions that were suddenly churning up her insides.

He began to curse, shocking her with the abrupt way he took his foot off the accelerator and turned his attention back to the stretch of curving Tarmac in front of them. 'I'm sorry. I didn't think. Obviously you will be nervous about being in a car after—'

'No.' She sighed, feeling just a bit guilty for making him think that she was. 'Not so long as the driver is competent—which you clearly are.'

At which point another silence fell, while he made himself concentrate on his driving and Samantha's mind went lurching off on an agenda of its own.

'So, tell me why the Tremount Hotel has been left to fall into such a miserable state,' he invited after a minute or two. 'It looked as if it must have been quite something once upon a time.'

'It was,' Samantha agreed, relieved to be given a more neutral subject to fill in the silence while they travelled. 'Victorian,' she said. 'Originally built to accommodate the upper echelons of British middle-class society of its time. And filled with some real architectural treasures if the right person knew where to look for them.'

'They would have to look hard.' André grunted.

'They would have to possess *soul*,' Samantha corrected, forcing André to respond with a rueful grimace at her set-down. 'It fell on hard times when the British holiday market shifted abroad. But now the market is coming back to its own shores places like the Tremount could have a lot of potential for the right developer. It has its own beach, and isn't too far away from the nearest resort town. Also, there is a large piece of land to the right of the main building you may have noticed as you came down the driveway. It was once a nine-hole golf course until it was left to fall into disrepair along with the hotel. With the right expert on the job, it could…'

André let her talk on, harshly aware she had no idea she was giving him a report on the hotel's potential that was as detailed and informed as any of his top surveyors could offer him. But, then, Samantha couldn't remember, and therefore had no idea that this kind of thing came as second nature to her. Or that, like himself, she had been involved in the hotel industry all of her life.

Nor was she aware that she was interspersing her words with his name, just as she'd used to do. And her hands—always the most busy tool she used to express herself—were motioning and measuring, long fingers pointing, marking, making those delicate circling movements with a twist of her slender wrists that were so familiar to him.

It made him want to hit something. Because the sensual sound of his name falling from her lips and the hand movements might belong to the old Samantha, but nothing else about her did. Not the priggish hairstyle, nor the dowdy clothes, nor the expression in her eyes—which should be animated while she talked but was as dull and flat as the tone of her voice.

The old Samantha was a vivid bright fireball of energy. This one was shocking him by her stillness, her lack of passion for anything—if you didn't count the moments they'd touched on the subject of their marriage. Then she'd revealed passion all right, he acknowledged grimly. A passionate horror that had had her fainting clean away.

It took over an hour to reach Exeter. But Samantha had been talking so much that she was surprised when the car came to a smooth halt in the forecourt of a hotel.

'So this is the famous Visconte Exeter,' she observed curiously. 'I remember reading in the newspapers about its big gala opening last year—'

Last year, she then repeated to herself, and began to frown as a sudden thought struck her. 'Did you come to the opening?' she asked sharply, the very idea that he could have been this close to her without either of them knowing it hurting her for some unexplainable reason.

Something in his stillness grabbed her attention. His eyes were hooded and his jaw line clenched. He answered her question, 'No.' And then he got out of the car to swing round the long bonnet so he could open her door for her.

'Why weren't you here?' she demanded instantly.

He began to frown. 'I don't understand the question.'

Her eyes flicked up, green and hard. 'Why weren't you here to attend the opening of your own hotel?' She spelled it out succinctly.

'Good grief.' He laughed, but it was a very forced laugh. 'I don't attend every opening we have.' Reaching down, he unfastened her seat belt since she had not got round to doing it herself. 'The Visconte chain stretches right around the world. I would have to be Superman to—'

'You weren't even in the country, were you?' Samantha cut in.

She could remember it now. The big party to celebrate the opening. The coverage it had received in local newspapers because of all the big-name local celebrities that had attended. My God, she'd had little else to do as she'd lain imprisoned in her hospital bed than pore hungrily over every article written in them.

Searching. She had been searching for something that might have jogged her memory. But it hadn't happened.

Why hadn't it happened? How could she have not even recognised her own married name when she'd read it so often?

Because she'd blocked it out, she realised painfully. Just as she'd blocked out everything else about this man until he'd come along today and had virtually force-fed the Visconte name to her.

So she could also remember the papers remarking on the fact that the owner himself had been expected to attend the opening but had pulled out at the last moment—because he'd been out of the country on other business.

Out of the country barely a month after her accident.

Her eyes lanced him with a bitter look. 'Did you bother trying to look for me at all?' she asked coldly. 'Or was our marriage already over by the time I disappeared?'

His face closed up tight. 'I'm not going to answer any of that,' he said, taking a firm grip on her arm.

'Why not?' she challenged, resisting his tug. 'Because the answer may paint you as less than the caring man you would like me to believe?'

'Because the answer may have you fainting on me

again,' he corrected. 'And, until we seek professional advice on that problem, we don't talk about us.'

With that, he firmly propelled her out of the car, then released a soft curse when he saw her bite down on her full lip as she placed her weight on her injured leg.

Having to concentrate hard not to cry out, Samantha grabbed hold of his arm for support. Once again her senses went utterly haywire, and she found herself standing there, not only having to brace herself against the pain, but having to brace herself against the feel of tensile muscles flexing beneath her grip. He was all power and hard masculinity, she likened hazily, watching images build in her mind of warm dark golden flesh and a disturbingly attractive sexuality that somehow merged with the physical pain she was experiencing until she couldn't distinguish one sensation from the other.

'Just how painful is the damned thing?' he rasped out angrily.

It stole the moment—stole a whole lot more—when she opened her eyes and found herself looking at a man who was *still* a stranger. And as she stood there, held caught in a sea of confusion, the physical pain separated itself from painful imagery like two lovers untangling, then became only a hard, tight, aching throb that completely obliterated the other.

Green, André was thinking. Her eyes were so green—a dark and pulsing passionate green colour they had only used to go when they were making love. But today there was something else there, confusion and pain and a terrible despair that made him want to hit something again.

'Answer me,' he commanded, aware that the violent emotions flailing around inside him had everything to do with the expression he had seen burning in her eyes.

'Damn painful,' she replied, lowering her gaze to

watch as she carefully bent and straightened the knee a couple of times before trying to stand on it again.

And he was glad that she had looked away. Much longer having to witness her expression was likely to have finished him. It had been hard enough controlling the urge to pull her into his arms and just kiss the pain away for her.

Not the wisest course of action to take when the woman in question had the clever knack of falling into a deep faint if he so much as touched on intimacy. He grimaced, clenched his jaw firmly shut, and watched in grim silence as she placed her foot on the ground then carefully transferred her weight onto it. This time it remained there, and the grip on his arm slackened. She released a sigh, then let go of his arm altogether.

'Okay,' she said. 'If you could just pass me my stick...'

It was like moving from a rock to a very hard place. No sooner had he managed to contain one set of angry emotions than another set erupted inside him. This new set having something to do with that damn stick and his fierce resentment of it.

'You will lean on me,' he determined.

'Not while I still have another alternative.' She hit back with throbbing venom.

'My God.' His breath left his lungs on a hiss of impatience. 'Why do you insist on seeing me as some kind of monster?'

She flushed, not with guilt but with anger. 'You were already out of this country within a month of my disappearance,' she charged. 'How else am I supposed to translate that?'

He refused to answer, withdrawing from the fight by flattening his mouth into a tight line as he shifted his attention away from her and with a snap of his fingers brought a blue-liveried doorman running.

End of discussion, she noted angrily, listening to him snapping out instructions to the doorman about her suitcase before he leaned past her to retrieve her stick. In grim silence he offered it to her and in grim silence she took it. Then in the same grim silence they began walking towards the hotel entrance—together but separate, like two polite strangers, with her challenge still hanging in the air between them like an omen of whatever was to follow.

CHAPTER FIVE

THE hotel interior was more or less what she had expected for a deluxe-class establishment. No garish splashes of yellow on purple here, but a soft blend of creams and greens, which contrasted beautifully with a subtle placing of a dark wine-red colour, set against the kind of unashamed luxury which made an absolute mockery of what they had just come from.

Though the quality of her surroundings was the last thing on her mind when, only a few minutes later, she found herself standing inside a suite of rooms with this man and at last began to feel the vulnerability of her situation.

Maybe he was beginning to realise the same thing, because he released a small sigh, then turned to face her. 'Okay?' he asked guardedly.

No, she wanted to reply. I'm not okay and I want to go back where I came from. But common sense, or stupidity—she wasn't sure which—stopped the words from coming.

'You've already been using this suite,' she remarked instead, having noticed the signs of habitation in the few personal items she could see scattered about.

'I arrived late last night,' he confirmed, 'in time to come up here and sleep off some of my jet lag before I came to find you.'

The late London train, as Freddie had suggested, Samantha realised, and smiled a little wryly as she turned away from him to pretend to take an interest in her surroundings—mainly because she couldn't think of another thing to say.

Another silence formed. She sensed him watching her as she moved around the suite, opening doors and closing them again before moving on to the next one.

'Found what you're looking for?' he enquired eventually, though he was sardonically aware of what it was, she was sure.

Well, the suite comprised two bedrooms with their own *en suites*, she confirmed. So there was no need to fight for her privacy. 'Yes,' she said—and diverted her attention to the view beyond the window, with her chin up and her green eyes definitely telling him he could mock her all he liked.

The telephone began to ring then. Samantha was never so relieved to hear the sound. While he strode over to a desk standing at the other end of the room, she reached for the handle and opened a French window that led out onto a large, private balcony. Stepping outside, she walked over to lean on the balcony rail and, after a tense little sigh, allowed herself the luxury of a few deep breaths of fresh air, only realising as she did so that it had been a long time since she'd breathed in and out properly.

Stress, tension. Tension, stress. Was there a difference between the two of them? she wondered bleakly, and decided that even if there was a difference the two had become one tight sensation to her.

Oh, why did I let myself be talked into coming away with him like this? Samantha asked herself, as the full weight of her own vulnerability tumbled down upon her head.

Then, You know why, she told herself grimly. He

knows who you are. He's the man who holds the key to all of your problems.

Or is *he* my problem? she then suggested, and felt a cold chill touch her flesh, as if fate itself was offering her an answer. She was married to him, she'd seen firm proof of that, so why didn't she *feel* married? Glancing down at her left hand, she saw no sign that a ring had ever resided there.

So, where was her ring? If she'd been wearing one at the time of the accident, it certainly hadn't been on her finger after the crash.

'I have to go out.'

His deep voice coming from behind her made her turn warily. He was standing, propping up the opening, studying her through heavily lashed hooded dark eyes. His hair was short and neat and black and he wore his clothes with a casual ease that belied their sophistication. Nothing wrong with his body, nothing wrong with his face. So what was it about him that she found so upsetting? She gave her own answer. The inner man. The inner man worries you; the outer one simply disturbs you.

'Business,' he explained, making her blink her eyes into focus on him. 'I should be back in a couple of hours. But I've ordered some lunch for you. Then I suggest you take a rest.' His black lashes flickered as he ran his gaze over the way she was leaning so heavily on the stick. 'Nathan said you spend every evening standing behind the bar at the Tremount; was that wise considering how weak that knee actually is?'

'The knee is fine so long as I pace myself,' she answered coolly.

He ignored what she had said. 'All night serving behind a bar. All day working behind a reception desk. It's no wonder you look so worn out.'

Her chin came up, green eyes beginning to burn with resentment. 'I have to eat, like anyone else.' She said it almost accusingly. He noted it with a sudden darkening of the eyes. 'And I liked my job,' she added. 'I will always be grateful to the manager of the Tremount for taking me on, considering how—worn out I look and how many hours I had to take off to attend the necessary hospital appointments. He was good to me.'

He rejected all of that deridingly. 'You were good to him, you mean. Neither of you knew it, but he was lucky enough to acquire one of the most experienced hotel executives in the game when he took you on.'

She was surprised to hear him say that—yet not surprised when she considered how naturally she had seemed to fall into hotel routine. It probably should have occurred to her sooner that she might have worked in the trade before.

'And the need to worry about where your next meal is coming from,' he went on flatly as he levered himself away from the door, 'is now well and truly over.' He eyed her critically. 'And priority number one, once I've dealt with this bit of—business, is to get you fitted out with some decent clothes. You're used to luxury, not tat, Samantha,' he said.

'Anything else about me which doesn't meet with your approval?' she mocked, stung.

'Yes.' His eyes began to glint. 'The way you're wearing your hair. It makes you look like a toffee-nosed prude when I know for a fact you're an absolute witch. It isn't fair to give wrong impressions about oneself to others. It means they fall into nasty little traps they can't get out of.'

'Is all of that supposed to imply something specific?' she demanded, stiffening at his criticism.

'Of course,' he drawled. 'But that's for me to keep to myself and you to find out for yourself.' Then he straightened. ' Now I'm off,' he announced. 'I'll be back as soon as I—'

'You said I don't have to worry about eating again,' she cut in, anger simmering nicely now. 'Does that mean I have you to rely on for food, or do I have money of my own stashed away somewhere?'

'You have a very healthy bank account,' he informed her, naming one of the big high street banks.

'So all I have to do is walk into one of the branches and prove who I am to get at my own money?' He confirmed it. She smiled. 'Then, watch out, *signore*,' she responded—acid-sweet. 'Because if I am the witch you call me, I may just decide to disappear on you for a second time. I wonder if you'll experience a sense of *déjà vu* if I do?'

He was standing in front of her before the last word had trailed into taunting silence. 'Just try it.' He growled. 'And this time I promise you I'll follow you to the ends of the earth if I have to!'

She defied the warning burning in his eyes. 'Why didn't you the first time?'

'Where is your evidence to say that I didn't?' He challenged her right back.

'You were out of this country barely a month after I disappeared; that says a lot, don't you think?'

'I was out of the country. Yes,' he hissed back at her. 'But why I was out of the country is just one more question you're going to have to search that—' reaching up he pressed a fingertip to her temple '—closed mind of yours to find the answer to.'

Her reaction managed to shock the pair of them. She shrank back from him so urgently that she almost toppled over. 'What was that for?' He snarled, automatically reaching out to steady her.

Once again she pulled away. 'I h-hate it when you touch me,' she choked with an awful little shudder.

His eyes went black, a furious anger suddenly flaring on the sting of her insult. 'Hate?' He flicked the word at her in a thin silken tone that had her throat closing over. 'Well, let's just try this as a little exercise to test the strength of this so called hatred—'

And the next thing she knew she was being held fast by a pair of angry hands and his mouth was against her mouth. Her senses went into a complete tail-spin, sending shock waves ricocheting through her body as the most horrendous feeling of familiarity completely overwhelmed her.

She knew this mouth. She knew its feel and its shape and its sensual mobility as it coaxed her own mouth to respond. His tongue ran a caress along the line of her tightly closed lips and she recognised the light, moist gesture as his way of making her open up and welcome him.

But, worse than that, she wanted to. She wanted to respond so much that she began to whimper, having to fight herself as well as the kiss as sensation after frighteningly familiar sensation went clamouring through her system. Heat began to pool deep down in her abdomen, desire licked a taunting flick across her breasts.

It was too much. She couldn't bear it.

Her stick hit the balcony floor with a hard clatter as her hands snapped up to push him away. But they didn't push, they clung to his shoulders. And she was being assailed by yet more hot waves of familiarity. She knew his height against her own height. She knew his width and the superior power in his much stronger body.

And she knew the pleasure in feeling small and frail and oh, so feminine when held against him like this.

Maybe he sensed it. Maybe he was reading her body language. Because his hands shifted from her shoulders and began to smooth their way down her back to her slender waist. She groaned as he drew her hard up against him because—God help her—she let him do it.

Let his lips crush her own apart and let their tongues make contact and let him taste her and simply surrendered the battle to this hot and seductive taste of passion.

He withdrew. It was so abrupt that she just stood there, leaning against his hard-packed framework staring up at him in blank incomprehension.

'Yes…' he hissed down at her in soft-voiced triumph. 'You might think you hate my touch, *cara mia*, but you cannot get enough of my kisses. What does that say about what is happening in here?' he posed, bringing the whole, wild episode back to where it had started by tapping a finger against her brow again.

And just like that the familiarity disappeared and she found herself looking at a complete stranger. A cruelly taunting stranger with eyes still glinting with a residual anger and a mouth that still pulsed from the damning kiss. It was no wonder she shuddered again.

'Also, no faint,' he mocked, adding insult to injury by stepping right back from her in a way designed to mockingly prove that she was indeed still conscious.

'You bastard,' she breathed.

His lazy shrug conveyed a complete indifference to the title. Then he turned and walked gracefully towards the window. 'See you in a couple of hours,' he said to accompany his careless departure. 'And make sure you take that rest. You look like you need it.'

Samantha simply stared after him, too deeply sunk into a slow-dawning understanding to know or even care what he'd said. He had kissed her in anger. It had been a punishment as well as a demonstration of his power over her.

'I'm to blame, aren't I?'

The shaky claim brought his feet to a standstill.

'I did something so unforgivable that I daren't let myself remember.'

'No,' he denied.

She didn't believe him. It had to be her fault or why else had he treated her as he had just now?

'Apportioning blame will not help the issue,' he added grimly.

'Then, what will?'

He shook his head. 'We agreed not to discuss the past until we'd sought professional advice.'

Her short laugh scorned that remark. 'That's rich coming from the man who's just imposed the past on me with about as much ruthlessness as he could muster!'

'All right!' he rasped, reeling round to catch her off guard again. She jumped as if frightened. His teeth showed white in angry acknowledgement. 'That,' he said, waving a hand at her reaction, 'is why I kissed you! Why I was angry—why I still am! We were lovers, Samantha!' And suddenly he was striding towards her again. Hands reaching up. Hands grabbing her shoulders. 'Hot, greedy, *passionate* lovers, who never could get enough of each other! So of course it damn well infuriates me when you jump if I so much as come near you! Being near you and *not* kissing you means I am denying myself—as if it isn't enough to have one of us doing that! So—' He bent, kissed her once more, like a terse punctuation. 'Get used to it. You're my wife. I like kissing you. Now I'm getting the hell out of here before I decide to convert all of this anger into something else I like doing with you!'

And with that he turned and strode away, leaving her standing there feeling shell-shocked and shaken by the barrage of emotion he had just thrown at her.

The suite's outer door closed with a controlled slam. She blinked, breathed, and only realised when she did it that she hadn't drawn breath throughout his last angry speech. Her lips were still burning from the power of his kiss and her body was trembling so badly she began to wonder if now was going to be the moment that she sank into a faint.

It didn't happen. Instead she managed to take a step forward—and tripped over her walking stick as she did. The trip jarred her knee and, wincing, she let fly with a few choice curses as she rubbed the offending joint and fervently wished she had never set eyes on André Visconte!

'Ever,' she tagged on fiercely to that wish.

André was standing in the hotel manager's office, shooting orders down the telephone as if he was conducting a bloody war.

It was late, and he'd just come away from an interview at the police road accident department which had left him feeling turned inside out. Guilt was devouring him, along with agony and distress and a blinding black fury that was threatening to swallow him whole.

'Just do it!' he growled out at Nathan when he dared to argue the point. 'If Samantha says it has the potential, then at least do her the honour of accepting that she knows what she's talking about!'

Nathan began to patiently explain that it wasn't Samantha's word he was questioning, but the wiseness of André making such a big corporate decision feeling as wound up as he did.

'Do *you* think the Tremount has potential?' André questioned coldly.

'Yes,' Nathan replied. 'But—'

'Then what the hell is it you're arguing about? Set up the damn deal and just let me know how much it's going to cost me.'

'For Samantha?' Nathan drawled.

'Yes!' he hissed back. 'It's for Samantha! And while you're at it, make sure that friend of hers—Chrissy—is taken care of.'

'Carla,' Nathan corrected.

'Carla, then!' he all but snarled. He wasn't in the mood for all of this. 'Put her on our payroll. Samantha worries about her.' And anything—*anything* Samantha worried about had to be eliminated!

Samantha…

'Hell,' he muttered, and slammed down the receiver, then slumped back against the desk to bury his face in hands that were shaking.

Now he'd seen the photographs he couldn't get them out of his head. The roadside carnage. The twisted wreck of burnt out metal that said more clearly than words what had happened to her.

Then there were the other pictures, ones that came without photographs but were still just as gruellingly graphic, of her waking up in some strange hospital, suffering from shock and pain and a total disorientation with the strange world around her.

And where had he been while all of this was happening?

Halfway round the world on a bloody wild-goose chase!

Now she was sitting upstairs, no doubt waiting for him to continue where he had left off earlier.

Imposing himself on her. Staking his claim. He shuddered and despised himself. He wouldn't blame her if she'd taken up her own threat and had made another bolt for it.

Oh, dear God. Had she—?

Dragging his hands away from his face, he looked down at his watch to find he had been gone for almost three hours instead of the two he'd told her he would be.

With a jolt, he sprang forward and made for the door in a hurry. Samantha could disappear into thin air with a few hours to do it in. He should know; he'd had previous experience. The lift took him upwards. He paused outside their suite and took a few moments to smooth out his wrecked emotions before slotting in the access key and quietly opening the door…

CHAPTER SIX

THE suite wore an air of hushed quietness. It chilled his blood—until his eyes alighted on Samantha. She was lying asleep on one of the soft cream sofas, looking as if she had been there for a long time.

Slowly he walked towards her, his footsteps silenced by thick green carpet. The lunch he'd had sent up still sat untouched on the table by the window. He frowned, then deepened the frown when he saw two packs of tablets sitting beside the lunch tray.

Picking them up, he read the labels. One lot of tablets he recognised as the named-brand painkillers she had taken earlier. But he felt his gut squeeze in dismay when he recognised the other as a famous-brand tranquilliser.

Had she taken these? Had she taken *all* of these? Had he finally managed to drive her into—

His head shot up and round, his eyes locking onto her in a moment of skin-crawling horror.

Then, No, he grimly calmed himself. She wouldn't be that stupid.

But he found himself checking out the pack and almost sinking to the floor in relief when he discovered none of the tranquillisers missing. Going to squat down beside her, he gazed into her sleeping face. She still looked pale, but some of the strain had eased away.

As if she was able to sense the very moment he came within touching distance, her eyes suddenly flicked open and he found himself gazing into sleepy green.

'Hi.' He greeted her softly, aware that he was already on his guard, ready to field a hostile response.

It didn't come. Instead she simply lay there looking at him as if she was searching for something she needed to see.

Remorse for his earlier behaviour? he wondered. Well, she had it. 'Sorry things got a bit out of hand before,' he quietly apologised. 'Believe or not—' he grimaced '—I am finding this situation as difficult as you must be.'

'I understand.' She nodded, then seemed to realise that she was staring and broke the eye contact by sitting and sliding her feet to the floor.

It was his cue to move away, and he did so, having no wish to give her reason to erect her defences yet again. Straightening up, he looked around him for something neutral to say. 'You didn't eat your lunch.' It was all he could come up with.

'I wasn't hungry,' she replied, leaning forward to stroke exploring fingers across her damaged knee.

'How is it?'

'Better.' She showed him by flexing it with an ease he hadn't seen before. 'I took some anti-inflammatories, then fell asleep while I was waiting for them to work. What time is it?'

André glanced at his watch. 'Five-thirty.'

She nodded and stood up. He was really surprised by the lack of stiffness in her movements. It was almost like the Samantha he used to know.

But that Samantha wasn't really here, he grimly reminded himself.

Her polite voice intruded. 'Did your meeting go okay?'

'Fine,' he said, then turned his back on her, grabbed

the back of his neck and just stood there staring into space while his mind played back a reel of still frames that would look great in a horror movie.

What was he thinking while he stood there like that? Samantha wondered warily. He'd seemed all right. The anger had gone, so too the desire to shock her into reacting. Yet he clearly wasn't comfortable with what had replaced it. Something must be bothering him or he wouldn't be standing there looking like a man at a loss to know what to do next.

'Are you all right?' she asked him reluctantly, not wanting to provoke a return of their earlier hostilities.

He released an oddly muffled laugh. 'Actually, no,' he said, then turned to wing a rueful smile at her. 'I came back here half expecting to find you'd carried out your threat and made a bolt for it.'

If he'd meant to make her smile, she didn't even come close to it. 'Where would I go?' she asked him bleakly. 'You may think I like being like this but I don't,' she added. 'I need to find out about myself and, as you rightly pointed out to me, you seem to be the only person who can help me do that.'

'I don't think anything of the kind about you.' He sighed. 'I don't doubt for one minute that you must be afraid of what all of this must mean.'

'Were we…?' she stopped, changing her mind.

'What?' he prompted.

'Doesn't matter.' She shook her head.

'You're going that dreadful shade of grey again,' he informed her levelly.

'I'm okay,' she said and discovered that it was her turn to turn away from him. 'I think I'll take a shower…'

'Good idea,' he agreed. 'I think I will do the same.'

Relief quavered through the atmosphere, put there because each was glad of the excuse to escape the other. 'My room is the one on the left,' he told her. 'They are both more or less the same, but if you want to swap I don't—'

'The one on the right will be fine,' she cut in, and began to limp towards it with no sign of the nagging pain. It was amazing what a couple of pills could do Samantha mused wryly.

'Food,' he said suddenly. 'We both need to eat. Let's make it an early dinner,' he decided. 'Say, seven o'clock?'

Samantha nodded in agreement, too eager to escape, now that she had an excuse, to start up a discussion on whether she could swallow a single morsel as her throat felt so tight.

'Seven it is, then,' he confirmed. 'I'll book a table in the restaurant. Unless you would rather eat up here?'

'No,' she said quickly. 'The restaurant will be fine.' The last thing she wanted was to be incarcerated in this suite of rooms with him for a whole evening. 'I...'

'What?' he prompted when she carefully severed yet another sentence.

She shook her head, aware of the explosive properties in dryly promising not to show him up by stepping out with him wearing polyester. 'I'll see you later,' she murmured, and found her escape in the bedroom she had already claimed as her own by unpacking her suitcase and hanging up her few clothes.

André watched the door close behind her and at last released the tense sigh he had been holding in check. This wary truce they had managed to achieve was harder to deal with than the constant lightning bolts they'd been delivering across each other's bows.

Would it last?

No, it wouldn't last, he acknowledged ruefully. She might be different, but she was still Samantha. A fiery temperament was as much a part of her nature as it was a part of his own. It was the reason why they'd fought so much, loved so much and, in the end, almost destroyed each other.

Well, not this time, he vowed as he moved across the room towards his own bedroom door. Samantha might not understand this yet, but the two of them had been given a second chance and this time they were going to use it wisely.

He was going to use it wisely, he then amended. Because he couldn't expect Samantha to be wise after an event she didn't even remember.

At precisely seven o'clock Samantha took a final look at herself in the mirror, drew in a deep breath, then walked towards the door, reasonably confident that he was going to be feeling quietly relieved when he saw how she was dressed.

For, despite his derogatory impression that her clothes were tat, she had a dress. A very expensive matt-black crêpe cocktail dress, kindly donated to her, among other items, by the wife of one of her doctors who'd taken pity on her—and who'd also gone up a couple of sizes since she'd bought the clothes.

Most of the other stuff she'd had replaced with new just as soon as she could afford to. But this dress had been too good to let go so she'd kept it, never really believing she'd ever get a chance to wear it.

But here she was, doing exactly that, and not only did she think the dress looked good on her but it also *felt* good in the way the beautiful fabric moved against her slender shape. She had washed her hair with the expensive toiletries in the bathroom, and had discovered that you truly did get what you paid for because, as she'd blow-dried her hair, it had been a pleasurable experience to watch the colour become more vibrant the drier it had become.

So she'd left it to fall free around her shoulders—mainly because she suspected he was expecting her to screw it up in defiance of his toffee-nosed prude remark. Also, she had applied some make-up, paying careful attention to the strained bruising around her eyes. The only thing letting her down were the low-heeled black court shoes she was forced to wear.

But otherwise she was ready to be seen out in public with him, she told herself firmly, and lifted her chin and opened the door.

André was already there, standing over by the desk with one hand braced on it as he leaned over some papers. He looked quite painfully gorgeous.

And he was wearing a plain white tee shirt, grey linen trousers—and that was it.

While she had been dressing up he had been dressing down, and the realisation almost shattered her carefully constructed composure.

Then he looked up, saw her standing there, went perfectly still, and her composure shattered anyway. For this man wasn't just breathtakingly attractive, he was dangerously so. Black silk hair, olive-toned skin, eyes like bitter chocolate which seemed to melt as they moved with an excruciating slowness from the top of her head to the shoes on her feet. His facial bone structure was perfect, his mouth essentially male, and the muscular configuration beneath that tight white tee shirt screamed sex at her—*sex*.

Slowly he began to straighten his torso, the hand sliding away from the desk the more upright he became. But what really took her breath away was the way his eyes gentled as they made contact with her own eyes.

He knew. He knew she was feeling at a loss to know how to deal with the obvious crossed wires in the communication. Yet all he said was, 'A punctual woman, and a beautiful one too.'

Then, reaching out to close the manila file, he picked it up and said lightly, 'Hang on just five seconds while I put this away, then we will go and eat...'

Stepping into his own room, he *was* only five seconds. But he still came out wearing a grey linen jacket that completely transformed him from a mere casual diner to a stunningly chic one.

Only a man with Italian blood running in his veins could have done it. Only a man with a great deal of sensitivity could have pulled it off with such quiet aplomb.

She was impressed. She was grateful. She was seduced. He won her full attention by hypnotising her with his deep-toned, smooth, sexy, American accent, and with the quick smile that would suddenly flash out, adding a dangerous charm to an already dangerously attractive face.

They shared a table for two in a corner of the restaurant, where they talked quietly about innocuous things, like food and wine and the leisure industry. His concentration on her and whatever she had to say was so intense that she felt it like a constant buzz of awareness from fingertips to head. His eyes never left her. And his well-shaped mouth was firm but edged with a sensuousness that persistently reminded her of that kiss.

A kiss she had known. A kiss she had enjoyed. A kiss she had responded to without having to think. Even now, as she sat here watching that mouth move as he talked, she could feel its pleasurable pressure burning against her lips.

Attraction. She was aware of a physical attraction pulsing softly in her blood. She liked it. She was beginning to like him. Samantha started to relax, lower her guard, and even caught herself laughing once or twice.

Then he ruined it by picking up his glass of blood-red wine, swirling it round in thoughtful silence for a second or two, and saying levelly, 'I have a confession to make.'

Her eyes leapt to his, the green softened by what had been happening to her sharpening into instant wariness. His mouth went awry, as if in acknowledgement that he was about to spoil what had so far turned out to be a perfect evening.

'When I said I had to go out on business this afternoon I allowed you to assume it was hotel business, but it wasn't,' he explained. 'What I actually did was spend some time with your doctor.'

Her coffee cup rattled as she put in back on its saucer. 'Why would you want to go and do something like that without me there?' she protested.

'Because I had some very sensitive things to tell him and I felt they would be better said without you there to hear them.'

'About me,' she presumed, her soft mouth tightening to hide a deep stab of hurt.

'About the both of us,' he said, making it clear.

Her eyes flashed with resentment. 'He isn't supposed to discuss me with anyone!' she said tightly, feeling hunted suddenly, strangely, frighteningly, *angrily* hunted.

'He didn't. He just listened while I talked, then advised me on the best course to take with this problem we have.'

This problem, Samantha repeated to herself. How good of him to let me know what I am. 'And his advice was what?' she prompted coldly.

'That we take it very easy from here on in,' he replied, watching her, his eyes never leaving her face for a moment. 'He agrees with me that your memory is not buried quite so deep as you assume it to be. Your reaction to me is enough to substantiate that. But he advises no brutal question-and-answer sessions. No intense probing, but to allow things to come out in a slow, natural everyday way because he thinks the fainting thing is worrying. So we have to tread very carefully if we are not to cause further problems. And he wants to see you before we go back to London. He—'

'London?' she interrupted. 'Who said anything about me going to London?'

'I did,' he said. 'It's where we live. Or one of the places we live, at any rate,' he wryly amended. 'I have a branch office there. We have a house. He suggests we go there and try to pick up the threads of our normal life so that you can—'

'What normal life?' she countered tautly. 'What is even vaguely normal about me going to London with a man I don't remember, to a house I don't remember, to a life I don't remember?'

'What is normal about *not* remembering?'

Her face froze over, her awareness that he was only speaking the truth filling her with her own sense of helplessness. But she hated him for making her feel that she had no right to direct her own life because she didn't have a functioning brain in her head!

'If, between you, you've both already decided on

what's best for me, then why does he want to see me at all?' Her voice throbbed with resentment.

He did not respond to it. 'He feels you may need—reassurance that I mean you no harm,' he explained.

'Really? Does that include some reassurance that he has my best interests at heart also?' Her green eyes flashed him a look of scorn. 'Well, forgive me for not seeing things that way!'

'Why are you so angry?' he questioned curiously.

If she didn't get out of here she was going to toss the last of her wine in his face. 'Because you went behind my back and discussed my situation without my agreement,' she sliced at him. 'And if that isn't devious, I don't know what is! And to make it all worse, *he* actually let you get away with it!' She could barely breathe she was so infuriated by that!

'I needed advice and he needed to be in possession of all the facts before he could offer me that advice.' The arrogant devil was shrugging it all off, as if his answer justified what he had done.

And it did in one way, Samantha conceded. But it certainly did not in another. 'You could have lied through your teeth to him for all he knows!'

'I told him the truth,' he stated quietly.

'So everyone knows the truth about Samantha but Samantha. How cosy,' she derided, and got to her feet.

'Running away again, darling?' he taunted dryly.

She didn't bother to reply—didn't want to, actually. Did not damn well want to! she told herself fiercely as she walked away.

And she did it without a hint of a limp, André grimly noted as he watched her go. She would probably pay for that bit of pride in the morning, he predicted.

Ignoring looks from their fellow diners, who had been

keeping a curious eye on them from the moment the altercation had begun, he hissed out a tense sigh, thinking, So much for believing there was safety in numbers. Then he lifted his glass to his lips to swallow what was left of the red wine before getting up to go after her.

As he had known she would be, she was standing by the suite door, bristling with frustration because she didn't have the means to let herself in so that she could complete her angry exit by shutting herself away in her room before he could get to her.

And he grimly wished she had been able to do that—not for his sake but for her sake. Because her inability to get into the suite without his help was just another example of how out of control of her own life she must be feeling right now.

And she was trembling, he realised as soon as he came up beside her and silently fitted the card into the slot. Stiff-backed, chin up, eyes staring fiercely ahead—but trembling like a fine slender leaf having to fight against the wind that was trying to blow her away.

'Samantha—'

'Don't speak to me,' she cut in, walking through the door the moment he released the locking mechanism.

He followed her inside, closed the door, and watched her stalk stiffly across the room and shut herself away.

Maybe that wasn't a bad thing, he told himself as a real bone-weariness began to pull at him. It had been a long and gruelling day for the both of them, and he was still suffering the remains of jet lag. A night's cooling-off period might do them both a bit of good, he decided. And, with a little bit of luck, by the morning she might be seeing the sense in what he'd done.

Not that he held out much hope of that, he then admitted with a grimace that was half a smile. Because he knew Samantha, even if she didn't know herself. She was hot and she was stubborn. And he was in for a battle.

A battle he fully intended to win. For there was no room to back down now. No going back. And the sooner Samantha came to terms with that, the better it was going to be for both of them.

CHAPTER SEVEN

HE WAS half right on most counts, André discovered the next morning when she appeared for breakfast wearing a dusky mauve outfit consisting of a skimpy camisole-type top and a tight little skirt in a darker shade of mauve. Both of which did hot things to his libido even though her icy demeanour was supposed to be freezing out all of that.

Her hair was back in its screwed-up knot, and she was limping again. It didn't surprise him but it damn well annoyed him. Would she ever learn to embrace caution?

No, he answered his own question. Caution had never been a word Samantha recognised.

'I'll keep that appointment,' she announced as she joined him at the table.

It was all he was going to get, and wisely he didn't try for any more, other than murmuring a relaxed toned, 'Coffee's hot, juice is cold, take your pick.' Then he returned his attention to the newspaper he had folded open on the table.

As for Samantha, she refused to react to his non-reaction, though she was pretty sure he was sitting there expecting her to. And even if he did look good this morning, in a bright white shirt and grey silk tie that matched the colour of the jacket hanging on the back of his chair, she still hated him and still fiercely resented the way he was orchestrating her life.

It was a resentment which hadn't faded one little bit

by the time she stepped out of the specialist's consulting room a couple of hours later.

She found André lounging on the corner of the desk belonging to the pretty receptionist, who was looking all smiling and doe-eyed at him.

The little flirt, she thought scathingly. And worse—he was enjoying it! Resentment turned into something really ugly that burned like acid in her chest.

'If you're ready,' she snapped with enough venom to make them both take note of the green sparking in her eyes.

The nurse blushed, but he didn't. In fact his eyes began to gleam behind the dangerous slits he had narrowed them into. Samantha ignored the both of them and walked as haughtily as she could with a limp towards the exit door, felt him come up behind her and had to fight to suppress the urge to spin round and scratch his flirting eyes out!

'Watch it.' The warning was spoken in silken threat right against her earlobe—and suddenly she froze like a statue as a desperate sensation of *déjà vu* went washing through her.

Sensing the change, he stepped around her so he could look into her face before releasing a soft curse and grimly taking hold of her shoulders. 'You've gone that funny shade of pale again,' he informed her huskily.

'Mr Visconte?' The receptionist's voice was pitched with fluttering concern. 'Is your wife feeling ill? Shall I—?'

'Just get me out of here,' Samantha breathed tautly. 'I need some fresh air.'

Without another word he folded an arm across her shoulders to lend support while murmuring a polite goodbye as they made their exit. As soon as they were outside, Samantha moved right away from him. She felt hot and stifled, and had to stand gulping in some much needed breaths of air in an effort to stave off the feelings of faintness while he watched and waited for her to get a hold of herself again.

'Well,' he said finally, 'are you going to tell me what brought it on this time?'

No, I am not, she answered silently. 'It was just too warm in there, that's all.'

'Liar,' he drawled. 'You were about to faint again and we both know it.'

Her colour returned—all her hostility returning right along with it. 'Do we really have to have an inquisition on every small gesture I make?' she flicked at him.

'No.' He shrugged, displaying a frustrating calmness the more irate she became. 'But if you feel fit to spit, I assume you also feel fit to walk?'

'Go to hell,' she said, and limped off down the shallow steps and onto the street.

He fell into step beside her, not touching but close enough to catch her if she decided to fall into a pathetic swoon.

They reached the car. He unlocked the door and saw her inside before going around to climb in beside her. The engine fired but the car didn't move. Sitting there beside him, staring fixedly ahead, she waited with gritted teeth for what was coming.

As if on cue, the first question arrived. 'What did the doctor say?'

'Exactly what you said he would say,' she replied. '"Be a good girl. Do as you're told and everything will be fine one day."'

Her tone dripped sarcasm. But she couldn't help it,

she felt as if she were fighting for her very life here—yet she did not understand why!

Again, he showed that uncanny knack of latching onto her thoughts by sighing heavily. 'Why do you feel you have to do battle against me all the time? Did the doctor offer you no reassurance at all about me?'

'He performed beautifully,' she assured him. 'He confirmed that you are indeed who you say you are and I am who you say I am. He then went on to ask me a lot of questions which I have to *presume* were supposed to give everyone else answers to what is wrong with me—since everyone seems intent on keeping me in the dark about myself! Then he went on to advise me to work *with* you not *against* you, because you only had my best interests at heart.'

'But you don't believe that?' he assumed from her acid tone.

'What right do I have to an opinion?' She laughed thickly. 'I'm just the headcase who can't trust a thing her instincts tell her!'

'And what are your instincts telling you about me?'

'They're telling me that for some reason, known only to you and your new friend my doctor back there, you are about to manipulate me to suit your own purposes!'

'In what way?' He wasn't angry, just curious—which only managed to infuriate her further, because she saw analysis in every question he asked her—just like the doctor.

'I tell you what.' At last she turned to lance him with a look. 'I'll make a deal with you. For every answer I give you, I get one back.'

He studied the glint of challenge in her eyes for a long moment; while she sat there, wishing he was as ugly as sin because it would make it so much easier to keep him at a distance then. But he wasn't ugly, he was beautiful, and her throat closed up on a block of tears because she wanted so much to reach out and touch him.

Touch him, taste him, lose herself in him so she didn't have to think, fight, worry whether or not he was a man she could place her trust in when she couldn't even trust herself to know what was right.

'Okay,' he quietly agreed. 'Ask.'

It wasn't the answer she had been expecting. It threw her into turmoil. Sucking in a tense breath, she held onto it as panic began to build with enough power to burst through her skin. Then she said, 'No.' She breathed out like a deflating balloon.

'Because you don't want to know the answers or because you don't feel ready to know?'

'Because I'm sick and tired of the whole stupid subject!' she cried, filling with hot, pressured air again. 'It's boring! You're boring! I've lost my memory, okay?' she tossed tightly at him. 'I don't know you, and for all I do know you could be some raving sex maniac I had to run away from or get devoured!'

He laughed! He had the outright gall to laugh out loud. 'If there are any sex-mad fiends lurking in this car then they're sitting in the other seat to mine,' he said dryly.

'That's an absolute lie!' She gasped, going prickly hot all over at the very suggestion that she could be like that!

For an answer he leaned across the gap separating them and kissed her. She ignited like brushwood as all those angry emotions running riot inside her swiftly converted themselves into something else entirely, and before she knew it her hand was claiming the back of his head in her urgency to keep his mouth joined with hers.

It was she who compelled their lips to open, she who hungrily deepened the kiss. And it was she who groaned with agonising pleasure when he let her do it all.

And it was also she who shrivelled up with shame when it had to be him who broke the heated engagement. Point well and truly made.

She was surprised when he said nothing but instead merely repositioned himself in his seat and set them moving with a smoothness that utterly belied the tension still sparking between them.

Sex-mad, she repeated to herself, and shivered. Could her brain be suppressing the shame of being raving sex-mad? Dragging her eyes away from him, she fixed them straight ahead and struggled very hard not to suffocate in a sense of self-loathing.

Bringing the car to a halt outside the main doors, he climbed out then came around to her side of the car to watch her alight. His jaw clenched as she paused to exercise the knee a little before trying to walk on it. But he said not a word, didn't attempt to offer help, and even Samantha was surprised when she reached out to place her hand on his arm as they began moving.

Hard muscle flexed again. She tried to ignore the effect it had on her. If she had any effect at all on him, then he ignored it too. Neither spoke; they just walked, hand to arm as couples do.

But as they walked through the hotel entrance he stopped, then muttered a couple of rich curses beneath his breath.

'Listen,' he said, 'you aren't going to like this, and I know I don't, but there is someone standing at the reception desk we both know.'

'Who...where?' she said, hunting the busy foyer at

the same time as a shaft of nervous tension straightened her spine.

'His name is Stefan Reece, and he's talking to a receptionist right on the end of the desk.'

She saw a tall man with fine blond hair and what looked like an easy smile, chatting pleasantly with the receptionist. Warily she moved a little closer to André's big frame. He responded by twisting round until he was half blocking her from view.

'Now, don't get jumpy,' he chided. 'He's a competitor, that's all.' And he named a hotel chain that she instantly recognised, before going on. 'He'll be here scouting. We all do it—check out the competition to see if they're offering a better service than we are offering ourselves. Since he's already seen us, we can't avoid him,' he added with a clip to his voice that said he wished otherwise. 'But it's up to you how we deal with this. We can pretend there's nothing wrong, exchange a few pleasantries, then get the hell away from him before he realises there's something different about you. Or we can keep to the truth and get into the complications of trying to explain it all.'

Which told her exactly which option he preferred and, frankly, so did she. In fact the very idea of trying to explain she couldn't remember her own name made her feel distinctly nauseous.

'He'll see the limp,' she said. 'And the scar...' Instinctively her hand jerked up to cover the side of her face.

Lifting his hand, André took hold of her hand and firmly lowered it to her side again. 'Stop it,' he scolded. 'The scar is barely noticeable except in your mind.'

'I haven't got a mind, remember?' she gibed. 'And he'll know that too the moment he speaks to me!'

'It's your memory you've lost, not your wits.' He sighed in exasperation. 'All you need to do is smile a reasonably convincing smile, and leave the talking to me. You can do that, can't you?'

Could she?

'André—Samantha!' a deep voice greeted. 'This is a pleasant surprise!'

Speak for yourself, Samantha thought childishly.

'Maybe a bigger one for us than it must be for you?' André suggested dryly as he took the other man's outstretched hand.

'Caught red-handed in the enemy camp.' Stefan Reece admitted it. 'What can I say? Unless I remind you that the boot was well and truly on the other foot the last time I saw you.' He grinned. 'Sydney, about a year ago if my memory serves me right. And you were checking out my establishment—but without this lovely creature along with you to make my day. Hello Samantha,' he murmured warmly, offering his hand to her next. 'You're looking as beautiful as ever, I see.'

'Thank you,' she said. If he'd noticed the scar he hid it well, she thought, and was grateful enough to find an answering smile. His laughing eyes darkened; it took him longer than it should have to release her hand again. And she felt the man standing beside her give a restless shift.

'How's business?' André asked, and it was so near to an angry rasp that she glanced sharply at him.

'Good—though not as good as you seem to be having it,' Stefan Reece was saying ruefully. 'Which reminds me.' He then turned to Samantha, his face lighting up. 'I went by the Bressingham the other day, expecting it to be open by now, but…'

Samantha had stopped listening. The name

Bressingham name had tugged at a chord somewhere deep down inside her, and she was suddenly experiencing such an overwhelming sense of grief that she could barely cope with the power of it. Her heart began to throb so slowly and thickly that her fingernails coiled into taut male flesh without her even being aware whose waist it was she was clinging to.

'Have you just arrived, Stefan?' The harsh rasp of André's voice sliced through whatever it was that was holding her.

The other man blinked, glanced quickly from one tense face to the other and seemed to realise he had made some huge blunder here, though for the life of him he didn't know what it was. 'Just checking in when I saw you two standing here, so I...'

'Then let me make sure they give you the best available suite. On the house, of course.' With a snap of his fingers André brought a hotel attendant running. With only a few terse instructions he had Stefan Reece settled in one of the best suites, and the arm he had resting across Samantha's shoulders had turned into a crushing anchor.

'It would have been nice if we could have had dinner together tonight, but Samantha and I are leaving for London this afternoon, and...'

So soon? The information was just another shock Samantha had difficulty coming to terms with.

'Shame,' Stefan Reece was saying. 'It isn't often we get a chance to...'

Her mind kept shutting off, she realised. Concentrating on full sentences seemed completely beyond her scope. She kept hearing the word 'Bressingham, Bressingham'. It hurt but she didn't know why it hurt.

The arm about her shoulders urged her into movement. She complied as if through a floating haze within which she could hear the two men talking. Yet she wasn't there with them. It was a strange experience, walking, hearing, yet feeling many miles away.

'*Cara*, Stefan is saying goodbye to you,' a voice prompted softly.

'Oh,' she said, and blinked but couldn't' focus. 'Goodbye, Stefan. It was nice to see you again.' The words arrived automatically. His reply was lost in the resuming haze.

The next thing she knew, she was standing in the lift being transported upwards and André was standing over her, literally propping her up against the lift wall.

'You don't have to do that,' she protested. 'I can manage on my own now, thank you.'

He moved away but she could tell he didn't want to. And all he did was move as far as to lean a shoulder against the wall right beside her. He was concerned, she could feel it, yet he didn't attempt to ask her what had brought the faint feeling on this time.

'You don't seem to have managed very well over the last year without me,' he murmured huskily instead. 'In fact, I would go as far as to say you've made one hell of a mess of trying to manage on your own.' And, to make his point, his hand came up, gently touching the puckered scar at her temple.

She reacted by flinching away from his touch so violently, this time, that she banged the other side of her face on the lift wall.

'You bloody fool!' he exploded. 'What did you think I was going to do to you?'

'Just don't touch me like that again!' she choked out,

green eyes flaring with bitterness. 'I hate you! I don't know why I hate you but I really, really hate you!'

'You're overreacting.' He sighed.

'M-maybe,' she conceded. 'But...'

But what? she asked herself helplessly. You *are* overreacting to a lot of things! Overreacting to a consultation with a doctor which was, in reality, the most common sense thing to have done in the circumstances. Overreacting to a kiss that shouldn't have happened but did *and* you enjoyed it! Then you overreact to the prospect of meeting someone you should know but don't and, to top it all off, you really overreact to a name you do know but cannot work out why!

'Bressingham,' she said huskily. 'What is the Bressingham?'

'Why?' He sounded about as uncooperative now as she knew she had been sounding since he'd stridden back into her life.

'Because I recognise it from somewhere but I can't remember where.'

'Story of your life.'

The lift stopped, the doors sliding open to allow two people to come in, stalling Samantha's desire to retaliate to that one.

So they smiled politely at the polite smiles they received, then stood stiffly beside each other while the lift continued on its way up. And the tension in the small confines of the lift was fraught—so fraught the other couple kept glancing warily at each other. And by the time the lift ejected the intruders on the next floor Samantha was beginning to wonder if her throat would ever open up again.

The doors closed and up they went again, with the same taut silence accompanying them. Another stop, and this time he stretched his arm out to hold back the doors in an indication that they had reached their floor.

Reluctantly Samantha limped forward. As she went to go by him, he stopped her with a clipped, tart, 'You don't hate me, Samantha. You just wish that you did.'

For some reason—she didn't know why—her hand snaked out and caught him a stinging slap across his face.

For what felt like a full minute afterwards, both just stood there staring at the other, her with a pain and hurt and anger she just could not comprehend, he with a black fury that said he was having to stand stock still like that or retaliate in some way.

Having just enough sense left to err on the side of caution, she turned and walked away. But once again she found herself having to wait for him to open the suite door for her, and she was trembling by the time that he did so.

Once again she took the direct route to her bedroom the moment she got inside, and once again André watched her make her escape while telling himself to just to let it go—while the feel of her fingers still stung his cheek.

Only this time he found he just couldn't leave it. This time he refused to be shut out by a closed door. Anger, pride, stupidity, you name it, he found he wasn't going to give himself time to think about his next action as he strode grimly after her.

CHAPTER EIGHT

SAMANTHA was standing in the middle of the room, desperately trying to justify what she had just done, when the door suddenly shot open.

Her heart began to thump somewhere in the region of her stomach. He was angry and she didn't blame him. Her fingermarks were still lying like an accusation against the side of his face. Remorse pushed her into speech.

'I'm sorry,' she said immediately. 'I didn't mean to do it. I don't know what came over me.'

He didn't even acknowledge the apology. The door closed with the help of his foot. The room was suddenly filled with the scent of danger. His eyes were black and his mouth hard. A warning chill went slinking down her spine. I've managed to set the devil loose, she realised uneasily, and decided that this could well be a good time to faint.

But she didn't feel in the least bit faint. In fact she felt disturbingly—

'N-no,' she stammered out, lifting up a trembling hand meant to ward him off as he began striding towards her. 'Stay there. Let me try and explain…'

He just kept on coming. It was like being stalked by an angry predator. Fear and an unexpected excitement began to war in her blood. He came to a stop a hair's breadth from her outstretched, trembling fingers. She saw it as a reprieve and rushed back into speech again. 'It-It's been a d-difficult twenty-four hours for me,' she explained unsteadily. 'I w-was overwrought, n-not thinking straight. I just—snapped. I didn't want to, but—'

'Well, guess who else has snapped?' he posed, caught the outstretched hand and used it to pull her towards him.

The softness of her breasts made impact with solid, male muscle. It was like making contact with pure electricity; a static charge lit up nerve ends so fiercely that she could actually hear them crackle. She tried to pull away but it was already too late; his other arm had snaked around her waist to hold her firmly against him. Even as she released a protesting gasp, his dark head was lowering.

Oh, she tried to fight him. She twisted and turned and went through a series of denying groans and quivers—and kissed him back as if she couldn't get enough of him. It was awful. She was appalled at herself, yet her mouth clung hungrily and her body writhed closer to the uncompromising hardness of his.

Because she wanted this. Wanted what she knew was going to happen with the need of a woman who had been waiting for this moment for much too long.

Too long…she repeated, and knew it was the truth. Too long hurting, too long wanting, and too long waiting for this man to come to her.

It was a knowledge which had another sob clutching at her throat. He felt it and lifted his head to look down at her. He was still angry. She could see it glinting in his eyes. She could see the passion too, the flame of desire that, angry or not, he couldn't manage to hide. 'You've vented your filthy temper on me many times, *cara*,' he told her thinly. 'But you've never raised your hand to me before.'

'I'm sorry,' she said again, but it was a different kind

of sorry. It was low and soft and unbelievably sensual—and spoken as she was twisting her fingers free from his so she could gently lay them against the marks she had placed on his face.

His eyes began to burn. Hers darkened in a dramatic surrender to what it was she knew she wanted here. The hand moved on, fingers sliding into his silk black hair and around his nape—before pulling his mouth back to hers.

'You bloody hypocrite,' she heard him breathe as they resumed that vital contact.

He was right, and she was. But it didn't stop the pair of them from enjoying a sensual feeding frenzy with frantic deep kisses and restless hands that touched and stroked and acknowledged no boundaries in their quest to taste the whole banquet.

It was hot and it was hungry. Samantha didn't know herself, the touch of his stroking hands and the passion in his kisses seeming to draw a completely different person out of her skin: a wild and wanton person with a throbbing, pulsing sensuality that demanded full attention and made sure she got it. Where he touched, she revelled in sheer, luxuriating pleasure. Where he didn't she writhed in restless demand.

He muttered something into her mouth she recognised as a signal to tone the whole thing down. But, no way, she thought feverishly, and ripped shirt buttons from their holes so she could place her hands against the hair-roughened beauty of burning, tight flesh. All hint of toning anything down faded in that moment as, with a deep shudder, he took back control by running his hands beneath her top. Dragging her mouth from his, she released a soft, shivering gasp as pleasure went singing along her skin where he began to caress her.

'You don't know what it is you're inviting here,' he growled darkly.

I do, she thought. 'Don't talk,' she commanded, terrified that speech was going to break the magic spell surrounding them.

Instantly his mood flipped back over, the moist tip of his tongue stabbing at her lips in an insistent command for her to part them again. When she did, he began to torment with short, slick, sensual forays into her mouth that made her light up inside.

This was the point where he began to seduce her in earnest, Samantha recognised from somewhere within the turmoil. His hands caressed, his mouth seduced, and her clothes began disappearing. She didn't care—in fact she welcomed their loss. He stroked her breasts, her back, the soft pink curve of her bottom. When she sighed out in pleasure, he rewarded the sigh with deep probing kisses to keep her submerged in a world of pure sensation.

When he decided to lift her up and carry her to the bed, her eyes came open to reveal the green, darkened by desire but alive to what was actually happening.

'What?' he questioned very softly. His tone was a measured seduction in itself. Laying her down, he came to lie beside her, leaning close to her pulsing lips to murmur, 'Tell me what you want and I will give it to you.'

He was speaking in Italian, low and hushed and intensely intimate. When she merely lay there and listened, with her eyes dark and vulnerable, he said gently, 'Do you want this to stop now?'

He meant it too. If she told him yes, she wanted it to stop, he would move away without a single protest. But it never even became an issue. Gazing deep into the desire darkened depths of his eyes, 'No,' she whispered.

He rewarded her with another long, soul-stripping kiss. But it was also a softly seducing, beautiful kiss. And it didn't stop there. He began to kiss her all over. He kissed her chin, her nose, the flickering lids hiding away her eyes. He slid that devastatingly skilled tongue-tip around the small scar at her temple. The gesture filled her with the most incredibly sweet sense of loving.

But when she began to caress him he stopped her with a silken, 'No,' and firmly returned her hand to the mattress.

It was his seduction, and he was determined to play it his way, she realised. And she just lay there and let him. Why? Because she wanted to be seduced. She wanted to simply lie here and feel—feel anything and everything he could possibly make her feel.

When his kiss began trailing down her throat she groaned as he paused, then bit sensually into the pulse-point leaping there. The feel of his mouth closing around one erect pink nipple lost her the last dregs of conscious reality. Her flesh was alive and demanding total concentration, the smallest brush with his mouth set a million nerve ends shimmering.

I know this, she found herself thinking hazily. I've been here before, been reduced to this beautiful state of boneless pleasure many, many times before. I know this man. I know his touch. I know what's coming, which is why I daren't so much as breathe in case I distract him.

This was living at its most sensual. When his tongue began slowly circling her navel, sensation fanned out in a heart-stopping ripple, followed almost instantly by an overwhelming stillness as a knowing finger made sliding contact with the very core of her sexuality, centering all that concentration on the one area as desire swelled, then burst like a flower opening up to the life-nourishing heat of the sun.

'André.' She sighed, and he felt the thick drug of power surge in his body.

This woman was *his*. Mine, he thought possessively, every sigh, every pleasurable quiver, every silk-smooth, sensual cell that made up her beautiful body. Even her thoughts—her damned hidden thoughts—belonged to him while he touched her like this.

But it wasn't enough. He wanted more. He wanted everything, he decided as the power of his own burgeoning desire grew too strong for him to contain any longer. Breaking free, he came to his feet beside the bed, saw her eyes flicker open in bewildered surprise then wince shut again as a shaft of afternoon sunlight struck into them.

In a single stride he had closed the curtains, diffusing the light in the room to a seductive softness, before turning back to find her eyes open again. Without a word, he began stripping his clothes off while she lay there half on her side, and saying not a word to try to stop this.

But then they were still making love—with their eyes and his body movements—and the way she lay there, following the removal of each piece of clothing with such devotion, flooded each newly revealed part of his compact muscle-structure with a burning sense of masculine arrogance.

'You study me with the curiosity of a virgin,' he murmured as he came to lie beside her.

She just smiled a bewitchingly provocative smile, and in the next moment he rolled her onto her back and punished the smile with a kiss that changed the whole tempo of what he had been creating before.

Samantha placed her hands on his body and this time he didn't attempt to stop her. Each touch became a deliberate torment, heightening the senses to a pitch that was almost savage in their quest to wring the most from the other. She stroked his arms, his back, dug her nails deep into the flesh which formed his lean, tight buttocks, and his teeth grazed tauntingly across a nipple then hungrily drew the whole stinging areola into his mouth.

And hot—he was hot. His skin was hot, his mouth—the moisture within it. She drew in a tight breath of air and found the scent of his body so intoxicatingly hot it turned the air to a thick, smooth, sensual steam she was reluctant to breathe out again.

When he came back to plunder her mouth, she responded by closing her arms around him and flattening her body up against his body, breast to breast, hips to hips—soft pulsing sex making contact with hard probing sex. He rolled with her until she was lying on top of him, her kissing him, her moving on him, her hair—having escaped from its knot long ago—tumbling in a silken trail of spiralling waves all around his face and shoulders.

Then her knee began to protest at the uncomfortable pressure she was placing upon it and, on a tiny groan, it was she who was changing their position, rolling onto the mattress beside him and trying to bring him with her. But he was too shrewd for his own good. He'd heard the groan and had recognised it for what it was. Before she realised what he was doing he was leaning down to kiss the hairline pink scars which criss-crossed the once smooth and perfect area.

'No,' she whimpered, strangely upset by what he was

doing, and she reached to grasp a fistful of his hair to pull him away again.

He let her do it, but came to lean over her with a face carved with tension. 'If you *ever* put your life at risk again, I will personally kill you!' he rasped at her furiously.

She still held tight to a fistful of his hair, and in reply she brought his mouth onto hers to kiss away the fear raking through him. And it *was* fear; she knew that instinctively. It filled her with a most peculiar feeling of warmth tinged with aching despair.

And, as if he knew it, he entered her like a man caught between two kinds of hell. It should have hurt it was so fierce and possessive. But it didn't hurt. It was in fact the most exquisite sensation she felt she had ever experienced. He thrust deep and she welcomed him like a long-lost, desperately missed lover.

'André,' she breathed again.

It sent him spinning over that finely balanced edge between control and sexual insanity. He drove into her like a man who was being given his last chance to experience this level of ecstasy. And she took each hot, lancing thrust with gasps of pleasure, growing shrill the closer she came to reaching the goal he was driving her towards.

Yet when she reached it she went quiet, and his hand trembled when it raked up to push the tendrils of hair away from her face, so he could watch this woman, who did everything with such frightening totality, absorbing each consuming wave of pleasure he was inducing, in a silence that pierced his heart with the knowledge that she was no longer of this world but floating on another plane entirely.

Then he joined her. With one more sweet, slow

plunge, his eyes drew closed and his features grew sharp as he began to spill out his own fierce pleasure.

Neither of them was aware of anything much for the next few, communal minutes while they made a slow return to a sanity that seemed more exhausting than the climb out of it.

Then he became conscious of his weight pressing heavily down on her and reluctantly decided to move. His careful withdrawal from her body caused a final mutual spasm of residual pleasure, then cool air touched their sweat-sheened flesh as he rolled onto his back beside her on the bed.

After that they just lay there, with eyes closed and bodies slack, waiting for reality to come filtering back in. It was the calm after the storm with another storm hovering in the near distance, threatening to roll in depending on what they both chose to do or say next.

Eventually he turned, moving onto his side to face her, and touched her cheek with a finger. 'Okay?' he asked huskily.

Samantha nodded, and though her eyes flickered open she couldn't seem to bring herself to look at him, so she stared at the ceiling instead while she admitted sombrely, 'I knew your touch.'

The finger stilled in its gentle tracing of her cheekbone. Reaching up, she caught the finger, clutching at it hard as she added shakily, 'I knew you.'

He didn't try to recover the finger. In fact he didn't do anything but lie very still. 'You say *knew* not *know*,' he remarked finally. 'Is that significant?'

She closed her eyes again, nodded and felt a tear creep out from the far corner of each eye. 'Nothing else,' she whispered. 'I just—know your touch, and for a while I knew you...'

Which was why she was gripping his finger so tightly, André pondered grimly to himself. And wanted to cry with her, it was that damned wretched.

'I'm so afraid it will be all I'll ever know now.'

On a sigh he gathered her in, kissed her brow, stroked his cheek over her tumbled hair, and left his finger right where it was, because—hell—if she did need to touch him then let her keep the finger! He didn't need it. But, God, he needed her.

'It will be okay.' He tried to sound reassuring, though he was no more certain of anything than she was herself. 'Trust me, *cara*, and I will promise to get you through this as quickly and as painlessly as I can.'

'It will be painful, then?'

'Yes.' He sighed; it was no use denying it. It was, after all, why they were supposed to be taking things so carefully.

And why they should not even be here like this.

Fool, he cursed himself. A ban on intimacy to this degree should have been a foregone conclusion to anyone with intelligence. Keep your hands off until you have a right to touch, he'd told himself, because he was acutely aware that he had lost that right twelve months ago. So what had he done? Within twenty-four hours of setting eyes on her again he'd tumbled her into the nearest bed and taken just about every liberty he could with her.

Well done, André, he mocked himself harshly. At least last time you managed to wait a whole week before you took her to bed. This time you could barely manage a full day.

Well not again, he vowed. Not until she recovered every last wretched memory! Then he almost groaned in frustration when she began absently stroking the tip of his finger over the softness of her lips. His body quickened. He shut his eyes and grimly forced his senses back into the cupboard they had been languishing in for a whole, miserable year.

'Come on,' he said, and got off the bed then bent down to lift her to her feet. Already he was getting used to waiting patiently while she used his forearms as support until she gained a reasonable balance.

'Okay?' he prompted when her grip slackened.

'Mmm,' she said.

Looking down to check for himself that she was indeed managing before he took his arms away, he saw long and slender naked flesh, pearly white skin and a cluster of fine ginger curls, which reminded him of certain sensual pleasures he still hadn't reacquainted himself with… Then he had to turn away before she could see what was happening to him.

'Right, go and have a quick shower, then pack your things while I do the same,' he instructed briskly, striding around the room to pick up his clothes. 'I would like to leave here within the hour if we can do it.'

'We're still leaving today?'

Her tone alone was enough to have him straighten, with his final piece of clothing, to see her still standing where he had left her, looking like a beautiful Titian goddess, wearing a lost and frightened expression on her face that cut him to the quick.

She didn't want to leave Devon and what she had come to feel safe with. And he had no choice but to insist they leave, because her past was in London—and his future, if she was going to let him have one once she recovered her memory, that was.

'Of course,' he said.

'London,' she murmured, and he hated to see that vulnerable expression hollowing out her lovely green eyes. It was impossible not to respond to it, and on a sigh he walked back to her, kissed her once, firmly.

'Home,' he corrected firmly. 'We are going home...'

CHAPTER NINE

THEY were an hour into their journey before either of them spoke more than a few frustratingly short syllables without a protective coating of politeness on their voices.

Home, he'd said, and instantly the barriers had gone back up between them. He'd erected his wall, Samantha suspected, because he wasn't going to change his mind and didn't want to argue about it. She had put her wall up because she wanted to argue but didn't seem to have any grounds to do so.

Home was home. Of course he wanted to take her back there, she reasoned. Or why else would he go to all this trouble to come and get her? Home probably also held a million clues as to why she was like this, and if she wanted to recover her memory then home was the most logical place to go and look for it.

But accepting all of that didn't stop her from dreading the moment. So it was easier to be silent than risk letting it all spill out.

Only, the silence was also causing the kind of tension in the small confines of the car that was obviously beginning to get to him, going by the frequent, tight glances he kept flicking at her.

'What do you think it is I am taking you to?' he exploded as if on cue at her last thought. 'Hell and damnation?'

Turning her face to the car's side window, she refused to answer, and he began muttering some really choice curses, most of them in rich Italian, which quite colourfully described his irritation with sulky females, the heavy traffic on British motorways, and the whole situation in general.

'Have you always had such a filthy temper?' she asked coldly when he eventually sizzled into silence.

'No, I caught it from you,' he replied, changing lanes and increasing his speed, mainly, she suspected, because it gave him something to do. 'With anyone else I am as cool-tempered as an arctic frost.'

'That surprises me.'

'Why should it?' he threw back. 'I run a multinational corporation. You don't do that efficiently when you let your emotions rule your head.'

'The Italian temperament is notoriously volatile,' was all she said to that.

It was like a red rag being waved at an angry bull. 'I make love in Italian too,' he gritted, drawing a parallel even he didn't understand.

'Your first name is French, though, isn't it?'

He nodded. 'My mother was French,' he explained. 'My father Italian. But I was born and bred in the city of Philadelphia. The Mongrel, you used to like to call me,' he added with a smile. 'So I used to retaliate and call you—'

'The Alleycat,' she said.

His foot slipped off the accelerator. She straightened in her seat and the ensuing silence was stunned.

'You remember,' he breathed, getting a hold of himself only enough to concentrate on his driving, while she continued to sit there staring straight ahead and looking pale again.

Seeing the sickly pallor, he began to get worried, 'Samantha,' he prompted, suddenly feeling trapped there on a three-lane motorway doing seventy miles an hour. 'Talk to me,' he commanded.

But it became clear that she couldn't. With a flashing glance in his mirrors, he indicated and began switching lanes. If the worst came to the worst, he decided, he could pull onto the hard shoulder now, without causing a multi-car pile-up.

His jaw felt like a piece of rock. Reaching across the central console, he took a tight hold on her hands where she held them knotted together on her lap. 'Speak,' he ordered tightly.

This time he managed to get through to her. 'I'm all right,' she insisted, but they both knew that she wasn't. 'I'm not going to fall into a hysterical fit.'

'Ask me the same question,' he mocked. Then he saw a sign up ahead warning of a service exit and threw up a silent thanks to whoever had put it there.

A few minutes later he was pulling them into a parking bay, shutting down the engine, then climbing out of the car and swinging around the long bonnet to open her door. She was still too pale, too still.

'Come on,' he said, firmly urging her out of the car and into his arms. The worst of it was that she went without a murmur, burying her face into his throat then just standing there, letting his warmth and his strength infuse a little bit of both back into her.

'Sorry,' she murmured eventually, straightening away from him a little. 'It was shock, that's all, to hear myself saying it and know I was speaking the truth.'

His hands came up to cup her face, lifting it so he could search her clouded eyes. 'It was no big thing,' he gently dismissed. 'I suppose we should be worrying if you *don't* have the occasional memory flash.'

'Is that what the doctor said?'

'Yes,' he confirmed. 'But I'm not supposed to push it, which I did just now by bringing up the past. So it's me who should be apologising, not you.'

It was such a sweet thing to say she wanted to start crying. Maybe he saw the tears threatening, because his tone suddenly became very brisk. 'Now we've stopped, let's go and find a drink and a sandwich or something.'

Subject over—put away. Samantha had no wish to argue with that decision.

Half an hour later they were back on the road, and the day was beginning to draw in around them. After a coffee and a sandwich she was feeling a bit better, less tense about the whole London situation, and definitely more relaxed with him. 'Tell me about Bressingham,' she said.

He glanced at her, then away again, and for a while she thought he wasn't going to answer. It was, after all, another part of that past he had made taboo between them. 'You remember something else?' he questioned eventually.

'Just the name.'

He nodded, and took another few moments to take this reply in. 'The Bressingham is a hotel,' he then announced. That was all, no elaboration.

Samantha began to frown. 'One of yours?' she asked.

'We occupy six major sites in London alone,' he supplied.

'Is that where I met you? Did I work at the Bressingham Hotel?'

'Yes,' he said.

'Which is why Stefan Reece specifically connected the hotel with me,' she therefore concluded.

'Just look at that,' he suddenly exclaimed, indicating the road directly ahead of them. 'We are about to be engulfed in one hell of a cloudburst, looking at the spray coming off the road.'

He was right and they were. It hit almost at the same moment they noticed it. 'No talking now, while I concentrate,' André instructed as the windscreen wipers leapt into life.

Sublimely unaware that she had been smoothly put through several diversions in the last sixty seconds, Samantha didn't even think of arguing when they were shrouded in a wet grey mist which cut visibility down to an absolute minimum.

To ease the silence, he reached out and switched on the radio, and two seconds later a preset pop station began singing out the latest rock ballad obsessing the pop charts at the moment.

He didn't bother to change the station and she didn't mind the music. So they drove on through the rain cocooned in their own small, dry world with the music and inane DJ chatter to keep them company, and the steady swish of the car wiper-blades slowly luring Samantha into a light slumber.

From the corner of his eye André saw her body relax and was at last able to ease some of the tension out of his own. There was a very fine line between telling outright lies and merely bending the truth a little, he observed very grimly. Reflecting on their last conversation, he couldn't quite clear it with his conscience that he had managed to tread that fine line all the way.

The problem was that the Bressingham was one of several major issues that had placed them in this situation in the first place. And, until he had decided which issue to tackle first, he had no wish to tackle any.

'Ever heard the adage that real life is stranger than

fiction?' The DJ's voice cut into his brooding. 'Well, listen to this…'

Go to hell, André thought, and switched stations. He had his own stranger-than-real-life situation tying him in knots right here. He didn't need to listen to anyone else's!

The rain stopped as they were driving down the Kensington Road. As if sensing the difference when the wipers fell silent, Samantha stirred, stretched, opened her eyes, and found herself staring straight into a pair of warmly familiar dark brown eyes.

'Hi,' he murmured softly, and her stomach turned over.

'Hi,' she responded, feeling shy beneath the intimacy of his gaze. Stupid she knew, after the kind of intimacies they'd shared this afternoon. But she still made quite a play out of sitting up properly to give her an excuse to break that eye contact.

'Where are we?' she asked, glancing out of the window.

'Stuck in traffic,' he answered wryly. 'You slept for over an hour,' he added as the car began crawling forward. 'Which had me wondering if you didn't sleep much last night.'

Last night felt a long way away to Samantha—several very long lifetimes in fact. 'The rain's stopped,' she said. It was her way of ignoring his question.

'Only just,' he replied, and turned off at the next junction, taking them past place names she recognised but didn't know why she did. If anyone had asked her she would have claimed never to have even visited London, never mind lived here.

'You have a house and—what did you say—six hotels in London?' she remarked. 'Wouldn't it be easier to simply occupy one of your own suites than take on the added expense of a house?'

'Oh, very prudent-thinking.' He grinned.

The grin sent her stomach flipping again, but the words didn't, because she was very aware that prudence had been her closest companion during the last tough year.

'Living in hotels all the time is like living on top of the job,' he explained. 'Hotels are fine if we only need to be somewhere for a couple of days. But in the long term we both prefer our own private living space.'

And Samantha didn't miss the smooth way he was including her into what he was saying.

'So we have an apartment in New York, where my head office is situated,' he went on. 'Another in Paris and one in Milan. And a villa in the Caribbean for when we feel the need to really get right away and crash out on a beach for a while.'

'Lotus-eaters?' she likened dryly.

'When the mood take us,' he agreed. 'But, as for the rest of the time, we work hard, travel far, and live out of suitcases.'

'In luxury penthouse suites, like the one in Exeter,' she provided.

'Perks of the job,' he said.

'Extravagant perks of the job.'

'Great lifestyle, though. You love it,' he added as a lazy tease.

'Me?' she turned to stare at him, not sure she liked the sound of the pampered, jet-setting person he was making her out to be.

The car slowed and made an abrupt right turn. Looking ahead of them again, she only had time to register a wide expanse of black wrought-iron railings flanked by a thick green neatly clipped hedge. Then they were coming to a stop in front of a pair of tall wrought-iron gates. Beyond the gates stood a house, a beautiful white rendered house that looked like a small Georgian mansion set in its own private grounds.

The gates began to open automatically. Tyres crunched on gravel as they drove through, then began passing between two beautifully kept lawns with neatly laid borders. He drew them to a stop directly in front of a shallow porch supported by two slender round pillars, either side of which stood two great stone urns, spilling with a shock of flame-red geraniums.

Opening her door, Samantha climbed out, then just stood there staring. In the grey and muggy half-light of a cloud-cast and damp summer evening it all looked very white, very pristine, very elegant, yet…

I don't like this place, she thought suddenly. And went so icy cold that she shivered.

From the other side of the car, André was grimly observing her response, so he saw the stillness followed by the telling little shiver, knew exactly why it had happened and wondered tautly if she did.

Tension pulled like a vice across his shoulders while he waited for her to say something. He needed her to give him a clue as to what was happening so he could then decide how to respond. The house could be the key to unlock the holocaust. Certainly, there was good reason for it to do so.

But then, he had believed that seeing him for the first time would have done it, but it hadn't.

Neither had the mention of the Bressingham.

'You and I actually *live* here?' she questioned unsteadily.

The vice gave way. He relaxed his shoulders. 'Yes,'

he confirmed, amazed that his voice could sound so steady when really he was shaking with relief.

'I'll get the luggage later,' he said and, without looking at her, he walked around the car and beneath the porch with his key at the ready. 'Are you coming?' he prompted lightly.

No, Samantha answered silently, not understanding why this house was having such a powerful, muscle-dragging effect on her. But the feeling was too strong for her to ignore it. So she remained where she was, clinging to the open door of the Jaguar, watching him place the key in the door, then send it swinging open.

Her breath caught in her throat and congealed there in a thick, suffocating ball. He too, had gone very still—no movement, no sign of anything. As if, like herself, he was waiting for something monumental to happen. Silence thumped and throbbed in the warm, muggy atmosphere, the complete stillness all aiding and abetting that silence to wrap tight pressure bands around her chest, until a roaring began to build inside her head.

No, she willed herself hazily. I won't faint away again—I won't!

Maybe he sensed her silent battle because he turned suddenly to face her. Big, lean and so devastatingly attractive. She felt sick with how strong her feelings were for him. It hurt, it actually hurt like a physical pain, because she just could not bring herself to believe that he felt the same for her.

'Tell me why you married me,' she whispered, having to squeeze the words past the ball in her throat.

His face seemed carved from stone. 'Why does any man marry a beautiful woman?' he countered levelly.

The 'beautiful' did not come into the equation. She didn't even want to hear it there. It changed the emphasis too much. Made the beauty more important than the woman.

Yet… She dropped her eyes from his and began to frown at the ground in blind confusion, because 'beauty' didn't seem to be her problem here. It was something else that was bothering her, gnawing at her, warning her. But what else? What—what else…?

'If I could marry you again tomorrow, I would do so.' A crunch of gravel and she looked up to find him walking towards her, the dark solemnity of his expression a hypnotic balm. 'If you ran away again I would look for you until the day I die.'

'But you didn't search the first time,' she whispered hoarsely, feeling as if she was trapped on a never-ending treadmill with that single question being the chain that held her there.

He smiled, if you could call it a smile. A twist of derision? Of mockery? Of grim, dark irony?

Then, with a lightning movement of lean, lithe muscle, he suddenly grabbed hold of the Jaguar door and the car bonnet on the other side of her, trapping her with his body, his strength—and with his anger. She gasped. His teeth glinted white between his stretched lips. And his eyes flashed like black diamonds, as hard as hell.

'It wasn't me who lost you, *mia cara*,' he incised very thinly. 'It was you that lost yourself.'

Sparks crackled in the air between them. Electric impulses began flashing in her brain. Doors opened, then slammed shut before she could so much as glimpse what was going on behind them. Her heart began to race. Her breasts lifted and fell in a hectic, shallow attempt at breathing.

She opened her mouth, tried to speak, found that she

couldn't because those angry eyes were forcing her to acknowledge what he'd said just now.

He was right—he was right! Her panic-ridden mind began screaming at her. Like some terrible coward she had run away and lost herself rather than face whatever it was she was scared of.

How pathetic, she thought scathingly, looking hard into those ruthless eyes that were making her face her own wretched cowardice. And willed—*willed* her mind to stop playing stupid games on her so she could solve the conundrum that made this man feel like her very soul mate and her worst enemy at the same time!

'I love you, don't I?' she heard herself say in a cracked little whisper.

The eyes went absolutely black. 'Yes,' he confirmed.

'And I hurt you badly. You implied that to me once.'

He didn't like that claim, it had the eyes flicking away from her on a flash of irritation before they came back to her face again.

'For a short while,' he confirmed very grimly. 'But if you are now thinking that I brought you here to exact retribution, then don't,' he declared. 'Because I hurt you a whole lot more than you even attempted to hurt me.'

Which implied that their marriage had not been all delight and happiness, she concluded. But then, they'd already settled that point in several ways during the last couple of days.

Both hot-tempered, both passionately volatile, both stubbornly determined to have their own way.

Glancing over his shoulder, she looked at the house again. It no longer filled her with frightened dismay—though she still didn't understand why it had done in the first place.

'I still don't remember,' she said, looking back at him. 'But I want to.'

Something stirred on those rock-solid features—a slackening of tension. 'Good.' He nodded, and straightened away from her. 'Then we are beginning to make some progress at last. How is the knee? Can you use it yet?'

Diversion tactics, she noted as she glanced down to find the right knee bent, so her weight was all on the other leg. Instinctive protection, she recognised dully, no matter how big the trauma, she could still protect the wretched knee.

Neither said anything more while she went through her usual exercises to loosen the stiffness out of the joint. Then, as if by tacit agreement, the moment her foot went on the ground she reached for his arm, at the same instant that he offered it to her. Slender fingers looped round cool buff cambric then curled into solid strength. Her senses leapt, then steadied. He waited to make sure that she was ready, then turned them both towards the house.

Home, he'd called it. Her home. *Their* home. 'It's looks a bit big for just two of us,' she remarked.

'It's a— It's been in the family for a long time.'

Something in the way he hesitated then changed what he had been going to say made her stop and look up at him. But all she saw was the silken curve of dark eyelashes covering his expressive eyes. Beginning to look away from him again, she caught a glimpse of his mouth as it moved, suddenly hardening into the kind of sneer that made her fingernails dig into his arm in puzzled alarm.

The action sent his eyelashes flicking up to reveal his eyes again. Something hot was burning there, something hard and so angry she drew in a sharp breath and tried to step right back.

The burn became a flash, followed by a full explosion. 'Oh, to *hell* with this!' he hissed, and bent and lifted her into his arms.

'What are you doing?' she cried out, feeling her heart jump to her throat as hard-packed muscle met with her shock-quivering frame. 'I'm not an invalid! I don't *need* carrying!'

'You are my *wife*,' he gritted back. 'I don't *need* an excuse to do *anything* with you!'

'My agreement would be nice!' she snapped right back as he strode angrily towards the house.

He stopped on the threshold, bent his head and kissed her with such untamed passion it was as if he actually meant to turn her bones to dust.

By the time he lifted his head again he knew he had succeeded. 'Yes,' he hissed. 'You might not know *who* you are but you will know *what* you are before this day is through,' he vowed.

'What's the matter with you?' she cried. 'Why are you so suddenly angry?'

'*Wife!*' he snarled as if that answered everything. 'My wife! *Ma femme a moi!*' he rasped in French. '*La mia moglie!*' he declared in a harsh Italian—staking his claim on all fronts like an impassioned new groom who was carrying his virgin bride to her fate.

Only she was no new bride, and nor was she a virgin, as they'd already well and truly substantiated once already today. Nor did whatever his intentions were frighten her in the slightest. If anything, she felt terribly exhilarated.

The door slammed shut behind them, and she gained a vague impression of a classical Georgian interior:

pastel silk walls; elegant cornices; oil paintings that must have cost the earth but went by in a blur as he kept on walking down a rectangular hall towards the stairwell.

'André—'

'Shut up,' he cut in, chin jutted and locked in grim determination. 'Don't so much as dare say my name until I've got you safely horizontal.'

'Why?' she asked curiously.

'Because you usually avoid saying it. In fact, you only say it when you don't realise you're saying it. It makes me wild,' he gritted. 'Makes me feel as though I only take physical form in the realms of your imagination.'

He began mounting the stairs while Samantha absorbed what he'd said and realised he'd said it perfectly. Touch him and she knew him. Stand apart and he became a shadowy figment she could never quite see in full, physical shape.

'Sorry,' she whispered, and touched an apologetic kiss to the rigid line of his jaw a kiss that immediately became something else entirely.

A bite, an open-mouthed, fully fledged, salacious bite, that sank its teeth into warm and living skin on bone and would have drawn blood—only that was not the objective. The objective was to flick a tongue over rasping skin in need of shaving and taste the man—taste him. It was compulsive. A desire that arrived from nowhere and completely took her over.

His shoulders flexed, his skin grew hot, and the air left his throat on a hoarse scrape. 'Witch,' he gritted. But he liked it. She could feel the pleasure rippling through him as another door opened and closed. Then he was leaning heavily back against it, and with a jerk he freed his jaw and paid her back by claiming her mouth with a kiss that was hot and deep and so hungry it wanted to devour.

Samantha was quite happy to be devoured. It was that elemental.

Even when he allowed her feet to slide to the floor, that kiss wasn't broken. This was need, hot and fevered. This was sex at its most animal. He grabbed the edge of her top and raked it up her body and over her head. She lifted her arms up to aid its departure, groaning in anguish when their mouths had to part to allow the top to pass between them.

He removed his own shirt with no help from her; she was too busy touching his hair, touching his face with hungry fingers. And after that she became lost in a world of male textures. Satin-smooth shoulders, springy black chest hair—tight male nipples that she took greedily into her mouth.

His breathing had gone haywire, chest rising and sinking in rapid rhythm with his heartbeat. And where his fingers slid in the most excruciatingly light caresses she became a live conduit to pure sexual pleasure. Her bra sprang free. With a boneless fluidity that defied the fact that she was standing on her own two feet, she stepped back and flicked the bra away, then stood, chin up, eyes like emerald fires, proudly offering him the chance to taste.

On a growl, he came away from the door. 'You haven't forgotten this, have you?' he gritted. 'You still remember how to seduce me out of my skin!'

She touched that skin. One long and slender arm made another fluid movement and her fingers were resting against a hair-free, satin, taut pectoral.

Hard muscle flexed beneath her fingers. She sent him a provoking smile.

It was a smile that made him lose touch with the last dregs of reason. 'You're not of this world,' he muttered rawly, wrapped his arms around her and lifted her back off her feet.

'Neither are you,' she replied. Then, 'André,' she murmured tauntingly into his hard, dark, handsome face. 'Are you real or aren't you?'

'You're about to find out,' he said, dropping her down onto a high, French-style antique bed; he pushed her to lie back, then with a few grimly economical movements began unfastening his trousers. Her shoes fell off, a set of bare toes came up to rub against the centre of his chest, and his eyes narrowed into glinting slits which threatened retribution as he stood over her and let her torment him while he rid himself of his clothes.

She didn't know that this was the real Samantha playing her old sensual games, André mused grimly. If she did know she would not be seducing him, but screaming at him like a maniac.

But instinct had taken over. And instinct was instinct, whether or not it had the memories to go along with it. And the real Samantha's instinct was to tease and to provoke and to play the seductress until she drove her poor victim crazy.

What lack of memory didn't tell her was that this poor victim had taken her measure a long time ago. Anything she could dish out he could give back tenfold. It was one of the major ingredients that had made their marriage so excitingly volatile. But, as with any volatile substance, it was also dangerously unpredictable. And it was just that unpredictability which had finally torn them both to shreds in the end—because neither had been able to trust the other not to behave like this with anyone else.

Mistrust led to suspicion, and suspicion to lies. When he'd first met her she'd had no less than three boyfriends in tow. Three other men knowing her like this? Three other lovers to share the addiction? The very idea had driven him into taking some desperate measures to gain exclusive rights to this beautiful, wanton, glorious woman.

Within the month he had married her, holding the arrogant belief that marriage was all it would take to tame the tiger that lived inside her. What he'd actually discovered was that he had his own tiger, waiting to leap out and roar. Despite discovering Samantha was a virgin, her tiger became an intense sexual appetite. His tiger was jealousy. He'd had to lose her to discover that her seductress act had hidden a vulnerable heart, which had only wanted him to love her but could not quite believe that he did.

Jealousy was love's natural predator. It was mean and cruel and naturally devious. So he'd fed her desire and had held back that which she had needed most from him—his love. In the end it had killed her—or as good as, when he saw what it had left her with. This… The desire for his body. And a fear so great, of the love resurrecting itself, that she preferred to remember nothing than risk going through that torment again.

So, what did all of that say about him? he finally concluded. Standing here in front of her—bold in his nakedness, with her foot circling exquisitely arousing caresses against his flesh as he prepared to begin feeding those desires again.

'André?' she murmured questioningly, because he'd been standing there too long doing nothing but stare at her.

André. Dear God, the name ripped him to pieces with self-contempt, disgust and a sickening dismay.

'No,' he uttered thickly, stepping back from the foot then turning his back on her so he didn't have to watch while she shattered.

She didn't say a word, not one word. Her silence cut into him like a nine-inch steel blade.

'We won't do this again unless we do so as equals,' he told her flatly.

'Equals?' he heard her whisper.

'Yes!' he barked, dragging up the zip over a burgeoning shaft which was making an absolute mockery out of his grand gesture. He swung round to sear her with the flame of his own filthy anger. 'Equals as in you saying my name and *knowing* this man called *André* who you are about to give your body to!' he all but snarled at her.

She was sitting up, hair a mass of crackling fire around her shoulders and coiling sensually over her lily-white breasts. But her face was whiter, and he saw her flinch, saw her beautiful eyes fill with the horrible glint of shame. Remorse almost choked him. He'd started this. He'd given in to temptation when he'd promised himself he wouldn't, done it all on the flimsy excuse to himself that he was diverting her attention away from what they had been discussing.

'I do know him,' she said quietly. 'He's a rat.'

She was right and he was. His anger melted down into grim self-mockery. 'Well, the rat is going to go scavenging in the kitchen,' he threw back satirically. 'Get dressed and come and join me when you're ready.'

With that he got out of there before she threw something lethal at him. Instincts were instincts after all, and Samantha's instincts were all damned dangerous…

CHAPTER TEN

SHE didn't go down. He had to be crazy to think that she actually would.

Or just plain arrogant.

What she did was remain sitting on the edge of the bed, silently drowning in a pool of her own humiliation. And it was all her own. Because she'd done it all by her stupid self. He might have started it but she'd certainly encouraged it. When she should have been pushing him away she'd kissed him, bitten him, lured him and provoked him like a sex-mad teenager without a moral in sight.

Sex-mad. She shivered, feeling goose-bumps of dismay break out all over her flesh. At least they had a strong enough effect to make her get up and gather up her clothes with the intention of putting them back on. Then she just stood there, looking around the bedroom with its beautiful French furniture as if none of it was even there. Then, without thinking twice about it, she dropped the clothes to the floor again, walked back to the bed and crawled beneath the cool white percale duvet, shut her eyes and sank into a deep, dark slumber filled with dancing nymphets and leering dark devils.

She awoke hours later, feeling heavy-eyed and so sluggish she could almost believe she had drunk herself into a bad hangover.

That would be a first, she thought with a smile, and got out of the bed to walk into the bathroom, where she showered, dried herself, strolled across the thick creamy carpet towards another door that led into the dressing room. Taking her time, she selected a long, emerald-green, Japanese silk robe, slipped it on and began tying the silk belt around her waist as she walked back into the bedroom. Her head was down, watching her busy fingers, and her movements were as smooth and relaxed as anyone's should be who was moving around their own bedroom, in their own home.

André was away, she was thinking idly. Raoul was out on the town somewhere. Which meant she had the whole house to herself to—

That was when she noticed the suitcase standing by the door, frowned at it—then heard a sound across the room and turned her head to see André, dressed in black silk trousers and a white silk shirt, standing by the window, with his hands in his pockets and his handsome face wearing a very sternly closed expression.

'You found your old clothes, then,' he said, and—slam. A door flew shut in her head and she sank onto the soft cream carpet.

The next thing she knew she was lying on a strange bed, wearing a beautiful green silk wrap she didn't recognise, and a complete stranger was leaning over her.

Youngish, good-looking. 'Hi.' He smiled pleasantly when he saw she was looking at him. 'Beautiful eyes. I'm glad you opened them.'

'Where am I?' she mumbled hazily. 'Who are you?'

'I'm a doctor.' He smiled again. 'The name is Jonathan Miles, though people I really like are allowed to call me Jack.'

It was only then that she realised he was lightly clasping one of her wrists, where the pulse was throbbing dully beneath his fingers.

'Now, stay still for a moment while I get close and intimate by looking deep into those beautiful eyes with this torch...'

Obediently she did as instructed. 'What happened?' she asked as he began flashing the torch into one of her eyes.

'You blacked out,' he explained, moving onto the other eye. 'André was worried, so he called me in to check you over.'

André. At last the mist clouding her brain began to clear.

'Do you know where you are?' he asked her quietly.

'Yes,' she mumbled.

'Can you tell me the last thing you remember before you blacked out?'

'I woke up. I knew who I was. Realised it and blacked out,' she replied with quiet economy.

He began to frown. 'What made you realise?'

Him, she wanted to spit. I hate him. I don't ever want to set eyes on him again. And, acting on that thought, she let her eyes drift shut again. 'I prefer not to talk about it,' she said.

The doctor sat back with a dissatisfied sigh. 'Too upsetting or too—private?' he quizzed.

Both, she thought and refused to answer. The silence dragged. Somewhere else in the room a body shifted tensely. The doctor's fingers lightly touched the fine scar at her temple. Her eyes flicked back open, hard green, sparking with warning.

'Nice job.' He smiled that pleasant smile again. 'A superficial laceration that should disappear completely given time,' he said in diagnosis. 'What about the knee?'

'The knee is fine,' she answered tightly. 'Like everything that's wrong with me, it just needs time.'

The doctor studied her angry, pale, defensive face for a few moments, then nodded. 'Point taken,' he conceded. 'Bearing that in mind, I suppose you won't agree to a head X-ray, just to check that there is nothing—'

'No,' she interrupted firmly.

'Yes,' another voice chipped in. 'If you feel its necessary, Jack, then she'll do it.'

The moment André made his presence truly felt, Samantha covered her eyes with a hand.

'This isn't your decision, André,' she heard the doctor say with a flat-voiced firmness that quietly impressed her. And if she'd been watching she would have seen him flash a warning look at the other man, which had him swinging away in grim frustration.

She would have also seen the doctor pick up her two packs of tablets from the bedside cabinet where, unbeknown to her, André had fished them out of her handbag and placed them. Jack Miles read the two pharmacy labels, grimaced, then opened one and flipped out a small white pill before deftly pocketing the rest and reaching for a glass of water.

'Here, take this,' he instructed.

The hand slid away. She frowned at the pill, recognised it and obediently took it from him, drank it down with the water then closed her eyes to wait for the mild tranquilliser to soothe away everything.

She felt the bed shift as the doctor stood up, then his hand gently resting on one of hers for a moment. 'André knows where I am if you need me, Samantha.'

'Mmm,' she said. 'Thanks.' And was just glad he was going.

The moment Jack gave him the nod, André strode for the door and the two men left quietly. He felt like hell, and by the expression on Jack's face he felt that André deserved it.

'I don't know what game you think you're playing here, André…' Jack Miles went on the attack as soon as the door closed behind him '…but I'm going to tell you that it's a dangerous one.'

'It isn't a game,' he threw back grimly.

'I'm glad you realise that,' the doctor said. 'But if you brought me here for my honest opinion, then I think you're in over your head. Amnesia is a tricky condition. We know very little about it. But I would say that she is beginning to remember. And, personally, I think she needs a controlled environment in which to do so.'

'No,' André refused instantly, and turned to walk towards the stairwell. 'You're talking hospitals, and though I might see the sense in her having a quick X-ray, I will *not* put her back into hospital. She's had enough of those to last her a lifetime,' he added with a tense shift of his shoulders.

'Which doesn't necessarily make you her best alternative.'

'I'm her *only* alternative!' he barked, swinging round to glare at the other man. 'She relates to me! She responds to me! She needs me to be here for her and I won't let her down again!'

It was possessive and it was passionate. Jack studied his tight, determined features, and grimaced. 'Your own personal crusade, André?' he suggested.

'Yes,' André hissed, and turned away again to stride down the stairs, wanting Jack to go now, since he wasn't telling him anything he didn't know already. In over his head? Hell, he knew it. Stick her in a controlled environment? Not while he still had breath left in his body to stop it from happening.

'Here…' At the front door, Jack fished the two packs of tablets out of his pocket and handed them to him. 'You keep these away from her,' he advised. 'Administer only when *you* believe they are necessary.'

'You mean—' His mouth went dry. 'You think she's…'

'I think she's in shock, damn it!' The other man suddenly exploded. 'When did you find her? Two days ago? How many times did you say she'd blacked out or almost blacked out since then? Who knows what's happening inside her head? I certainly don't. You obviously don't. And I don't think that she knows either! Tonight, for instance,' he continued furiously, 'she goes to sleep, wakes up—and starts using that bedroom as if she'd never spent a year away from it! Then all of a sudden, wham, she somersaults back from the past into the present—it's no wonder she blacks out!'

'I get the picture,' André said roughly, grimly pocketing the tablets and wanting to shut him up so that he would just go. 'Thanks for coming out at such short notice, Jack. It was appreciated.'

'But not the opinion, hmm?' Jack Miles noted dryly. 'Well, just one last piece of advice before I leave,' he went on. 'If you feel you must deal with this problem yourself, then take it easy. Give her comfort, support and just be there for her. But no probing,' he warned with deadly seriousness. 'And maybe, just maybe, you'll get lucky and the memories will simply float gently to the surface and emerge without causing her further trauma.'

'But you don't think it will be that easy.' André grimaced, reading the doubtful tone in his voice.

Jack shook his head. 'As she's proved already, things are coming back in disjointed flashes. And you are the trigger, André. Don't, for goodness' sake, squeeze that trigger, or the gun might backfire in your face.'

It backfired twelve months ago, André thought heavily as he closed the door on Jack Miles's departure. Sighing, he turned and walked into the sitting room, then aimed directly for the whisky decanter. As he poured the drink, his eyes caught sight of a framed photograph sitting on the top of the antique bureau which was the only piece of furniture Samantha had brought with her into the house when they'd married.

Stepping over to it, he picked up the photo frame and stood staring down at the faces of two laughing young men. Then, with a violence that erupted out of nowhere, he threw the frame to the floor, smashing it to smithereens.

The next morning Samantha came down the stairs and turned towards the back of the house, following the aroma of toast and freshly ground coffee. In truth, her stomach was beginning to think her throat had been cut, it was so long since she'd swallowed anything more substantial that a pre-packed sandwich at a motorway café.

But it still took courage to open the door she presumed led into the kitchen, not at all sure who she was going see on the other side of it. Stranger or half-stranger?

Half-stranger, she discovered. A very dark, very attractive one, wearing a v-necked sweatshirt and a pair of stone-washed trousers. He was standing in front of a very impressive stainless steel cooking range, feeding slices of bread into a rotating grill. Glancing round, he saw her standing in the doorway, and a short tense stillness followed in which she gazed warily at him and he stared warily back.

Stalemate. Neither knew what to say to the other. Neither knew how the other was going to react. He broke the deadlock first by dipping his eyes over the simple corn-yellow blouse she had teamed with a pair of pale olive trousers and a matching gilet. And if he recognised them as items from the wardrobe upstairs, this time he had the caution to say nothing, and with a smooth-spoken, 'Hi,' he turned his attention back to what he was doing. 'Did the smell of the coffee get as far as your room?'

'The toast, actually,' she replied, striving to sound as relaxed as he did. 'I'm starving,' she admitted.

'I know the feeling. I didn't eat much myself yesterday. Sit down,' he invited. 'Sustenance will arrive in about ten seconds.'

Well, that was the most awkward part over, she mused as she did as she was told and went to sit down at the large, scrubbed kitchen table that dominated the room. Then, to stop herself from looking at him, she made herself take an interest in her surroundings.

The kitchen was gorgeous, packed full of individually standing, old, scrubbed pine furniture you would only expect to find in a traditional farmhouse. 'Who did the interior decorating for you?' she questioned curiously.

'My mother,' he replied, deftly stacking hot slices of toast onto a hot plate. 'Hence the French influence in just about everything you see.

His mother. Her heart sank. 'Does she live here as well?' she asked, silently pleading for him to say no.

He went many steps further than her plea with a quiet, 'She died several years ago.'

Which made her feel really mean for what she had been thinking. 'I'm sorry,' she murmured.

He just offered a shrug as he turned to put the plate

of toast down on the table, followed by a big old-fashioned coffee pot. 'The two of you never met,' he told her, and turned away again.

'Your father?' She felt compelled to ask next.

Two serviceable white coffee mugs and a couple of white side plates arrived on the table along with milk, sugar and butter dish. 'He died when I was ten years old.'

'Oh, I'm sorry,' she said again, then clamped her mouth shut. And because they were both aware that it was a natural progression for her to go on and ask if there were any other members of his family, a very loud silence fell.

But she couldn't ask—though she didn't understand *why* she couldn't.

In an attempt to fill the gap, she reached for the coffee mugs, carefully lining them up in front of her while she racked her brains for something else to say. 'I would have expected a house the size of this to have a small army of servants to keep it so nice,' she remarked.

'They come in on a daily basis during week days,' he explained, pulling out the chair opposite hers and sitting down. 'Today is Saturday,' he added, for no reason that Samantha could see other than to keep the conversation moving.

'Should I know any of them?' she asked, picking up the coffee pot.

'Mrs Saunders, who keeps the house, you knew. As to the rest, I have no idea.'

'Oh,' was all she could find to say to that. So she turned her attention to pouring coffee into both of the mugs, adding sugar to one and milk to the other, then she slid the sugared black one across the table towards him.

'Thanks,' he murmured a trifle thickly.

She nodded in acknowledgement, took a sip at her coffee, selected a slice of toast, placed it on one of the white side plates, then just sat there blankly staring at it.

'What?' he said gruffly. 'Something wrong? Something I—'

'Knife,' she explained.

It was his turn to look blank as he stared at the table for a few seconds before he got up and went to a drawer, coming back with several knives which he placed down on the table.

'You've hurt your finger,' she observed, noticing the heavy plaster wrapping encasing the index finger on his right hand.

'I dropped a glass,' he lied, 'and cut myself when I was picking up the broken pieces. While I'm up, do you want marmalade or jam?'

Samantha shook her head and he sat down again. Picking up her coffee, she sipped at it for a while. He did the same. When she buttered her slice of toast so did he. It was awful, she decided glumly. Neither of them had a single thing worth saying. Strangers did not even cover what they were to each other any more.

'Did you—?'

'Have you—?'

Both began speaking at once, and both stopped at once.

'You go first,' he invited.

Great, Samantha thought! She'd forgotten what she had been going to say.

Story of my life, she mocked. 'I think I'll have that jam.' She plucked the words out of thin air.

He got up. Her temper began to fray under the stress. 'I didn't expect you to get it for me,' she snapped. 'All you needed to do was point me in the right direction and I would have managed to find it myself!'

The jam pot landed with a thud on the table. 'No problem,' he clipped.

Lying swine, she thought, and came to her feet. He was still standing. 'Where are you going now?' He sighed the words out impatiently.

'It's you who's been jumping up and down,' she threw back.

'Just—sit and eat,' he commanded. Not looking so smooth around his own sleek edges now, she noticed waspishly.

'I'm not hungry—'

'Sit down and *eat*!' he repeated angrily.

'I can't!' she cried. 'I feel as if you've got me pinned under a microscope!'

His sigh seemed to rake over ever inch of him. 'Okay,' he said. 'Point taken. I'll eat later. But for goodness' sake,' he added angrily, 'eat something, Samantha… Eat!'

With that he strode out of the kitchen, making her feel miserable and guilty for driving him away. So she ate—force-fed herself, in fact. She drank some coffee, then got up and made fresh of both coffee and toast, placed them on a tray and, on a deep breath for courage, went looking for him.

He was easier to find than she'd expected. She simply followed the muffled sound of his angry voice and found him sitting behind a desk in a beautiful study, lined wall-to-wall with brass-grilled bookcases which looked as old as the house.

He was talking on the phone, but the moment he saw her come through the door he broke the conversation and returned the receiver to its rest.

'Peace offering.' She smiled nervously, carrying the loaded tray over to the desk and setting it down. 'I'm sorry I caused all of that…strife, in the kitchen.'

'My fault,' he said instantly.

'No it wasn't.' She refused to let him be that gracious. 'It was mine. I was nervous—still am as a matter of fact,' she admitted

'Pour the coffee,' he instructed.

Grimacing at the way he had coolly passed over her carefully planned apology, she did as he bade and poured the coffee, then silently handed it to him. She received no thanks, only a glinting look in those wretched eyes that could have held amusement as he took the coffee mug from her.

'You're a hard man, Signor Visconte,' she informed him dryly, and turned to leave.

'And you, Signora Visconte,' he returned, 'are the most amazingly unpredictable woman I know.'

'Compliment or censure?' She mused out loud.

He laughed. 'Oh, most definitely a compliment,' he assured. 'No—don't go,' he added when she made to do just that, and the husky warmth of his voice vibrated on her senses, bringing her to a very wary standstill.

What now? she wondered, already beginning to pull up her defences again—just in case.

'Give me two minutes to consume your…peace offering and I'll reacquaint you with the house, if you like…'

Her defences fell again, that tentative 'if you like' helping to tumble them. She nodded her agreement. The telephone rang. It helped ease them through the next, few, awkward seconds. He answered it; she wandered off to peer inside the brass grilles at the selection of priceless first-edition books she could see locked safely out of reach.

'Has anyone bothered reading them?' she asked when the phone went down again.

'Not in my lifetime,' he drawled. 'They belonged to my grandfather on my Italian side. This house belonged to *his* English mother. The melting pot of culture swimming in my blood is astonishing when you think about it,' he mocked.

The true mongrel, Samantha thought, and smiled to herself because that blood had to be a rare mix of very old money when you put all the evidence together.

'They should be in a museum,' Samantha remarked.

'The books or my family?'

'The books.' She laughed, swinging round to toss that laugh at him.

His eyes dilated; she saw it happen as his attention riveted on this first laughing response she had offered him. Her heart-rate quickened, sending a rush of awareness surging to her head. Then, with a blink of his long lashes, he recovered, her heart-rate slowed and the awareness faded.

'The books belong to the house.' He continued with the conversation as if the stinging moment in between had never been there. 'I am only their guardian. Even my very French mother, who respected nothing if it wasn't French, didn't dare lay a finger them.'

'You say that very cynically. But she married an Italian who lived in America. Surely that says she must have loved your father very much.'

'That was her first marriage. She married her second husband the year after my father died. He was as French as she was.'

Samantha frowned. 'But I thought you said you were brought up in Philadelphia?'

'Not by her choice but my father's choice. He was the one with the money and therefore the power—even from the grave.' Suddenly the cynicism was really pronounced. 'If my mother wanted to keep her hands on the money then she had to agree to keep me, as his sole beneficiary, where that money was generated.'

'You didn't get on with her,' Samantha murmured softly.

'You are mistaken,' he said coldly. 'I adored her. She and Ra—'

He stopped quite suddenly, snapping his lips together on whatever he had been about to say. Yet another of those strained silences fell round them, making Samantha frown and André look angry.

The ring of the telephone actually startled the pair of them as it pealed out its demand. He snatched it up. 'What?' he rapped out, then sat there frowning and listening while Samantha hunted through the conversation, looking for a logical reason for the sudden silence. The books? The mother? The stepfather whose name he didn't quite finish?

'Right now, you mean?' he questioned sharply. 'Okay, that's great.' He stood up. 'No, now is fine. I'll have to change into a suit, but set it up and I'll be there.'

The phone went down.

'I have to go out,' he said to Samantha. 'I'm sorry. Would you mind showing yourself around the house?'

'Of course not,' she assured him.

'Thanks,' he murmured. 'I shouldn't be long.' He was already striding for the door. 'Feel free to make yourself at home while I'm gone.'

'I thought it *was* my home,' she whispered into the

empty space he had left behind him, and felt slightly offended by the speed with which he had made his escape—almost as if he'd been relieved by the excuse to get away from her for a while.

No, she scolded herself. The man is important. He runs a multinational business. Of course he has to keep his priorities in perspective.

And that was the second lot of toast and coffee he had walked away from this morning, she thought with a rueful smile. Sighing to herself, she picked the tray up again and carried it back to the kitchen, thinking, Now I am even beginning to feel like a wife. Unappreciated and put to one side.

'I've just thought…' His voice came at her from behind. 'You will wait here, won't you? You won't be tempted to go out, without me to—'

'Keep an eye on me?' she finished for him, turning to throw him a fiery glare.

A glare that fizzled out when she saw him standing there in a grey suit, white shirt and blue silk tie. In the space of what felt like only five minutes he had transformed himself from casual man about the house into hard-edged man of the City.

Handsome, sharp. Powerful—sexy…

'I just don't think I should be leaving you alone right now,' he explained.

Samantha frowned. 'Go to your meeting,' she told him. 'I'm not stupid. And I have no intention of doing anything stupid.'

'And that,' he drawled sardonically, 'is most definitely my cue to get out of here before we start yet another row.'

He went to leave; her eyes began to hurt. 'Was it always like this between us?' she asked thickly.

'Yes,' he admitted. 'We fight as we make love: with no holds barred.'

His beautiful mouth moved on a grimace and Samantha grimaced herself. 'No wonder our marriage barely lasted a year, then,' she said. And, seeing his hesitation, his desire to say something in answer to her last comment, Samantha turned her back on him again, with a, 'See you later,' gauged to finish the discussion before, as he'd predicted, it developed into something else.

He clearly thought the very same thing, because he left with only a flat, 'Sure.'

It was a relief to have him gone. A relief to have time to walk through the house without feeling under the constant surveillance of a pair of dark eyes that seemingly expected everything she saw to be the magic key that opened the floodgates to her memory.

The house didn't do it. Walking from room to room, the only thing she did learn was that his mother had possessed a truly unimpeachable eye for what was the best in good taste and classical styling. One room blended smoothly with another in a flow of pastel shades and exquisite furniture pieces that must have cost the earth.

By the time she arrived back where she'd started from, Samantha had to ask herself why she had been so afraid of coming into this house yesterday. Because, on the whole, she'd found the house an absolute pleasure.

Nothing had hit her as scary, nothing vaguely sinister—if she didn't count the room upstairs, which had given her a couple of uneasy moments when she'd tried the door only to find it was locked. Or the beautiful walnut roll-top bureau in the sitting room she had caught herself gently stroking as if it was a long-lost friend.

But other than for those things she simply loved every inch of the place. A point that added to the puzzle as to why she would want to turn her back on it all as if it had never existed.

Or turn her back on the man who came with it, she then added with a faint quiver she knew was more sexual than threatening.

With a small sigh, she suddenly decided to pick up the phone and call Carla at the Tremount. She'd promised she would keep in touch, and right now she felt she needed to hear a friendly voice… A truly familiar friendly voice, she extended.

But the conversation wasn't quite as comforting as that…

CHAPTER ELEVEN

LETTING himself back into the house, André paused in the hallway to listen for signs of life. Hearing none, he began searching rooms, giving himself a few uneasy moments when he couldn't find Samantha anywhere—until he had the sense to look where he would have expected to find the old Samantha.

Sure enough, even as he strode through the door connecting the sitting room with the elegant glass-domed swimming pool, he saw her cutting through the water with the smooth, clean glide of a natural-born swimmer. She was a mermaid; she always had been. Give her time to herself and she would usually find a pool somewhere to dive into, and it filled him with a real burst of pleasure to see her truly back where she belonged like this.

His first instinct was to strip to his micro-briefs then dive in there and join her—only he was wryly aware that she probably wouldn't appreciate the gesture right now, when natural responses had to be contained to their minimum.

Presuming, of course, that the Samantha swimming in the pool was the new Samantha, he then thought frowningly. He didn't think even she knew how often she'd slipped back and forth through time. He hadn't begun to realise himself until this morning, when he'd watched her pour his coffee without needing to be prompted on how he liked it. As she'd pushed the drink towards him it had finally begun to dawn on him just what was happening to her—and had been happening from the moment he'd walked back into her life.

The journey to Exeter from the Tremount, for instance, when she'd spent the whole time talking to him as if they'd never been apart. André this, André that. It had driven him crazy at the time, hearing her say his name so comfortably while still believing he was a complete stranger. Then there were the times when they'd touched or kissed or made love, he recounted with a fine, tight, sense-twisting shudder. She'd known him then, all right, and had slipped into the old Samantha mould just as naturally as she was cutting through the water right now.

So—which one was swimming in the pool—the old or the new Samantha? he asked himself.

Hell, he didn't know. But he was not going to risk finding out the hard way, by shocking her into another blackout in the middle of a pool of deep water.

So, instead of making her aware of his presence, he turned away with the intention of leaving as silently as he had arrived… Or would have done if a rather sarcastic voice hadn't stopped him.

'Well, well.' He heard her drawl. 'If it isn't the very busy, hotshot tycoon taking time out of his busy tycoon schedule to say hello…'

His skin began to prickle, the tone alone telling him that whichever Samantha it was she was angry about something. Turning round, he saw her treading water dead centre of the pool. 'Was there something specific you meant to convey in that remark?' he enquired narrowly.

'Yes,' she replied, then slid gracefully onto her back to stroke smoothly away.

Still not certain who it was he was talking to, André

stepped to the edge of the pool. 'Then, explain,' he suggested.

'I was commenting on your very busy life,' she informed him as those long slender arms lazily propelled her through the water. 'Picking up a hotel here, picking another up there… Tell me,' she begged, the sarcasm echoing high into the glass-domed roof, 'because I'll be really interested to know, is there an actual point where you can ever envisage saying to yourself that enough is enough, I don't *need* another hotel, no matter what its money-pulling potential is?'

She was talking hotels. His flesh went cold. 'Get out of the water!' he commanded harshly.

'I beg your pardon?' She gasped, and stopped swimming to stare at him.

'You heard me.' He began striding down the length of the pool with his senses on alert and his mind gone haywire. 'I want you to swim to the side of the pool and get out! I mean it, Samantha!' he warned when she made no move to comply. 'If you don't get out of there I'm coming in to drag you out!'

And to suit threat with action he pulled off his jacket and tossed it aside.

Puzzled, more than anything, he suspected, because she could see he was so deadly serious, she swam to the other side of the pool and pulled herself out. Water streamed from her body, leaving behind it a long, slender nymph with skin like a pearl and a lilac one-piece swimsuit that revealed more that it concealed… And he still didn't know which Samantha it was that turned to glare at him across the width of the pool.

'What's the matter with you?' she demanded crossly. 'I can swim like a fish! I don't need—'

'And if you'd had another blackout while you were

in there?' he raked back. 'What good would your swimming proficiency be to you then?'

Slender hands went on slender hips. Old or new? Both would challenge him with that pose. 'You're just trying to divert my attention away from what I was talking about,' she accused him. 'Do you think I haven't noticed how you like to do that? Well, forget it this time, André, because it isn't going to work—'

André. She'd just called him André.

'So let's talk about hotels,' she went on in a voice still dripping sarcasm. 'And let's talk about sneaky tycoons who move in on people as well as hotels and take them over without—'

Hell, she knew who she was all right. 'I did *not* move in on the Bressingham!' He angrily denied the charge. 'And I did *not* move in on your father! In fact it was the other way round, if you'd only...'

Something changed inside her. Samantha felt it happen. A sudden icy confusion that made her feel very peculiar as she tried to make sense of a misunderstanding which oddly didn't feel like a misunderstanding but more like a horrible—horrible case of *déjà vu*.

'I was talking about the Tremount and Carla,' she murmured very slowly. 'I rang her while you were out. Sh-she told me you...'

Her voice trailed away. Her eyes went blank. Her father—the Bressingham, she found herself repeating. Goose-bumps began to break out all over her wet skin. Then, no, Carla and the Tremount, she corrected herself.

'Y-you bought it,' she continued with a perplexed frown. 'Carla s-suddenly thinks you're the bees-knees w-when only hours before she...'

She stopped again, frowning that perplexed look across the pool at André, who was standing taut and still and looking very pale. 'I n-need to sit down,' she said, and did so, stumbling over to the nearest pool chair and dropping into it.

Cold, she felt icy cold, and nothing seemed to be functioning. Heart, lungs, the blood in her veins—they'd gone very silent and still, as if they were gathering themselves ready for some kind of major eruption.

'Samantha…' That was André's voice, she recognised as if from a great distance. There were his footsteps she could hear echoing like thunder on the hard tiled floor. '*Cara mia*, listen to me…' And he sounded odd, rough and thick and…

'Why is there a door locked upstairs?' she asked him.

The footsteps stopped. She looked up, saw him standing stock-still about four feet away. 'It's a storeroom,' he said. 'I keep my personal files locked away in there…'

'Liar,' she said, and looked away again. He kept the door locked because it was Raoul's room.

Raoul—!

Oh, dear God! She jerked to her feet, jarring her knee in the process so she couldn't help but wince. André took a giant step towards her but she held him off with a trembling hand. 'No,' she said. 'I'm all right. I'm not going to black out. Just don't come near me for a minute while I…'

Once again the words dried up, flailing in a muddy pool of confusion she couldn't quite seem to clear.

'You're not all right,' he refuted hoarsely. 'You're beginning to—'

'Remember—' she finished for him. And just like that it finally happened, roaring up with the abruptness of a flickering flame sizzling in the short grasses of her memory, suddenly erupting into a column of fire.

'Oh, my God.' She gasped, and began shake. André, her father, Raoul, the Bressingham. 'André,' she murmured painfully.

And he was there, coming from behind to drop her robe about her shoulders then holding it there with hands like vices that began firmly pulling her back from the edge of the pool as if he was afraid she was going to topple right back into it.

Maybe she *was* about to topple. She didn't even care. The flame of truth was a roaring column inside her head. It began leaping, flicking out long lethal fingers across huge empty gaps to ignite other memories.

'You lied to me,' she whispered.

'By omission, yes.' His deep voice confirmed.

'You deliberately set out to cheat and deceive me.'

His hands tightened fractionally. 'I wasn't like that,' he denied. 'You were given only half the picture. The rest was—'

Without trying to listen she broke free, somewhere in the recess of her burning mind surprised that he actually allowed her to do it. She limped off towards the door that opened into the beautiful sitting room. Behind her, André followed in grim silence as she crossed the room to the walnut bureau, tried to open it and found it locked.

'You took the key with you when you left here,' he quietly informed her.

Key, she thought, and bent to feel around under the bureau's base, then came back up with a fine-worked gold key stuck to the middle of a piece of sticky tape. It was a spare key, originally taped there by her mother and allowed to remain in its secret place when the beautiful piece of furniture came to Samantha. She had been fifteen years old at the time, and inconsolable with grief. But to touch the smooth walnut wood had been like making contact with her mother. She did the same thing now, gently stroking the wood and immediately feeling that special sensation.

Then tears flooded into her eyes, because she suddenly realised she didn't have a single thing like this to remind her of her father. Not any more anyway. André had taken it all away from her.

Holding back the tears, she concentrated on fitting the key into the pretty ornate lock and easing back the roll-top lid. It slid into its housing with a smooth familiarity that clutched at her heart.

Inside the bureau were more memories. Precious, special, deeply personal memories slotted neatly into a row of finely worked cubby-holes. Letters, birthday cards, photographs…it was a diary of memorabilia spanning her whole life.

Then there were the other things. Things which didn't belong in here. But she'd thrown them in and had locked them away just so they were out of her sight.

The flame burned brighter. She had no control over it. It showed her the Bressingham, her father, Raoul, then the Bressingham again, planting faces, buildings, snatched little scenes into her head like picture post-cards, before burning each one of them up in a sheet of fire to replace it with another. She saw herself on her wedding day, dressed in white and smiling. Dressed in black at her father's funeral and inconsolably sad. A hotel foyer virtually reduced to a pile of rubble. André scowling. Raoul smirking. Typed words written on pieces of paper she couldn't quite focus on well enough to read.

'You betrayed me,' she whispered.

'No, I didn't,' André denied.

'Where's Raoul?' she asked next.

'In Australia.' He seemed prepared to answer her questions as they came. 'He's been there for the last twelve months.'

There was a significant reason why he'd offered up that last piece of information, but Samantha did not have the ability to work out what that reason was right now. She was too busy remembering other things: painful truths with wretched conclusions.

'He tried to rape me, right here in this house,' she murmured thickly. 'And you let him get away with it.'

No reply came back to answer that particular charge, she noticed. And she found she wasn't really surprised. When André had stopped himself from finishing his sentence this morning it had not been his stepfather he had been about to declare his love for—but his half-brother, Raoul.

Raoul, the younger one, the spoiled one, the mean and shrewd, manipulatively sly one... Though big brother was not above being manipulatively sly himself, she recalled.

The tears attempted to flood again. Lodging them back into her throat, she reached out and with trembling fingers picked up the set of angrily discarded papers. Not once had she looked at André since they'd faced each other across the swimming pool, and she didn't attempt to do so now as she turned to offer the papers to him.

'These belong to you,' she said. 'Raoul gave them to me.'

Lean brown fingers slowly took them from her. Her heart felt sluggish as she watched those fingers begin flicking through the copied pieces of evidence documenting the events leading up to André Visconte gaining full ownership of the Bressingham Hotel—on the same day that he'd married Samantha Bressingham.

'Quite a dowry, when you think about it.' She smiled on a tight piece of self-derision. 'The Bressingham came really quite cheap for you, didn't it?'

'Don't make judgements when you are not in possession of the full facts,' he grimly advised.

'You mean I still have some more ugly memories to look forward to? How nice.'

'Not all of them are ugly.'

'They are from where I'm standing,' she said, and walked away, out of the room and across the hall then up the stairs.

As she travelled along the upper landing she passed by the door to Raoul's room. Last time she had stepped through that door she had gone to confront him about those papers. Now she was glad the door was locked. She never wanted to cross its threshold ever again.

Shutting herself in the bedroom, she stood for a moment with her face covered by her hands. Her insides were trembling and her flesh was shivering, and her head was aching so badly she wanted to crawl beneath the duvet and go to sleep.

But that was exactly what she had been doing for the last twelve months, she told herself. She had been sleeping to hide away from the ugly truth that she had fallen in love with a man who had deceived and lied to her right from the start.

Their whirlwind courtship and hasty marriage had been a smooth, slick manoeuvre on his part to seal the deal of any hotelier's dreams of gaining possession of the Bressingham. And why had that been? she asked, slowly sliding her hands away from her face to stare bleakly at this next ugly truth.

Because the Bressingham was special. No one would ever try to dispute that. Old as it was, and tired as it was, it possessed a reputation for old-world grace and charm that had been capturing the hearts of anyone who walked into it for the last one hundred and fifty years.

Mention the Bressingham and people's eyes lit up, no matter where in the world it was that you mentioned it. It was that well known, that warmly thought of. That special.

It was why Stefan Reece's eyes had lit up when he'd mentioned the Bressingham. And it was also why he had directed his comments about the hotel directly to Samantha. Family-owned and run, from the day it had opened its doors to its first paying guests. And Samantha was now the last living member of that family.

But none of that silly, soft sentimentality gave the reason why people like André and Stefan Reece would do almost anything to own the Bressingham. No, for them its importance lay in two very simple elements.

Its premier location in a premier city and, quite simply, its name.

To buy the Bressingham name was to buy a dead-cert winner. So if push came to shove, and the daughter had to be bought along with the name, then, what the hell, why not? She was young, she was good-looking, she was great in bed.

'Oh, God, I hate myself.' Samantha groaned, and pushed her hands to her face again—only to drag them away almost immediately when a knock came at the door.

Nausea clawed at her stomach. 'Go to hell,' she said, and forced herself to move, walking on stiff legs into the bathroom.

She heard him try the door handle as she was shutting herself away, and wasn't surprised he'd ignored what she'd said. The man was immune to other people's feelings. Which was why she had locked the bedroom door so he couldn't come in. In that way, at least, she knew the man. He was no coward when it came to facing problems.

As opposed to herself, she likened sombrely. She had made a wretched vocation out of refusing to face hers!

Almost as if she'd just thrown down a challenge, her mind began to replay that ugly scene from twelve months ago. While she'd been shut away in this same room, taking a shower, Raoul had calmly walked into the bedroom she'd shared with André and had left the stack of documents on her bed, then gone to his own bedroom to await the outcome.

She'd known why he had done it. Only an hour before he had propositioned her, and she had slapped him down with the coldest little refusal she could use.

The papers had been his retaliation. So she'd read them, with a sickened disgust at how low Raoul had been prepared to go in his quest to cause trouble between her and André. Then she'd walked into Raoul's room to tell him what he could damned well do with his papers of lies.

But it hadn't turned out like that. Raoul had been clever; he had known exactly what he'd been doing when he'd lured her into his bedroom that night. Tall like André, dark like André, but younger, more like her own age, and with a mean streak a mile wide that he was oh, so careful never to show André.

'Oh, come on, Sam,' he murmured dryly. 'We all know you're a hot little thing. Even my macho brother never knows whose bed you're sleeping in when he's away.'

'That's a lie,' she said, going white at the poisonous suggestion. Then, 'Don't do that!' she snapped when his hands came up to touch her. She knocked them away and started backing up.

He smiled a lazy smile. 'But you're family,' he murmured tauntingly. 'And we all know how big brother likes us all to get our even share. It makes him feel good and in control. "You want money, Raoul? Sure you can have money. You want a car? Sure, here's the cheque. You want to live in my house? Sure, live in my house; make yourself at home, what's mine is yours."'

'Think again if you dare to believe he was including me in that,' she told him coldly.

'And why not you?' he jeered. 'Those deeds of ownership on the Bressingham tell you exactly where you stand in big brother's plan of things. You were a very un-hostile takeover, Samantha.' He spelled it out cruelly. 'Came with the fixtures and fittings. One feisty wife. Pain-in-the-neck flirt. Install her in family home. Use at will.'

'God, you're a nasty piece of work, Raoul.' She retaliated. 'I own the Bressingham!' she declared angrily. 'It came to me in my father's will!'

'Did it?' He sounded so sure of himself. So absolutely positive that he was right, it started her doubting her own mind right there and then. 'Did it actually say, "I hereby bequeath my precious daughter the Bressingham Hotel and enough money to return it to the proud place it used to be"?'

He knew it didn't; she began to shake. Her father's will had merely stated that everything he possessed would go to her. André had taken care of the rest. And why not? She trusted him with her life, never mind her father's business affairs. She had been so grief stricken. So lost without the man who had been her mentor and her hero from the day she'd been born. She hadn't even known he was ill. He'd kept so much from her.

Had that included letting André buy the Bressingham?

Now she could see her own face as it must have looked that night in Raoul's bedroom. See the slow dawning of a realisation that Raoul could be right take the colour from her face. And if he'd been right about one thing, he could have been be right about the others. Maybe she had come with the deal. Maybe André had married her because her father had insisted that the Bressingham must remain with the Bressingham family.

Beginning to shiver again, she reached out to switch on the shower, then dropped her robe to the floor so she could begin peeling off her wet swimsuit. She didn't want to remember any more, but her mind decided otherwise. As she stepped beneath the shower's hot spray, the rest of the dreadful scene began to fill her head.

Raoul trying to touch her, her slapping his hands away, him enjoying the minor skirmish, smiling, taunting her with words and gestures until she could barely breathe as panic began stir. He was big, he was strong; she had been no match for him. What followed had been a horrible experience that had continued as a frantic struggle on Raoul's bed—when André had walked in on them.

And that is about as far as I want to go with this, she told herself on a sick little shudder. What she really needed to do was get to away from here—right away, she decided, on a sudden upsurge of panic that had her stepping quickly out of the shower. She needed to give herself some time and space to get her head together. Because, right now, she didn't know who she was, what she was, or even why she was!

* * *

André knew when he saw her coming down the stairs that he had a big problem on his hands. He had been standing here in the hall waiting for her, half expecting to see her wearing a cold mask instead of a face. But it was worse than that. She was dressed in stark, mourning black, and was carrying that damned suitcase she had brought with her from the Tremount.

Samantha was about to bury their marriage.

'Going somewhere?' he questioned silkily.

She didn't bother to reply. Neither did she make eye contact as she attempted to walk straight past him as if he wasn't there.

His hand snaked out, wrenching the suitcase from her. It brought her to a stop on a sharp little gasp. He was very happy to watch the anger flare in her blank green eyes. 'We need to talk,' he said.

'No,' she refused. 'I have nothing I want to say to you.' And she kept on walking—without the suitcase. Head up, body stiff, only that small limp to ruin her cold, stiff exit. It was almost a shame to spoil it, he acknowledged. But *he* was going to talk, he determined grimly. *She* was going to talk!

'Have you ever heard that old saying, if I had my time over, I would play that scene differently?' He fed the words coolly after her. 'Well, this is your chance, *cara*,' he said. 'Don't miss this rare opportunity you've been handed by playing the scene the same way again.'

Watching her pull to a stop, he felt the tight sting of triumph. She might hate the very thought of it, but she knew he was right. 'I can't talk about it all now,' she murmured unevenly. 'I need time to—'

'Time,' he grimly cut in, 'is something you've been wasting for twelve long, miserable months.'

'Okay!' She spun on him so abruptly that, even

though he had been deliberately provoking her into it, he didn't expect the speed with which she decided to take him on. 'You want to play the scene a different way?' she challenged. 'So let's play it a different way!'

And if he'd thought her cold a moment ago then she certainly wasn't now. She was burning with anger, with bitterness and a hatred that tried to sear off his skin.

'You walked in here that night, took one look at what was going on in that locked room upstairs, and instantly blamed me for it!'

'It was Raoul's room!' he threw back. 'His bed you were both tangled upon! Look at the evidence, Samantha. How would you have responded if that had been me with another woman in there?'

'Oh, no.' She shook her head. 'You are not going to divert the blame by shifting the argument. You were there. You saw. You drew your conclusion… I needed your help!' she cried. 'Instead I was called a whore!'

The truth cut deep; he went white. She was whiter. 'It was spur of the moment.' He defended himself. 'I lost my head.'

She wasn't impressed. 'Raoul said you never knew whose bed I was in when you weren't here,' she told him tightly. 'I didn't believe him. But it was the truth, wasn't it?'

'No.' He denied it, but he couldn't look her straight in the eye as he did so because, damn himself to hell, he had suspected she might *wonder* what it would be like to make love with other men.

The downside of marrying a virgin and finding himself landed with a feisty, flirtatious witch for a wife was that he just hadn't been able to trust her not to fly with her instincts and give those other guys a try.

'You didn't have to walk out of here the way you

did.' He heard himself grind out, and immediately acknowledged how weak that argument sounded.

Her eyes flicked green scorn at him. 'What else did you expect?' she asked. 'You threw Raoul out, then you returned to cut me into little pieces before slamming out yourself! I wasn't hanging around here to see which brother decided to return first and finish what he'd started. So I got out.' Her voice was shrill. 'What sane woman wouldn't?'

'I went to the Bressingham,' he explained. 'Spent the night in your father's old office getting drunk. Around dawn I had to finally admit that I had made a mess of the whole thing. So I came back here. You'd already packed and gone—so had Raoul.'

'At which you drew your own conclusions,' she inserted with a bitter little smile. 'No wonder it took you a year to stumble over me.'

'It wasn't like that.' He sighed. 'I—'

'I don't want to know.' Stiffly she turned back to the door.

'Devon,' he said, aware that he was clutching at straws now, to keep her here. 'Why did you choose to go to Devon?'

'Place of happy childhood memories,' she mocked without turning. 'We used to spend our holidays there. Staying at the Tremount Hotel, of all places,' she added with heavy irony. 'Which was probably why I felt so comfortable working there... Now you've bought it,' she said, and her voice began to thicken. 'Carla thinks you are wonderful and everyone is happy.'

'Except for you,' he responded gruffly.

'Yes.' She nodded. 'Except for me.'

'But why not?' he questioned frowningly. 'I thought you would understand that I bought it for you.'

She turned her head at that. 'Like you bought the Bressingham?' she posed, then smiled a wretchedly bleak smile and turned away again, and this time he could see she intended to leave.

Frustration licked through him. They had resolved absolutely nothing. She hated him. He had no defence. If she left now, it would be over. He was as certain of that as he had ever been about anything.

'Even a condemned man is allowed his moment to speak on his own behalf, *cara*...'

As he stood there, waiting to see what she would do, one of her hands fluttered up to touch her right temple. It was a gesture of uncertainty; already he had come to recognise it as such.

'I just can't stay here,' she whispered unsteadily.

'Fine,' he said immediately. 'Then we will go somewhere else.'

But the moment he began striding towards her she began to stiffen. 'I want to be on my own,' she murmured stubbornly.

'No.' The refusal was absolutely rock-solid. In any other situation he would have just taken hold of her and kissed her senseless, since he knew without a doubt that kissing was one sure way he could make her respond to him.

But that was just another scene they had played before, which now needed playing differently. So he sighed heavily and, ignoring her muttered protest, firmly turned her to face him.

'Have you any idea how frail you look?' he murmured gently. 'Give yourself a break, Samantha. Give me one!' he added. 'One split-second swoon and you could be under the wheels of the nearest car out there. So I am asking you, please, to let me come with you...'

He wasn't sure whether it was the *please* that did it, or the touch of his hands, or the way his eyes wanted to swallow her up whole. But something caused the wistful sigh of surrender.

'Come if you want.' She capitulated, then pulled out of his grasp.

Without hesitation he reached around her and opened the front door. Sunlight flooded into them. She stepped outside and paused to wait while he pulled the door shut behind them.

'Where shall we go?' he asked as he came to stand beside her.

'The—the Bressingham,' she responded unevenly. 'I n-need to see what you've done to it...'

CHAPTER TWELVE

FROM the moment she stepped through its heavy oak and glass doors, Samantha felt the tears threatening to fall once again. Beside her, André stood silent and still, waiting for her first response.

'It's finished,' she whispered.

'With the greatest test yet to come.' He smiled briefly, following her as she walked forward until she was standing in the middle of the foyer where she began to turn in a slow circle, taking in every dearly loved, perfectly reproduced detail as she did so.

'Nothing's changed.' She breathed out eventually, in a fantastical voice that drew another mocking smile. 'Okay.' She allowed. 'So everything has changed. But…'

She was truly overwhelmed by what she was seeing. In fact she found she couldn't quite believe it. The last time she had been standing right here the whole place had been reduced to a building site. She had not long since buried her father, and it had felt like the end of a special era.

Now everything was back right where it should be. The same look, the same smell, the same aged patina on the same pieces of oak, felled centuries ago and since preserved by layers of lovingly applied beeswax, many of which she had applied herself. Even the same lazy old staircase ambled up to the mezzanine dining hall, she saw, whereas the last time she'd been here there had been only a great ugly hole.

Drawn towards it by a power stronger than will, she walked up a few steps with fingers trailing the rich dark wood banister as if she was making contact with a long-lost friend; then she turned to take in the scene from this new position.

Born in the hotel, she had lived here and worked here from the time she had been old enough to carry a plate without dropping it. Her soul resided here in this great old building. Her birth name hung above its doors. She knew every quaint nook and cranny, every piece of wood, every vase and ornament or gold-framed painting on the walls.

And everything, everything was back where it should be.

'So...what do you think?' André prompted.

It was like asking a new mother what she thought of her baby. 'It's...perfect,' she whispered.

Oh, she wasn't so lost to sentimentality to ignore the fact that there were, in truth, many changes. Having felt the weight of the two-inch-thick health and safety report, she was well aware that, behind this outer dressing, the hotel had been virtually gutted and rebuilt. But what had risen from the rubble turned her heart over.

'I can't believe it,' she said, referring to what the architects and designers had managed to achieve.

'Why?' André's deeply dry voice queried. 'Did you expect me to put the *Visconte* stamp on it the moment your back was turned?'

If nothing else, his remark made her focus on him for the first time since they'd arrived here. He was still standing where she had left him, a lean, languid figure wearing an impeccably cut suit and a cynical smile.

Her own expression changed, cooled and hardened fractionally. 'I would rather do this by myself if you're bent on spoiling it for me,' she said coolly, watching his cynical look change to a grimace in acknowledgment of her chilly set-down, and she looked away from him again.

'Who took over the project after I—left?' she asked after a moment.

He began walking towards her. 'The whole thing came to a halt for a while,' he confessed. 'Then the contractors starting yelling at me to let them get on with it, so…' He shrugged, paused to look around him. 'The final result is pretty impressive,' he opined. 'I'm pleased that you are pleased with it.'

'Is the rest of it as impressive?'

He declined the invitation to give an opinion. 'I'll let you be the judge of that.'

'You didn't answer my question,' she said as he drew level with her.

'Which one was that?' he posed.

'About who took over the project after I left it.'

'Only one other person was qualified to do so,' he drawled with a self-mocking smile which sent her eyes wide in surprise.

'You mean—*you* took it over?'

'Don't sound so shocked.' He scolded. 'Being the very busy, hotshot tycoon does not absolve me of the right to a few small pleasures in life.'

Her frown came back, along with a sigh in exasperation. 'Is it me or yourself you're mocking when you talk like that?'

'Both of us, I think,' he said, then added more neutrally, 'Come and take a look at what we've done with the famous Bressingham dining room.'

He placed a light hand to her lower back to urge her to turn. Her spine arched away from the heat in his fingers. Without comment he dropped the hand again, and together they walked up the rest of the stairs with her body still tingling from the briefest of touches.

Nothing had changed here either, she saw, drawing to a stop at the top of the staircase to simply absorb what was to her the loveliest room in the building. This was where life happened at the Bressingham, she recalled poignantly. A place where the hum of conversation blended with the chink of silver on china, and people relaxed in comfortable chairs while enjoying food prepared by gifted magicians. And it all took place beneath the great crystal chandeliers hanging from the ceiling, now beautifully restored to their original glory.

The old grand piano still stood in its corner. The same brick-dust-red paint still warmed the walls. All it needed was covers placed on the tables and she would almost believe she was standing here, by the same *maître d's* station, waiting to be seated for a romantic dinner.

With the man she loved…

The tears threatened again, pressing like weights against her throat in their desire to escape as a new set of memories suddenly rose up to haunt her.

'This is where we first met,' André murmured, telling her that his own memories were coinciding with hers. 'I'd come here for dinner and you were playing *maître d'*…'

She'd glanced up from her table plan to find herself looking at the most gorgeous man she had ever set eyes upon. Samantha progressed the memory. Smooth and suave, breathtakingly sophisticated in a black silk dinner suit, he'd tossed a devastating grin at her, had touched a long finger to her black bow tie and had said, 'Snap…'

'You took my breath away.' André took back the moment. 'So much so that I think I said something really stupid, like ''Snap'' and touched your bow tie…'

Samantha swallowed. So did he.

'As I drew my finger away it brushed the underside of your chin, and it was like touching a small piece of heaven…'

'Don't,' she whispered unevenly.

'Why not?' he demanded. 'Don't you think the ruthless rat of a tycoon should be allowed any sentimentality?'

'I just don't want to talk about it,' she answered painfully.

'Well, I do—' And before she could do more than gasp out a protest, he placed his hands round her waist and, with the minimum of effort, picked her and plonked her back down again, right behind the old-fashioned *maître d'* station.

Her eyes leapt up to his and her mouth parted to issue a stinging rebuttal. But instead the words clogged in her throat and she found herself locked into a painful replay of one of the most precious moments in her life.

'That's right.' André growled. 'Look all wide-eyed and startled, just as you did that evening, and remember, *cara*, just who it is you're looking at!' His hand came up, a finger settling beneath her chin. The skin there seemed to actually preen itself. 'For I am the guy who took one look at you, with your glorious hair and sensational eyes, and skin like the smoothest substance I've ever known, and fell so head-over-heels in love with you that he would rather cut his own throat than *ever* hurt you!'

Angry—he was stunningly angry, she realised belatedly. All that cynicism and mockery had been hiding a deep and burning anger, which was now spitting out at her from eyes as cold as black diamonds in a face chiselled from the hardest rock.

'Then, why did you?' She hit right back at him, and if his eyes were hard hers were harder. With a toss of her head she dislodged the finger. 'I gave every single *cell* of myself to you—and you threw it all right back in my face! That isn't *love*, André! How dare you even call it that!'

'Are we talking about Raoul here, or the Bressingham?' he gritted.

'Both,' she said. *'Both!'*

A door opened somewhere below them. André turned like a serpent sensing attack as a woman in an overall walked across the foyer and disappeared through the door by reception.

'Who was that?' she questioned shakily.

'A cleaner,' he replied, swinging his eyes back to her with a new frustration burning in them, because the interruption had ruined the moment, and he knew he would never get it back. 'There is a whole army of them around somewhere,' he added, withdrawing his aggressive stance with a sigh. 'Where to now?' he asked coolly.

She shook her head, still shaking from their confrontation. 'I don't know,' she confessed. 'I—y-you choose...'

But André didn't want to choose. He wanted to grab her by the shoulders and shake some sense into her! 'Can't you see—can't you tell what I've tried to do here?' he bit out angrily.

'Kept to the letter of your contract with my father.' She nodded.

He sighed in frustration. 'Any second now,' he gritted,

'I am going to kiss that closed mind of yours right out into the open.'

'It is open,' she declared.

The glance he threw her actually made her skin flinch. 'No, it isn't,' he said, and threw her completely by walking away from her.

Watching him go, she felt a moment of sheer terror. No! she wanted to cry out. Don't walk away! Don't give up on me now, when I need you to justify your part in everything!

He stopped. She held her breath. Had she actually shouted those words out? Turning, he flicked her a lean look that told her nothing. 'Are you coming?'

Her heart clattered into action, relief swimming about her head while another part of her wanted to remain aloof and defiant. 'I—yes,' she said, and stepped away from the *maître d'* station. He turned his back and started walking again. She started to follow, acutely aware that, somehow, somewhere, control had shifted from her to André.

'Wh-where are we going?' Weakly she tried to grab it back again.

She hadn't got it, she realised as soon as he answered. 'Somewhere less…emotive to finish this conversation.' He supplied, as if throwing down a gauntlet.

But there was no such place inside this building. The moment they stepped into her father's old office, André realised his mistake, seeing the change come over her face. Maybe he shouldn't be doing this now, he pondered grimly as he watched the memories close around her. Maybe he should wait, give her the time and the space she wanted to recover properly, before they dug into the real issues clamouring around both of them.

Damn it, he cursed silently. How could she start to

recover without the full truth to help it to happen? Turning angrily away from his moment of uncertainty, he walked over to the place where anyone who had known the late Thomas Bressingham would also know he kept his private store of spirits. It was too early for whisky; André realised that. But right now he needed something.

'Has this room been touched at all?'

Her voice sounded thick with unshed tears. Grimacing, André added an extra tot to the glass. 'Other than being brought up to Health and Safety standards, no,' he replied, failing to add that it had been his strict instruction that nothing in this room must be touched unless it was absolutely necessary.

Strangely, though, he hadn't issued that instruction out of consideration for Samantha's feelings. He had done it for his own. He might possess a long string of premier-class hotels, but even to him the Bressingham was special… Just as Thomas Bressingham had been a special kind of man. This overcrowded, very male-orientated, private office held in its very walls some part of what had made his father-in-law special. He could never put his finger on exactly what that was, but he could always feel it when he stepped in here.

A little as his very tactile wife was feeling it now, he likened when he turned with his glass to find her wandering about the room, gently touching things with the caressing hand of a lifelong lover.

But then, she belonged in here too. A Bressingham. The last in a long line of Bressinghams.

'Let's talk about your father,' he said.

A light came on in her eyes then was instantly doused again. 'He loved this place.' She sighed out tragically.

Grimacing at the claim, André mentally took a deep

breath—and went for broke. 'But he loved you one hell of a lot more, *cara*...'

If he'd put a whip to her hide Samantha could not have been more offended. 'Because he was prepared to buy me the man I loved by giving this place to him?' she suggested painfully.

That was it. He might as well have said it. Samantha watched him put down his glass and close the gap between them with a swiftness that sent the breath deep into her lungs. Hands gripped her shoulders, heat speared through her body, catching fire...catching fire as it always did when he touched her. His eyes glittered down on her like black storms of biting fury and, with a small shake, he compelled her to listen and believe what he was about to say to her.

She wanted to refute it, even before she'd heard it; she knew she desperately; desperately needed to refute what was coming. When he opened his mouth to speak she almost, almost flattened her own against it just to stop him from speaking.

Then he began, his voice hard-edged with honesty. 'Your father did not give me this place to *buy* me, Samantha,' he told her very precisely. 'He gave it to me because he was broke.'

Full stop. No elaboration. His eyes said, Believe it. His silence said, Accept it.

'No.' she choked the denial of both.

'Yes,' he insisted, not angrily but so calmly that she knew it was the truth. 'He knew he was sick. He knew he was broke, and he knew that Health and Safety were threatening to close him down if he didn't spend millions bringing the hotel up to modern standards. So who better to pay the price than the very wealthy, very besotted future son-in-law?'

The cynicism was back. Shocked horror contracted her pupils until there was nothing left but dark green circles of truth. 'You think I set you up!' She gasped.

He released a hard laugh. 'I am not that short on self-esteem,' he returned then let go of her and turned to walk back to his drink.

But his hand was shaking as he lifted the glass to his lips. 'I don't believe you.' She charged him. 'It's the reason why you didn't trust me… Why you could believe Raoul's version of what happened that night instead of mine!'

'Let's stick to one problem before we starting dealing with another,' he clipped.

'If you drink one more sip of that whisky, André, you will have to suffer me driving you home!'

He rounded on her furiously. 'Who said we are leaving together?'

It shook her to the core. On a wave of hollowing weakness she stumbled into the nearest chair. The air throbbed, the anger roared like a lion in the sudden silence. He set down his glass; she pushed trembling fingers to her brow, where the muddle of memories were still struggling to sort themselves out.

'Ex-explain about the Bressingham, then,' she prompted eventually, taking his advice and trying, trying to stick to one problem at a time. But it was difficult, because they merged like two parts of the same whole and she couldn't seem to separate them.

On a harsh sigh, he sank down onto the edge of her father's desk, shoved his hands in his pockets, then sighed again.

'Your father knew he was ill. He needed money. So naturally he came to me.' His voice was no longer harsh, but just heavy. 'I offered to bail him out—no strings attached. But he was too damned proud to let me do that. So he came up with his idea of an acceptable alternative,' he explained, his tone alone telling her that it hadn't been as acceptable to him. 'He would give me the Bressingham on the promise that I would do what was necessary to keep it open. And I was to mention none of it to you,' he added wearily.

'But why?' she questioned.

'Why do you think?' He sighed. 'His precious daughter must be worried by nothing. Her wedding day was coming up. She had caught her prince. He wanted to—'

'If you don't stop tossing words like insults at me, I will probably pick up something heavy and throw it at you.' Samantha cut in.

'The old Samantha would have just gone ahead and done it.'

But the old Samantha died on a road in Devon, Samantha thought bleakly. And the new one was still struggling to evolve from what was left. 'Please, go on,' she invited stiltedly.

'There is very little left to say,' he murmured with a shrug. 'We came to an agreement where I would do as he asked. But because I had my own pride to consider here, I refused to take possession of the hotel until you and I were officially married—hence the date on the documents you were given,' he defined. 'It helped me to justify what I was doing.'

'Beginning our marriage with lies,' Samantha inserted.

'I'm sorry,' he said.

But it wasn't enough, because it was hard to forgive someone— No, she then amended that. It was hard to forgive the *two* people she'd loved most in the world for deceiving her the way they had.

'Was I so weak, so pathetic that you both felt you had to protect me from the ugly truth?' she asked painfully.

'It was the deal.' He looked away. 'I couldn't in all honour break it.'

'So instead you broke the vow to honour that you made with me,' she concluded. Then she remembered that André had actually suspected she was a party to her father's deal.

A silent conspiracy. She smiled bleakly at the idea. Even her father's will had been carefully worded, with a simple one-liner leaving everything *he'd possessed* to her. André had dealt with the details. She had never thought to question him. He probably saw that as further proof of her involvement.

Oh, what a tangled web, she mused emptily, and came to her feet. 'If that's it,' she said huskily, 'then I think I'd like to go now.'

'Go where?' he asked.

'Back to the house,' she told him. 'To pack.' Pack and leave the open way this time, the calm way. 'I don't think there is anything left to be said.'

'That's where you're wrong,' he countered gruffly. 'We haven't even touched the tip of the iceberg as far as explanations are concerned... And if you think I am going to stand by and watch you walk out on me again, Samantha, then think again.'

'You never watched the first time.'

'Raoul,' he breathed. 'It always comes back to Raoul.'

Raoul, yes, Raoul, Samantha agreed wearily. Who'd come to live with them in London only weeks after their wedding. Raoul who had played adoring half-brother while secretly resenting André for everything. His wealth, his power, his new English wife. Raoul, the poor relation, born to the wrong parent, he'd used to call himself—out of André's hearing, of course. He had wanted to be a Visconte but had had to make do with being a Delacroix.

'He's sorry, if it means anything to you.'

'Sorry?' Looking up, she sent him a huff of scorn.

'Deeply ashamed of himself.' He extended.

The fizz of anger began to rise again. If she could have stopped it she would have done, because she knew, by now, that she had taken more than she could safely manage to deal with.

'He abused my hand of friendship, my hospitality, my marriage and me,' she spelled it out coldly. 'I hope he will live with his shame for the rest of his life.'

'He will,' André confirmed.

'And you want me to pity him for that? Is that what your expression is saying?'

'Pity is better than bitterness, *cara*. And I should know,' he added heavily. 'Look what my bitterness did to us.'

So he was actually admitting that he *had* believed her to be a party to her father's overall plan? 'I think I hate you,' she breathed, turning away.

'Only think?'

'Go to hell, André,' she incised. And with that she walked, shaking, limping—hating herself for that limp because it ruined an otherwise precise exit.

Out on the mezzanine the chandeliers had been lit. As she walked down the stairs she could see the whole ambience of the foyer had begun to pull on its evening cloak. If the piano suddenly began playing behind her she knew she would be truly done for.

'He went to Australia,' a deep voice said quietly, stopping her as her foot made the foyer floor. 'I thought you'd gone with him, so I chased after the pair of you.

I went to kill him,' André admitted. 'Then I was going to strangle the lovely life out of you. Or at least,' he added, 'that was the plan.' Samantha sensed rather than saw the accompanying grimace. 'It didn't quite work out like that. I found him hiding out on a cattle station in God knows where because he knew I would be coming after him.' He released a short sigh. 'But it was really you I'd gone for. Except you weren't with him. So instead of killing him I broke down and wept like a baby... Does that help ease your pain to know that, *cara*?' he questioned levelly. 'It made a man out of Raoul, as twisted as that may seem. He broke down and wept right along with me. Then he told me the truth about what he'd done, and while I was trying to come to terms with the bloody mess I'd made of everything he disappeared again, leaving me alone to deal with the lousy, rotten truth of what the pair of us had done to you.'

Australia. At last she managed to recall where she had heard Australia mentioned before. Stefan Reece had seen André there twelve months ago. 'You were in Australia when I had my accident.'

'For two months.' His voice was coming closer. 'It took me that long to track Raoul down. And thirty seconds to realise what an unforgivable fool I had been. By the time I got back to London your trail had gone cold, and between wishing you in hell for leaving the way you did, and wishing you would just call me to let me know you were okay, I—lived—I think.' He sighed. 'I don't remember much about the long, empty months in between. Then Nathan Payne called me in New York with news about you, and my life suddenly kick-started again.'

'And Raoul?' she asked.

'Still in hiding in the outback, waiting for redemption to ease his guilt. I hear from him now and then, but nothing that says he has come to terms with the man he discovered himself to be.' His breath touched her nape and she quivered slightly.

'You've forgiven him.' She realised.

'After I had learned to forgive myself.'

'Don't touch me,' she said jerkily, hearing him move behind her. When he touched her she lost touch with her common sense.

'I'm not going to,' he replied—because he already knew what his touch did to her, and he was now trying to play fair. 'I just want you to consider forgiving Raoul some day, even if you cannot bring yourself to forgive me.'

And forgiveness was an essential part of her own healing process; that was what he was trying to say.

Funny that, she mused hollowly. But she had already forgiven André for some though not all of what he'd done—though she hadn't realised it until now. As for Raoul? She could now feel sorry for him, she discovered. But forgive? He'd scared her, seriously scared her, when he'd pushed her onto his bed. And it was the lies he'd told André about her, in an effort to save his own skin, she couldn't forgive. Those lies had helped to ruin her marriage—her trust in the one person left in the world she'd felt she could rely on—and had ruined her in a way.

'He gave me the copies of your deal with my father to hurt you too, you know,' she murmured.

'I know,' André confirmed, and didn't attempt to justify what Raoul had done.

A throb began to pound at the back of her eyes. A deep, pressure ache, which was trying to tell her she just couldn't think any more right now. On a slow, weary sigh her shoulders drooped, her body losing the will to want to her upright any more.

'You've had it,' André murmured huskily. 'Come on, let's get you home.'

Home, Samantha repeated silently, and didn't try to argue. She stepped forward; he followed, still maintaining his no-touch policy, she noticed.

The headache became so bad on the way back to the house that she could barely walk unaided up the stairs. Yet still André didn't attempt to help her. It was as if it had become a point of honour for him to make no physical contact without her permission.

But he remained right behind her all the way into the bedroom, and only left again when he'd watched her swallow two of her painkillers he'd produced from his pocket. After that, she pulled off her clothes and slipped beneath the duvet, frowning slightly because she had only just realised that the pills should have been in her bedside drawer; so how had he got hold of them?

She fell asleep thinking about the attractively innocuous puzzle.

CHAPTER THIRTEEN

ANDRÉ was sitting behind the desk in his study. Head back, eyes closed, bare feet propped on the desk top, and the soft light from a single table lamp just managing to diffuse the hardness from his weary profile. Since leaving Samantha to sleep away some of the strain of the day he had been working steadily, using it as his way of putting their problems aside, for a short while at least.

But now he'd had enough. Work could go to hell. It was his marriage that really mattered right now, and if he felt like wallowing in his own misery for a while then...why not? Across the room somewhere, Puccini's *La Bohème* was quietly filtering through the silence. His mood suited the music's dark mood, and one set of long brown fingers were idly rotating his black fountain pen to a rhythm he had unconsciously picked up.

But the fingers went still when he heard the first soft tread on the stairs.

His eyes slid open, but he didn't move. Lounging there, he stared at the gap in the half-open door, listened and waited to find out what she was going to do.

Go right past the door or step into the room? She had to see the light, hear the music. She must know he was in here. The new Samantha was as unpredictable as the old one, but he would lay heavy odds on the old one being unable to pass by that door without putting her head in here—no matter how reluctant she might be to do so. It was a point of pride—of defiance, if you like—

not to turn away from potential confrontation. She had done it only once in his experience, and that had been the time she'd left here one night a year ago, without hanging around long enough to have the whole ugly scene out with him.

Nothing happened. She hadn't moved towards the kitchen; she hadn't moved towards the front door. The muscles encasing his stomach began to tighten, trying to urge him to get up and go and check what she was doing out there. But he refused to give in to it. This was Samantha's move. He would wait here to see what that move was, even if it was killing him to do it.

The annoying, provoking, beautiful witch.

A sound at last. His heart stopped beating. His fingers curled around the pen. The door began to swing wider. Dressed to go or dressed to stay? he asked himself as a tingle that began at the back of his neck spread out to infuse his whole system with a state of readiness to move like lightning if she was dressed to leave.

Then she appeared in the opening, and he had to narrow his eyes to hide their expression as relief turned the tingle to liquid until his bones felt like wax.

She looked as she'd used to look in the mornings, all warm and soft and still a little sleepy. She was wearing one of her old short silk wraps in a soft shell-pink the same colour as her warm, bare toes, and her hair was lying in an unbrushed silken tangle about her face and shoulders.

'Hi,' she murmured awkwardly. 'I'm going to make myself some breakfast, if that's okay.'

'It's nine o'clock in the evening,' he said, frowning down at his watch.

'I know.' She offered a tense little lift of one shoulder. 'But I fancy porridge with honey… Do you want some?'

He shook his head. 'No, thanks,' he murmured, only to immediately wish he'd answered differently when she just nodded and disappeared again.

The first real invitation she'd offered him and he'd turned it down. What a bloody fool, he cursed himself. Now he had no real excuse to go after her. No excuse to get close, get *warm*—since he hadn't felt warm all day thanks to this wretched war of nerve ends they were waging on each other.

Closing his eyes, he relaxed back into the chair, cursed himself some more and managed to stay like that for all of five minutes, thinking of her wandering around the kitchen in that thin little wrap, and with nothing on her feet, and—

With a growl of frustration, he gave up trying to be strong, slid his feet to the floor, got up and went looking for her. She was standing by the microwave, watching a bowl of porridge rotate.

'Your father would disown you if he could see you making porridge that way,' he remarked lazily.

She looked up, smiled briefly, then looked away again. 'He *thought* he got his porridge the old-fashioned way every morning, but he didn't, the poor, deluded soul.'

'Found the honey?'

'Not yet.'

He went off to hunt it down in a cupboard, saw the kettle was coming to the boil with the teapot standing at the ready beside it. 'I'll have a cup of that, if you don't mind,' he said lightly.

'Sure,' she replied, and moved to pour boiling water onto the tea bags, took the pot to a ready-set table, before going back to get her porridge from the microwave.

Finding himself a cup, he sat down. She sat down. He

loosened the top on the honey pot then set it down in front of her. She picked it up and took the lid off completely, then picked up her spoon.

And because he couldn't help it, he started grinning. 'Finishing the day as we started it.' He explained the grin.

'One hell of a lot went on in between,' she dryly pointed out.

'How is the headache?' he queried belatedly.

'Gone,' she said. 'The sleep gave my head a chance to put its filing system in order, I think.' Twisting a spoonful of honey out of the jar, she then let it spiral its way down onto her porridge.

His mouth began to water. He didn't know why, but the warmth suddenly heating certain parts of his body told him that his mouth *wasn't* watering because he fancied the look of the honey!

It was the woman and what she was doing that was making him feel—

'You were right about something you said today,' she murmured.

'Only one thing? I must be slipping.' He grimaced. 'What was it?' he asked, lifting his eyes, up to her eyes to find them watching him from underneath her long dark gold-tipped lashes.

She licked the honey spoon. It could have been deliberate—but probably wasn't. Whatever, he felt his body stir, his own eyes darken in response.

'Bitterness hurts almost as much as the reason for it,' she said. Then she licked the darned spoon again with the full flat surface of her pink tongue.

'So you've decided to do what?' he prompted from somewhere way at the back of his overactive hormones.

'Try to put it to one side, I suppose.' She shrugged.

She dipped the spoon into the porridge now, and began eating it.

In dire need of something casual to do, André picked up the teapot and began pouring. Then he thought, To hell with it, and threw caution to the wind.

'You know, I've been thinking too,' he said, pushing a cup towards her. 'Has it occurred to you that if you hadn't had your accident and lost your memory you probably would have come back here eventually?'

'I know it.' She surprised him by admitting it. Then surprised him again with an impish smile. 'Got the memory back,' she reminded him. 'It's telling me all sorts of things I'd forgotten about.'

Meaning what? He wanted to ask, but didn't dare in case he didn't like the answer. So he stuck doggedly to the point he had been trying to make. 'Well, don't you think that if you had come back we would have gone through more or less what we have been doing for the last few days? Only, you would have been angry instead of frightened and bewildered,' he added. 'And I would have been digging my own grave by maintaining my lofty position as victim, because pride would not have allowed me to accept I was in the wrong when it would have meant my grovelling at your beautiful feet.'

'Would you have done—eventually?' She looked really curious to know.

'Haven't I been doing that in one way or another?' he countered ruefully.

'When?' Putting down the porridge spoon, she replaced it with the teaspoon from her saucer. 'When have you actually got down at my feet and grovelled for forgiveness for anything?' she demanded, calmly using the teaspoon now to dip into the honey pot again.

His loins began to tighten in anticipation of another

round of sensual torment. The porridge was gone, which meant there was only one place that spoonful of honey was meant to go. His eyes suddenly felt as hot as the rest of him.

'Put that spoon in your mouth and I will give you a full demonstration of how a man grovels.' He growled at her.

The spoon became suspended halfway between honey pot and her parted mouth. The air began to sizzle. His body was infused with that tight tingle of readiness to move like lightning if she forced him to. All it needed was for that spoon to finish its journey and there was no way, now, he could back away from a challenge he had thrown down without thinking it through first.

Spoon in mouth, I go for her. Spoon laid down, I stew in my own damned frustration.

Her eyes began to glow. His began to burn. The spoon went into her mouth. He was around that table before she had a chance to do more than drop the spoon and shriek, 'André, no!'

'André, no—you little liar,' he gritted, lifted her to her feet and kissed her hotly.

She melted as the honey had melted into the hot porridge. Slow and smooth, sensual and sweet. She couldn't even hold herself upright. His arms tightened around her; his mouth lifted free. He tasted of honey, she tasted of honey, the air swirled with its seductive scent.

'You've been gunning for this reaction since you came down the stairs,' he accused, his voice like gravel.

'That isn't true!' she protested.

'No? Then, why the skimpy robe?' He challenged. 'Why are you wearing nothing beneath?' Her cheeks grew hot. He grinned like a tiger with his prey all neatly tied up and ready to eat. 'You knew I was sitting down here worrying about you. You knew I'd be waiting like some slavish lap-dog for you to give me permission to leap. So I've leapt,' he gritted. 'Now let's see if you like what the lap-dog turns into when he's aroused.'

'You are no lap-dog!' She flashed the words at him scathingly. 'More a scavenging wolf, feeding on the remains of those weaker than you!'

'Are we talking about the Bressingham and your father again?' He sighed out wearily.

'And the Tremount. And the lies!' Her eyes flashed all hell and damnation at him. 'And the arrogant belief that you only have to touch me to make me bend to your will!'

'The lies, I apologise for. The Tremount, I don't,' he said. 'And the last little truth is your own cross to bear, *cara mia*, not mine!'

And to prove it, he kissed her again. She bent, she melted, she groaned and cursed him and kissed him back as though her very life depended on it. He picked her up in his arms and started walking, mouth to mouth, giving her no chance to come back down to earth again.

Out of the kitchen, down the hall and past the study, still bathed in soft light and the sound of Puccini. Half sobbing in his arms, she was so annoyed with herself for letting him do this. He walked the stairs with his lungs beginning to burst—not from the work of carrying her, but because he needed her so badly he was barely managing to control himself.

The bed awaited, still with the cool white duvet thrown back and the imprint of her body pressed into the sheet. Laying her down on that same imprint, he finally broke the kiss so he could straighten and begin taking off his clothes.

The little witch just lay there and watched him, bold

as brass. 'If you want this to stop, say so now,' he gritted on a sudden twinge of conscience.

'What's the use?' she said. 'When we both know you only have to kiss me to change my mind again?'

Had there been resentment in that voice? No, he decided, not resentment, but resignation to her lot, and the eyes were dark and languid, luscious and green and sensually wanting.

'Take the robe off, then,' he instructed.

She didn't even bother to object to his autocratic tone! She simply did it, wriggling herself out of the silk and casually tossing it aside so she could go back to what she had been doing—which was watching him undress.

Her eyes fluttered down as he began releasing his trousers—and remained there watching with the sensual blatancy of a woman who knew what was to come.

He was very aroused and, like her, he was quite blatant about it. As he stepped up to the bed, she reached out a hand and stroked him. That stroke said, Hello, you're mine. And the passionate way he responded said, Yes, I know.

Even as he eased himself down beside her she was welcoming him, arms up, eyes dark, hair a shimmering splash of fire on snow-white percale. 'I think you set me up for this, downstairs,' he murmured suspiciously.

'Mmm,' she said. 'What did you expect? A grand announcement that I'd given up the fight and decided to forgive you?'

'Why the sudden change?' he asked, gently tracing the delicate oval of her face.

'I just woke up and I wasn't angry with you any more,' she explained. 'So I decided to seduce you. It always worked in the past, when we'd had a row.'

'This was no ordinary row, though, was it?' he pointed out.

'No.' Her eyes clouded for a moment. 'But I also woke up remembering how much I love you.' She sighed out soulfully. 'I'm victim to my own emotions. It's really very tragic, when you think about it.'

'You little liar,' he gritted. 'You woke remembering how much *I* love *you*. Don't think I don't remember that smug look in your eyes over the honey spoon.'

His hands reached out to draw her so close that their mouths were almost touching and their eyes had nowhere else to look but straight into each others.

'I loved you more than any man deserved to be loved,' she whispered sadly, 'and you threw it all right back in my face.'

'I know.' And he did know. It was a truth of his own he'd had to bear the weight of for twelve long, miserable months.

'But I fell so fast and deep for you that it knocked me for six,' he confessed. 'There you were, a completely new phenomenon to me. You were younger than I was used to, more impulsive, as unpredictable as hell...' His hand came up to touch a lock of silken fire. 'You flirted with any man who would let you; you teased the life out of me—I was both fascinated and infuriated by the easy way you had other men flocking around you.'

'I worked in a hotel,' she reminded him. 'It was my job to be friendly to people.'

'You were a flirt in your cradle,' André dryly responded. 'I have that on authority—from your father no less. It made me so filthy jealous to watch you behave like that with anyone else but me, that sometimes you were very fortunate I didn't turn caveman and drag you off by your beautiful hair!'

'None of that gives you the right to say what you did to me when you found me with Raoul,' she said painfully.

Releasing a sigh, André kissed her. It was an apology; neither of them saw the kiss as anything else. 'It wasn't only your head Raoul messed with,' he admitted heavily. 'I couldn't seem to move without him slipping in with some remark about the men he had seen you with. It was okay. I had no problem with his suggestive remarks when it was always my arms you slept in each night. But then your father died only a few months into our marriage. You were so inconsolable you wouldn't let me near. I resented that, *amore*. I resented you shutting me out yet seemingly being quite happy laughing and joking and smiling with other men.'

'They didn't expect to sleep with me,' she responded. 'And I could sleep with you but I couldn't—' She stopped to swallow the tears again.

'I know. I understand.' His hand moved on her hair again. 'You were having to cope with too many other emotions to have room left for what it was you thought I wanted from you.'

'It was always sex, André,' she whispered thickly. 'Every time I looked at you I saw desire burning in your eyes, and I…'

'You're wrong, you know,' he murmured. 'It wasn't the desire for sex, it was the desire to share your pain with you. And, as for the sex, I gave you what you only ever seemed to want from me—which made me feel like a damned good stallion but did absolutely nothing for *my* emotional needs. I only wanted you to love me.'

Unable to remain still any longer, she was so angry, she sat up and away from him, while André bent an arm beneath his head and watched her spark.

His other hand came up to rest on her back. It had been meant as a soothing gesture, but she turned on him like the unpredictable firecracker she was. Coming to lean right over him, she hissed into his face, 'I loved you! How dare you imply I didn't love you? I lost a year of my life because I believed I would never be allowed to love you again!'

His hand moved, caught her nape, long fingers tangling with her hair and, without giving her a chance to say another stinging word, he brought her mouth down onto his own—and quite simply shut her up.

His hands found her body and hers found his. He kissed her slow and he kissed her deep and she sank seductively into it. No more talk; it wasn't needed. This said it all for them, despite what they had been saying only minutes before. They couldn't argue with desire when love surrounded it. It was different, special. It was the true elixir of life.

So they made love like tender lovers, touching, tasting, slow and easy, hot and deep. Their senses knew each other. It was why Samantha had responded every time he'd come near; her mind could shut him out but her senses could not.

For André it was oh, so much more arousing to make love to her mind as well as her body. To look into her eyes and know she was seeing him—the man she'd married. The man she'd loved enough to do that.

So he made love to her in Italian. He made love to her in French—because she'd always loved him doing it and he wanted to give her back every single thing she had forgotten in the last empty year.

And she listened—hell, she listened with every single cell. As he slowly smoothly entered her he had never felt so energised in his whole life.

Afterwards he kissed her slowly back down to reality. He kissed her soft mouth, her closed eyes, the scar at her temple. When she opened her eyes they were heavy, liquid and loved.

'If I run away again, you'll come and find me, won't you?' she whispered, so very earnestly.

'Always,' he replied.

She sighed at that.

They slept in a close love-knot. When André eventually woke up, he glanced at the time and slid stealthily out of the bed, let himself out of the room and quietly went downstairs.

When he came back she was sitting up with the duvet trapped around her breasts. 'Don't tell me you've just bought another hotel in between orgies?' she said.

'No.' His smile was rueful because of her unwitting connection with what he had actually gone downstairs for. Coming to stand over her by the bed, he placed two packages down in front of her, then bent to murmur. 'Happy anniversary...'

It took her a moment to realise what he was talking about. Then her cheeks bloomed with colour, her eyes turned black. 'I forgot,' she said, and sounded as if she was going to start crying.

'Take it from me, I've got what I wanted.' He smiled. 'Here...open this one first, because it belongs to last year's anniversary...'

Fingers trembling, Samantha did as he said, tearing the plain pink paper away from the flat package folded neatly inside. Opening it up, she read the words on the piece of paper until the tears blurred them away. It was the deeds to the Bressingham. 'No.' She sobbed. 'You don't have to do this.'

'It was done a long, long time ago,' he quietly replied.

'About an hour after your father signed the Bressingham over to me, to be precise,' he added gently.

Her eyes flashed and, as unpredictable as ever, she turned on him like an angry cat. 'Why didn't you tell me this before, when I was spouting out all of that rubbish to you?' she cried. 'I feel an absolute fool now!'

'Good,' he said, and kissed her again. 'So you should, for doubting me.'

'And you didn't doubt me?'

'We aren't getting into this one again,' he ordained. 'It's our anniversary. So open your second package.'

Not sure she wanted to, Samantha did as he said. A sigh heaved from her. 'I don't believe this,' she said breathily, staring down at the deeds for the Tremount Hotel.

'I think these two might make you an official member of the tycoon club,' André drawled, then added lazily, 'Here, I think this is a good moment to put these back where they belong…'

These turned out to be a simple gold wedding band, which he slid onto her finger, following it with a glowing emerald circled by a ring of diamond fire.

Samantha sat staring down at the rings she'd left behind for so long that she wasn't really surprised when André prompted ruefully, 'Don't I even get a thank-you kiss?'

'I'm going to cry,' she told him with a shake of her lowered head.

'Will it make you feel any better if you do?' he questioned gently.

'No.' She shook her head again.

'Okay,' he murmured and reached out to push her down onto the bed then came over her to claim his own kiss.

When it was over, he remained poised above her, looking deep into her swimming eyes, with his own eyes very sombre. 'The Bressingham was always yours. I never considered it mine from the moment your father concocted his deal. But the Tremount is different,' he admitted deeply. 'The Tremount is to say thank you to it, for looking after you when I should have been doing it. And to say I'm sorry for ever doubting you.'

'Raoul is your brother and you loved him—just as I loved my father.' Reaching up, she placed a kiss to his sombre mouth. 'Neither of us expected either of them to deceive us, André.'

'Your father's deception was well meant. Raoul's lies were not. And I deceived you too, don't forget.'

'But I want to forget,' she insisted. 'With the freedom to choose, I want to forget it all now. Can we do that?'

Her green eyes pleaded. His began to burn. 'Sure,' he agreed. 'Anything you say while you look at me like that… And the honey was a killer, by the way.'

A diversion, Samantha recognised, and let him keep it.

'I saw it done on TV once,' she confessed with smile. 'I always meant to try it out on you but never seemed to get the chance before today.'

His sleek brows arched. 'Anything else you would like to try out?'

'Lots,' she breathed, her eyes darkening in line with the challenge. 'Anniversary present number one coming up,' she announced. 'I think you'll like this.'

And he did.